To Another Beautiful
Woman in my Life.
Always the Best!
Timothy L Daniels
2009

A TARGET RICH ENVIRONMENT

A Novel By
Timothy L. Daniels

Copyright 2007

Eloquent Books
New York, New York

Eloquent Books
An imprint of AEG Publishing Group
845 Third Avenue, 6th Floor – 6016
New York, NY 10022
www.eloquentbooks.com

ISBN: 978-1-60693-442-5 1-60693-442-2

Printed in the United States of America

Book Design: D. Johnson, Dedicated Business Solutions, Inc.

A TARGET RICH
ENVIRONMENT

SAN DIEGO, CALIFORNIA HAS THE LARGEST PORT OF ENTRY BETWEEN ANY TWO COUNTRIES IN THE WORLD. ON A TYPICAL DAY APPROXIMATELY 50,000 CARS CROSS INTO THE UNITED STATES FROM MEXICO.

OPERATION ALLIANCE IS A REAL BORDER DRUG TASK FORCE THAT HAS BEEN INVESTIGATING NARCOTICS SMUGGLING/TRAFFICKING FOR THREE DECADES. OPERATION ALLIANCE IS CURRENTLY COMPRISED OF SPECIAL AGENT CRIMINAL INVESTIGATORS FROM U.S. IMMIGRATION AND CUSTOMS ENFORCEMENT (ICE, FORMERLY LEGACY U.S. CUSTOMS AND THE U.S. IMMIGRATION SERVICE), THE DRUG ENFORCEMENT ADMINISTRATION, BORDER PATROL (CUSTOMS AND BORDER PROTECTION), ATF, NCIS, FBI, CHULA VISTA POLICE DEPARTMENT, AND THE SAN DIEGO POLICE DEPARTMENT.

WHILE THE CHARACTERS DEPICTED IN THIS STORY ARE SAID TO BE ASSIGNED TO OPERATION ALLIANCE, AND OPERATION ALLIANCE IS A REAL NARCOTICS TASK FORCE, IT SHOULD BE NOTED THAT THIS IS A WORK OF FICTION. SOME OF THE INCIDENTS THAT MAKE UP THIS STORY ARE VERY LOOSELY BASED ON REAL CASES, HOWEVER, ALL CHARACTERS ARE FICTIONAL AND THIS WORK IS NOT INTENDED TO DEPICT ANY PERSONS, LIVING OR DEAD. THIS STORY IS WRITTEN FOR THE ENTERTAINMENT OF THE READER AND FOR NO OTHER REASON.

ANY COMMENTARY ON PRODUCTS OR SERVICES ARE SOLELY THE OPINION OF THE AUTHOR AND ARE INTENDED ONLY TO FURTHER DEVELOP THE CHARACTER(S) DEPICTED.

CHAPTER . . .

1

The sun would soon be up. There was a hint of light on the horizon to the southeast. Jimmy Maxwell pushed out his legs in a vain attempt to stretch inside the cab of his Ford Expedition. Despite his cramped condition, he knew he was lucky to have been assigned the SUV. At six feet, three inches, it was the only vehicle in the U.S. Customs fleet that really fit him.

Jimmy ran a hand through his light brown hair and exhaled audibly. He was starting to get a little gray around the temple area; nothing unusual for men in his family. He had a goatee as well and had been thinking about shaving it off, as it was nearly half-gray. At least he was lucky enough to still have a full head of hair. He knew a lot of thirty-six-year-olds that were going bald. It was becoming a more acceptable, maybe even stylish look but one for which he had no desire.

He'd been sitting point on the surveillance for the last hour, watching the front of 314 Ashbrook, Chula Vista, California. Jimmy hoped it would be worth the discomfort, and looked forward to actually kicking in the door of this place. His confidential source had assured him that Angel Garcia was in the house. The source had been pretty reliable in the past and Jimmy felt confident that this was one of Garcia's stash houses. He just hoped that Garcia was there when they made entry.

Garcia had been indicted by a federal grand jury six months earlier for drug trafficking. Most federal investigators believed he'd retreated to Mexico in order to avoid arrest but Jimmy now had good reason to hope he was within reach.

When Jimmy had asked his source, Jesus Fernandez, aka Chuey, about how he knew Angel was going to be at the residence, he admitted to having delivered a load of marijuana to the residence the previous day, seeing Angel while unloading the car.

"What the hell are you thinking?" Jimmy asked Chuey. "Why didn't you call me? If you get caught moving dope without our permission, you will go to prison and I will be the first to testify against you."

"Hey, man, I tried, but your cell phone was off," Chuey said.

"Bullshit. Did you try to call Deron?" Jimmy asked.

Deron Morris was Jimmy's partner. Deron was thirty years old, having come over to Customs after having spent a couple of years as a Naval Criminal Investigative Service Special Agent. Since starting with Customs, Jimmy had seen at least half of the new hires into the criminal investigator position come over from other agencies. Deron had been with Customs for three years, initially assigned to Jimmy as a trainee, but the two had hit it off almost immediately. Deron had street smarts. He was a natural at dealing with people. In an interview with a suspect, he had that uncanny knack at getting someone to talk to him and admit knowledge of their part in what they'd been arrested for.

Chuey was a typical confidential source. He was a problem child. He could make cases because he ran around with good crooks, but he was hard to control. He gave you second- and third-hand information and claimed it was first-hand; he exaggerated; he disappeared when you needed him. And, of course, he whined and needed money constantly. He was a teenager in a man's body.

"I was with those guys. How can I call when I'm with those guys and they want me to drive?" Chuey asked. "I told you yesterday morning that I had something big coming up."

Jimmy hadn't known whether to believe him or not. At this point, it really didn't matter. The deed was done and at least Chuey had called him shortly after the delivery with the address and filled him in as to what was in the house. He'd also claimed that he'd seen Angel Garcia while he was unloading the dope. Jimmy hoped it was true. If he had been there, Jimmy wondered if he actually lived at the house or was just checking on his merchandise. Jimmy found it hard to believe that Angel actually lived there, but Chuey believed it.

Jimmy had initially hoped that the magistrate judge would have given them night service on their warrant. Jimmy had drafted most of the affidavit for the warrant but had sent Deron to track down the judge to get it signed. The judge had reminded Deron that there was no exigency for night service other than what they had created for themselves by letting their informant deliver the car containing the drugs to the residence.

Judges could afford to be patient and sticklers with the rules. They didn't have to sit out on houses full of dope all night watching to make sure none of it headed up the road.

Deron had waited several hours in front of the judge's house in Rancho Penasquitos for the duty judge to return home from some sort of social function she'd gone to. Deron told Jimmy later that when she'd finally come home he'd walked over to her as she was exiting her car.

"May I help you?" she'd asked as he approached.

"Judge, Special Agent Morris from the Customs Service. I'm hoping you'll sign a search warrant for me."

"I will if you've got probable cause," she replied in a droll, matter-of-fact tone. Deron followed her into her house, not knowing whether to laugh or be annoyed.

Jimmy remembered a Saturday some months earlier when he'd had to track down a judge to have a criminal complaint reviewed following a Friday night arrest. Agents were required by law to have a judge review their probable cause statement within forty-eight hours of an arrest, something known to them as the 'Forty-Eight Hour Rule.' The probable cause statement gave the judge the facts surrounding why the arrest was made, assuring them that there was reason for the arrest. Jimmy mused that had the judge who made that ruling been a golfer, or perhaps into yachting on weekends, he or she would not have counted weekends or holidays in the ruling.

The judge had been on the golf course and Jimmy had to borrow a golf cart in order to track him down. Jimmy found him on the ninth hole and got him to sign the complaint on the back of his golf cart.

All the judges Jimmy knew really hated being bothered on the weekend. He also couldn't remember a judge ever ruling

that there wasn't probable cause for an arrest. Oh well, someone had probably made a bad arrest somewhere in the past,
screwing it up for everyone else.

Jimmy tried to stretch again. His left leg continued to try to
cramp. "Hey, Bill, I'm going to need you to relieve me in another ten minutes so I can join the rest of the entry team when
we brief up," Jimmy put out on the radio.

Bill Anderson was a new agent who had been assigned to
the group about five months earlier after graduating the basic
academy in Brunswick, Georgia. He was a big burly kid with
reddish hair cut in a crew cut. He was a little on the heavy side
and still had some freckles splashed across his nose, probably
left over from childhood. Everyone, including Jimmy, liked
him almost immediately. Jimmy's only real criticism of the kid
was the fact that he was so naïve.

Like all agents on probation, Bill wasn't allowed to par-
ticipate in warrant entries until he made probation. Everyone
knew that if something went to shit, there was often a firestorm
of questions and usually controversy, and if you were on probation, it was very easy to just have the agency fire you, whether
you screwed up or not—not that they necessarily would, but
why take the chance.

The fact that probationary agents took a minimal role in
enforcement action allowed them time to be exposed to how
things were done. For example, they got to see first-hand how
long it took the team to brief and stack for the warrant, and
then finally deploy. The probationary agent usually took a perimeter position and was sometimes able to watch the breech-
ing and entry process, and the occasional problems those pro-
cesses presented. Sometimes the security doors or double doors
on a house took a bit of finesse to open. In any event, Jimmy
thought it a good idea to give new agents time to grow into
their positions and not get screwed out of a career due to inex-
perience or bad luck.

Jimmy remembered that a few years earlier, a senior agent
and a probationary agent were involved in a drug destruct with
some evidence custodians at a burn site in Texas. The narcot-

ics had been placed in an incinerator and a fire started. The agents and officers stayed on site for several hours, then locked up the facility and left the area with the fire still smoldering. They had been oblivious to the fact that they had been under surveillance by others not so well intentioned. Following the departure of the agents, those who had been watching broke into the facility, put out the dying fire, and then made off with what later appeared to be a significant amount of yet unburned packages of drugs. The follow-up investigation that ensued found everyone at fault, including the probationary agent who was just doing what his senior training agent had directed. The probationary agent was fired, while everyone else was able to keep their jobs thanks to their civil service protections.

Jimmy had been on some of those drug destructs himself. The Customs Service had twenty-four-hour periods at the ports of entry when they approached thirty significant narcotics seizures, all of which came with a corresponding number of felony arrests. Of course, with all those seizures there had to be regular drug destructs and the special agents who investigated those cases had to provide security for them. It wasn't unusual to see fifteen or twenty thousand pounds of dope burned every three or four weeks.

"I'm on my way to your location," Bill put out on the radio.

There should be plenty of time to brief up and do the entry before the traffickers in the residence get up, Jimmy thought to himself. Most drug traffickers didn't really get up and start moving until late morning or sometimes even early to mid-afternoon, doing a good deal of their business during the cover of darkness, and oftentimes partying with their product well into the night.

As this thought crossed Jimmy's mind, he noticed an old Dodge Colt station wagon pull up to the front of the residence. Jimmy looked at his watch. It was 6:05 a.m. Jimmy was parked about four houses away on the opposite side of the street in the point position. He had a good view of the front of the garage, but couldn't really see much of the rest of the house due to parked cars and trees.

"Surveillance from Jimmy, we just had an arrival at our target location. Standby."

"These assholes must be very busy, working this early," said Tom Phillips, the group supervisor.

Tom had seen it all. He was in his late forties and was one of those unusual federal agents that had spent his whole career in San Diego. His hair was gray and he was overweight but he still had a fire inside to do the job. Jimmy wondered if he regretted taking the promotion to group supervisor a few years earlier. Tom much preferred being out on the streets with the troops to dealing with administrative matters and attending management meetings.

"Yes they must," Jimmy replied over the air.

The driver of the Colt honked once. A moment later, the garage door opened and the car pulled inside. Jimmy used his binoculars to see boxes stacked on both sides of the garage.

"The car is in the garage. It looks like we might have a good one. There are a lot of boxes in the garage. I'm betting that some of them contain a green, leafy substance," Jimmy transmitted to his fellow agents.

"Bill, get up here and park in this space behind me. Let us know if there's any other movement," Jimmy radioed.

"I'm coming around the block. Be there in about twenty seconds," Bill replied.

The garage door closed behind the Colt. Bill drove up and parked against the curb behind Jimmy. Jimmy waited a minute, and then attempted to start his car to leave. All he got was a rapid clicking noise.

"Shit, my battery is dead," he said to himself. He'd been sitting for hours with his car in the accessory position in order for his radio to work. Apparently the radio had used more power than he'd expected and he'd drained his battery. Jimmy exited his car and walked back toward Bill.

"What's up?" Bill asked.

"Hey, I need a jump. My battery died."

"Great timing, huh?" Bill stated with a big smile. He popped the hood and started to get out of his car.

"Bill, get your vest and raid jacket off before you get out, okay. Let's not compromise this thing before it gets started."

"Sorry, Jimmy," Bill said, starting to take off his raid gear as quickly as he could in the confines of his car.

"Actually, just stay in your car," Jimmy said, deciding to simplify the issue. "Keep your vest on. Just pull up alongside me," Jimmy stated. Bill started his car and pulled up alongside Jimmy's Expedition. Jimmy opened the back of his SUV and started to remove a set of jumper cables from among several boxes he kept that contained everything from ammunition to batteries, blank cassette tapes, film, flares, his bulletproof vest, and even a few MREs, as well as other assorted treasures important to a federal agent.

Jimmy pulled out the jumper cables and started towards the front of his Expedition, looking over towards the target house. As he opened the hood of his vehicle, the garage door opened. Jimmy knew that agents were suiting up several blocks away in preparation for executing the warrant, but it looked as though the Dodge Colt was going to be leaving a little earlier than expected. *No sense in letting it leave*, he thought. Who knows what it might be leaving with—or who. He pulled the jumper cables off Bill's battery and closed his hood.

"Bill, head towards the driveway and block the car from leaving. Put out on your radio that we need all agents here now. Go, go, go! I'm with you."

Jimmy grabbed his Sig Sauer, Model 229, .40-caliber pistol off the front seat of his Expedition, along with a Stinger flashlight and started running for the stash house. Bill stopped in the driveway blocking the Colt from leaving.

Jimmy was only a few seconds behind Bill who was throwing his radio mike back on the seat of his car. Bill stood behind the opened driver's door of his car, using the door as cover, while he aimed his service weapon at the driver of the Colt.

Jimmy passed Bill, running to the Colt with his weapon aimed at the driver.

"Police! I want to see your hands. I want to see your hands. Out of the car!" Jimmy commanded.

Jimmy didn't wait for the Hispanic male occupant to respond. He opened the driver's door and reached in for the driver, pulling him by the top of his shirt.

"Out, out! Sordo! I said get out!" Jimmy again commanded.

Jimmy pulled the occupant out of the car and proned him out on the side of the driveway. Bill continued to provide cover and watched the front of the house.

In what seemed like a several minutes, but was probably less than thirty seconds, agents began to arrive at the residence. Initially there was no other movement readily apparent at the residence as agents began to stack for their entry; however, that changed quickly.

"There's movement in the house!" Jimmy yelled. "Someone looked out the blinds!"

The agents had stacked and were nearing the front door as Jimmy finished yelling. Sal Fierro, one of the larger agents in the office, crushed the door with a battering ram. In one continuous motion, he threw the ram aside into a flowerbed and the agents began to flood the house.

"Down, down! Police . . . Policia! Get down!"

Jimmy continued to cover the occupant of the Colt at gunpoint, listening to the familiar sounds of numerous heavy feet thundering through the house, along with the continued yells of 'Police!' and 'Down!'. You could hear the inner doors being slammed open. About fifteen seconds into the entry, Jimmy heard glass break.

"Someone's running out the back! Does anyone have him?"

It sounded like Tom Phillips' voice.

Shit, Jimmy thought. It occurred to him that with the rapid deployment and entry, there hadn't been time to get any perimeter people around to the backyard. Bill Anderson was still with Jimmy, covering the subject in the Dodge Colt.

Agents train that the entry team doesn't chase people out of a house. It was the perimeter agent's job to catch runners. Perimeter agents are trained not to enter a house, even if there is a call for help. So whoever had just run out the back was gone, unless the agents got lucky and the subject was stupid enough to hide in the immediate area.

Jimmy had that fleeting thought that many law enforcement officers have. *We only catch the stupid ones.* Not always true, but often enough the case. If it was Angel Garcia, stupid or not, he was gone.

You weren't necessarily smart to begin with, being in the drug trafficking trade, especially at Garcia's level. Still, that didn't make you stupid either. Most of these people were lucky to make it into their mid-forties. The majority of the cartel members died brutal deaths, or ended up in prison for the rest of their lives. Despite this fact, there was always someone there ready to take their place. But Jimmy had a feeling that Garcia wasn't stupid, and he knew that he was as ruthless a person as one could imagine if he'd made it to this level in the business.

"Don't you move!" Jimmy commanded the driver of the Colt, re-focusing on the present after noticing the Colt driver moving. He couldn't tell if he was just trying to get more comfortable or whether he was attempting to get up from the ground. The subject just looked at him like a deer in head-lights. Jimmy drew his pistol back towards his body, wondering when someone was going to come out of the house with a set of handcuffs. *What a bitch having to hit the place before you were ready*, Jimmy thought. *I should have been there on the entry.*

"Bill, you can come over here now. Come on."

Bill holstered his gun and tentatively moved up to Jimmy's position.

"Handcuff this idiot; then I want you to do a good pat-down on him. Once he's cuffed, get some I.D. from him and put him in your car," Jimmy directed.

Bill nodded. Jimmy waited until he was handcuffed, then headed towards the house.

"Are you guys Code Four?" Jimmy called from the open front door.

"Yeah," Tom Phillips stated, looking back over his shoulder from a position at the entrance to a hallway visible from the front door. Jimmy entered slowly, looking around at the controlled chaos.

"Tom, come back here when you get a chance," Barbara Burke, another agent in their group, yelled from a position towards the back of the house.

Tom turned and disappeared down the hall with Jimmy following. Greg Thompson was keeping an eye on several handcuffed subjects seated on a dirty sofa in the living room. The house was filthy, sparsely decorated with a few simple pieces of furniture.

As Jimmy started down the hall, he looked in one bedroom to see Shirley McCue and Sal Fierro getting two small children up from a urine-stained mattress laying on the floor in a small bedroom with no light other than that coming in from a window, which was mostly covered with taped-up newspaper.

Jimmy entered the master bedroom at the end of the house to see Tom Phillips, Barbara Burke and Deron Morris standing over several boxes visible at the closet. Jimmy walked closer. The boxes were full of cash.

"Nice hit, Jimmy," stated Deron. "Looks like your source is going to have a good payday."

"Let's get another agent in here. Guess we should get a few more agents rolling this way so we can get this cash out of here and start transporting prisoners to the office," Jimmy said.

"We need photographs before we move or disturb any evidence," Tom said.

"How much do you think it is?" Barbara asked. "Looks like mostly one hundred dollar denominations."

"I don't know. Should be at least a few hundred thou," Jimmy said. "Pretty unusual, having this kind of cash in a stash house. I'll bet it wasn't meant to be here very long. Somebody's going to be pretty pissed about this. You know, I think I'll go let the guys watching out front know to be paying extra attention in case we get some unexpected visitors."

Jimmy headed out front and advised Bill of the discovery of the cash.

"Sweet. Can you get me spotted out here so I can go in and take a look?" Bill asked.

"Yeah, but give me another few minutes. I need to go check out the garage," Jimmy said.

Jimmy returned to the house, again noting the two subjects seated on the sofa.

"Have you run them yet?" Jimmy asked Greg.

"No. I've got their I.D.s. Gary went to get some 202s, the personal history form agents filled out whenever anyone was arrested.

"Let me know if any of them are famous for anything when you get done," Jimmy told Gary. "That chongo on the left looks familiar."

"Jimmy, Garcia isn't here. I did check I.D.'s enough to know that."

"Shit! It figures. That guy has more luck than any damned . . ." Jimmy didn't finish the sentence. "Let's get the interviews going, ok? I'd really like to know if he was here, and if not, who that guy was that went out the back."

Jimmy headed towards the garage, passing through the kitchen that smelled of old beans and overused lard. Several roaches scurried along the kitchen counter past dirty dishes piled high both in the sink and along the countertop. An old brown rag with a patch of mold growing on it hung over the water faucet.

The scene in the garage brought a smile to Jimmy's face. Mitch Corrick, Gary Burns and Jesus Sanchez were going through boxes and pulling open cabinets and drawers. Stacked against every wall were boxes full of duct-taped, brick-shaped packages of marijuana.

Mitch looked up from a box, holding a folding knife in one hand that had a white powdery residue on the tip of the blade.

"Dude. This is sweet! It looks like some of this shit is coke," Mitch stated.

"Tom called to have some more guys head this way, but I guess I better have him ask the RAC for a few more," Jimmy replied. "Some additional security out front might be in order."

Jimmy had been involved in a lot of seizures, many that were fairly large. Seizing a couple of hundred kilos of cocaine, or a ton of marijuana was not unusual. The San Ysidro Port of Entry was the largest land border port between any two countries in the world and there was more dope coming into the U.S. through that port than anyone could possibly imagine.

Jimmy wondered what kind of hornet's nest he was stirring up with a case like this. Management and Customs Headquarters in Washington D.C. were sure going to be paying attention, if only for a few days. Jimmy loved his job, and was good at it. He knew there were many better investigators, but few that were as tenacious as he was. What he didn't like was dealing with Headquarters and the politics involved in federal law enforcement. Most federal agencies involved in drug law enforcement fought over jurisdictional issues and wanted a piece of any significant investigation.

There would probably be some interest in a press release, something Jimmy really didn't want. Normally the Customs Service stayed away from press releases, but Jimmy figured this seizure was definitely going to raise more eyebrows than the typical port seizure and arrest.

Press releases were fairly common among most of the other law enforcement agencies in the area. The Border Patrol, local police departments and even the DEA and FBI usually went out of their way to pat themselves on the back for significant seizures, while the Customs Service seldom did—maybe because it was so routine.

Agents didn't really mind the lack of press releases the agency allowed. It had its benefits. There were so many people in the smuggling and distribution end of this business that oftentimes the narcotics were passed through several levels before hitting the border, and then a few more levels before hitting the streets. Sometimes the narcotics moved through people's hands on credit. When law enforcement was able to seize some dope, someone ended up owing someone. When you owed too much, or if there was some suspicion that the loss was due to negligence, or through someone suspected of being a snitch, whether they were or not, those people were oftentimes killed. So, although law enforcement usually only arrested a transporter or 'mule,' there was usually other forms of justice being doled out by the cartel. Bodies were found dumped along the roadside, or in the trunk of a car, sometimes tortured or disfigured before their demise. Someone was paying for the loss of drugs and the money it represented.

As Jimmy opened boxes to do a quick check of the contents, Tom entered the garage and walked over to him. "Nice job, Jimmy. Congratulations."

"Thanks, Jefe."

"Did you invite anyone from DEA to come out on this?" Tom asked.

"Yea, Hector Dominguez. I told him it was a marijuana case. I don't think he wanted to be up all night. He told me to give him a call if it turned into something worthwhile."

Tom smiled and shook his head. "It figures. But, good, I'm glad you invited someone from DEA because, you know, they're probably going to raise a fuss. Almost every time we end up with a significant seizure like this they want to know why they've been left out. You know they'll want to latch onto this case."

"It sure is bullshit that we have to let them come poach on our cases, especially when they do almost nothing to help us with them. It's also bullshit that we seem to always get left out of any of the cases they initiate," Jimmy said.

"Life in the big city, buck-o. You've been around long enough that you should be used to it."

"I know, but it's still bullshit."

Jimmy look around, estimating the garage contained well over a ton of marijuana and probably close to five hundred kilograms of cocaine. Even in terms of wholesale value, Jimmy estimated that the dope in the garage was worth over eight million dollars. Someone would get whacked over this. There was no doubt in Jimmy's mind over that fact.

CHAPTER . . .

2

The alarm clock went off at 6:00 a.m., waking Jimmy from a troubled sleep. In his dream, he'd been in a gunfight, but when he tried to pull the trigger of his gun, it wouldn't go off. He awoke frustrated and in a sweat.

Jimmy sat up and rubbed his eyes. He looked over at his wife. Shirley lay on her side, the bedding coming up to her ears. Jimmy just looked at her a few minutes as he slowly came awake. He had married Shirley ten years earlier when she was twenty years old and he was twenty-six. She was a good-looking woman, tall, blonde, what some people might refer to as a trophy wife. She probably could have been a model when they married, but she'd gained a few pounds after giving birth to their daughter. Nothing significant, but enough that modeling was out. Jimmy actually liked the few extra pounds Shirley had put on as half of them had gone to her breasts.

Reaching over, he touched Shirley's bottom beneath the comforter.

"Let me sleep," she said, rolling away from him.

Jimmy lay back down and tried to snuggle against his wife.

"Go to the bathroom and take care of yourself," Shirley snapped. "I'm trying to sleep."

The frustration Jimmy had felt when he woke snapped back as he felt his anger rise. Their relationship had become more strained over the years with Shirley becoming increasingly moody and insistent on her way. Jimmy knew she resented his career choice, maybe even him for staying in his career. They'd talked about it countless times but with no resolution to the issue.

Jimmy didn't really understand his wife. He made good money, and sure, there were long hours. But it was a good job with good benefits. More importantly, it was something Jimmy had worked years for and something that gave him satisfaction and fulfillment. In short, it made him happy, at least most of the time.

Shirley didn't think they had enough time together. From Jimmy's perspective, they spent as much time together as most working couples. The difference being that the time they did spend together usually consisted of an evening or weekend that was regularly interrupted by frequent calls on his cell phone.

"Don't answer it," Shirley would plead.

"Honey, I have to," Jimmy would respond.

They always had a deal going, or there was a confidential source that had some information on a new trafficker or some other deal about to go down. Of course, there was a fair amount of time dealing with some confidential source that needed money, or talking to a cop that was at a source's house because he'd smacked around his wife or girlfriend. Jimmy would have to intercede and convince them not to arrest the source because he was involved in some critical upcoming deal. Controlling a source was like being a father, brother and priest all at the same time.

Jimmy got up and went to look in on their daughter, Nikki. She was the love of his life, although Shirley might argue that she was second to his job. Nikki was five years old, as cute as little girls come, with red hair and freckles splashed across her nose. Nikki was beginning to stir but was still asleep. Jimmy closed her bedroom door as quietly as he could and went back to his room to get dressed so he could go for a run. He'd been so busy the past few days he hadn't had a chance. Quietly heading out the front door, Jimmy looked up, shook off the frustration of dreams and wives, and smiled. There was a slight breeze from the west. It was nearing seventy degrees; the sky was clear, blue and beautiful except for a thin layer of haze trapped by the inversion layer that San Diego usually experienced most of the year.

The run felt good, the first half mile being the toughest. His moderately long brown hair was held in place by a San Diego Padres ball cap to keep it from constantly being in his face while he jogged. Jimmy liked running, having been a football player and wrestler in high school. He hadn't had time for sports in college, having gone to college after a stint in the Navy.

During his run, thoughts of the previous few days at work kept crowding into his mind. Man, he'd been so close to arresting Garcia. Still, not a bad gig all in all. There was nearly 3,100 pounds of marijuana in the garage, as well as 640 kilograms of cocaine. The money count wasn't yet officially back from the bank, but the initial bundle count indicated they'd seized $600,000.00.

Jimmy smiled as he thought of what he'd been told about these kinds of cases. Big cases, big problems, little cases, little problems, no cases, no problems. He wondered what kind of big problems were ahead of him.

He also thought about another thing he'd been told. One of his training officers reminded him that dope cases were a lot like a relationship with a beautiful woman. There were those moments of ecstasy, like when you kicked in the door of a stash house and made that initial discovery of dope or money. It was a lot like trying to get into a beautiful woman's pants. A lot of effort, then sex that was over way too quickly. Then there remained days of paperwork, follow-up, court and dealing with evidentiary issues. You had to keep the bosses and the prosecutor happy. That was like the rest of the relationship with the beautiful woman—a lot of work to keep her happy.

An hour later, Jimmy stepped out of the shower. Shirley came into the bathroom and started brushing her teeth, initially ignoring her husband.

"When you get dressed I need you to help me clean up this place," she said.

"I can help you for about an hour, then I've got a date to go shooting with Bill," Jimmy replied. "He's been struggling to qualify and I'd like to see him make probation."

"Bullshit! You need to stay home and help me. Bill can go shoot by himself," Shirley said.

My God. I really don't need another day of her crap, he thought.

Just before he said something, Nikki came into the room.

"Hi, Daddy!"

"Hi, sweety. What are you doing today?"

"I'm going to help you with your chores," Nikki replied. Her smile was contagious, melting his heart. He'd been starting to get angry with his wife, but Nikki's diversion had kept him, at least momentarily, from saying something that would have escalated the conflict between them.

"That would be great. I could sure use your help," Jimmy said, sweeping her up and into his arms. Jimmy gave her a big hug, an Eskimo kiss, and then swung her around in several circles. Nikki squealed in delight. Shirley watched with an emotionless stare, but managed a smile when Nikki looked over at her.

"Daddy, put me down. We have a lot of work to do," she said, trying to sound grown up.

"I think we should go on a bike ride," Jimmy suggested.

"You're going to help me with this house," Shirley stated matter-of-factly.

If he let himself think about his wife's demands, he'd become irritated. He worked sixty or more hours per week while Shirley stayed at home. She was a housewife and mother, something he realized was a full-time job. But why she couldn't, or wouldn't, keep the house up really bothered him. It was nice that she was around for their daughter, and she usually had a meal prepared when he got home, but she would leave roughly half of the housework for him. Jimmy had brought up this fact several times, only to wish he hadn't. His wife would not discuss issues that bothered him, only issues that bothered her. If she disagreed with him she'd just raise her voice, try to intimidate him and then spend the next few hours explaining how what she did at home was a lot more difficult than going out and playing cops and robbers.

According to Shirley, he was out having fun with his friends, able to come and go as he pleased, while she was stuck at home. He sometimes wondered if saving housework for him was some sort of punishment for his being the provider of a decent income. Jimmy felt himself getting irritated again but decided to suck it up and not let his day head off to the shits.

He reminded himself that arguing would only prolong the agony, also rationalizing and reminding himself of his Christian principles. 'Blessed are the peacemakers.' He believed it, knew it to be true, but sometimes wondered if his motives weren't as much mental self-preservation as being Christian.

"Where do you want me to start, dear?" he asked.

"Knock off that 'dear' crap. You know it pisses me off. You don't have to be condescending."

Jimmy and Nikki spent the next few hours vacuuming, dusting and straightening up the garage. He'd called Bill and pushed off their shooting date until later in the day—maybe.

Nikki wasn't much help, but she was great company. Jimmy had to laugh when she tried pushing the vacuum. The vacuum cleaner looked like it weighed two hundred pounds in her little hands.

By mid-afternoon, they had finished their chores. Shirley entered the garage and asked Jimmy where the closest Sears store was located. She knew where all the stores were located, she just couldn't remember which one was closest.

"The Chula Vista Shopping Center," Jimmy replied. "We'll go with you. We're tired and thirsty and need some ice cream or something, don't we Nik?"

"Yeah! Daddy, I want a root beer float," Nikki pleaded.

"You guys can come, but we're not going to the Chula Vista Sears," Shirley said.

"Why not? You're going to have to drive all the way to El Cajon for the next closest Sears," Jimmy said.

"My girlfriend Sally is a Chula Vista cop, and she told me that there are a lot of cars getting stolen from that shopping center parking lot," Shirley stated.

"I'm sure there's an occasional theft from the lot, but so what? The odds of losing your car there are at least several thousand to one on a bad day," Jimmy said.

"You're just a fed. Sally is a real cop, and I believe her. Besides, I don't really like shopping with all those Mexicans and gang bangers," Shirley stated.

"Oh, please!" Jimmy said, unable to contain himself any longer. "You live in southern California for god's sake. You've got friends who are Hispanic. What the hell is wrong with you today?"

"You're what's wrong. I can't even talk to you anymore. It's so frustrating. I tell you something and you instantly argue with me. You're always right and I'm always wrong. I can't even have an opinion," Shirley stated, on the verge of tears.

"Don't be sad Mommy," Nikki said, standing at her mother's side, head even with her mother's waist, looking up at her.

"Look, I'm sorry if I have an opinion that I feel compelled to voice sometimes. You certainly feel more than free to voice your opinions, and I usually say nothing, if for no other reason than to keep the peace."

Both adults stood looking at each other, allowing a moment of silence to regain their thoughts and composure.

"Nikki, why don't you go with mommy and keep her company at the store. I'm sure she'll get you a good treat, won't you, honey?" Jimmy asked.

Shirley stood looking at her husband without saying anything for a few more seconds, and then turned and walked away.

Jimmy started feeling a little guilty about the disagreement and wondered if Shirley really had wanted him to go shopping with her. "Honey?" Jimmy called out. Shirley turned and looked at him. "I do love you and I'll go with you to any store you want."

"Only if you really want to," Shirley replied, waiting for him next to their car in the driveway.

"Let me grab my sunglasses and use the head real quick," Jimmy said, returning to the house.

"I always have to wait on you!" Shirley said to him as the door to the garage closed between them, momentarily silencing her.

That night in bed, Jimmy read from his Bible. He made it a point to read I Corinthians 13, the love chapter, at least once a week. He liked to remind himself that love wasn't a feeling, it was a deliberate act that involved kindness, patience and sacrifice. Then he tried to finish his reading with a Psalm. They offered him a certain peace as he read them. However, tonight, like many nights of late, Shirley came into the room in one of her moods. The beauty of her naked body was overshadowed by the ugliness of her demeanor. She pulled the sheets back and got into bed.

"Turn the light out," she demanded.

"Can I finish my chapter first? It'll only take a couple of minutes."

"Then go read in the other room," she said. "I'm tired and I need to get some sleep."

Jimmy sighed, sat up and placed his Bible on the nightstand. He turned and looked at her a moment then turned the light out. "Night, hon," he said. There was no reply.

CHAPTER . . .

3

"Nice caper last week," Neil Bradley told Jimmy as he walked by. Jimmy smiled and nodded. "Thanks," he replied. He turned the corner into his section of the office bay, walked into his cubicle and sat down at his desk.

Better get to work on the report, he thought to himself. Jimmy had started the report at home over the weekend but knew he had a lot of work still ahead on this case.

Before he could even get his computer powered up his telephone rang. "Maxwell," he answered.

"Jimmy, it's Tom. Hey, you need me to assign someone to get that dope to the lab for you?" Tom asked.

"No thanks, Tom. I can get it to the lab tomorrow morning," Jimmy said.

"We have duty tomorrow," Tom reminded him. "What happens if it's a busy day?"

"Shit! That's right. Man, just when you get something good going the duty pops up and bites you in the ass," Jimmy remarked.

"No whining. You know that's our lot in life here on the border," Tom said.

"I know; and you know that normally I don't mind at all. But you have to agree that trying to do proactive investigations is a little tough when you have the duty every week," Jimmy stated.

There were six U.S. Customs, Operation Alliance groups, each with nine or ten agents, and one Group Supervisor. The groups rotated on a daily basis, handling all of the drug seizures made by inspectors at the San Ysidro, Otay Mesa and Tecate ports of entry, along with their related follow-up investigations. Initial processing of these cases usually took several days, leaving very little time to work proactive cases brought from confidential sources, not to mention the time it took

21

to do the follow-up investigations related to the port cases or other cases Customs was brought into for help from other law enforcement agencies.

"I'll get you replaced on the duty tomorrow, but I'm still going to have Sal and Bill get your dope to the lab.

"Tom, I'll stand my duty. I don't want the group thinking I'm someone special just because I took it upon myself to get wrapped up in a proactive investigation. Seriously, I can handle duty. But thanks, I do appreciate the thought."

"Well, if you change your mind and find out you've got too much to do, let me know," Tom said. "And please, get as much knocked out on your case this week as possible."

"I'll get most of it done by week's end."

"Oh, and by the way, you need to bring me your undercover driver's license."

"Why?"

"Another new rule," Tom said. "The RAC wants all the u/c licenses turned in and locked up in the office safe. You can check it out if you need it for a deal."

Jimmy suspected that the Resident Agent in charge of his office had probably received the order to secure the IDs from headquarters, and really hoped it wasn't just her own office policy. Still, where the hell did those widget-ordering idiots in management come up with these ideas.

"Are you kidding me?" Jimmy replied. "What's the deal: Don't they trust us with our u/c identifications? What happens if I'm in the field and I run into someone I've been undercover with before? If they confront me and I get sucked up into having to talk with them, or go have a drink with them or something, I'm screwed."

"I guess if you see someone like that headed your way, you better walk across the street or whatever to avoid them," Tom said.

"I can't believe it! Uncle trusts me to drive around with a sub-machine gun all day, but doesn't trust me with my u/c license. I'm tempted to just turn it in and refuse any more u/c assignments."

Tom knew Jimmy was just blowing off steam with his re-mark. Jimmy was too good an agent to refuse an assignment, let alone the opportunity to work u/c, something most of the Anglo agents seldom got the chance to do. Most of the u/c opportunities were assigned to the Hispanic agents that spoke Spanish.

Several hours later, Jimmy was finishing the initial draft of his report of investigation, or what the agents referred to as an R.O.I. The initial complaint following an arrest contained a probable cause statement issued with a complaint or charge sheet. Those documents, along with copies of the defendant's prior criminal history, photographs, and reports from other parties, such as a canine officer's report of how his drug detector dog alerted to the odor of narcotics, were filed with the court and served as an initial basis to hold someone in custody. A more detailed report of investigation had to be provided to the U.S. Attorney's office or District Attorney's office within ten days. Jimmy liked to get his reports done in a day or two, when everything was still fresh in his mind. Besides, Jimmy always seemed to be jumping from one shit storm to another. He often started working on a new case before he finished cleaning up all the things he had to do from the previous case. It wasn't that he necessarily looked for the cases that dropped in his lap—they just did. San Diego was a target-rich area with far more drug traffickers than cops to deal with them..

Part of the reason for Jimmy's success had to do with his personality. He was one of the senior agents in his group. His reputation had developed early in his career. He didn't try to avoid work, and did as good a job as time allowed. As a re-sult, the bosses came to him with some of the sexier cases. The inspectors at the port liked him and called and referred both general information and potential informants to him because he treated them like equals. He was friendly, and he always got back to them to let them know how the information panned out, thanking them for the referral.

Jimmy also firmly believed he had many good cases com-ing his way because he prayed daily: "Lord, bring those drug

traffickers across my path. Use me to get drugs off the street."
Jimmy rarely shared the fact that he prayed this prayer, but he
firmly believed that it was having an affect.

As Jimmy was saving his report on the computer, his telephone rang.

"Maxwell."

"Hey Jimmy. This is Mitch. I just got a call from one of my
sources that may interest you. I'm on the cell so I don't want to
talk too much about this. How about meeting me at the Starbucks on Dairy Mart?"

Mitch Corrick was one of those agents in Jimmy's group
that had a lot of potential but never really seemed to get much
done. He had five years on the job, was married and well liked.
He was a solid agent when it came to handling his port duty
assignments, but he'd never really done much proactive work.
When he would come across proactive information from
the occasional source he happened into, he'd always seem to
be able to pass it along to someone else to work. That aside,
Jimmy always figured he'd be in management someday because
he looked good and said the right things to the right people.
He also had good common sense and didn't cause anyone any
problems. Someone with those characteristics always seemed
to go far in the service.

"I can be there in about twenty minutes. What's it in regards
to?"

"You know your guy who got away last Friday? I may have a
local address for him."

"Angel? Sweet! I'll be there in fifteen minutes," Jimmy said.

Jimmy parked his Expedition in the Starbucks parking lot
twelve minutes later. He looked down at his watch. *Must be a
new record*, he thought. Jimmy was often criticized for usually
being a little late everywhere he went. Even with good intentions and fairly good planning, it just always seemed to take a
little longer than he planned to go anywhere or to get anything
done. Sometimes it was the traffic, which seemed to be a little
worse each year, or sometimes he just tried to get too much

done prior to leaving for an appointment. This time he decided to just stop everything and leave.

The outside seating area was about half-full of people who'd decided to have their lunch in the afternoon sunshine. There was a Rubio's restaurant next door as well as a Nextel store. Jimmy looked down at his Nextel. *Yeah, that's what I figured,* he thought to himself. *No signal. These things are the biggest pieces of shit. If it wasn't for the radio function these pieces of garbage would be absolutely useless.* Someone had to be getting kickbacks in Washington over some of the crap the agency bought. Jimmy remembered using 'WordPerfect' for a number of years, a word-processing system that worked very well. Then suddenly the agency switched to 'Word.' It was a giant step backwards in most agents' minds. But someone had to keep Bill Gates rich. *Oh well, such was life,* Jimmy thought.

Mitch pulled up in his gold Monte Carlo, parking a few spaces away. For some reason he didn't see Jimmy. He and a Hispanic male about twenty-five years old got out of the Monte Carlo and walked over to a small table outside the Starbucks and sat down. Jimmy recognized the source as 'Tonio,' short for Antonio Macias. Tonio sat nervously looking around the area.

Jimmy got out of his Expedition and smiled as he walked over to meet the two. He'd met Tonio on a few prior occasions. He smiled, mostly to himself as he sat down, finding it amusing because Tonio seemed to always wear the same clothes every time they met. Nothing was different today. He sported a long sleeve, cowboy-style shirt, plaid with a lot of pink, and a pair of dirty jeans and beat-up cowboy boots. His other standout feature was a thick handlebar moustache that gave him an almost Italian look. It seemed odd to have that thick of a moustache, or to sport that style at his age. Jimmy continued smiling, thinking that all Tonio needed was a monkey on his shoulder to be a cowboy organ grinder.

"Hey, Mitch. Hey, Tonio. Nice to see you," Jimmy said, extending his hand to shake hands with Tonio. "Can we go sit in my truck or something? There's an awful lot of folks hanging out here today."

"Sure," Mitch replied, getting out of his car. Tonio got out as well, still looking around nervously as the three men walked over to Jimmy's SUV.

Jimmy could tell that Tonio felt better about moving as well. He hadn't looked comfortable seated in public in the middle of the day, especially this close to the border. Jimmy took a mental note to talk to Mitch about it later. Mitch just didn't have much experience dealing with sources, and with a source, comfort levels were a big thing.

Mitch and Tonio sat in the back of the Expedition, hidden for the most part from the public due to the heavily tinted windows. Jimmy sat in the driver's seat and got out a small notepad given to him by one of his Chula Vista P.D. buddies, then turned to look at Tonio.

"Tell him what you told me," Mitch directed his source.

Tonio started speaking in his best English, but his thick accent made him very difficult to understand if you didn't pay close attention. It had taken Jimmy a number of years to filter out the accent so he could hear all of what was being said.

"Angel has an old lady that lives in Chula Vista. I used to run with some of his guys and I met him a few times over some *cervezas*. Don't know if he's there all the time, but I heard him say he's got a kid. I know he visits him some."

"What's his old lady's name?" Jimmy asked.

"I think its Carmen. Yeah, it's Carmen. I'm pretty sure."

"Where's she live?" Mitch asked.

"I went by the house about six months ago looking for Angel with a couple of his guys. I don't know the address, but I know how to get there," he said.

"Let's go," Jimmy said, turning around and starting the car. "Where we going?"

"Head over to Orange, then go north towards Palomar Street."

Jimmy moved out of the parking lot and headed north. A few minutes later, they were eastbound on Orange.

"Down this street," Tonio directed.

"Oleander?"

"Yeah, I'm pretty sure. It was kinda dark, but . . . yeah, go down here," Tonio said, his brow wrinkled as he looked around, seemingly getting his bearings.

Several turns later, as Jimmy slowly moved down the street, Tonio spoke. "That's it. Don't stop, that's it."

"I'll have to go to the end of the street and flip a U," he said. "Mitch, get ready to write down the numbers and see if we can get any license plates."

"1561 Ravenwood. There's a silver Maxima in the driveway. Couldn't get all the plate. Dude, you're going to have to go by one more time," Mitch stated.

"Shit," Jimmy muttered to himself. He didn't like going by a target address more than once.

Several minutes later, the three were on their way back to Starbucks. Mitch was on his cell phone with Sector Communications, their dispatch office.

Mitch hung up the call. "The plate comes back to Carmen Beltran at that address."

"Looks like you did good, Tonio," Jimmy said.

Tonio smiled, showing a capped gold front tooth between two brown-stained teeth.

"Jefe," Tonio said, looking at Mitch. "I know you got me a little money last week, but I could really use a little help. My rent's already three days late."

"What do you think we can get him, Jimmy?" Mitch asked.

"How much money did you give him last week?"

"Five hundred bucks. He gave me a license plate to have stopped at the border. It only had about thirty kilos of weed or I would have got him more."

"I think we can get you a little more in a few days, but you know how it works. The paperwork we have to do takes a day or so, and then it has to get signed off by the bosses. We can maybe get another few hundred, but if this address turns out to lead us to Angel, you'll have a real good payday. In the meantime, you need to learn to be a better money manager."

"Jefe, I got to buy groceries."

"I feel your pain, Tonio, but you've got to learn to save a little for those thin times. Maybe you should think about a job."

"I've been collecting cardboard and aluminum cans," Tonio said.

"You know, you might consider some new clothes. If I get you an extra hundred bucks, how about buying a new set of threads," Mitch suggested. Tonio hung his head a little and nodded. Jimmy smiled, happy that he wasn't the only one who'd noticed Tonio's one-outfit wardrobe.

"And make sure you're not spending your money on nose candy," Jimmy said.

Tonio looked up at Jimmy. "I don't use drugs. No way," he replied, acting a little hurt. "I'm here to work with you guys."

Probably helping eliminate the competition, Jimmy thought. One thing he'd learned over the years was that sources were crooks. Oh, sure, there was an occasional concerned citizen that could provide something useful to them, but the good sources were traffickers themselves. That's why they were good sources. They knew the business, and those in the business. They worked for the government because they were trying to work time off an upcoming sentence, or they saw the chance to eliminate competition, or they were on the outs with their particular organization and still needed to make money or they were out to get revenge for some wrong done to them by old colleagues. Whatever the case, the vast majority of sources didn't provide information because they were good citizens.

The truth was, half of the drug traffickers Jimmy had encountered didn't use drugs themselves, but Tonio had the look of someone who put a lot of profits up his nose. His constant sniffle and wiping of his nose with the back of his hand was one telltale sign. Still, as long as the information was good, no one in drug law enforcement was going to get too concerned over a little drug use. The agents frequently warned their sources against the use of drugs, but they couldn't be with them all the time and it was counterproductive to give them too hard a time about it.

Most agents were frustrated at the constant lack of ability to do their job the way it should be done. Every year there were new rules and more restrictions on how you did business. The disincentives were plentiful and some of the rules absolutely tied your hands from doing what needed to be done. The war on drugs was lost. All people in law enforcement could do was help control the bleeding, and try to hurt the cartels' pocketbooks a little.

Jimmy pulled into a parking spot a few spaces from Mitch's G-ride. He turned around and looked over his seat at Tonio. "I know you're here to work with us, Tonio. And we appreciate you helping us out. We'll get you what we can, but what I said earlier still goes. It's going to be the end of the week before we can get you anything so be patient and don't do anything stupid. Okay?" Tonio nodded a yes.

"And I'm reminding you that you're not to tell anyone what you told us today. Okay? Not your wife, your girlfriend, anyone. *Comprende?*" Mitch said.

"I'm not crazy, Jefe," Tonio said, getting out of the SUV.

"I hope that guy knows what he's talking about," Jimmy said as Tonio walked away. "We're going to have to get a surveillance set up. I want to spend some serious time at that place."

"Cool. It's all good with me," Mitch said. A few seconds later he remarked, "Some of the guys aren't going to be too happy about it though. You have to admit, we've been busier than hell the last couple of months."

"I know. But that's why we get the big bucks." Jimmy winked. Mitch smiled back and got out of the Expedition, heading for his Monte Carlo. "Besides, it's always better to sit out on a surveillance than to sit in the office, right?" Jimmy called out to Mitch.

Mitch turned, smiled and nodded his agreement but kept walking away.

CHAPTER . . .

4

Jimmy walked in the door of his modest Chula Vista residence just before 7:00 p.m. He lived in an older area of east Chula Vista on a cul-de-sac just off Hilltop Drive. His forty-five-year-old house had been remodeled just before he purchased it five years earlier. It was only 1,700 square feet but had an enclosed back patio that wasn't counted in the original square footage. Its large backyard was full of mature eucalyptus trees, one of which had a tire swing hanging from a lower branch.

During the remodel, its living room and family room had been converted to a great room with the removal of a portion of the wall. Jimmy had just installed a large potbelly stove in a corner of the great room facing the patio. The stove had a large face that opened enough to give the feel of having a fireplace if you didn't close its door.

Jimmy carried in his MP-5 submachine in a black canvas carrier designed to look like a tennis bag. In his other hand was his briefcase. The briefcase contained dozens of different forms, duty rosters for judges and prosecutors, computer discs with go-by's for every kind of report or warrant used in narcotics law enforcement, and a tube of toothpaste and a toothbrush. In the back of his car was another bag containing a change of clothes. In this line of work, you never knew when you'd start a surveillance of a bad guy with a load of dope and end up on a road trip.

"Hi, Honey," Jimmy said as he walked into the kitchen and kissed his wife.

"Hi," she said, returning his kiss, then returning to some pasta cooking on the stovetop.

"Daddy!" Nikki said, running to him from the family room.

Jimmy set his bags down and swept Nikki up, swinging her around over his head in an arc. It was getting a little tougher to get her up that high as she grew and got heavier.

"How's my baby girl?" he asked.

"I'm not a baby, Daddy," she stated.

"You'll always be my baby girl," came his reply with a big hug and kiss on the cheek.

"Daddy, you have to come see the picture I'm drawing," Nikki said, grabbing him by then hand and dragging him toward the family room.

"Don't leave those bags in my kitchen," Shirley called after Jimmy.

Jimmy pulled free of Nikki for a second and turned to grab his bags. Just before he picked them up, he swatted his wife's backside in fun.

"If you want a pot of hot water thrown at you, keep it up," she remarked.

"Lighten up, dear, I'm just playing," Jimmy replied.

"And knock it off with that 'dear' crap," she snapped.

Later that evening, after Nikki went to bed, Jimmy sat on the sofa drinking a Bohemia, his favorite Mexican beer. He'd turned on NYPD Blue, one of his favorite television shows. Jimmy acknowledged that the show, like all other cop shows, was totally unrealistic, but he loved it anyway. There really hadn't been any good cop shows since 'Police Story' went off the air in the late 70s.

If we could only get away with some of that stuff, he'd remarked on occasion.

"Yeah, I bet you'd like that, getting to bully and threaten people," Shirley said. Jimmy just shook his head but said nothing. It amazed him at times how little she knew him after all the years they'd been together. He knew he was a kind and gentle person, but he also knew he'd do whatever he needed to do if someone threatened his life or others.

Shirley didn't like most of the television shows Jimmy liked, and he in turn hated the programs she watched on TV. Their marriage, like many others he guessed, had become a compromise, giving in to each other on things like television shows, food choices, and the like. On those occasions when they couldn't agree on what to watch, well, thank goodness there was a TV in the bedroom.

The two really hadn't had much time to talk with each other prior to the start of the program, as there'd been dinner preparation, then dinner, during which Nikki received most of the attention. Then there was the kitchen cleanup and finally getting Nikki off to bed.

As the show progressed towards its conclusion, Shirley asked, "So how was your day?"

"Pretty good, babe. How was yours?" Jimmy continued watching the show but failed to look over at his wife during the exchange.

"You know, this is one of the reasons why I'm always pissed off at you," Shirley said. "Your damned TV show is more important than me. I'm trying to have a conversation with you."

"If you wanted to talk, why didn't you say something earlier? I could have recorded the show or something," Jimmy said.

"It's just a TV show."

"Honey, you know I like this show, and now that I've invested fifty minutes in it you want to talk. I'll be all ears the rest of the night, but I'd really like to finish the last ten minutes of the show," Jimmy pleaded.

Shirley got up without saying a word and went into the bedroom.

Shit, Jimmy thought to himself. *Guess I've done it again. But good god, why is it always about her?*

Jimmy finished the show, then rose and went to the bedroom. Shirley was already in bed with the light out.

"Honey?" he said in a semi-whispered voice. There was no response.

Jimmy closed the door and went back to the living room. He sat in silence for about ten minutes thinking about how to handle the growing tension between him and his wife. Finally, he rose and walked to Nikki's room. She lay in her bed, clutching a stuffed monkey she'd had since she was three. She was so beautiful. It always seemed to take his mind off his problems, at least for a time, watching her sleep peacefully.

I've got to hold this marriage together, Jimmy thought to himself. *That little girl means everything to me. I can't let her down.*

Growing up in a family and not knowing your father was tough. Going through a stepdad or two was even tougher. Jimmy knew what that was like.

Jimmy had to admit to himself that he was a bit of a dichotomy. On the one hand, he was a romantic; on the other, he was supposed to be the tough cop. From his teens, he knew he wanted to be married and have children. He wrote poetry and thought he knew what love was all about. He believed in family values, Christian principles, God, and the fact that marriage was supposed to be forever.

However, he also knew that there were certain things in life that, as a Christian, you didn't do. He believed in hell and punishment, right and wrong, and the fact that you deserved the consequences of your bad actions. That's why he didn't mind carrying a gun. The world needed peacemakers, peace officers. The world was full of hate and evil and someone had to be there to stem the tide of it all.

When he first started in law enforcement, Jimmy believed that everyone had some redeeming value, that despite what they'd done in life it was probably as a result of some bad thing they'd experienced or been forced into earlier in their life because of their environment or other circumstance outside their control. Within a few months of entering law enforcement, he knew his theory was wrong. There were people out there who were just plain evil. All they cared about was themselves. If they had had redeeming values at some point earlier in their lives, those values had been lost. These people were takers, users, and destroyers. He didn't know why they'd allowed themselves to become what they'd become, but he knew for a fact that there were those who enjoyed doing incredibly evil things. As far as he was concerned, they wasted the air they breathed and the world would be a better place without them.

Once he'd figured this out it finally made sense when he read those passages in the Old Testament where God told the Israelites to go into a land and kill everyone, or when he read of Elijah killing all the prophets of Baal. It wasn't that God wanted to kill anyone—it was necessary for the protection of the good. Bad apples really do spoil the whole barrel. From that perspective, taking someone off the street and locking them up meant you were protecting the rest of the citizens.

Jimmy returned to the family room and sat down on the sofa. So much was on his mind that it was hard to focus on any one thing for very long. Family issues, work issues, his relationship with God; all had suffered a bit, but none more than his relationship with God. It was hard to say when it started to deteriorate. The problems with his wife weren't helping, and with all the work of late, there didn't seem to be the time anymore to spend reading his Bible, or even going to church. He'd lie in bed at night and start to pray, but fall asleep in exhaustion before really getting started.

Well, there was nothing he could do about anything tonight. Jimmy went to the kitchen and got himself another beer, his third of the night. *May as well have a few more*, he thought. *I've got duty tomorrow so I won't get one then, and the wife's already asleep.* He opened his liquor cabinet and poured a nice double shot of Knob Creek bourbon.

He'd started receiving a bottle of Knob Creek from Shirley's parents for Christmas after they got married. The gift had become a tradition throughout their marriage. During the first few years of marriage, the bottle had lasted most of the year. As the years slipped by, Jimmy had become fonder of the drink and his taste for good bourbon had grown to the point where he was going through a bottle of Knob Creek every three or four weeks.

He returned to the great room and sat down to think about his warrant and Angel Garcia. It amazed him how he'd managed to land in the middle of a major drug trafficking investigation while working as an everyday border response drug agent.

He took a sip of his Knob Creek and started thinking about the case. There was Alberto Ruiz-Barraza. He was pretty well known, at least among the federal agents along the border working narcotics investigations. The news channels periodically ran stories about him. He headed a drug cartel responsible for the importation of hundreds of millions of dollars worth of drugs from Mexico into the United States. The cartel also made several million dollars a month through kidnappings. This money helped offset the money lost to drug seizures made by law enforcement.

Ruiz was a murderer, one of those people that wasted the air they breathed. He was responsible for killing dozens of people every year who got in his way, or who didn't pay his taxes for moving their drugs through Baja California, Mexico, or who stole from him, or who just pissed him off.

There was Jose Leon-Gamboa, a lieutenant in Ruiz's organization, a man who oversaw smuggling operations for the cartel. He had been a state judicial police officer for about ten years. Now he made a living by providing protection for Ruiz's stash houses, and occasionally providing escort services for some of the larger narcotics loads as they came up to the border. Leon had left his position as a police officer following a politically motivated corruption investigation, but he'd avoided prosecution by paying the Governor of Baja half a million dollars.

Then there was Angel Garcia. He worked for Leon, ultimately responsible for running a number of the stash houses in the Tijuana and San Diego area. No one really believed Garcia spent much time in these houses. They assumed he stayed in Mexico most of the time, organizing movements of drugs and overseeing the hiring of those who did run the houses, occasionally visiting some of them to check on employees and inventories, conducting various audits, and making sure that merchandise wasn't disappearing. But Garcia wasn't in Mexico—not now at any rate. Jimmy wondered why.

Jimmy took another sip of his Knob Creek. He let his mind wander, thinking of all of the people the cartel employed. There had to be at least several hundred people in the Tijuana and

San Diego alone, not to mention other distribution areas in the United States. Then there were the farmers who grew and harvested marijuana in the west central area of Mexico. There were transportation workers, including those who both drove and flew drugs from Central America and northern South America, as well as from central Mexico. Then there were politicians, soldiers, judges, prosecutors and Mexican law enforcement officers. It was a billion-dollar-a-year business.

There were even a few U.S. law enforcement officers who worked at the border for the cartel. A simple nod and wave of the hand sending a truck or car up the road without inspection could earn an Immigration and Customs Inspector as much as fifty thousand dollars. Who would know? What was your integrity worth? Was it worth risking your freedom, maybe your life?

Jimmy fell asleep on the sofa after several drinks, his last thoughts of the evening centered around wondering who was getting killed down south over all that dope and money he'd seized from the cartel.

CHAPTER . . .

5

At 6:15 a.m., the telephone on the nightstand rang, bringing Jimmy out of a troubled sleep. He'd consumed a six-pack of Bohemia and had several double shots of Knob Creek the night before. He couldn't even remember going to bed. The telephone rang again as Jimmy struggled to feel around for it. On the third ring, he found it and then struggled again to find the on button, finally pushing the correct one.

"Sorry to wake you, Jimmy. This is Angie at Sector. You need to call Inspector Sharp at the Otay Mesa Port. They have a marijuana load."

"Okay, Angie. Thanks," Jimmy replied.

"You need the number?" she asked.

"No, I've got it."

Once he took a drink of water to clear his throat he spent a moment trying to wake up and gather his thoughts. It took him a minute to locate a piece of paper and pen out of his nightstand. Once done, Jimmy returned the call to the port, speaking briefly with Inspector Sharp. The subject they had in custody was a lone Mexican male who was allegedly driving a friend's car that just happened to have a gas tank compartment full of marijuana. The inspectors estimated it to be somewhere between seventy and eighty pounds, but they hadn't taken the vehicle apart yet.

Jimmy authorized the dismantling of the vehicle. Agents had worked out a system with the inspectors where they were supposed to check with the agents prior to tearing up the vehicles loaded with drugs. This was done in order to allow the agents the opportunity of trying to cooperate the defendant driver so that a controlled delivery of the drugs to the owners or intended recipients could be attempted. In this instance, it was way too early to have enough people available or in the area to attempt a delivery.

The time factor in these cases was critical to their success. There were often spotters who would advise the drug owners whether or not a vehicle had been sent into secondary inspection, and the drivers were on a pretty tight schedule to arrive at their intended destination. Since it was going to take close to an hour to get to the port, Jimmy told Inspector Sharp to go ahead with processing the vehicle.

Jimmy finished his short conversation, sat up and spent another minute trying to get enough energy to get out of bed. He finally kicked off the covers and headed for the bathroom thinking to himself, *Well, it's job security. It's just like housework, it never seems to end.*

Arriving at the port about an hour later, Jimmy ran his criminal history checks and other computer queries in TECS, the Treasury Enforcement Communications System, a system that allowed investigators to input suspect information as well as confirmed criminal history information. The checks on the driver had all been negative.

Jimmy exchanged pleasantries with Monique Reardon, a San Diego police officer assigned to work with Customs agents under a special program assisting in interviews as a Spanish translator. Monique had been working with Customs for about a year and had a very good reputation as someone who knew how to push all the right buttons in someone in order to get them to admit knowledge of the drugs. She was an attractive woman who came across sweet enough that most defendants she spoke with almost felt obligated to tell her the truth. Jimmy knew she could be pretty hard as well, but she hid that side of herself, at least during these types of interviews.

Once advised of his rights, Jimmy began the interview of the defendant with Monique. He too was normally very good with interviewing. It was pretty rare that he wasn't able to break a defendant. He and Monique had great respect for each other in this regard. Of course, there would always be the occasional defendant who invoked their rights to speak with an attorney, or who just didn't want to make a statement, but it was a bit unusual if Jimmy couldn't get someone to talk to him, and once they started talking, they admitted knowledge of the drugs they were smuggling or buried themselves so deep in lies that they were easy to convict.

As the interview progressed, it became apparent that this was one of those times when the smuggler just wasn't going to break. Thirty minutes into the interview, things were going nowhere and Jimmy was getting frustrated. He never allowed himself to show his frustration to a defendant, but it was there.

Interviews with Spanish speakers were always tough on him. You couldn't control the interview nearly as well when you had to depend on someone else to pose your questions. You also didn't know when to interrupt or cut someone off when they started lying, and you didn't know when to push them back towards the truth when they wandered off on tangents. Jimmy comforted himself with the fact that at least he had Monique with him. If she couldn't get someone to talk, they probably wouldn't talk to anyone. The defendant claimed he'd borrowed the car, and was sticking with the story.

Jimmy knew that the U.S. Attorney's Office would usually dump a case without an admission of guilt, even though everyone in this business was aware that if you crossed the border in a vehicle loaded with tens of thousands of dollars worth of drugs, it was extremely unlikely that you didn't know they were there. The logic was money-based. Why would an organization risk all that drug money on an unwitting driver who, if they discovered the drugs, would either steal them or turn them over to law enforcement?

There was also the risk that if someone tried following an unwitting driver across the border and was referred for inspection, the owners wouldn't know where their dope went. One just couldn't predict where an unwitting driver was going. They may tell you that they're going to their mother's house, but change their mind and end up going somewhere else.

The U.S. Attorney's Office was aware of these facts as well, but they also knew, as did Jimmy, that most of these cases didn't have good jury appeal. Most of the defendants were down and outers who agreed to smuggle dope because they couldn't make their rent, or their child or parent needed medical care, or some other financial crisis loomed in their present or near future. Juries regularly acquitted without a confession, and would probably feel bad about convicting with a confession if the person looked pathetic enough. The mentality of most southern Californians was, 'It's only dope. It's not like it's a real crime.'

Two hours into the interview, Jimmy gave up and decided to just print the defendant and get him ready for jail. Following the printing process, the defendant was locked up in a holding cell, and Jimmy sat down in the agent's office to work on the booking paperwork.

"Hey, Jimmy," Barbara Burke said, walking into the office.

"Hi, Barbara. What's up?"

"I just finished interviewing two seventeen-year-old males that smuggled 150 pounds of weed in a false compartment built into the roof of a Plymouth van. I think the driver's uncle is the registered owner."

"Did they do the right thing?" Jimmy asked.

"Oh yeah. Had them eating out of my hand," she said with a smile.

Jimmy smiled, picturing how her interview must have gone with her two young defendants. They probably would have told her anything she wanted just to try and make her happy. Barbara was in her mid-twenties, a very good-looking brunette who wore clothes that fit her every curve. She caught stares from just about everyone present when she entered a room. On top of her good looks was the fact that despite having been on the job only a few years, she was smart and she had a knack at interviewing.

"Any luck with your guy?" she asked.

"No. Pisses me off too. He almost broke twice, but then reverted back to his bullshit story."

"That makes it easy," she said.

"How's that? All it really means is that the idiot will spend a couple of days in jail and then probably get kicked," Jimmy said.

"Haven't you heard?"

"Heard what?"

"We're doing deferred prosecutions now," she said.

"So what does that mean?"

"It's this new program they just instituted. If you have a Mexican national, and they aren't the registered owner of the load vehicle, and they have no prior arrests, and they get caught with 150 pounds or less of marijuana, we can just turn them over to INS who will cancel their documents and send them south."

"What happens if they confess?" he asked.

"If they confess, they get arrested and go to jail."

"What a bunch of shit. Let's give them an incentive to be truthful and honest with us," he said sarcastically. He paused a moment then continued, "And what about some of our fellow agents who are already less than motivated to do a good job interviewing to begin with?"

"I know, I know," she said. "I'm just telling you about the program, not giving you my opinion as to what I think about its merits."

"Well I'm not letting this guy go. He just smuggled in about seventy pounds of weed. Matter of fact, I need to go check with the inspector and get the final count."

"By the way, what about American citizens? Any incentives for them to tell the truth or lie?" Jimmy asked.

"Nope. If they're a U.S. citizen they go to jail."

"Unbelievable!" Jimmy said. "Wow, I can't believe some-one would come up with tell the truth, go to jail, tell a lie, go home . . . if you're a Mexican, that is. I can already name a bunch of agents who will be whispering in the ears of their defendants not to admit anything. You know, Andy Terrell told me a few months ago that when the defendant admits knowledge to him, his interview is over. He doesn't give a shit about investigating these cases. Fortunately there aren't a lot of guys like him, but with this kind of incentive, who knows what some of them will do."

"I think management is just looking at it from the stand-point that with the jails being overcrowded, and the cost issues associated with trying to prosecute these folks, something new had to be tried. It makes some sense that if the person has lost their immigration status, and they can't come up here and smuggle or break our laws anymore, that it's the right thing to do to avoid wasting time and money."

Jimmy gave a little disgusted laugh and shook his head. "Yeah, but you know that a bunch of these folks will be back anyway. Many of them have reported border-crossing cards lost or stolen and gotten replacements in order to have a duplicate, and most of the rest will just be smuggled back in if they really want to come back. Besides, they lose their immigration status even if they go to jail. Screw it, all my guys are going to jail, even if the U.S. Attorney's Office does kick them the next day."

"I kind of figured that's what you'd say," Barbara said. She smiled, shook her head and then turned and walked out of the office.

Jimmy picked up the telephone and called MCC, the Metropolitan Correctional Center.

"Hello. Agent Maxwell from U.S. Customs. Hey, I need to get a window for a male adult that I just arrested for drug smuggling," he told the MCC guard on the telephone.

What a way to do business, he thought. *Having to make an appointment to book someone into jail.* The federal jail facility was so undermanned that they only took new prisoners between certain hours, those hours amounting to four or five hours out of twenty-four, and you had to call ahead to make sure there was space available for them. There were times when you couldn't get someone booked into custody because the jail was full. Jimmy found it amazing that there were times you couldn't get a drug smuggler booked into MCC because the jail was full, mostly of alien smugglers and undocumented criminal aliens who'd returned to the U.S. and been caught.

I wonder how the FBI feels when they can't get a bank robber booked into custody because a bunch of illegal aliens are taking up all the bed space, he'd thought on occasion.

Jimmy was also glad that his defendant didn't appear to have any significant medical issues. What a pain in the ass it was to arrest someone with TB or some other communicable disease, or when the arrestee was addicted to drugs, or had some other malady. The jail would refuse to take them and you would have to either take them to an emergency room and get them treated and released by a doctor, or book them into a detoxification center and stay with them until a contract guard service could dispatch someone to come take over babysitting them.

The rest of the duty day went by without significant incident. It was busy, the day shift getting nine or ten cases. All of them were marijuana cases until mid-afternoon when one of the supervisory inspectors ran into Jimmy with a smile on his face.

"Jimmy, I think you're going to like this," Dean Jenson stated.

"What you got?" Jimmy asked.

"We have a lone Hispanic female in a car with a shitload of heroin," he said.

"Cool. Where is she now?"

"Got her in a holding cell," Dean said.

"Why a cell already? No chance of trying to deliver the car cold?" Jimmy asked.

"No. It was a floor compartment and we had to do some cutting to get to it. I didn't think there was going to be any way you guys would be able to deliver it. Not to mention the fact that she's already been here over an hour."

"Too bad. You're right. Sure wish we could get some of these out of the port though," Jimmy said.

Jimmy headed over to the security office and holding cell area.

"Hey, Jimmy," Sally Arkin said, greeting him. Sally was one of those older Customs Inspectors that had spent over twenty years working at the port. Everyone knew her. She was thin and had been attractive in her youth, but her age and many years working outside showed in her weathered skin. Sally was also a smoker, giving her voice that gravely sound. She reminded Jimmy a little of Marlene Dietrich

Sally sat at a computer terminal located behind a large, stainless-steel-covered counter in a room adorned with what looked like a large picnic-style bench attached to the floor, stretching all the way around the perimeter wall. Half a dozen disheveled people sat on the bench about four or five feet apart from each other.

"What cell is our customer with the heroin staying in?" Jimmy asked.

"The first wet cell on the left," Sally replied.

Jimmy walked over to the cell door, knocked once in case the woman was using the toilet, and then opened the door.

The woman sat on a small wooden bench in the corner of the five-by-five cell wrapped in an old brown, wool army blanket. The woman was in her mid thirties, about five-foot eight, and two hundred pounds. She wore a pair of loose-fitting shorts and a very small top with spaghetti straps that showed a lot of her large saggy breasts. The clothes were filthy, and her hair was a mess. Despite this fact, Jimmy guessed she had tried to dress provocatively hoping to distract the inspector on the primary inspection station with the view of her breasts rather than with checking her car. It might have worked better had she been an attractive woman. She had large breasts, but she was not even slightly attractive. Jimmy suppressed a shudder at the thought of her trying to appear sexy.

Showing his credentials, Jimmy asked, "Has anyone told you why you're here yet?"

"No," she replied.

"Well you're here because we've found drugs in your car."

The expression on the woman's face didn't change, telling Jimmy that she knew of the drugs.

"What's your name?"

"Maria Brice," she replied.

"Where do you live?"

"Los Angeles."

"Where were you born?"

"Santa Ana."

"Brice isn't your maiden name, is it?"

"No. It was my ex-husband's name."

"Well, let me give you some advice. You're in a lot of trouble. I've got some administrative things to deal with before we talk, but when I get back I want to advise you that if you decide to talk to me, and I hope you do, be truthful. You're not here by accident. We all know that you knew of the drugs," Jimmy snuck in the lie in an effort to encourage her to talk to him and be truthful.

"Can I get a drink of water?" Maria asked.

"There's a button on the side of the toilet. Push it," Jimmy directed.

Maria got up and after managing to flush the toilet accidentally, figured out where the fountain button was located atop the sink area of the stainless-steel fixture.

Jimmy turned, locked the cell door, and then returned to the security office. Once there he found a lunch-box-sized plastic tub under Sally's side of the counter. The container held the woman's purse and a few other personal effects. Most of it looked so disgusting that he was tempted to go put on a pair of rubber surgical gloves used by the inspectors for their pat-downs.

Going through the wallet in the purse, Jimmy discovered a gas receipt dated about a month earlier. It was one of those older receipts that not many businesses used anymore where the credit card was placed in a holder and a receipt was placed over it and swiped. The receipt showed a vehicle license plate number.

"Hey, Sally, what was the plate on the vehicle with the heroin?"

"Hang on," she said, picking up a clipboard to look.

"Looks like 7GXX246," she said. "Sure wish some people had done a little better in their penmanship classes," she said smiling. "Yeah, pretty sure it's a seven. Doesn't make sense that it was a T anyway."

"Cool," Jimmy said. The plate matched that on the gas receipt.

Jimmy finished going through the personal effects and then returned to the investigator's office in west secondary. Running Maria's criminal history, Jimmy noted several arrests for being under the influence of heroin.

Shit, he thought. *Hope she's not a hype.*

Twenty minutes later, Jimmy had Maria in an interview room. Barbara sat in the room as witness as Jimmy filled out a personal history form, obtaining information about where she lived, her family, employment status and the like. When he was finished, he pitched her to be truthful with him if she agreed to talk to him. Jimmy then advised her of her rights. Maria stated that she understood her rights and agreed to speak with the agents.

Like so many other interviews Jimmy and his peers began, Maria began to concoct a story that was full of half-truths and out-and-out lies.

"No, really," she said. "I got a ride down to TJ yesterday from my friend Adam, but he had to be back to work this morning so he dropped me off at my aunt's house so I could borrow her car," Maria explained.

"So how long has your aunt, Lupe wasn't it, had this car?" Jimmy asked.

"I think she bought it recently, like in the last few weeks sometime. I don't really know because I only get to see her every few months."

"When was the last time you drove this car?" Jimmy asked.

"This is the first time. She didn't even have this car last time I was here," she replied.

"Does she have any other cars?" Barbara asked.

"No, just this one."

"You guys must be close, what with the fact that your aunt Lupe is letting you take her only car all the way to LA. When are you bringing it back?" Jimmy asked.

"Probably next weekend," Maria stated.

"What if I told you that I know you've been driving this car for over a month?" Jimmy asked.

"I don't know how you could know that, when I just saw it for the first time last night," she replied.

Jimmy opened a folder sitting on the table in front of him, took the gas receipt out and laid it down in front of Maria.

"Guess where I found this?" Jimmy said.

Maria gave a little gasp, and stared at the receipt with her mouth open.

"You're going to have a tough time getting a jury to believe your story when I show them this," Jimmy said. "So, here are your options. You tell me the truth and I'll see what I can do for you. What I'd like to do is write a report indicating to the prosecutor and judge that all that heroin in your car isn't yours. What I'd like to write is that the heroin belongs to someone else, that you've been unemployed for a long time, and that you were just trying to make some money to live on. You know, we all need to make money. The courts understand that. So it would be better for you if I write in my report that you're just a person who made a mistake by letting someone talk you into driving a car across the border for some money. But if you continue to lie to us about this I can tell you what the prosecutor and judge are going to believe. They'll think that you're way more involved in the drug trafficking organization than you are, and that you may even be the owner of the heroin."

Maria sat quiet for a minute.

"Come on, Maria. We're not going to sit here and waste much more time on you. This isn't a tough case for us to prosecute, and we've got other customers waiting," Jimmy said.

"They told me it was just marijuana," Maria said, hanging her head.

"How much were you supposed to get?" Barbara asked.

"Five hundred bucks," Maria replied.

It always amazed Jimmy how little money it took for someone to decide to ruin their lives. There still wasn't a final weight on the heroin, but there had to be close to fifty pounds of the stuff from what Jimmy saw being unloaded. Maria was looking at about ten years in prison without some serious help based on further cooperation.

Jimmy finished his interview of Maria then took care of the rest of the booking process. As he got ready to transport her to the federal jail, he noticed she was looking a little pale.

"How much of a habit do you have?" he asked.

"What do you mean?" Maria asked.

"Are you going to get sick on me?"

"No."

"You sure? I've seen addicts before, Maria. Honestly, you can tell me the truth. I promise you're not going to be in any more trouble."

"I'm all right."

Jimmy handcuffed Maria and seated her in the front seat of his Expedition.

"Sector, this is Alpha 353. Transporting one female from India 290 to MCC, mileage 54,355," he put out on his radio.

"A353, Ten-Four. Call us on arrival," they replied.

Jimmy looked over at Maria as he sped up I-5. He pushed the vehicle in the traffic, keeping his speed between eighty and ninety mph, trying to get to MCC as quickly as he could. Maria laid her head against the passenger side window and began to moan.

"Maria, lift up your head a bit," Jimmy said. Once she did, he rolled the window down, hoping the fresh air would help. Maria then began spitting out the window every few seconds in a less than ladylike manner.

Fifteen minutes later, Jimmy pulled his vehicle down the driveway entrance to MCC. Reaching the bottom, a jail security guard met him, checked his ID and radioed in that a prisoner had arrived. Jimmy looked over at Maria. She was starting to rock back and forth, moaning more loudly. Jimmy knew the look, knowing she was about ready to throw up.

"Hang on!" he yelled, running around and opening the car door. Just as he got her out of his vehicle, she threw up. Some of the vomit splattered on Jimmy's shoes and the bottom of his pants legs. Maria stood over her vomit and continued to spit into it for another minute.

"I'm ok now," she said. "Sorry."

"Come on, let's go in," Jimmy said, shaking his head in disgust.

"Hope they have a bathroom inside. I really have to pee," Maria said, sounding like she was feeling better.

Jimmy escorted her over to the large metal roll-up door that provided access to the facility. Another guard looked out a window, this one also checking his credentials. After closely scrutinizing the picture in the credentials against Jimmy's face, the guard radioed someone in the control center to open the door.

Once inside the facility, the three rode an elevator to the second floor where they met several other guards and a physician's assistant.

"I really got to pee," Maria told one of the guards.

"Hang on lady," he told her. "It's going to be a few minutes."

"Any medical issues?" the PA asked.

"She's not reporting anything, but I have a feeling she has a heroin habit," Jimmy said reluctantly. He knew what was coming next.

"We can't take her like that," the PA said, raising his voice an octave. "When was the last time you used?" he asked Maria.

"I only chip occasionally," she said. Jimmy shook his head, angry that Maria was just now finally admitting her habit.

"That's not what I asked. When did you use last?"

"Last night. But man, I need to use the bathroom," she said.

"You're going to have to wait," he said, turning to Jimmy. "We can't take her. You're going to have to take her to a detox facility."

Jimmy had yet to un-cuff her, and without saying a word, he took her by the elbow and escorted her back to the elevator.

Once at his car he unlocked it, put his gun back in his holster and then grabbed his cell phone. He dialed the number and called with his back to Maria.

"Hon, I'm not going to be home for dinner. I really thought I would be, but something came up," he said.

"Jimmy, I really have to go to the bathroom," Maria said.

"What's her name?" Shirley asked in an accusatory tone.

As Jimmy started to respond, he noted movement behind him and turned to see that Maria had hooked her thumbs in her shorts and was pulling them down. She squatted and began to urinate on the ground between him and the front passenger tire of the Expedition, the urine running into her pool of vomit.

"I can't talk now," Jimmy said, hanging up and shaking his head in disbelief.

When Maria finished, she stood up but was now unable to pull her shorts and panties up with the handcuffs on.

"Jimmy, can you help me?" she asked.

Jimmy turned his head away from the sight before him, but reached down and grabbed the corners of her panties and shorts with just the tip of his index fingers and thumbs, and grimacing, he pulled them up, his face turned away.

"Thanks, Jimmy. I'm sorry, but I really had to go."

Jimmy wondered what he'd tell his wife when he got home. She wouldn't believe a word of what just happened if he swore to it.

CHAPTER . . .

6

Jimmy spent the next day and a half writing reports and submitting drug samples to the DEA lab for analysis. He had really wanted to get out and spend time sitting on 1561 Ravenwood in the hopes of finding Angel Garcia, but he knew his first responsibility was to deal with his port duty arrests and getting the paperwork completed and filed.

He remembered when he'd been hired and his first boss had sat him down to give him the new employee pep talk. In the sharing of his wisdom there was no talk of being careful, no talk about integrity or what kinds of problems you could have with informants. There hadn't been officer safety-related issues raised or reminders about being responsible with his authority or being safe with firearms. No, his boss talked to him about the things any boss might bring up: putting in a full eight hours a day, giving the taxpayer his money's worth, and all that. But most of all, Jimmy remembered a phrase he used. 'Publish or perish,' he told Jimmy. How true. Agents spent a lot of time writing, memorializing what they did in the field, memorializing the details of warrant entries, surveillances, meetings with sources, arrests and interviews.

It wasn't until the mid-afternoon hours that Jimmy was able to grab a handful of agents, brief them and head out to the Ravenwood address. Jimmy called NIN, the Narcotics Information Network, to advise them of the surveillance. It was standard protocol to advise NIN about things such as surveillances, warrants, or other contacts or law enforcement activities in the field. NIN was a central clearinghouse for the various law enforcement agencies in the county that worked narcotics. They tracked addresses and people that were under investigation in order to prevent what was referred to as 'blue on blue' issues. You didn't want an informant from Customs setting up a dope deal with an informant from DEA. There had been times before the NIN was created that a Customs' agent would believe they were going out to arrest a smuggler who was really a DEA undercover agent or informant, and the next thing you knew a bunch of cops were pointing guns at each other.

NIN also prevented agents from stepping on each other's investigations. There was nothing worse than having invested six months or a year working a trafficker, maybe being up on a wiretap, and then having someone from another agency go arrest him for having a pound of marijuana when he was supposed to deliver five hundred kilograms of cocaine to your informant the next day. By calling NIN prior to making a contact at a residence, you avoided those types of issues.

Jimmy remembered that just a few months earlier, he'd had a case at the border where he arrested some knucklehead with a load of dope who'd been driving someone else's car that was registered to an address in San Diego. He had decided a few days later that the prudent thing to do to would be to visit the registered owner of the load vehicle to inquire if they knew the smuggler, or to ask them why their car would have been used to smuggle drugs. Maybe he'd even be lucky enough to find a house full of dope when he got there. However, in route to the residence he'd called NIN to run the address. In that case, following the protocol had paid off. It turned out that DEA was up on a wire at the residence and search warrants were being prepared for execution the following week.

During their pre-surveillance brief prior to setting up on Ravenwood, Jimmy had advised that if they got a chance they would arrest Garcia either arriving or leaving the residence. If it was determined that they couldn't grab him on foot in front of the residence, they would covertly follow him in a vehicle and radio for a black and white to pull him over on a traffic ruse. Once stopped, they could scoop him, hopefully without a pursuit or other incident.

Once at the residence, agents set up around the neighborhood, each in a position to cover one of the four directions of travel he might take if he managed to go mobile from the area prior to the agents being able to put the *habeas grabus* on him.

"I'll take the eye for awhile," Jimmy put out on the TAC channel they were using. There was not sign of activity at the home. The silver Maxima was not parked in the driveway, and the blinds were closed.

Everyone settled in, finding a spot they could try and blend into without drawing too much attention to the residents of the neighborhood.

It was not uncommon for agents to be contacted by the police while they sat static on a surveillance. Quite often, a resident would see one of their cars, then call in a 'suspicious vehicle' parked in the area. Occasionally, the resident, being nosy and not necessarily thinking about their own safety, doing their perceived neighborhood watch duties, would just walk up to them and knock on the window and ask them what they were doing.

The afternoon passed quietly. Most of the agents had to leave their cars running with the air conditioning on in order to stay cool enough to be able to sit in their cars. As they sat waiting, the only break in the reverie was when someone advised that they'd be unavailable for five or ten minutes while they left for a bathroom break. Fortunately, there was a public park with restrooms just a few blocks away.

Jimmy was thinking about calling the surveillance and sending everyone home when just after 5:00 p.m. Sal put out over the radio, "Silver Maxima is southbound on Brandywine. If it's your car it should be turning west on our target street in a few seconds."

"Driver is indicating a westbound turn. Committed westbound," Shirley put out on the air.

"I have her," Jimmy said.

The Maxima passed Jimmy's parked Expedition and pulled into her driveway, six houses from Jimmy's location. Jimmy ducked down in his seat a little as the Maxima passed, grateful for his tinted windows.

"It's our car. She's parked in the driveway."

A good-looking Hispanic woman in her early thirties exited the driver's side in what appeared to be an expensive blue business suit. The woman retrieved some dry cleaning from the back seat area of the car as well as a soft leather briefcase. The passenger door opened and a young boy of seven or eight exited the car, struggling with a heavy-looking backpack that Jimmy guessed probably carried schoolbooks. At the front door, the woman struggled with her keys in her attempt to gain access to her home. Jimmy felt a momentary urge to offer assistance.

"They're entering the house," Jimmy transmitted. "Surveillance units, let's meet in the Von's parking lot off Telegraph Canyon Road."

Five minutes later, the agents parked, exited their cars and gathered together.

"Wow, pretty exciting afternoon, Jimmy," Shirley said with a smile and wink. For a woman nearing forty, Shirley still looked pretty good. She was single, blonde, physically fit, and had great legs, although a bit smallish in the chest for what Jimmy thought to be the ideal build of a woman. She still liked to flirt with some of the guys and was much more playful than any woman her age Jimmy had ever known. On top of her other good qualities, she got along with virtually everyone. Jimmy sometimes wondered why she was still single.

"Don't listen to her, man. Anyone who's got the same name as your old lady . . ." Sal didn't finish his comment after getting a glare from Jimmy. Jimmy liked to tease as much as anyone, but he seemed to always stick up for the women in the group. More importantly, he didn't like bringing up problems he had at home at work. It was bad enough having to deal with those issues at home. Work was his sanctuary and he wanted to keep it that way.

"What's the plan?" Mitch asked.

"You guys want to sit out here until midnight in the hopes that our boy will show up?"

"Not really," Greg Thompson said. "I promised my wife I was going to take her out to dinner tonight. I cancelled on her a couple of days ago and don't really want to again."

"I don't care," Jesus said. "But if we stay late, we come in late, right?"

"I'm not your supervisor, dude, just the case agent. You can do whatever you think you can get away with." Jimmy paused, but he'd already made up his mind. "Let's call it a night and be back out here around 6:00 a.m."

"Oh, man! I've got to get up at 4:00 a.m. to be here by 6:00. Why so early? I need my beauty sleep," Mitch complained.

"I really don't think the sleep's been helping," Shirley said. Everyone laughed.

"You know I live in Oceanside," Mitch started to say. Jimmy cut him off.

"So move to Chula Vista. Besides, the traffic won't be an issue leaving at 5:00 a.m., so you might even be able to sleep in an extra fifteen minutes. Besides, we're out here on information from your snitch. You're the last person who's getting a pass on this surveillance."

"Just one of many reasons to love informants," Mitch sighed.

"I've got a complaint that has to be filed before 9:00 am," Barbara said. "I can be here but I'm going to have to split around 8:00 a.m. so I can go to the office and get my paperwork."

"That's okay, don't worry about it. Just come in at your normal time, file your case and hit us on the air. If we're out rolling around somewhere, we'll advise."

Jimmy looked over at Bill Anderson who had yet to say a word.

"You good for 6:00 a.m.?"

"Sure. Hell, I'm the rookie. What good would it do me to complain?"

"I like your attitude. And you're right, it wouldn't do any good," Deron said.

"One of many reasons I picked him for my partner," Jimmy said with a smile.

"No, seriously, I'm just happy to be out here with you guys. Besides, she's a good-looking woman from what I saw. I'll be her professional stalker anytime," Bill said.Jimmy refrained from commenting any further, knowing that Bill was trying to fit into the group by picking up on the smart-ass quips.

"Hey, Jimmy, I'm not sure I'm going to make it in the morning," Deron said. I'll try but our last duty day kicked my ass. I've got to get some complaints over to the duty magistrate tomorrow. We'll see how much I can get knocked out when I get home."

Jimmy shook his head and smiled. "Okay, dude. Do what you have to do." He looked around at the rest of the troops. "Anyone else buried ass deep in work? Speak now or forever hold your peace." No one responded. "Okay, thanks you guys. See you in the morning."

The agents dispersed into the heavy afternoon commute.

Jimmy toyed with the idea of going home, but decided he'd return and sit on the Ravenwood address a little longer.

An hour later, Carmen Beltran exited the house in a pair of sweats and got into her car. Jimmy had been parked down the street watching the house. He let her pass him, make the corner and disappear before he started his vehicle, made a U-turn in the street and followed. She drove to a YMCA fitness center a few blocks away.

I should probably have hit the gym on the way home myself, he thought.

As he watched her walk from her car into the building, he was drawn to how incredibly attractive a woman she was. *How did she end up with a crook like Angel Garcia?* he thought. *Money?*

A little over an hour later Carmen left the gym and headed back home. It was getting dark. Once Carmen was back in her house, Jimmy decided to call it a night and head home. He knew he was going to have a long day tomorrow.

Chapter . . .

7

The alarm went off at 4:30 a.m. and Jimmy sat up, turning it off in the dark. He looked over at his wife who continued to sleep. He sat still for a minute and tried to focus his thoughts, first on why he was getting up so early, then on what he had to do for the day. His head pounded and his mouth was dry.

God, I've got to quit drinking so much, he thought. His drinking had slowly increased over the past several years and he knew it was starting to get excessive. His whole life had started to evolve in ways he would have never believed a few years earlier.

He had been raised in the church with a strong belief in God that had never changed, but he was unhappy in his personal life. He had never liked dating and had never been a party guy. When he met Shirley in college, she seemed like an answer to his prayers. She was good looking, smart and seemed to want the same things in life as he did.

The first few years of marriage were pretty good. They seemed to be even better when Nikki had been born. She was the love of Jimmy's life. Jimmy knew that his wife dearly loved their little girl as well, but her birth had started a change in their relationship, or so it seemed. Jimmy was never home enough. He didn't help around the house enough. Shirley just seemed so stressed about almost everything. She'd initially wanted more attention than he could give, but after not getting it she withdrew, growing ever colder towards him. It was for these reasons, along with the increased pace in Jimmy's work, and to some degree his drinking, that a wedge was being driven between he and his wife.

It was only natural that the longer you were on the job, especially in this area, getting more proficient in what you did, developing more sources of information, more relationships with your peers and other law enforcement contacts, that you were going to draw more work your way, and with the work came longer hours. Shirley hated it, hated the time it took away from them. She didn't understand why he wasn't off work when he got home. The constant ringing of the cell phone infuriated her. Her short temper over this and other issues caused Jimmy to shut down communication with her. He was tired of listening to her whine. So he drank more, oftentimes just to be able to fall asleep without laying in bed having dozens of thoughts flood his mind. Even his language had begun to slip, something he'd always kept in check.

Jimmy gave his sleeping daughter a kiss on the forehead and headed out the door at 5:30 a.m. The aspirin was kicking in and as he drove away from his house, he felt a little excited about what the day held in store.

"Wow. You made it on time and with a smile on your face," he remarked to Mitch.

"Didn't even get pulled over by a Chippy on my way south," he said.

"I guess that's a good thing." Jimmy looked around. "Who we missing?"

"I think we're all here. I even talked to Deron last night. He's caught up enough on his work that he's going to join us. He'll be here in a minute."

Fifteen minutes later, the agents were set up around the Ravenwood residence again. Despite the hour, the neighborhood was pretty busy. People were getting into cars and driving away in a rush, garage doors were opening and closing, and neighborhood cats were dodging some of the cars as they presumably headed back to their homes to be fed after an evening of carousing.

No unusual vehicles were visible at the Ravenwood residence, just the silver Maxima parked in the driveway. At 7:20 a.m. the door opened and Carmen Beltran and her little boy exited the residence. The boy carried the same backpack he'd carried into the house the night before. Carmen was wearing another nice-looking business suit, this one cream in color, accentuating her brown skin, and was again carrying her leather briefcase.

The surveillance team followed them away, and as expected, the little boy was dropped off a mile away at the Brandywine Elementary School. The surveillance continued, following Carmen to the Kearney Mesa area where they watched her park at Hemisphere Business Products. They handled all kinds of business electronics, from computers to photocopiers and fax machines. Carmen entered the business, disappearing as the door closed behind her.

Well, now what? Jimmy thought.

"What's the game plan?" Mitch asked over the air.

"Let's give it a bit, and see if it looks like she's here for the day. If she is, I'll call it so you guys can get out of here," Jimmy responded.

An hour later, Jimmy terminated the surveillance.

Now what? he thought.

Jimmy decided to go back and sit on the Ravenwood address for a bit by himself. Once there, he found a spot in the shade, rolled down his windows and settled in. It was a quiet, peaceful morning, with lots of birds chirping as spring began to kick into full bloom. San Diego, America's finest city, as it was known to its residents, was an awesome place to live. While much of the rest of the country was still going through winter-like conditions, it was already in the high 70s, with blue skies and just a whisper of a cool breeze off the ocean.

Thirty minutes or so after parking, Jimmy watched two undocumented Mexicans come out of some bushes that lined an area between the street and an arroyo that paralleled the area between Interstate 805 and Brandywine Avenue. The two men, who were probably in their mid 30s, looked tired, dirty and disheveled. One of them carried an old, soft-sided suitcase, while the other carried two, one-gallon plastic milk jugs, one of which had about an inch of water in it.

The two men looked around and then started down the sidewalk. They walked about half a block, then the man with the water bottles trotted up into a yard and turned on a garden hose connected to a spigot on the side of a house. The man filled up his water bottles, then turned off the water and trotted back to his friend. Just as the two men started to walk away, a resident from a house near them came out and called to them. The men looked at the Hispanic resident. They initially seemed frightened, but stood listening to what was being said to them in Spanish. Then Jimmy noticed the men relax a bit, and slowly walk towards the residence while the resident went back inside.

A few minutes later, the resident returned to the front porch area, finding the men seated on the steps leading to the porch. The resident handed each of the men a sandwich and an apple. The men took the food, thanked the man, then turned and walked away. The resident went back inside.

Just another day in paradise, Jimmy thought to himself.

Jimmy continued his lone surveillance through the morning, but as lunchtime approached, he began to get restless.

This is a bunch of crap, he thought to himself. *Let's try another approach.*

Jimmy started the Expedition and drove down to the Brandywine Elementary School. Once inside the office, Jimmy identified himself to one of the school secretaries and asked if there were any yearbooks from the previous school year. He really didn't want to give away any specifics about whom he was interested in, but told the lady that he was trying to locate a child who'd been taken in a custody dispute. He told the woman that the parent who had taken the child was involved in drug trafficking. The secretary disappeared into the back for a minute and then returned with the 1997 yearbook.

Thumbing through the pages, it only took about five minutes to find a picture of Carmen Beltran's son. His name was Raul Garcia. He was in the third grade, making him about a year older than Jimmy had guessed. Jimmy pretended to look awhile longer, going through quite a few more pages. He then closed the yearbook and handed it back to the woman who had stood watching him.

"Find who you were looking for?" she asked.

"No. I'll bet he goes to Havenhurst Elementary over off Max. Guess I'll go over there and bother someone else," he said with a wink and a smile.

"No bother. Good luck."

"Thanks."

Jimmy headed out of the parking lot of the school, initially heading towards his office.

Sweet, Jimmy thought. *Okay, little Raul is likely the son of Angel Garcia. He isn't using his mom's name. So, now that I've verified the connection to the residence how do I handle this? I still don't know if Angel is living there, although it seems unlikely. Still, he probably visits sometimes if Raul is his kid. I need a break on this so I don't have to sit out here for heaven knows how long.*

Jimmy turned on the 'good-times' radio station in his Expedition. Thinking about his next course of action, he changed his mind about going back to his office.

I am not going back to the office, he thought. *Think I'll head over to Chula Vista P.D. and find someone to run some ARJIS checks on Beltran and her address for me. Maybe I can find a connection to Angel with the computer.*

ARJIS was the 'Automated Regional Justice Information System,' a county computer system designed to store a variety of information useful to any investigator. The system stored information about traffic citations to include the driver of the car, license plate number of the car, location stopped along with the date and time. It contained field interview and contact information. When a police officer stopped a suspicious person, typically someone like a gang member or the like, it documented their contact, with whom it was made, as well as the date and time. It also contained information on subjects that had been arrested, as well as the victims and witnesses to crimes reported to the police.

If the police had contacted Angel in the past, Jimmy might be lucky enough to find a real address in the area that he provided the police. Maybe he got a ticket in a car that could be identified and located. If Carmen Beltran had been the victim of domestic violence, it might show Angel as the suspect and a date and time he was last at her house. There were many possibilities.

Jimmy had started his law enforcement career working nearly four years as a Chula Vista Police Officer. When he got married, he decided to move over to the feds in order to avoid the shift work. He reasoned it would be better to be home in the evenings and have most weekends to spend with the family. It sounded good then, and there was certainly more opportunity for being home in the evenings with his current job than on the P.D., but he spent way more hours working with Customs. Then there were all those calls to his home every evening. One of the good things about being a police officer was that when the shift was over, it was over.

Once he exited the freeway, it was only a two-minute drive until he turned south on Guava, a one-block-long street that ended in the back lot of the police department. Jimmy parked and went up to the employee entrance. Punching in the access code, which hadn't been changed since he worked there eight years earlier, he entered the building. He walked past the Watch Commander's Office and stuck his head in the door.

"Hey, Lieutenant," he said to Lieutenant Richard Stark.

"How you doing, Jimmy?" Lt. Stark asked.

"I'm good, L.T. Just thought I'd come by and see if I can find someone around to run an ARJIS check for me."

"Should be someone back in the detective's bay," he said. "Matter of fact, I think Patricia Ely is back there."

"No offense, L.T., but that woman is as fucked up as a soup sandwich when it comes to computers."

The Lieutenant laughed and remarked, "Yeah, you're right. Ah, hell. Go back there and see who you can find."

Jimmy walked back towards the detective's bay. The main office was almost deserted and Jimmy looked at his watch to reassure himself that it wasn't past five o'clock yet. Nope, it was only 1:45.

Maybe everyone is taking a late lunch, he thought.

Rounding a corner, he saw one of his old buddies, Dan Cummings. He was sitting at a computer terminal with a stack of reports next to him. He was obviously doing some computer checks of his own.

"Hey, Dan. Looks like you're knee deep in something that smells bad."

"Jimmy! Dude! Good to see you. What brings you around the old stomping grounds?"

Dan got up from his chair as Jimmy walked over to him. The two gave each other a quick embrace.

"I came by to ask if you could run a quick ARJIS check for me on a doper address here in town."

"Man, we don't have any drugs or crime in our city. And if we do, it's because you hot-shot Customs guys didn't do your job and catch it at the border like we taxpayers pay you to do." Both men laughed.

"Riiigghhttt. It does look like you're busy. I could leave the name and address so you can run it later when you have more time."

"There's never enough time. I may as well do it now. I need a break from this crap I'm working on anyway."

"Anything good?"

"Just a murder. Some guy came home and found his wife shot full of little .25-caliber holes. We interviewed the husband who called it in, and who, by the way, is the prime suspect. He said she had been having an affair and that it was probably her boyfriend. Allegedly, the husband and she were going to work things out so she was going to break it off with the boyfriend. He allegedly didn't want it to end. You know, same old bullshit. I think it was the husband."

"Wow. I guess no one told him that if you really want to kill someone, you shouldn't use an ear, nose or throat gun."

"Nope. But in this case, it was enough."

"So I guess you have to do your magic and figure out if he was elsewhere at the time of the murder, or there's some other alibi?"

"What I need is a DNA test but this cheap-ass department won't pay for it."

"Why not?"

"Man, how soon you forget. You know. The City Manager tells the Chief that if he can keep his budget under a certain amount for the year he will give the Chief a big fat bonus at the end of the year. The Chief wants the bonus, so he keeps us short staffed, driving cars that should have been surveyed a couple of years ago, and won't let the lab spend any money on things like DNA testing. Of course, he and the two captains got new cars last month."

"No one said that life was fair. You want some more advice?" He continued before Dan had a chance to respond. "Remember, my friend, that politics are everything . . . almost."

"So, what does that have to do with anything?"

"If you ever want out of detectives, you know, to promote, don't piss off management complaining about stuff that won't change." Jimmy knew what Dan's response would be and had just made his comments to get a reaction out of his friend.

"Dude, I could care less about promoting. I got into this line of work to do law enforcement, not become some guy that sits behind a desk in the front office and orders pencils for the troops."

"That's my boy. Don't ever change."

"Yeah, yeah. So what's this address you need run?"

Jimmy pulled a little notebook out of his rear pants' pocket and began writing down the name Angel Garcia and 1561 Ravenwood on his notepad. When he finished, he ripped out the page and handed it to Dan. "Hey, can you get me a few more of these notepads? I'm just about out of them."

"Sure," he said as he took the piece of paper and started the query on the address. "That's the one thing we still have plenty of around here." Dan ran several queries as Jimmy stood behind him, looking over his shoulder.

"Nothing on the name. Could he be using any other last name?"

"I don't really know. Try Beltran."

Dan looked up a few seconds later. "Nada, senor. But let me try the address."

"There's only one hit on the address. Looks like officers responded to a disturbance call about two years ago, but when they arrived, they found a Carmen Beltran alone in the house with a split lip. She didn't provide any suspect information."

"Didn't, or wouldn't? Don't answer. It's a rhetorical question."

"Sorry man, but that's it, unless you've got something else to run."

"How about her plate," Jimmy remarked.

A minute later, Jimmy found out that Carmen had received a ticket about a year earlier for speeding. The ticket was issued early in the day so Jimmy surmised that she was probably running a little late for work that morning and had pushed the envelope a bit getting there.

"Oh well. I'd really hoped for a little more, but such is life," Jimmy remarked. "Thanks."

"So, you going to tell me what's so special about this place and, or this woman?"

"Don't you remember hearing the name Angel Garcia?"

Dan thought for a moment before speaking. "Some big-time doper guy, right? Seems we had a homicide a year or so ago that he was a possible suspect in."

"Yep, that's him."

"So what's your interest in him?"

"He's supposed to be a lieutenant in the Ruiz-Barraza organization. He manages a lot of their stash houses."

"What's his connection to Ravenwood?"

"His old lady lives there. At least I'm pretty sure she does. I was hoping he was staying there as well. I've got an arrest warrant for him. We took off a stash house about a week ago with a shitload of dope and he ran out the back door. I'd like to say that my crack perimeter team missed him, but to tell the truth, we didn't even have one. Anyway, it's a long story and the short version is that our guy's in the wind."

"Well, well. You found more dope you guys missed at the border?" Dan said with a smile.

"Yeah, like 640 kilos of white, about 3,000 pounds of weed and about $600,000.00"

"Holy monkey!" Dan said. "That is a lot of dope."

"Guess I'll look into a wire since nothing else is working out, although I'm pretty sure I won't be able to get one because we don't have any dirty calls connected to the residence."

"They're pretty hard to get anyway, even for you guys, aren't they?"

"Yeah. It's pretty funny. I was listening to some talk show host yesterday while I sat out on surveillance. This knucklehead was expressing concern about some new law that makes it a little easier for us to get wiretaps. I guess they think we're going to be listening into everyone's conversations or something. What a schmuck. I guess they don't know how tough it is to get up on a wire. If people only knew that you have to have exhausted all other investigative avenues in order to even apply for one, plus spend a whole lot of time and money to get one. Man, you have to apply for a pen register and then analyze all the calls it tracks from the number you want to go up on, then show a judge that there's calls being made from the phone you're interested in to documented crooks. Then we have to spend another ton of money going through the process to get up on a line. You know, I'll bet there's probably not more than a couple of dozen wires going in the county at any one time by all of the federal agencies combined. So in a county of over two-and-a-half million, the average Joe is probably safe from having somebody listen to him talk dirty to someone else's wife."

Dan laughed and remarked, "Yeah, but at least you guys have the money to spend."

"A little maybe. We don't have the politics of the city, but money is limited. If it wasn't for living in a HIDTA area, we wouldn't be able to do any wires, let alone have money for equipment like night vision goggles or laptop computers."

"HIDTA?"

"Yeah, you know. Uncle has classified certain areas in the country, particularly along the southwest border, high-intensity drug trafficking areas. Because we're in one of those areas, they throw us more cash in order to fight the 'alleged' war on drugs."

"Well sneak me $1,800.00 from your HIDTA money so I can run a DNA test, will you?"

Jimmy and Dan finished their conversation with a few pleasantries, and then Jimmy headed out the back to his vehicle.

Later that evening, Jimmy sat at home watching a Disney movie with Nikki on his lap and his wife by his side. Shirley was in a better mood than she'd been in for awhile. These were the types of evenings Jimmy enjoyed, free from the stress of dealing with family problems.

Jimmy sometimes wondered why he could seemingly take on any problem handed to him during the course of the day at work, but have such a struggle with every problem at home, particularly those involving his wife.

Shirley spoke quietly with Jimmy about her day as the movie played in the background, mostly sharing things that seemed of little consequence to him relative to what he'd been going through. He tried to listen and stay focused, but it was a chore. Jimmy smiled and nodded and agreed with her about how expensive beef was becoming and the fact that she wanted to buy a new vacuum cleaner. He agreed with her that they needed a new vacuum cleaner and offered to do the dinner dishes as soon as the movie was over.

As the movie ended, Jimmy looked down to see Nikki asleep in his lap. His left leg was asleep too. He carefully lifted his little girl and headed to her bedroom when his cell phone rang, waking her up.

"Crap!" Jimmy put Nikki down in her bed, but she sat up almost instantly.

"Daddy, it's not time for bed yet."

Jimmy smiled and put his index finger to his lip in a shushing gesture. As he did so, Shirley came into the room with a look of exasperation on her face.

"Don't take that call," she said, almost in a pleading way. Jimmy shook his head.

"Maxwell."

Shirley turned around and stormed off.

"Jimmy. Hey, this is Henry Rojas. Got a minute?"

"Sure. What's up Henry?" Henry was a San Diego Police Detective in their 'Street Teams' unit, a detective unit that worked street level drug dealing. Jimmy had worked with him a few times in the recent past.

"Hey, I've got a walk-in source that has some information that maybe you can do something with. Got any time to meet with her in the near future?"

Jimmy really didn't feel like he had time, but was never one to let anyone down if they needed anything.

"How about tomorrow morning?"

"Let's meet over in the Mission Valley area around ten. Maybe over near the IKEA store."

"Call me in the morning when you get close."

The call ended as quickly as it started and Jimmy closed his cell phone and clipped it back into the holder on his belt.

"Daddy, when do I get a phone like yours?" Nikki asked.

Jimmy laughed. "Not for a while, sweetie."

Jimmy tucked his little girl in bed, then sat next to her and said her prayers with her. He then said a little prayer of his own, asking God that when he went into his bedroom, his wife wouldn't be angry with him.

CHAPTER . . .

8

The following morning, Jimmy drove down to the Mission Valley area to meet with his SDPD buddy Henry Rojas. Jimmy pulled into a spot on the east end of the IKEA parking lot just west of Qualcomm Stadium and dialed Rojas on his cell phone.

"Where you at?"

"Right around the corner."

"I'm about two rows over from the front door of IKEA, almost all the way down from the entrance," Jimmy said, looking around for Henry and trying to get a better bearing on where he was exactly.

"I'll find you, man. I'm a trained investigator."

Jimmy chuckled a little as he hung up. A minute later, Henry tapped on the side window of Jimmy's Expedition. Jimmy hit the unlock button and Henry slid into the back seat with an attractive Hispanic woman about thirty-five years old.

"Jimmy, Angelica. Angelica, Jimmy," he said by way of introduction. "This is the agent I told you about, Angelica. He and I used to do some work together, and I trust him like a brother," Henry said. "Jimmy, Angelica has a friend that is having some trouble that you might be able to help with."

"I can't promise you that I can do anything, except maybe give you some advice," Jimmy said. He sighed a little too loud following his remark, and immediately regretted it.

"Jimmy, I think you're going to be interested in what this lady has to say," Henry said, giving him a little scowl. "Go ahead, Angelica."

There was a momentary pause where Angelica looked into Jimmy's eyes, searching him for a sign that he was worth sharing her concerns with. Jimmy regretted the sigh, wishing he had shown more concern for the lady's troubles, whatever they were. He knew that Henry wasn't going to bring him just any old flake. Henry knew that Jimmy's time was valuable, so there must be a good reason why the lady was here.

"I'm sorry, Angelica. I am interested in helping you if I can. I have a lot going on right now, but Henry was right when he told you about our trusting each other like brothers. If he thinks your problem is important, I'm sure I will as well. Honestly, if there's something I can do to help, I will."

Angelica continued to look into Jimmy's eyes, searching for something. Jimmy looked back at her, giving her time to organize her thoughts. It took about ten seconds, but finally she spoke.

"I have a friend who has some trouble."

"What kind of trouble?" Jimmy asked.

"She is being threatened."

"By who?"

"I don't know the man's name, but I think he is involved in bringing drugs across the border."

"What is the name of your friend, and where does she live?" Jimmy asked.

"Carmen. Carmen Beltran. She lives in Chula Vista."

Jimmy's mouth dropped open and he looked over at Henry, somewhat taken aback.

"You know the name?" Henry asked.

"I've heard the name," Jimmy said. "So, Angelica, tell me what you know about these threats."

"I don't want any trouble for Carmen, mister. Can you promise me that you won't make any trouble for her? She isn't a bad person."

"I'm not here to make trouble for anyone. Most people make trouble for themselves. But tell me, how well do you know her?" Jimmy asked.

"She's been my friend for, like ten years. She and her son live by themselves. They don't bother anyone, and she works hard. She's very smart."

"Is she a U.S. citizen, or Mexican?"

"She is Mexican, but she lives here legally."

"So she's a resident alien?"

"I think she's a U.S. citizen. She's at least a resident alien. She works in the marketing department for a copier company."

"Like Xerox?"

"I'm not sure the name of the company but that could be it. I know she's never had a problem with the law."

"So why is she having trouble now?"

"Her husband . . ."

"I thought she lived alone with her son?"

"Yes. But sometimes, once in awhile, he comes over to see the boy."

"Does he cause problems?"

"Well, I think he has before. But, listen Mr. Jimmy, what I'm going to tell you isn't Carmen's fault. She really is a good person, okay?"

"I'm sure she is."

"I think Carmen's husband . . . his name is Angel, yeah, Angel . . . like I said before, is involved in bringing drugs across the border. Carmen's trouble is with one of the men Carmen's husband works with. I don't really know the relations . . . relationship," she looked questioningly at Jimmy who smiled and nodded yes, "of the men, but there's one guy, or at least one guy, who thinks Carmen's husband has stolen from them or something, and he is trying to find Angel. They went to her house once and asked where Angel was. She said she didn't know and they threatened her. They told her that they would kill her if she was lying to them. They really want to know where he is, and bad. She doesn't know," Angelica said with a hint of desperation. "They've also called her house twice to ask if he's there. They say they are coming back soon, and she better tell them where he is or else. I think they mean it."

"So is his name Angel Beltran?" Jimmy asked.

"I think his name is Angel Garcia."

"If they're married, why don't they have the same last name?"

"Well, I think Carmen refers to him as her husband, but I'm not sure they ever really got married. I don't really think they did or she would have told me. The boy's last name is Garcia."

"Okay. Did they say when they'd be back?"

"No, but it could be any time. What if they come back and hurt or kill her? Can you do anything?"

"Do you think she would talk to me?" Jimmy asked.

"Yes. Yes."

"Do you have a number you can reach her at now?"

"I have her cell phone number."

"Call her right now, let her know it's you, then tell her there's someone who wants to speak with her."

Angelica dialed the number, then looked up at Jimmy before pushing the send button.

"Mr. Jimmy, don't let anything happen to her or the boy. She's probably going to be mad at me for talking to you guys, but I'm doing this because she's my friend, and she really is a good person."

Angelica pushed send, hit the speaker button, and waited for the phone to ring.

"Hi, this is Carmen," Jimmy heard as Carmen answered.

"Carmen, this is Angelica. I have someone here who wants to talk to you." Angelica handed the phone to Jimmy.

"Carmen, this is Special Agent Jimmy Maxwell. I am a criminal investigator with the Customs Service. There's also a San Diego Police Officer with us listening in."

There was no response and for a moment, Jimmy thought the call had dropped.

"Carmen? Can you hear me?"

"Yes. I'm here. Angelica shouldn't have called you."

"I think Angelica cares for you and contacted us because it's in your best interest."

"I'm at work and this isn't a good time to talk," Carmen replied.

"Can I come by your house after you get off work and talk to you in person?" Jimmy asked.

There was another pause. Carmen started to say something, then caught herself and responded, "Yes, I do need to get some advice. I assume that Angelica told you what's going on?"

"We have a general overview of the problem, but I would really like to get more details. Then maybe we can come up with a plan as to how to best deal with this issue."

"Do you know where I live?"

Jimmy started to respond, but caught himself and answered, "No. What is your address?"

"I live at 1561 Ravenwood, Chula Vista. I usually get home a little after 5:00, but I have a parent-teacher conference at my son's school tonight. Can you come by about 7:30?"

"I'll see you then. Bye."

Angelica flipped her phone closed and seemed to relax a bit.

"It'll be okay, right?"

"I think so. You did the right thing by telling us about this, really," Henry said, opening the door to the Expedition.

"Angelica, here's the keys to my car. Get in and relax for a minute. I just need to talk to Jimmy for one quick second."

Angelica exited the SUV and walked away.

"So how do you know her?" Jimmy asked.

"She owns the beauty salon where my wife gets her nails done. She was venting to my wife about a friend of hers having trouble with some drug traffickers, I think trying to figure out how she was going to handle the problem on her own. My wife mentioned that I was a cop who used to work trafficking organizations. I went down to talk to her last night, but after listening to her story I knew I wasn't going to be able to deal with it based on my management and current resources and time available. So guess what? I thought of you."

"Well that's very nice of you. Normally I'd probably think you were taking advantage of my good nature, but in this case—well, let's put it this way, the good Lord works in mysterious ways."

"Really?"

"Man, we just did a warrant a little over a week ago, got a shitload of dope, and barely missed arresting none other than Angel Garcia, hubby of Carmen Beltran. I know exactly where she lives because we've been following her around off and on the last week."

"No shit!"

"Do you remember when we arrested Jesus Negrete a couple of years ago and got that 1,500 and something pounds of weed out of that little house in Nestor?"

"Was that the bald guy with the bad skin?"

"Yeah. He worked for Angel Garcia. Angel runs all the stash houses for the Ruiz-Barraza cartel, which means he's probably got control of about eighty percent of the stash house in San Diego county."

"That's right. I remember Negrete told us during our interview of him about working for Angel somebody."

"He said Angel Garcia. You're just getting old, or maybe you've lost too many brain cells drinking all that cheap Mexican beer you like," Jimmy said with a smile.

"Man, this sounds interesting. Sure wish I could work it with you, but such is life. He paused for a second then continued. "So do you think that that someone looking for Angel is really that pissed just because they lost a little dope? I mean, we take off stash houses around here quite regularly. Not to mention that he's one of their top lieutenants who's been working for them a long time. Seems to me that should count for something. Cops take off dope sometimes. It's just the cost of doing business."

"Dude, I think this time they're really pissed and someone's got to pay. We hit them deep in the wallet with that warrant. We got 640 kilos of cocaine, about 3,000 pounds of weed and $600,000.00. "

"Wow! I hadn't heard. You guys are still doing a good job of keeping the lid on your capers, aren't you? No press release of any kind?"

"Not a word. You know how it works. Our cases make the press when they get turned over to one of the local departments, or when we call border patrol to have a load taken off at a checkpoint. I always get a chuckle out of seeing our dope seized by someone else in the news."

"Sounds like you don't appreciate us as much as you should."

"Quite honestly, it used to bother me a little, but now . . . man, you know me. I honestly appreciate you guys more than you know. We need you. I'd have had several of my snitches killed by now if it wasn't for being able to blame the cops for getting lucky and catching those badass traffickers."

"I know, Jimmy," Henry said with a little laugh. "Just giving you a hard time."

"It does still bug me a little when we have to call the border patrol to have them stop a car at one of their checkpoints for us. We call them, they take off our dope and then they hold a press conference to brag about their seizure. Those guys just love press releases. Do you know that if we're following a bad guy with a load of dope up the freeway, we have to call ahead and get their permission to drive through their checkpoint?"

"No shit?"

"Yeah. And to make matters worse, there's only one or two guys in the whole county that have the authority to bless us going through. It gets worse. We were tasked with providing security on a drug destruct a few weeks ago, so we're following a big panel truck up the freeway with like fifteen or twenty thousand pounds of dope, heading for a burn facility in L.A. and when I call border patrol to give them a head's up that we're coming, they tell us that without approval from their boss we can't come through."

"You laughed at the guy, right?"

"I was too stunned. I mean, it's like 5:00 in the morning, and this guy that's supposed to bless our passage through their precious checkpoint isn't answering his telephone. We're getting closer, and we keep calling to check on whether we're okay to go through, and they keep threatening that if we try to go through their checkpoint they'll stop us and seize the dope. I was tempted to just let them seize the dope, then they'd be stuck having to burn the crap."

"They'd probably do a press release on the seizure," Henry said laughing.

"You're probably right. Well, good talking to you, Henry, and thanks . . . I think."

Henry pulled out a little note pad and wrote down a telephone number, then ripped the page out of the pad and handed it to Jimmy.

"Angelica's telephone number, in case you need to reach her for some reason."

"Thanks. Hope you wrote down your name next to the number and not hers. My wife goes through my wallet every so often and I don't want her finding the name Angelica with a phone number. She'll go over and kick her ass, then mine, without even asking me why I have the number."

"Nope. It says Angelica."

"Oh, screw it," Jimmy said with a smile, tucking it into his wallet.

"Be safe. And don't forget to pass along any information you come across on stolen cars to yours truly." Henry smiled and gave Jimmy a wink as he got out of the Expedition. He turned and stuck his head in the open passenger-side window. "And by the way, maybe you should look for a change, you know, get out of the dope business for awhile. You don't see me out at 5:00 a.m. anymore."

Jimmy laughed. "Dude, it's what I'm good at. Besides, I'd be bored silly doing something else." Jimmy started his vehicle. "Hey, you be safe too," he said to Henry as he turned and walked away.

CHAPTER . . .

9

Barbara Burke sat with Jimmy in his Expedition across the street from Carmen Beltran's residence at 7:30 that evening, waiting for her return from the parent-teacher conference. She drove into her driveway at about 7:45 and got out of the car alone. Jimmy and Barbara opened the doors to the Expedition, got out and started across the street to her location.

"Hi. Ms. Beltran?" Jimmy inquired in an attempt to maintain the illusion that they weren't sure who she was. He walked up to her and held out his hand. Carmen turned and stared at Jimmy for a moment, then tentatively reached out and shook his hand.

"We spoke on the phone this morning. I'm Special Agent Jimmy Maxwell. This is my partner, Special Agent Burke."

Agent Burke reached over and also shook hands with Carmen. Carmen nodded and turned towards her house, reaching into her purse to retrieve her set of keys. Finding them, she headed towards her door. Jimmy and Barbara looked at each other and shrugged, then followed a few steps behind. Jimmy took a quick look around the area, scanning quickly for any signs of someone else watching or approaching. There wasn't any noticeable activity.

"Sorry I'm late," Carmen said as she unlocked her front door. "I decided to drop off my son with a friend before meeting with you people. I didn't really want him exposed to any of this business."

"I understand," Jimmy replied.

Jimmy and Barbara followed Carmen into her home. She walked over to a table near the kitchen and put down her purse, then walked into the living room and sat down in an easy chair, motioning for Jimmy and Barbara to sit on the sofa. Jimmy noticed that the house was immaculately kept.

"So, you people work for U.S. Customs?"

Jimmy pulled his credentials from his pocket and showed them to Carmen. Barbara Burke followed his lead and retrieved her credentials from her purse.

"My suggestion to you in the future would be to ask to see some sort of identification from anyone approaching you outside your house, or elsewhere for that matter, before you tell them who you are, or let them in your home. There are a lot of evil people in the world who may want to do you harm or take advantage of you, and they aren't going to want to do it out in front of the neighbors most of the time."

"I'll remember that," she replied.

"So, I understand that you have had some people threatening you?"

"Yes."

"Can you give me the details?"

"Well, it started about a week ago. Two men drove up to me as I was getting home from work. They wanted to know where Angel, that's my ex-husband, was. I told them I didn't know. You see, we've been separated for seven or eight years. They told me that they'd be back, and that I better not be lying to them."

"Do you know why they wanted to see your ex-husband?" Barbara asked.

"No, not really."

Jimmy sensed some hesitation in her voice.

"Ms. Beltran, did the men ever come back?" Jimmy asked.

"Several days later they were waiting again when I returned home from work. That time they came up behind me as I was opening my door. They pushed me inside. One of them picked up my son and held him as the other started going through the house, room by room. They didn't say anything initially; they just looked around for about five minutes, then one of them asked for my address book. I showed him where it was and he took it. They hardly said a word, but on their way out the man who took my address book turned and said, 'If you don't want anything to happen to your boy, you better tell Angel to come see us. And believe me, you don't want to call the police.'" Carmen paused a moment, a hint of fear showing on her face as she recounted the incident. "It was the most terrifying thing I've ever experienced."

"I'm sure it was." Jimmy paused for a moment. "So you didn't call the police?"

"No."

"And have you seen your ex-husband, or spoken with him about these men?" Jimmy asked.

"Agent Maxwell, my ex-husband and I are not close. I see him about once a month when he comes by to see Raul, his son. He comes unannounced. I don't know if Angel even knows these people. They didn't tell me their names or give me a telephone number to reach them at, or anything."

"My guess is that your ex-husband knows who they are, and knows how to reach them," Jimmy said.

"Ms. Beltran, haven't you even tried to call him to find out what this is about?" Barbara asked.

"I haven't seen him in about a month. I do have a cellular number for him, but he hasn't been answering it. I think it's turned off."

"Is it unusual for his phone to be turned off?" Barbara asked.

"Not really. I don't call very often. Sometimes it's on pretty regularly when I call, and other times I get no answer. I imagine I'll be able to get through eventually. I just hope it's before those men come back. I've been really worried. When they were here last, I was very frightened. So was my son. It took me hours to get him to sleep that night. He's very confused and keeps asking where his father is."

"What is the full name and date of birth of your ex-husband?" Barbara asked.

Jimmy watched her closely, trying to size her up. If they were truly separated, and she knew what he did, why not tell them? Was she trying to protect him? Was it for the boy, or was it because she just wanted to hide her head in the sand and stay uninvolved?

"His name is Angel Aurelio Garcia. His birthday is February 5, 1962."

"So how long have you two been divorced? You said you were separated, but you're using different last names. Why?" Jimmy asked.

"We've been divorced since my son Raul was born. I wanted Raul raised in the United States. Angel's ties are in Mexico with his family there. He would spend time visiting us, but would never stay around very long. It created a lot of strain in the relationship and he eventually moved away permanently. I filed for divorce when Raul was a year old."

"Has he ever been arrested?" Jimmy asked.

"I don't know. I don't think so."

"What do you know about your ex-husband that you can tell us?"

"We hardly see each other anymore. He just comes around to see Raul once in awhile."

"You don't know what he does?"

"Not really."

"What did he do when you two were together?"

"He was an auto mechanic."

"Ms. Beltran. We've been investigators for some time now. We're going to find out if your husband has been arrested and probably a whole lot more. My guess is that we'll even find out his occupation. There's no reason not to be totally up front with us about him, your relationship, or any other details about his or your life, especially if you want us to help you." Jimmy paused for a moment then asked, "Unless there's something to hide?" He paused to give her a chance to answer. When she didn't, he continued.

"Ms. Beltran, strange men don't come over to people's houses and threaten them for no reason. They don't come over and threaten people to find auto mechanics. They don't force themselves into someone's house, and then look around for someone without a good reason. They committed a felony. They risked going to prison, being shot by you, the homeowner, and all without stealing anything, raping or murdering you or your son. That tells me that they must have some other very important reason for being here. So I'm asking you, why would they do that?"

Carmen hesitated again, looking away and squirming a little in her chair.

"Honestly, Ms. Beltran, we're not here to create problems for you. We're here to help you if we can. So unless you admit to us that you've killed someone, or have done some other terrible deed, you have nothing to worry about from us. We're not here to judge you, and we don't believe you're a terrible person. What's to be concerned about? You don't think everyone makes mistakes in their life?"

"I'm pretty sure he's involved in drug trafficking," Carmen said weakly.

"That would have been our guess too," Jimmy said with a calm, understanding tone.

"I mean, I really don't know for sure, but I hear things from friends down south." She paused again. Jimmy and Barbara gave her time to collect her thoughts and continue.

"He's changed so much over the years. He used to be kind. I mean, he was very non-committal, even a little weak willed. He's not that way anymore. He can be brutal. I get scared sometimes when he's around."

"Everyone gets scared at times," Jimmy said. "Especially if they have a spouse who is involved in domestic violence. How many times has he hit you?"

Carmen looked up at Jimmy, her eyes starting to water. She looked surprised at his question. At the same time, he sensed sadness, and loneliness in her. It seemed odd in someone as beautiful and intelligent as she seemed to be.

"I know he's hit you. How often does it happen?"

"Look, for all practical purposes, I'm a single mom. I'm trying to raise my son the best way I know how. I work, I come home and help Raul with his homework, maybe watch a little TV, and go to bed. I don't want to be involved in Angel's life. I don't really want him around. But Raul is his son too. He provides a little support, not that much usually, but what right do I have to keep him from his son? And, Raul really enjoys the time he does get to spend with his father."

"You avoided the question. How often does he come over and how often do his visits result in him striking you?"

"Let's put it this way, it's happened more than once. But that's not why I agreed to have you come see me," she said a little indignantly.

"I know. Ms. Beltran, we're trying to find out all we can about your ex-husband in order to fully evaluate the nature of these threats against you. We need to know what kind of man he is, and what he's involved in. I know you don't know us from Adam, and I know that most people don't trust law enforcement officers, but honestly, we're here to help you."

Jimmy caught himself smiling as he finished the statement. He caught himself and tried to erase the smile, but Carmen caught it and looked at him quizzically.

"I'm sorry. I don't mean to make light of anything being said here, but I just realized I used the oldest line in the book for a government agent. You know, 'I'm from the government and I'm here to help.'"

Barbara smiled, but Carmen just gave a curt nod and put her head down. Apparently, she hadn't heard that one, or she was just too caught up in her thoughts or the situation for the humor to have registered.

"Ms. Beltran, we investigate drug trafficking organizations. We know a lot about how they operate. You have some reason to worry, but the odds are good that you won't see these men again for at least a few days. If you are truly not involved in drug trafficking, and we don't have any reason to doubt you, they will probably leave you alone. They want Angel, for whatever the reason, and they know that if they hurt you they will bring a lot of attention to whatever it is they're doing."

"Why do you think they want Angel?"

"Usually these things are driven by money. They probably lost some money and they think Angel knows where it is, or has it. Or they may think he has stolen something—money or drugs—from them. They may even think he's working for another cartel, or even the police. Now some of these things can be worked out. If he owes money, they may let him pay it back and move on. If they think he's working for their competition, or for the police, the odds are that they do mean to harm him."

"I have a job. My son has school. I can't just put a halt to my life because of this. What happens to us if they come over here to do him harm while he's with us? What about the effect that will have on Raul? My god, what has he done to us!"

"Do you have any vacation time?" Barbara asked.

"All of my vacation time is spoken for. We have a trip to Cancun planned for mid-summer. It's already paid for."

"Can you reschedule it?" Barbara asked.

"Look," Jimmy interjected. "It's like I said. You're probably not going to be revisited by these guys for at least a few days. I think they took the address book in order to check with your other friends and family to see if Angel is with them. They know that he knows this would be an obvious place for him to hide. If Angel doesn't want to be found, he's not going anywhere they'd know to look. These people aren't stupid. Just the same, when you come and go, pay attention to what's going on around you. You have a cell phone, right?"

"Yes."

"Do you know most of your neighbors, or at least what they drive?"

"Yes."

"Okay, so if you see something unusual, a car you haven't seen before, someone following you an inordinate amount of time, something like that, try to jot down the license plate and give Barbara or me a call."

Jimmy took out a little notebook and jotted down both his and Barbara's cell phone numbers, then ripped out the page and gave it to Carmen.

"Please call us if you hear from Angel, or if you have any other problems with those people who've been over here threatening you. Also, remember to look around before you get out of the car. Make sure you know who and what is around you. If you have a serious problem, like someone is coming over to you that you don't recognize, or if it's one of the guys you saw before, dial 911. Even if you get suspicious about someone or something, put 911 in the phone and keep your finger on the send button, just in case you need to dial quickly.

"I'd also like you to give me your number and the cell phone number you have for Angel. Maybe we can figure out where he is from the number. Do you know the billing address for his number?"

"His bill comes here."

"Well, we'd still like to have his number. Maybe we can find out if he's calling someplace locally where he might be staying. You don't have a current cell phone bill we could have, do you?"

"I think so." She walked over to a hutch and started going through some papers. As she looked she asked, "What are you going to do if you locate him?"

"At the very least we'd like to talk to him and get his take on why his *compadres* are so intent on locating him."

"Are you going to arrest him?"

"We just want to talk to him at this point. What would we arrest him for anyway?" Jimmy lied. Carmen looked at him for a moment, then went back to looking for his number.

"We'll try to spend some time watching your house ourselves, " Jimmy said. "So if you see a bunch of white folks in cars with tinted windows, it's probably us. Don't shoot us or anything, okay?" Jimmy said with a little smile and wink.

For the first time since they contacted Carmen, a flicker of a smile crossed her face. She looked back down and pulled the cell phone bill from a stack of envelopes. She then walked over to Jimmy and handed it to him.

"You don't have any guns in the house, do you?" Barbara asked.

"No, not that I'm aware of."

"Well, are there any you might not be aware of?" Jimmy asked, somewhat more official sounding after her answer.

"No, I really don't think so. Angel does keep a small safe in the spare bedroom closet, which is where he stays when he's here. I don't have access to it. It's kind of small. I can't imagine a gun fitting in it, and I have never seen him carry a gun, so no, I don't think there's a gun in the house."

"Can we see the safe?" Jimmy asked.

"Yes. I suppose," Carmen said. She stood and led the agents to Angel's bedroom.

Carmen slid the closet door open and pushed aside some men's clothes hanging in the closet. The clothing was high-end attire, mostly designer attire by Versace and Armani. She then bent down and moved several shoeboxes, one of which contained a pair of alligator cowboy boots, exposing an inexpensive, Sentry-type safe a little bigger than one of the shoeboxes.

"I guess it's a little larger than I remembered. I don't really come in here very often," Carmen remarked.

"Ms. Beltran, believe me when I say that this safe is plenty big enough to hold a handgun. Are you sure you don't know how to open it. I'd really like to be sure there are no weapons in the house."

"I really don't have the combination. There is one place I could look though."

Carmen left the room with Jimmy and Barbara following close behind. Officer safety habits dictated to Jimmy that he keep his eye on someone in unfamiliar surroundings, especially where they knew where everything was located and he didn't, and especially if they were crooks, or connected to crooks.

Carmen walked into her bedroom, pausing briefly and turning to look at the two agents.

"I'm sorry to invade on your privacy, Ms. Beltran, but since we don't know each other all that well yet, and since we all want to go home safely tonight, we're just being cautious and making sure of what you're getting. Please forgive us."

"I understand," she said with minor trepidation.

Jimmy looked into her room from the open bedroom door. On the wall over her bed was a full-sized framed photograph of Carmen Beltran. She was partially nude in the photograph, with one of her breasts showing. She was on her knees, posed like a 1940s or 50s pinup girl done by Gil Elvgren. It was stunning. Jimmy tried to look away, but was so struck by the picture that he continued to study it for a moment.

"Uh, hem," Barbara voiced, nudging Jimmy with her hip.

I'm sorry. Really, I'm sorry to embarrass you, Ms. Beltran."

"Yes, and he's sorry he embarrassed himself too," Barbara stated.

Jimmy looked over at Barbara with a frown.

Carmen sighed. "I wanted something that would capture my youth, something I could look at and smile at when I turned fifty or sixty." She looked at the picture a few seconds, then turned away and went to her dresser. Opening the top drawer, she fished through some papers and then removed an envelope.

"I don't know if I should open this or not. Angel told me to open it if anything ever happened to him. I really don't want him angry with me if he finds out I opened it prematurely."

"May I see it?" Jimmy asked.

Carmen handed him the envelope. It was just a plain business-sized white envelope.

"You can reseal the contents in a new envelope after we've looked, can't you?"

"I suppose."

She stood staring at Jimmy, who paused a moment, then ripped open the envelope. Inside was a letter from Angel addressed to Carmen. It was written in Spanish.

"What does it say?" Jimmy asked, handing the letter to her.

Carmen read through the letter with a blank expression on her face. Jimmy watched her, but occasionally stole glimpses of her photograph on the wall.

"He's telling me that if I've opened this letter something bad has probably happened to him. He's telling me he that he wants Raul and I to be okay. The combination of the safe is listed, as well as a bank name and address, and safety deposit box number. He says there's a key to the safety deposit box in the bedroom safe."

Jimmy wondered why she'd never been curious enough to open the envelope before, knowing that inside there was likely the combination to the safe. He would have guessed that most people in her position would have wanted to know what someone like him would be keeping in their house. Maybe she knew or suspected and just didn't want to confirm her suspicions.

"I'm afraid of the man," Carmen said, reading the question on Jimmy's mind.

"That would have been one of my guesses," Jimmy muttered quietly to himself as he followed her back to the spare bedroom. Barbara didn't say anything, but shook her head in mock amusement at the comment.

Carmen pulled the safe from the closet and worked the combination, glancing several times at the letter she'd laid on the carpet beside her. Within a minute the safe was open.

"May I?" Jimmy said, as he bent over and picked up the safe, placing it on the bed.

He pulled the door of the safe open and looked inside. Reaching in, he pulled out a Colt pistol. It looked like a 1911-model government .45, but it was, in fact, a 38 Super, one of the favorites of drug traffickers who wanted to align themselves with the big shots of the 1970s and 80s. Jimmy ejected the magazine and pulled the slide back, discovering that the weapon was loaded.

Behind the handgun were seven or eight large bundles of currency. Carmen stared, wide eyed, without saying a word. Jimmy did a bundle count, estimating that there was about ten thousand dollars in each bundle.

"You didn't know any of this was here?" Jimmy asked.

"No. Really, I didn't. Maybe I thought there was a few thousand, and I know Angel has a safety deposit box, so I may have guessed he kept the key to it there, but I had no idea he kept this kind of cash around. And I really didn't know about the gun. My god, he really is involved in drugs, isn't he?" she said, starting to sound excited.

"Settle down," Jimmy said. "You told us you suspected he was, based on what you'd heard from others, so this shouldn't really shock you. These are the kinds of things we regularly find when we conduct search warrants related to narcotics traffickers. You know, we're going to have to seize these items, at least until we get a chance to talk to Angel and have him explain how he came by these things."

"What if he comes home and wants them?"

"Reseal the letter in a new envelope and put it back in your dresser."

Jimmy turned to Barbara. "Do you have a search warrant kit in your G-ride?"

"No. But I have most of the paperwork we use on warrants. Want me to go get a receipt and inventory form and a 60-51?"

"Thanks. If you don't mind."

The CF-6051 was a chain of custody form that accompanied seized property. It documented what the item was that had been seized, the date and time of the seizure, case number and name and signature of the officer who had custody of the property at that time. The original form stayed with the property, but carbon copies could be left with the person from whom it was taken as a receipt. It also contained a box at the bottom of the form that, if signed, authorized abandonment of the property to the government.

Jimmy turned back to Carmen.

"Ms. Beltran. Honestly, you don't want this in your house. The gun is illegal for Angel to possess, and the currency is, as I'm sure you know, proceeds of your ex-husband's illegal activities."

"No, I know. I'm just worried about him coming home and finding this stuff all gone. He's going to be angry. I don't know if I can deal with him or not."

"You tell him that the police came by with a search warrant and seized the items. We're going to leave you some paperwork to show him if that happens. In the meantime, I mean it, if you hear from him, either by him calling or showing up here, you need to call me right away. Okay?"

"Yes, yes I will."

•

Chapter . . .

10

Jimmy woke early, got up and went to check on Nikki. She was sleeping peacefully, holding her stuffed ET doll that she'd had since she was two. He started a pot of coffee, then went back and got into bed next to his wife. She rolled away from him as he attempted to get closer to her.

"Go away," she said with a muffled voice due to her face being half-buried in her pillow. She could feel him press up next to her.

Jimmy moved back then lay still for a minute, not touching her with his body. He then simply tried to rest a hand on the small of her back.

Shirley sat upright, angry.

"What the fuck do you want?"

"I just wanted to be close to you."

"I've told you, I don't know how many times, leave me alone in the morning."

"Yeah. Most of the rest of the time as well," he said, getting up and grabbing a robe.

"What the fuck does that mean?"

"Why can't you be just a little affectionate? I'm not trying to jump your bones. I just wanted to lay next to you for a few minutes."

"You, cuddle? That'll be the day. I know what you really wanted Jimmy, so don't you lie to me."

Jimmy got up without saying anything else and headed for the kitchen. He heard his bedroom door being slammed behind him.

Just great! he thought. *Another peachy fucking day in paradise.*

He was angry and it really bothered him that Shirley didn't believe him. It wasn't that he didn't like sex in the morning; in fact, it was his favorite time of the day for that sort of thing.

But he hadn't snuggled next to her that morning just to jump her bones. He'd given up on expecting sex from her at any time. He'd mentioned in jest to a few of his closest friends that since he was married he got sex once or twice a month, whether he needed it or not. Sadly, he made the comment trying to be funny, but there was much more truth to it than he wanted there to be.

Jimmy poured a cup of coffee and went into his office. He sat down in his desk chair to reflect, and perhaps pout a little. As he sipped his coffee, he thought about his situation. He had really wanted to be married, to have a family, and someone to come home to. What he hadn't wanted was what he had.

Despite the fact that Shirley was an attractive woman that he cared about, he hadn't really been madly in love with her when they got married. They'd met in college and hit it off together the first few times they'd gone out. He was attracted to her and liked her family. He never really liked dating so when he discovered that she seemed to need him, he started getting interested in marriage. Ten months into their relationship he'd popped the question, believing the marriage would work out.

It hadn't really been nearly as easy as he'd expected. The first few years were all right. Then Shirley began to get restless. She claimed she wasn't fulfilled in her job at the department store. Jimmy had a good job, so he'd told her that if she was unhappy, she should quit. She did. She wanted a baby. Jimmy was pleased with the decision, as he wanted to have children as well.

Following the birth of Nikki, things were all right for awhile, but then Shirley became unhappy again. Jimmy wasn't home enough. She was always stuck at home with no life other than the baby. Jimmy spent a lot of time on the phone, and when Shirley called to vent, or just talk, it always seemed to be when he was busiest. Having to be abrupt, he'd ask if there was an emergency, and upon finding out that there wasn't, he'd have to cut her off. It always infuriated her but Jimmy didn't know what else to do. He hoped she'd get the message not to call him at work unless it was really important.

Jimmy did try to call her when he had some downtime, but that usually didn't work out well either. She'd be busy with Nikki, or out shopping. Their timing just wasn't that good on the telephone. Then Jimmy would come home tired, hoping to unwind, only to have to deal with some mini-crisis that often led to several hours of trying to talk things out with her.

Despite these difficulties, along with the fact that their intimacy had fallen to a level that would be totally unacceptable in most relationships, Jimmy hung in there and tried his best to be a patient, committed husband. His Christian values, along with his childhood experiences, dictated that he not give up in trying to keep his marriage together. He prayed regularly although for shorter and shorter amounts of time, but he believed marriage was a serious commitment that was supposed to be forever.

He knew he had grown a bit complacent about going to church regularly. That, with his drinking, and the fact that he let his mouth run away with him more than he should, caused Shirley to remind him of his shortcomings fairly regularly. She'd called him a hypocrite more times than he could count. She didn't seem to understand that going to church didn't mean you were perfect. He told her it was a hospital for sinners but she just didn't buy that.

Then there were times when Shirley was just downright mean to him. When he confronted her with her actions, she would tell him it was payback for his treatment of her. But he often wondered how he could treat her any better. Yet despite their problems and the way she treated him, he didn't cheat on his wife and was committed to his wedding vows.

The marriage woes were easier to deal with when Jimmy thought about his daughter. She was truly the love of his life.

As Jimmy reflected on what he was to do about his unhappy marriage, the telephone rang.

"Hello."

"Jimmy. This is Brad at Sector. Hey, there's a marijuana load at San Ysidro. Can you call Inspector Harris at 4820?"

"Sure. Boy, I'd forgotten we had duty today. Who's my backup?"

"Hang on a minute . . . It's Deron Morris."

"Do me a favor and give him a call and ask him to meet me there."

"No problem."

Jimmy made the call to the port and asked for Inspector Harris.

"Inspector Harris? This is Agent Maxwell. I understand there's a load of weed waiting for me?"

"Yeah. Let me get the paperwork."

About thirty seconds later, Inspector Harris returned to the telephone.

"What would you like to know?"

"How many people in the car, and does anyone speak English?"

"Just an old white woman. She's got to be in her seventies. She's all alone."

"Wow. We don't get too many of those, now do we? Where was the dope hidden?"

"It's just laying loose in the trunk. Looks like twenty or thirty pounds."

"Okay. Can you hold off on processing it until I get down there?"

"Sure."

About forty-five minutes later, Jimmy made the U-turn at the end of Interstate 5 and pulled into the west secondary lot. As Jimmy parked, he looked over and noticed several inspectors boxing up the packages from the trunk of a white Ford Taurus.

Jimmy exited his Expedition and walked over to them.

"Where's Inspector Harris?" he asked.

"Dude, I don't know. I think he went back on the line."

"I asked him not to process the dope until I got here."

"Sorry, man. He didn't say anything to me," the senior inspector said.

Jimmy shook his head and started walking towards the office. "Guys, can you put on some gloves?" Jimmy asked. "I may need to try to get prints off those packages and I'd just as soon not find yours."

"Yeah, okay," the Senior Inspector said as Jimmy shook his head. The two inspectors looked at each other and shrugged as he walked away, then continued processing the vehicle.

It always amazed Jimmy, and most of the other agents who responded to drug loads at the port, at how poorly the inspectors had been trained at being true law enforcement professionals. Some of the inspectors were pretty good—when they wanted to be—at finding drugs hidden in the ingeniously made false compartments the smugglers had installed in cars. But most of them didn't have a clue about what it took to prosecute cases, let alone what it took to take the case further by getting the drugs from the port so you could attempt delivery to its intended recipient.

Jimmy entered the office used by the duty agents after getting the identification of the detained defendant. According to her driver's license, her name was Edna Jones. She was seventy-two years old. There weren't many old folks smuggling marijuana into the United States. There were even fewer old white folks. *This should be interesting*, he thought.

The criminal history and address checks all proved to be negative. Maybe her social security just wasn't cutting it anymore. Jimmy went over to the holding cell where Edna was being detained.

"Ma'am, I'm Special Agent Maxwell," Jimmy said, showing her his credentials. "Please follow me."

Jimmy watched her as she got up and walked out of the cell.

"Do I need to handcuff you?" he asked.

"No. I'm not going to give you any trouble, officer."

"I appreciate that," Jimmy said, turning his head away from her and smiling.

Jimmy led Edna to an interview room and asked her to sit.

"We need to talk, Ms. Jones. Since we may be a little while, do you need any water, or to use the restroom or anything?"

"No, I'm all right."

Jimmy began the booking process, taking down biographical information. When he got to the question on the DEA Form 202 that dealt with her height and weight, he asked Edna her weight. He guessed it to be about 120 pounds, but he asked the question anyway.

"Ms. Jones, how much do you weigh?"

"A lady doesn't discuss her weight, especially with handsome young men," she said with a coy smile.

"I know, but please humor me. It's just a question I have to fill in on this form."

"There's no one that really needs to know. You know some things are personal."

"Well, I guess I'll have to take it off your driver's license information."

"I wouldn't tell those folks either. They must have just guessed."

She paused for a moment, then asked, "How much did they put down?"

"Well, let's see," Jimmy said, searching through a small stack of papers in front of him. "Looks like—here it is—135 pounds."

"Well I never," she said with some exasperation.

"Well, that's why we ask, so we don't have to guess. But if you won't tell me, I'll have to guess too. Let's see . . ." he said, looking her up and down. "I'm going to go with 130."

"Young man, just because you're arresting me and taking me to jail doesn't mean you have the right to be mean."

She stared defiantly at Jimmy as he stared back at her, trying to keep a straight face.

"If this stays between you and me I'll tell you."

"It just goes on the form, ma'am. The form goes in a case file that no one will probably ever look at."

"I weigh 117 pounds. It's the same weight I was when I married Charles 51 years ago, God rest his soul. Charles passed away two years ago around Thanksgiving."

"I'm sorry to hear that."

Jimmy finished with her biographical information, put the form aside, and then took out his rights' card and advised her of her rights.

"You've been very nice, Agent Maxwell, so I'll answer your questions."

"Good. So who does that car belong to that you were driving?"

"It's my friend's car. His name is Ralph Williams. He and his wife own a bar in Lakeside. I've know them for nearly twenty-five years."

"Why are you driving his car?"

"They invited me to dinner last night. We went to Senor Frog's. We were all having such a nice time."

"Wow. Sounds like it. So were you up all night?"

"Almost. I had a few glasses of wine with dinner, but Ralph and Lauren, that's his wife, were drinking margaritas. We didn't think it was safe to drive home after drinking so Ralph got a room nearby. I took a short nap on the sofa but did need to get home to feed Miss Kitty. That's my cat, you know. Ralph and Lauren said they were too tired so he gave me the keys to his car and told me to go. I think they're taking a cab to the border later, then they'll probably take the trolley home."

"And how do you think all that marijuana got in the trunk of their car?"

"Honestly, Agent Maxwell, I have no idea."

"Are you sure you're telling me the truth?"

"Yes. Yes. I just went down for dinner."

"Well, the car is registered to Ralph Williams, so I will be talking to him. Does he still live at 1553 Lincoln Place, Apartment 122?"

"Yes, I think that's the number. But it's not an apartment. He lives in a mobile home park."

"Oh, okay. I tell you what. I'm going to give you a notice to appear in court about a month from now. If I let you go home, will you promise me that you'll show up in court next month?"

"Of course. I have nothing to hide, and really, no where to go."

"Okay, then you go home and get some rest. If what you're telling me is true, I'll contact you before your court date and let you know whether or not you have to show up. If you don't hear from me then you just show up in court."

"All right."

"Do you have the money to get home in a cab, or do you have a friend to call who'll come get you?"

"I can take the trolley most of the way, then I'll take a bus."

"You need to do one more thing for me, okay?" Jimmy said, looking directly at Edna. He paused for a few seconds to make sure she was focused on him. "Do not call Ralph or Lauren. This might have upset you and you might be very angry about being placed in this position, but I don't want you to call them. I know you probably want to ask them about the marijuana, but I think it's better if you don't initiate the call. If they call you, and I'm pretty sure they will, you can tell them what happened, but only if they call you. If they or anyone else gives you any problem, you call me at this number."

Jimmy opened up his pocket notepad and wrote his cell phone number down on a piece of paper. He tore the sheet out of the pad and handed it to her.

An hour later, Edna was walked out of the facility and Jimmy watched her depart the area on the trolley. Returning to the secondary inspection office, Jimmy began to collect the reports from the inspectors who'd been involved in Edna's case.

"This has to have been a first for you," Deron said to Jimmy.

"What? My first white grandma arrest, or what?"

"No. It's got to be the first time you actually may have believed someone who told you they didn't know there was dope in the car and let them go home."

"I don't know if I believe her or not. I think I do actually, but dude, I wasn't going to book her into jail. Besides, it's only like twenty-something pounds of weed and she's really not a flight risk. She'll stick around, if for no other reason than to collect her social security check."

Deron laughed. "You're probably right."

"So what you doing Monday morning, bright and early?" Jimmy asked.

"No plans."

"You have plans now. I'm thinking we should pay a visit to the Williams' residence in lovely downtown Lakeside."

At 10:00 a.m., Monday morning, Jimmy and Deron drove into the Lakeside Manor trailer park on the north edge of Lakeside. The park was located about as far out of town as you could get without being in the Blossom Valley area of the county. Bill Blankenship, a narcotics detective from El Cajon Police Department, accompanied them. He occasionally worked with them on traffickers who lived in El Cajon. When Jimmy called him and told him the facts of the case, he laughed.

"Sure, man. I'd love to help you investigate the geriatric cartel," he said. "But how am I going to earn my Spanish pay?"

There were literally hundreds of mostly doublewide mobile homes in the park. The first hundred yards of roadway was littered with signs every twenty or thirty feet. One said something like, 'Senior Living at its Best,' while another warned, 'Speed bumps ahead.' The speed bump was a car length ahead. There was also a speed limit sign that read, ten-and-a-half miles per hour. Jimmy smiled and shook his head, remarking that he wondered how someone had come up with the ten-and-a-half mph speed limit.

After driving down several rows of mobile homes, nearly bottoming out on the ridiculously rough speed bumps that you practically needed an off-road vehicle to drive over, they pulled up to number 122. Jimmy waited until everyone was out of the cars, then walked up to the front door. Before knocking, he stepped to the side of the front door, then pulled his badge out from inside his shirt and let it hang center chest from the chain he kept it on around his neck. He looked over at his partners, making sure they were ready. They both nodded at him and he knocked on the door.

Following the second knock, he could hear footsteps approaching. A few seconds later, the door opened to a sight no one was expecting. Jimmy glanced at Bill and Deron and fought to suppress a laugh. A little old man with tiny bird legs, about five feet five inches, stood before him in a pair of leopard-skin bikini briefs. The elderly gentleman's bulging stomach hung over the front of the briefs, hiding the crotch area of his briefs from view. What little hair he had was snow white, with the top of his head bald. He was wrinkled, covered with liver spots, and was exceptionally skinny except for his stomach. Jimmy noticed three or four long, silver-colored chest hairs. It was a sight to behold. He almost shuddered as he looked at the shriveled form in front of him.

"Mr. Williams?" Jimmy asked with a gulp.

"Yes," he replied, stepping out on the porch in his scantily clad attire.

Jimmy held up his credentials for examination.

"May we come in? We'd like to ask you a few questions," Jimmy said.

"What's this about?"

"Sir, can we come in. I don't think you really want your neighbors knowing of our visit, do you?"

"All right," the elderly Williams said as he turned to go back inside. The investigators followed close behind. As they were entering, Jimmy continued.

"We're here about your white Ford Taurus." There was no immediate response. "You do own a Taurus, correct?"

"Yes, yes."

"Mr. Williams, is anyone else home with you?" Jimmy asked.

"My wife, Lauren."

As he was answering, a somewhat heavyset woman who appeared to be in her late fifties appeared from a darkened hallway. She entered the room wearing a thin white t-shirt that barely covered her pubic area. Her large breasts sagged somewhat, but didn't droop too far down her torso despite the lack of support of a bra. The t-shirt was very thin, her nipples and most of the rest of her body showing immodestly through the material.

"Ralph, who are these people?" she asked.

"It's the police, dear."

"Oh," she replied as she walked closer and offered her hand, first to Detective Blankenship, then Deron, and finally Jimmy.

"Can I get you gentlemen anything?" she inquired.

"No, thank you," Jimmy replied. "Mr. Williams, would you like to go get a robe or something?"

Mr. Williams suddenly seemed to notice his attire and nodded yes. He turned and started to head back to what Jimmy believed was his bedroom.

"You don't have any weapons in the house, do you?" Jimmy asked.

"No," he replied, walking away.

"Deron," Jimmy nodded and whispered. "Go with him." Deron nodded and quickly followed.

As he caught up, Jimmy heard him saying, "I'm sorry, sir, but I need to go with you."

"How about you, Mrs. Williams, do you need to grab a robe or anything?"

Lauren smiled at Jimmy and Bill, then walked to the sofa and sat down facing them.

"No. I'm fine, officers."

As she sat, her t-shirt pulled up. She crossed and uncrossed her legs several times, at each movement, revealing a little of her naked pubic area. Maybe it was his imagination, but Jimmy noticed her nipples hardening, pushing the thin cotton of the t-shirt out even more. It was difficult not to stare.

"You sure you don't need a robe?" Jimmy asked again.

"No, no. I'm fine."

About a minute later, Mr. Williams returned to the room wearing a dark blue satin robe. He walked to the sofa and sat next to his wife.

"Gentlemen, gentlemen, sit down . . . please."

"So, Mr. Williams, I assume you know why we're here," Jimmy said.

"I assume it has to do with the incident at the border."

"Good guess. I assume then that you've spoken with your friend Edna since you parted company Friday night in Tijuana?"

"Yes, I called her late Saturday afternoon. She told me what happened to her. I guess that's why you folks are here, right?"

"Yes. We need to ask you a few questions about how all that marijuana ended up in the trunk of your car."

"Well, to be frank with you, Agent?"

"Maxwell."

"As I was saying, Agent Maxwell, it really is remarkable. You see, there was no marijuana found in my car."

"Come again?" Deron said.

"No, really. I did give Edna my car keys and told her to take the vehicle home. But when Lauren and I came out of the motel early that afternoon, there was my car parked on the street. We looked around for Edna but she was nowhere to be found."

"Mr. Williams," Jimmy stated with a smile forming on his face, "We have your car, your registration document, and even a few personal effects taken from the car."

"No, sir. My car was still parked on the street in Tijuana when we came out of the motel on Saturday."

"Mr. Williams, I would urge you not to lie to me. Believe me when I say that we have your car."

"Nope. No you don't."

"You said you gave Edna the keys to your car, correct?"

"Yes."

"Well then, why did those keys work so perfectly in the car Edna got stopped at the border in?" Jimmy paused for a moment to study Ralph's face.

"You also said you called Edna late Saturday afternoon. If she didn't take your car, and she's your friend, why would you wait until then to check on her?"

Mr. Williams looked blankly ahead but said nothing.

"Do you know what a VIN is, Mr. Williams?" Deron asked.

"No sir."

"It's the vehicle identification number. They stamp it into a plate and attach it to your car so that your car can be positively identified. It's like a fingerprint for a car. There is only one number assigned to each car made. No two are alike. And guess what? The one on the car we seized Friday is registered to you."

"Maybe whoever put that marijuana in that car followed me around, knew my patterns, knew what establishments I frequented. They probably found a car like mine and when we parked he switched that plate that has that number on it with the one on my car."

Jimmy continued to smile and shook his head no as he stared at Ralph.

"Look," Jimmy said. "If you really want to convince us that we have the wrong car, show us your car."

"I'd be happy to."

"Good," Jimmy said, standing. "Where's it at?"

"It's still in Mexico. But I can go get it later today and have it here tomorrow."

"Mr. Williams, you're trying my patience," Jimmy said.

"Honestly, Agent Maxwell. I can get you the car tomorrow. We're honest people, not involved in drug trafficking. Look at us. Do we look like drug smugglers?"

"No, but that really doesn't mean anything to us. We see all kinds of people in this business." Jimmy had been looking around the room as he spoke. "All right, Mr. Williams, I'm going to give you until tomorrow to come up with your car, despite the fact that I know where it is. What I want from you then is the opportunity to look around your home and make sure that there are no drugs here, okay?"

"Yes, yes. Feel free to look around," Ralph said, standing up.

Lauren quickly stood also. Jimmy noticed that her face went a little pale and she looked nervous. He fixed his gaze on her until he caught her eye.

"What's wrong, Mrs. Williams? Is it okay with you if we take a look around?"

"Well, yes. But I have to say, gentlemen, that I . . . Well, we're all adults here, right? I mean to say, well, I'd be a little embarrassed if I were . . . Well, there may be some things you fellas will find that are, let's say, adult in nature." She paused a moment, looking at all three investigators. "Oh, come on," she said.

Lauren led Jimmy and Deron towards the back of the house. Bill asked Ralph to show him a cabinet just off the living room.

As they entered the master bedroom in the rear of the house, Jimmy immediately knew why Lauren had been nervous. The room was poorly lit, as the couple had thick curtains hung over the windows that were still closed. At the foot of the bed was a video camera mounted on a tripod that was pointed at the bed. A small Jacuzzi tub was also set up in the room.

At the side of the bed on the far side of the room was a bookcase full of videos. Jimmy walked over to the bookcase and looked at the collection. Most of the videos appeared to be homemade. There were titles like, 'Me and Ralph Having Fun,' 'Lauren Pleasuring Herself,' and 'Letting My Fingers Do The Walking.'

"You know, Agent Maxwell, if you'd like to borrow some of those, you're more than welcome."

Jimmy turned to look at Mrs. Williams, who was smiling and licking her lips in a seductive manner.

"I appreciate it, Mrs. Williams, but I don't think that will be necessary."

"It doesn't have to be for any official reason."

Lauren smiled and winked, then let her hands fall to her side. She then slowly lifted the bottom of her t-shirt just a few inches, trying to tease him by exposing a small area of her pubic area again. Jimmy quickly looked away.

"Mrs. Williams, I'm sure your husband probably wouldn't appreciate your behavior. How about letting us get our work done," Jimmy said with a scowl.

Lauren seemed to pout a little, then turned and walked out of the room.

"Geez, do you believe that woman," Deron said with a smile.

"I guess she really likes her sex, or something," Jimmy said.

"I'm sure that even you look good next to her old man," Deron teased.

"Thanks, I appreciate that."

"Besides, old what's his name probably can't even get it up anymore."

"Well, you can borrow one of his video's and find out," Jimmy said.

"Ooh, scary. I think I'll pass."

The two agents continued to look around the room, opening drawers and looking under the bed. A few minutes into the search, Deron slid open a closet and pulled out an electronic parabolic dish with attached headphones.

"For listening to the neighbors, would be my guess," he said, pushing them out of the way so he could continue his probe into the closet.

Jimmy walked over to a small closet door in the darkest corner of the room. He grabbed the doorknob and pulled the door open. As he did, the figure of a person began to fall out towards him.

"Hey! Hold on!"

Jimmy drew his .40 caliber Sig Sauer handgun and jumped back several feet, extending his shooting hand towards the advancing figure. The body fell forward, seemingly in slow motion. The rigid, naked and lifeless form hit the floor. When it hit, it bounced several times.

Laughter roared from Deron as it became apparent as to what had happened. The body was that of a blowup doll that had been stood up behind the closet door.

"Shit man, that was great! I can just see it now. 'Federal agent shoots blowup doll as it attacks.'" Deron was laughing so hard he could probably be heard next door.

"If you'd have shot that thing it would have went flying around the room like a balloon full of air someone had let go of," he continued.

Jimmy reholstered his gun as Detective Blankenship entered the bedroom, closely followed by Lauren and Ralph, to inquire about the commotion.

"It's okay," Deron said, still laughing. "Jimmy was just introducing himself to your friend."

The Williams looked around at everyone, not knowing if the agents were making fun of them or not.

"I think we're done in here. You find anything?" Jimmy inquired of Detective Blankenship.

Bill shook his head no, giving Jimmy an inquisitive look.

"Let's go," Jimmy said. "Thank you folks for your cooperation. Mr. Williams, we'll be by tomorrow afternoon."

"Come by the bar," Ralph said. "Lauren and I will be working there and I'll bring my Taurus over so you can see it."

"Okay," Jimmy said, thinking to himself, *yeah, right.*

Once outside and away from the front of the residence, Bill asked, "What was going on in the bedroom, guys?"

"It was the funniest thing I've ever seen," Deron said, starting to laugh again. "Jimmy almost shot the frigging blowup doll."

Even Jimmy began to smile.

"I opened this closet door and this body began to fall out on me. Scared the crap out of me for a second. It took a second to realize it was a stupid sex doll. I came about half a second from shooting the stupid thing. I thought it was attacking me."

Bill and Deron were laughing, with Jimmy joining in as they got into their vehicles to leave.

CHAPTER . . .

11

Driving back to the office, Jimmy and Bill continued to laugh about the Williams' search. The weather was perfect, sunny and in the mid-80s, with a few cumulus clouds scattered across the blue sky. Traffic was light now that the morning commute was over.

"Shit," Jimmy said, looking in his rearview mirror.

"What?"

"Chippy coming up fast."

Jimmy looked down at the speedometer. He was doing about eighty-five.

"Yeah. It's me, unfortunately," Jimmy said, heading towards the shoulder of the slow lane.

A minute later, the CHP officer walked up to the passenger side of Jimmy's Expedition. Deron rolled down the window.

"License and registration please, sir," the officer stated in an emotionless tone. Jimmy already had his credentials out, but had been waiting for the officer to ask for his license before showing them. He started to hand over his credentials when Deron spoke.

"I told him several times to slow down, officer," Deron said in a very dry, matter-of-fact voice.

Jimmy looked over at him for a second in disbelief. A second later, he broke out laughing, followed a second later by Deron. The CHP officer looked at them in disbelief, obviously trying to figure out why two grown men would be laughing and making jokes when he was about to scratch them a ticket.

"You gentlemen haven't been drinking, have you?" the officer asked.

"No, no, nothing like that, officer," Jimmy said, handing his credentials over to the less than amused CHP officer. "My partner and I had a humorous experience earlier this morning

and I guess he's just decided to stay in his stupid mood. Sorry.
I didn't realize I was going quite so fast."

The CHP officer looked at the credentials, then shook his
head, frowned and handed them back to Jimmy.

"I think I've stopped every one of you assholes in the last
month. You need to slow down."

The officer walked back to his black and white, started the
car and sped away almost before Jimmy could put his creds
back in his pocket.

"Do you think he was pissed because he didn't get to write
the ticket, or because we were laughing about the situation?"
Deron asked.

"Maybe both," Jimmy replied, "But I guess most of us do
drive a bit faster than we should."

"Well, God bless him for his professional courtesy. Too
bad we can't get the same consideration out of MCC," Deron
stated.

"I don't think we'll ever see professional courtesy at the federal jail," Jimmy replied.

Jimmy accelerated and began to merge back onto the freeway.

"Some things never change," he continued, looking over his
shoulder and then checking his mirrors. "But at least it's been
a few months since they just out and out refused to take one of
our prisoners."

"Yeah, but now they want us to call in advance and make
an appointment to bring them a prisoner. I called them two
hours in advance on this chongo a couple of days ago only to
show up and have to wait two hours before someone would
come down and take the guy. I swear, I almost handcuffed the
prisoner to their door and left."

"Hey, I showed up with a female prisoner last month at
about eight o'clock in the evening and they asked if I could
bring her back after midnight because they didn't have any female guards working the swing shift."

"Dude, I had a guy there last month who I'd been with for six
hours. Arrested him with like fifty pounds of weed and all during

my processing he was fine. We showed up at MCC and had a short wait of about twenty minutes to get in. When the physician's assistant came down and started asking him health questions, my idiot said he thought he had TB. The PA asked him why he thought he had TB and my guy says, 'well I've had a cough for a week that doesn't seem to be getting any better.' The PA rejected him and made me go get him a chest x-ray and clearance from a doctor before they'd take him. I swear those guys are getting to the point that they'll reject someone who has a hangnail."

Jimmy laughed.

"I was with Jesus last week at the port when he called MCC to reserve a bed for this guy. When the PA asked over the phone if there were any medical issues, Jesus says, 'He just got done watching a sad movie and is a little depressed. You guys want me to have a shrink check him out before I bring him?'"

"No shit! That's great! What did the PA say?"

"That's not funny man," Jimmy mocked in a deep voice.

"Sure it is," Jesus said. "You assholes just don't have a sense of humor."

"Alpha 353, Sector."

Jimmy picked up his radio microphone to respond.

"Sector, Alpha 353, go."

"Alpha 353, Alpha 315 is requesting your assistance at 4727 Broyles Court."

"Ten four, Sector. Advise him I'm about ten minutes away," he responded. "I think," he continued, trying to remember where Broyles Court was located. "Hey, my map book is lying on the back seat floor. Can you check that address for me? I think it's in the Paradise Hills area, but I'm not sure now that I think about it."

Deron retrieved the map book and began looking up the address.

"Close, but no cigar. There's a Broyles Street in Paradise Hills, but Broyles Ct. is in Shell town."

"Oh, well. Can't be right all the time. Well, we're still about ten minutes away. Hope you didn't have anything pressing you needed to be doing back at the office."

"Just five or six ROIs," Deron said.

"If the arrest report with the court isn't late, the report of investigation will wait. At least that's my motto," Jimmy replied with a smile.

"You should be a poet, dude."

"I am."

Jimmy kicked it back up to eighty-five, keeping a close eye in his rearview mirror for additional Chippy's.

When Jimmy and Deron arrived at the Broyles Ct. residence, there were numerous unmarked cars and several black and whites. Customs Group Supervisor Angelo Brown was on a cell phone to someone. He smiled, nodded and kept talking, while pointing towards the front door of the residence.

Jimmy and Deron walked up to the front door, meeting Special Agent Ron Harris who was coming out. Ron was about Jimmy's age, having roughly the same time on the job. Jimmy didn't think too highly of him but knew he'd probably be working for him some day. Ron never seemed to be able to make a case on his own, but he looked good and hung out with all the bosses. He was really good at riding the coattails of other agents who developed good cases. He was helpful, pleasant and seemed to say the right things when he was around management. Jimmy thought of him as a kiss ass.

"Hey, Jimmy," he said.

"Hey, Ron. Is Miguel inside?"

"Yeah. I think he's talking to a lady that lives here in one of the back bedrooms. Hey, before you go see him, go take a look in the garage."

Ron walked off towards Angelo. Jimmy looked over at Deron, sighed and shook his head, and then the two stepped forward into the living room. Deron smiled back at Jimmy.

"Give the poor guy a break. He tries," Deron said.

"Yeah. Coming in!" Jimmy called out loudly as he and Deron entered the living room.

There were three adult males seated on the living room sofa, hands handcuffed behind their backs. A small girl, about six or seven years old, sat in a recliner next to the sofa. One of the three handcuffed men stared at Jimmy as he moved through the room. The other two kept their heads down.

"Looks like a defiant little shit, doesn't he?" Deron remarked.

"Yeah. I wonder who he is," Jimmy said.

The two agents walked through the house. There were several agents in each room conducting searches. Most were wearing surgical rubber gloves, going through drawers and closets. Like most homes subject to police searches, this one was messy, not nearly as dirty as some, but not clean by most people's standards. The agents were making it even messier, as drawers were being emptied onto beds, and items from closets were being piled in corners as agents sifted through everything from shoeboxes to coat pockets.

Jimmy noticed clear plastic evidence bags sitting on beds and floors, some containing documents. One contained some personal-use marijuana. On the laundry room floor, towards the rear of the house, was a large electronic scale.

Jimmy and Deron opened the door into the garage. When they stepped inside, the smell of marijuana was overpowering. Looking around, there were cardboard boxes and bags of marijuana everywhere.

"Holy shit!" Deron said.

"Guys, open the garage door, why don't you. This shit stinks," Jimmy said.

"We don't want someone seeing how much dope is in here, particularly the press, should they get a call from someone," Al Blackstone said, walking up to Jimmy and Deron and shaking their hands. Al was in his mid-thirties with long, wavy black hair. He'd been in San Diego about five years now, originally from New York, having come into Customs from the FBI. He'd retained his accent and his attitude, but everyone who worked with him liked him. He was a good investigator with a good work ethic.

"Hey, Al," Jimmy said, nodding and smiling. "How about a compromise. You could open the little side door to the place, and crack the garage door a foot or two. Get some circulation going in here. Just a thought."

"I guess you're right. It is pretty stinky shit, huh?"

"You think!"

Jimmy started walking around the garage, poking into boxes and looking into cupboards. There was marijuana everywhere. It looked like about two tons of weed, if Jimmy had to guess. Not a bad hit.

Jimmy walked over to a table saw in one of the corners of the garage. It had a large exhaust hood built over it that was probably four feet by four feet at the base, tapering up to about a one-foot diameter pipe that vented to the roof of the garage. Jimmy wondered if there was a switch that went just to the exhaust fan, thinking if there was he'd turn it on to aid in the venting of the fumes in the garage. He looked around the sides of the table saw, then around the top area, then to the exhaust hood. Looking under the hood, Jimmy jumped back, drawing his handgun for the second time that day.

"Get out of there!" he yelled in a loud, commanding voice.

Several agents looked at Jimmy, then drew their own side arms and approached cautiously.

"Get out of there! Man, you don't want to do anything stupid. You better listen to me and get your ass out of there!"

Jimmy continued staring at the exhaust hood, weapon pointing at it, while the other agents crept closer. Seconds ticked by with no response from the man in the exhaust hood.

"There's a guy hiding up in the exhaust hood. Keep an eye on it."

Jimmy moved in closer to the exhaust hood, retracting his .40 to a tucked-in position almost under his right armpit. With his left hand, he reached under the exhaust hood and caught hold of the previously hidden subject by his belt. Jimmy began pulling him with sharp tugs.

"Let go, you idiot," Jimmy commanded. The exhaust hood was rocking a bit on its anchors.

"Okay. Hey, hey, hey. I don't want to come down on that saw blade. Hey, let go. I'll come out."

Jimmy kept pulling. A leg dropped out of the hood onto the top of the table saw, then the other leg came down. As his body dropped, and he went into a crouched position to clear his head, several agents swarmed him and dragged him to the ground where he was immediately handcuffed.

Jimmy holstered his gun and took a deep breath.

"How long you guys been here?" he asked.

"About an hour," Al replied.

"You might want to take another look around this place and make sure you don't get any more surprises. I can't believe that idiot has been holding himself up there for an hour."

"He's always bossy like that," Deron said to Al with a smile. "Be thankful you don't have him in your group."

"Do whatever you want, but if someone gets hurt, or gets away, don't say I didn't tell you so," Jimmy said with a very uncharacteristic snarl as he walked back into the house. Deron followed.

"Hey, man. What's wrong? Dude, I was only kidding about you being bossy."

Jimmy stopped and turned to his friend.

"Look. Just give me a minute and I'll be fine." He paused, then turned to face Deron before continuing. "That guy scared the shit out of me, if only for a second. That's twice in one day that someone's been where I didn't expect them. I don't like surprises."

Deron smiled again.

"Hey, the first one doesn't count. It wasn't a real person."

Jimmy's demeanor began to change from a scowl to a smile. He stopped and turned to face his friend.

"Let's keep this morning's story to ourselves, at least for the time being."

"Maybe that's a good idea. I might need a favor someday."

"You're a federal agent. No bribes. It's against the rules."

Jimmy and Deron walked up to a partially closed bedroom door. Looking inside, he noticed Miguel standing at the foot of a bed talking to a woman seated on it. As he pushed the door open, he noticed Special Agent Tammy Jones standing off to the side of the woman. It was quite a contrast, the dark skin of the Hispanic woman to that of Tammy who sported bright red hair with a ruddy Irish complexion and a face full of freckles.

"Hey, Mike. How's it going?" Jimmy said to Miguel.

"Jimmy. Glad you could make it." Miguel turned back to the woman seated on the foot of the bed.

"Maria, this is Special Agent Maxwell. He has a special interest in you. My suggestion to you is that you cooperate with us. There's a lot of dope in this house and someone is going to be very pissed off when they find out they don't have it any more. Now what do you say, Maria? Can you tell us where Angel is, or when he'll be home?"

Jimmy's ears perked up at the mention of Angel. He looked over at Miguel who returned his look, shrugged and turned towards the woman as he began his narration for the benefit of Jimmy and Maria.

"When I got the tip on this place I started watching it, and lo and behold, last night I saw a car show up and back up to the garage. I ran the plate and found it had crossed the border about an hour earlier. Probably got dropped at one of the pay parking lots there next to the port of entry. Anyway, it honked and the garage door opened. It was so dark I really couldn't see into the garage, but I did see packages coming out of the trunk and going into the garage. Presto, change-o, warrant time.

"I got the troops to sit out here all night while I wrote paper on this place and tracked down a judge. You know, it's funny how when we have the duty we have to stay available in case we get called. Judges are special, I guess. They have duty and then can't be found. I paged my judge, who was kind enough to call me back about an hour later to inform me he was at a cocktail party and wouldn't be home until 10:30 or 11:00. When he got home he wouldn't authorize night service, so we were stuck not being able to hit the place until this morning. Anyway, I digress. I'd seen a kid here yesterday and so we sat on the place for a few hours this morning, waiting for her to go to school so she wouldn't be here when we hit the place. Unfortunately, she didn't go to school today, so we hit the place about 9:00 a.m.

Entry went without a hitch—no problems—and I assume you've seen what we found so far. I started doing my thing, working on the personal history 202s, and starting interviews. One of the guys in the living room gave it up, stating they'd all been involved in unloading and moving dope. They unload the dope being smuggled across the border, then, about once a week, a truck shows up and takes the dope up to L.A.

I get to this little sweetheart and she starts threatening me. Says her boyfriend, Angel Garcia, will kill us all for doing this to him again."

"Does she speak English?" Jimmy asked.

"I think she does, but she's playing dumb and making me talk to her in Spanish. I know she understands some because she's reacted to some of the directions I've given to others when they've stopped by to ask me questions."

"Maria," Jimmy said. "When was the last time Angel was here?"

"Go fuck yourself, *puto*," Maria spat towards Jimmy.

"See, she does speak English," Miguel said.

"Women that talk dirty like that turn me on," Deron said. He turned to look at Jimmy who was shaking his head at him for the inappropriate remark.

"I think I'll go check out the rest of the place," Deron said, turning and leaving the room.

Jimmy turned back to Maria. "Doesn't sound to me like she wants to talk about anything," Jimmy said, looking at her as she stared at him defiantly. "I think we'd be wasting our time on her."

"Yeah, probably," Miguel said.

"You think she knows how much time she's looking at spending with us based on what you've got here?" Jimmy asked, continuing to stare into Maria's eyes.

"Nope." Miguel looked over at the woman. "Your little girl's going to be all grown up by the time you get out of jail. You might want to consider talking to us," Miguel stated. Maria looked away without saying anything.

"Well, let me know how it goes if you don't mind, and thanks for the call. You guys have enough help? We can stay and help for awhile if you need us," Jimmy offered.

"I appreciate it, but I think we're covered. You could check in with Angelo if you want before you leave," Miguel said.

Jimmy looked again at Maria, staring at her without saying anything. Maria sensed his look and turned to look at him, staring back defiantly. After about ten seconds, he broke his stare, then shook his head in mild frustration and started to walk out of the room. After taking a few steps he stopped, then turned again to Miguel.

"So, Mike. What's the deal with the little girl in the living room? I assume that's Maria's kid?"

"Yeah. She's been living here with mom and Angel ever since they opened for business. That's my best guess, anyway."

"Sounds like a child endangerment charge along with the drug trafficking charge to me. Don't you agree?"

"Yeah. So I guess she goes to the Polinski Center today, then after mom gets deported, following her conviction and prison sentence, the child gets sent to Mexico. Well, unless a foster family wants to keep her."

Maria's look of defiance rapidly turned to shock. She stared a moment at Jimmy, then turned and gave a pleading look to Miguel.

"Have a good one, Mikey," Jimmy said as he turned and walked from the room.

As Jimmy walked through the living room towards the front door, he looked over again at the six- or seven-year-old girl seated in the recliner. The light bulb went on and he redirected his steps towards the little girl. Deron was standing in the living room waiting for his friend.

"Hey, Deron. I'm going to go have a quick chat with the little girl."

"No problem, man. I'll go out and check in with Angelo and see if there's anything we can do to help before we take off."

Jimmy nodded then walked over to the little girl as Deron exited the residence.

"Hey, sweetie," he said. "No school today?"

The little girl shook her head no and kept rocking in the chair.

"You know, I have a little girl too. She's about your age and she's really pretty like you. So why didn't you go to school today? Not feeling good?"

"I don't always go to school, you know," the little girl said. "Besides, my daddy is supposed to come pick me up and take me to get a frozen yogurt."

"Yeah? What's your daddy's name?"

"Angel. But he pronounces it An-hel. It's the way Mexican's talk, you know."

"You're sure smart. What's your name?"

The little girl smiled. "Guadalupe. But you can call me Lupita."

"Can you tell me what time your daddy was supposed to pick you up today?"

"He's not going to come now. I know he doesn't like the police, and with all of you here, well, he's not going to come home right now. But it's okay. I understand. He'll come get me later."

Jimmy knew the little girl was old enough to know more about the world than most people would give her credit for, but he hadn't counted on her being old enough to have such candor. He hoped she wasn't old enough to know all the terrible things her father was involved in. He decided not to press the issue of Angel any further.

"So, Lupita, do you have any brothers or sisters? You know, at school or anywhere?" Jimmy asked.

"No. There's just me and my mom. I do have a *tio*, Alfredo."

"Really? What's your uncle's last name?"

"It's Saenz. He's my dad's half-brother. They had the same mother, you know. He lives in Tijuana."

"Wow. I didn't really know that. I bet you really like him?" Jimmy said, trying to keep the conversation going.

"He's all right. We don't see him very often."

Well, Lupita, it's been a pleasure to meet you. I'm sorry we had to come to your home and disturb your day with your father. Maybe we can meet again sometime under better circumstances."

Jimmy extended his hand to Lupita. She reached out and took it, giving it a tender shake. Jimmy smiled, then turned and walked away.

Deron met him in the front yard. He'd been talking to Angelo. Jimmy walked up and joined them.

"You think this place was being run by your guy?" Angelo asked.

"Yeah. But I can't figure out how, if the cartel is looking for him, that they, or someone, didn't know about this place. I mean, there's a lot of dope in this place. You probably have about two million bucks wholesale in weed in the garage. If any of the people who work for Ruiz or Leon were really looking for Garcia, how could they not have found out about this place? It makes no sense, unless our theory about them being pissed off at him for the big loss a few weeks ago is all wrong."

"You're probably right. Maybe they were pissed, but have realized it wasn't his fault, that it was just a business loss. Who else are they going to bring in that has his trust and power to control things over here?"

"Geez, Angelo, I have no idea at this point. I know the cartel. These guys aren't forgiving. They'd just as soon shoot you in the head as not if they think you cost them any significant money. And what's always amazed me is that as many of them get whacked on a continual basis, or end up in prison for extended stays, there's always someone else willing to step into their spot as soon as it becomes vacant."

"I know. It's always amazed me too. Still, we must be missing something because obviously Garcia is here working."

"Sure seems to be. Hey, Angelo, I really appreciate you guys calling me and letting me come over and snoop around. Is there anything we can do to help before we take off?"

"No. We have a bunch of folks here. Once we got in and saw what we had, I called the seized property folks. They're en route with a truck. I think we have it. Unless you just really want to stick around."

"I wouldn't mind, but Deron here says he can't wait to get going on some reports."

Angelo smiled and nodded. Jimmy turned and began walking away.

"Now don't be shooting any naked rubber girls," Angelo called out to him.

"You rotten scumbag," Jimmy said, looking at Deron. "I thought you weren't going to say anything." Deron was laughing too hard to answer. "Just wait. I'm gonna make you pay," Jimmy said, kicking playfully at Deron's backside as he ran towards the Expedition.

CHAPTER . . .

12

When the weekend finally arrived, Jimmy was more than ready for it. He tried sleeping in Saturday morning, but at 6:30 a.m. Nikki woke him up. As he opened his eyes, he found her nose against his. Focusing and backing up a little, he saw that she was smiling.

"Morning, sweetie," he said with a yawn.

"Daddy, come on, get up. I found your favorite on TV."

"Which favorite is that?"

"Rocky and Bullwinkle."

"Really? I haven't seen them on TV for a long, long time."

"I think you already got the tape of the one that's on," Nikki said.

"I think you already *have* the tape," Jimmy corrected his daughter with a smile.

"If you two are going to talk, go do it in the other room," Shirley said in a muffled voice, her face half-buried in her pillow.

"Mommy, why don't you come watch Rocky and Bullwinkle with us?" Nikki suggested.

"I'm going to sleep in a little longer, darling. You go watch with Daddy." Shirley looked over at Jimmy with a look that told him that he'd better take Nikki and leave if he wanted any kind of peaceful day.

Jimmy slipped from the covers and headed for the bathroom.

"I'll meet you in a minute, sweetie. How about turning the coffee pot on for me."

"Daddy, I already did that." Nikki almost sounded offended that her father would have thought she'd forgotten to do the obvious.

An hour later, Jimmy decided he'd go for a run. Nikki put on her pink bike helmet and followed him around the neighborhood on her bicycle. There was a nice sea breeze that made it comfortable. *A perfect day*, he thought. Clear blue skies, and at 8:00 a.m. it was 72 degrees. It would probably hit the mid-80s by the afternoon.

As he ran his thoughts drifted. One thing on his mind was Carmen Beltran. She was beautiful and smart. He wondered why someone like her had hooked up with someone like Angel. Well, at least Angel Garcia had good taste in women. As he continued thinking about her he wondered why he hadn't heard from her in nearly a week. He decided he'd give her a call later that day to see how she was doing.

He also wondered about Angel's other family. He wondered which relationship came first, the one with Maria or the one with Carmen. The two children, Raul and Lupita, were pretty close in age, although Raul was probably a year or two older. He wondered if the two women were aware of each other and their respective children.

Back at his house, he showered and then sat with Nikki and ate a bowl of cereal. Nikki sat with him long enough to have a banana, then returned to the television set for more cartoons.

Shirley joined him just as he was finishing the last few bites of his cereal.

"Morning, honey," he said as she walked into the kitchen.

"Morning . . . Hey, slow down. You don't have to eat like a pig."

Jimmy shook his head, wishing he could have finished eating before she joined him.

Shirley looked over at him as she poured a cup of coffee.

"What? You're not going to talk to me now because I said something? You eat way too fast. Why don't you slow down and enjoy your food?"

"Why don't you just let me eat the way I want to eat? Does it bother you that much?"

"Jimmy, you really need to have some manners. You know, you embarrass me sometimes with your manners when we're out with friends. I don't think your parents ever taught you anything about manners or any of the social graces."

"My parents did fine. You know, it's funny. I'm out with my co-workers nearly every day, having lunch or whatever. None of them have ever said a word to me about my manners. I have a lot of friends who seem to think I'm pretty good company, and none of them have ever even remotely suggested that I'm socially inept."

"Well, they're not your wife. They don't have to live with you, and see you the way I do day in and day out. Look, I don't want to fight. Let's have a nice day together, okay?"

"Okay."

"So tell me what happened with that weird, old, sexual, deviant couple."

"I ended up arresting Mr. Williams," Jimmy said.

"That's it. What happened? Why'd you arrest him?"

"Well after our visit to their house, Deron and I stopped by their bar the following afternoon. Mrs. Williams kept trying to get us to have a drink, while . . ."

"And you had one with her, right?"

"Hey, I'm trying to tell you what happened. And no, I didn't. Anyway, I finally got Mr. Williams to show us where his car was parked. It was the funniest thing. He leads us over to this door that opened to a field behind the bar. When he opened the door he looks out and then tries to act surprised while he says, 'My car! What . . . what . . . my car! It's gone! It was right here. I swear it was right here.' I kept trying to look serious, but it took every ounce of control not to laugh at the little shit.

"I initially told him he'd better call the police to report the theft, but while he was on hold with El Cajon P.D. I told him that it was also a crime to make a false police report. While he was on hold I explained to him that I could prove his car wasn't stolen, and that smuggling twenty-two pounds of marijuana wasn't that big of a deal. He finally confessed that one of the semi-regular patrons of his bar had talked him into getting involved in bringing the weed across the border in one of his cars. So he goes to jail and now has a felony conviction. He's going to end up losing a car worth a few thousand bucks, have a felony conviction, a bunch of court costs, maybe lose his liquor license, and all so he could make five hundred bucks."

"Some people are just greedy, aren't they?"

"Yeah, and stupid. For a few hundred bucks they risk being in jail and totally screwing up their lives forever. I can understand it for a lot of the people we arrest. They live in Mexico in poverty; they have nothing, and need money to keep a roof over their heads, or to pay for an operation for a family member, or something. But these idiots who have jobs and income, and just do it so they can have money to party on, or buy new sex toys or whatever, those idiots really need to examine their priorities in life. Its too bad things aren't a little more like the old days, when cops could take them down a back alley and tune them up a little."

"Come on, Jimmy. The police aren't there to be your parents or the social conscience of society, or the punishers of injustice or any of that crap. They enforce the law, and that's it. The courts, with the aid of a jury of your peers, decide on what should be done to the law breaker."

"The courts have become way too political, and they're bogged down with so many cases that they just slap hands in order to keep the system from getting backlogged to the point of coming to a grinding halt. And juries are composed of people that spend way too much time watching stupid television shows that show the police being able to do way too many things that they can't do in real life. Either that or watching television news and opinion shows that show some random cop somewhere doing some boneheaded thing that they show over and over in order to inflame the public into thinking that all cops are that way. Then the stupid juries decide to cut a crook some slack when he really needs to be in prison because they think he's just a victim of all that abuse that everyone supposedly gets from all those rat-bastard police officers."

"Look. I agree with you to a point. But a lot of cops get caught up in thinking they are the purveyors of justice. Look at what those L.A. cops did to Rodney King a few years ago."

"Look at what Rodney did to cause it to get to that point. Cops are human. You think that after a lengthy pursuit, and with him striking one of them first, and then not complying with simple commands, that they're not going to have their emotions maybe get a little jacked up. But what really pisses me off about the Rodney King thing was the fact that a jury of their peers tried those cops in court and acquitted them. Then, to satisfy the minority public in L.A., almost all of which go nuts and burn half the city down, the president caused them to be re-tried, federally, for civil rights violations. To be re-tried would have never happened to anyone but a cop. So lives and careers were ruined over some shithead who deserved the beating he got. That loser of a human being continues to be a drain on society."

"Let's change the subject, okay?"

"Fine. I don't need my blood pressure any higher anyway."

"My mom wants us to come over later this afternoon. You don't have to work or anything, do you?"

"Not that I know of, but you know that things come up sometimes."

"Well, just don't answer your phone today, okay?"

Jimmy ignored the comment.

"I want to go to church tomorrow," he said as he got up to head out to do some yard work.

"Okay," Shirley replied.

Several hours later, as Jimmy was finishing with mowing the lawn, his cell phone rang.

"Maxwell," he answered.

"Agent Maxwell. It's Carmen Beltran. I'm sorry to bother you on a weekend, but there's a car parked down the street watching the house with two men inside. I can't see them well, but they must be here watching my house. They've just been sitting there for the last hour."

"Ms. Beltran, you just stay in your house and keep an eye on them. Don't worry. I'm going to have a police car come by shortly and check them out. If anyone gets out of the car and starts towards your house, dial 911."

"Can you come by?" Carmen asked.

"Sure. It may take a bit to get over there, but let me go so I can get the police to come check out those men. What kind of car are they in?"

"It's a big dark blue car. I'm not sure what kind. It looks a little like a police car, but it isn't."

"Can you see the license plate?"

"I can't read it from here, but it's a Mexican plate."

"Okay, I'll have someone come by. You just wait inside and keep your phone handy, okay?"

"Okay. Bye."

Jimmy called Chula Vista Police and advised the dispatcher of the situation. All units were tied up responding to other calls, but they advised they'd respond as soon as they could, which probably meant it was going to take awhile. Jimmy tried to think of an agent that lived close by, but couldn't come up with anyone.

Shit, he thought. *I'm going to have to head over there.*

Jimmy went into the bathroom and grabbed a washcloth and began to give himself a quick wipe down. He was in the bedroom changing into clean clothes when Shirley came into the room.

"What's going on?"

"You go ahead and take Nikki over to your mom's. I have to go take care of a problem, but it shouldn't take too long. I'll just meet you over there."

"Why do you have to go in? Can't someone else take care of whatever is going on? You work harder than most of those people you work with. Let them go in for a change."

"Shirley, I've been around longer, so it's only natural that I would have more going on. It's the nature of this business. The longer you're around the more sources you pick up, the more contacts with other law enforcement you make, and the more things just seem to gravitate towards you. I'm sorry, but it's the nature of the beast."

"You used to tell me that it was ten percent of the agents that do ninety percent of the work. So if that's true, call one of the ninety percent and let them go in today."

"Look. It's true that some agents end up doing a lot more work than others. That's besides the point. I'm involved in a case that no one else knows enough about to be able to take care of right now. Even if I could find a willing agent to go in, it would take more time to bring them up to speed on this than to just go take care of it myself."

"So what's going on that's so important?"

"There's a witness to a very important case that has been threatened. Some men are over at her house. It's possible that they are there to kidnap her . . . or worse."

"Her? Her? Who's this her?" Shirley looked at her husband with both hurt and anger in her eyes.

"What is wrong with you?" Jimmy asked. Shirley started to respond but Jimmy cut her off, taking a few minutes to give her a thumbnail version of his investigation with Angel Garcia. By the time he'd finished, Shirley had finally seemed to get hold of her emotions.

"I don't know why you just can't turn your phone off sometimes. Or just not answer it once in a while?"

"Honey, I can't ignore my phone. They pay me extra money and give me a take-home car in order to be available if I get called. Get the crooks to break the law only Monday through Friday between nine and five and I'll be happy to be home on the evenings and weekends. As a matter of fact, you know they have sentencing enhancements for things like using a gun, or dealing dope within one thousand feet of a school; you know, stuff like that. Well I think they should have sentencing enhancements for breaking the law after five and on weekends. How about calling our congressman. I think Duncan Hunter would probably go for it." Jimmy gave Shirley a smile, a wink and kiss on the cheek as he turned away.

Jimmy grabbed his handgun and tucked it in his belt. He headed for the kitchen, grabbed his car keys off the hook by the garage door and turned to find his wife right behind him.

"I'll hurry, okay. I love you," he said, intending to give her a quick kiss. Instead, his wife threw her arms around his neck and held him tight for close to a minute. She then gave him a long, sensuous kiss. Finally releasing him, she looked him in the eyes and said, "Be careful."

Jimmy walked out to his G-ride and sat for a moment trying to figure out why his wife had reacted like she had. After about fifteen seconds, he shook his head, started the Expedition and headed over to Carmen's home.

As Jimmy rounded the corner to Carmen's house, he noticed a dark blue Crown Victoria parked on the west side of the street. Two Hispanic males sat inside. The car had Baja California plates that Jimmy jotted down.

"Chula Vista Police, 185," the dispatcher answered.

"This is Special Agent Maxwell with U.S. Customs. I called about twenty minutes ago and asked about having a unit check out two subjects who are stalking a witness of ours who lives at 1561 Ravenwood. Could you check on the status of the unit and give me an idea of when someone might be clear to respond?"

"One moment."

The dispatcher came back on the line about twenty seconds later.

"There's a unit that should be clear in about five minutes. They're a few minutes away from the location. I'll send them as soon as they clear."

Jimmy gave the dispatcher his cell phone number then said, "Please advise them that the suspicious vehicle is a dark blue Crown Vic, Baja license Adam Henry 43121. It seems to be occupied twice with Mexican males. I'm in the area in plain clothes in a green Expedition. I'm wearing jeans and a blue t-shirt with U.S. Navy printed on the front."

Jimmy could hear her putting out the descriptions over the air as he hung up. Now if he could just hang in there discreetly until the unit arrived. He had parked down the street where he could watch the sedan. Several times over the next few minutes he saw one of the subjects in his target vehicle look over his shoulder at him.

Relax, boys, Jimmy said quietly to himself.

Several more minutes passed with the looks at him becoming a bit more frequent.

Jimmy noticed the car start and the backup lights come on briefly as the vehicle was put into gear. The driver of the Crown Vic started away from the curb.

Shit, Jimmy thought. "Never a cop when you need one," he said aloud, putting the Expedition in gear.

Jimmy pulled out into the street at a ninety-degree angle to the curb, effectively blocking the street and the escape route of the vehicle. He pulled his badge out from under his shirt and let it hang from its chain around his neck.

"These assholes are not just driving away until I know who they are," he thought aloud.

As the Crown Victoria turned and headed towards him, Jimmy got out of his SUV on the opposite side of their approach and drew his sidearm. The Crown Vic stopped a car length from him. The occupants seemed to be assessing their next move. Jimmy had a position near the front of his vehicle that afforded him some cover, and a position that would afford him some protection if the driver of the Crown Victoria decided to accelerate and ram him.

"Police! I want to see your hands, fellas!" he yelled as he pointed his gun at the windshield of the sedan.

The driver of the Crown Vic put the car in park and kept his hands high on the steering wheel.

"Passenger! I said I want to see your hands. *Habla* English?"

The passenger put his hands up and shook his head yes. Jimmy waited patiently for about thirty seconds, hoping the police unit would round the corner and assist him in his contact. It was obvious that the men in the Crown Vic were nervous, probably wondering what this one *gringo* was doing just standing there pointing a gun at them. Jimmy decided to approach and contact them. He slowly moved around the front of his SUV and walked towards the passenger side of the big sedan.

"Agente Aduana. Do you speak English?"

"Si. A little, mister. What do you want with us?"

"I'd like to see some identification."

As the men reached towards their wallets, Jimmy said, "Slowly, gentlemen. And you better come out of those pockets with a wallet or you won't like what happens next."

The movement of the two men slowed. Wallets came out and as the passenger opened his wallet to retrieve his identification, Jimmy noticed a badge.

"What you're doing over here?" he asked as they started to produce identification. They didn't answer.

As the men removed their identification, the police unit finally came around the corner. Jimmy turned his body towards them and with his non-gun hand displayed his badge to the approaching officer as the unit came to a stop. The police unit turned on the first stage of his overhead lights, displaying a flashing red light. The officer got out of his unit and approached Jimmy, his weapon drawn. Jimmy took several steps back and spoke in a low voice so as not to be heard by the occupants of the Crown Vic.

"Ed Brown," the officer said, introducing himself.

Jimmy nodded and said, "Jimmy Maxwell. These guys were Code 5 on 1561. I have a witness to a pretty important narcotics investigation living there who was getting pretty nervous. I don't know who these guys are, but when I asked for I.D., I saw a Mexican badge of some type in the passenger's wallet."

The officer nodded his head that he understood, and then started his approach to the driver's side of the car.

Jimmy increased the volume of his voice to the officer as he walked towards the sedan.

"I just made the stop. They haven't been out of the car and no one has been patted down."

The officer slowed a bit and with his weapon in one hand, he keyed his radio microphone with his free hand and said something in a low voice to his dispatch.

"Turn off the car and hand me the keys," the officer said to the driver. The driver complied.

The officer looked at identification from the driver while Jimmy watched momentarily before he started jotting down the I.D. information from the passenger.

A few minutes later, Jimmy and the officer were standing together, comparing notes and exchanging information.

"They're both Tijuana police officers. The driver, Mauricio Moreno, says they were waiting for the passenger's grandmother to get home. The passenger's name is, let's see, Alberto Orozco. Grandma allegedly lives at 1544."

"He's a lying piece of shit."

"Yeah, I know. I had dispatch run the address and put in a call. The people who live there are Anglo and said they've lived there about five months. They think a Hispanic family lived there before them, and there is a Hispanic family name of Aispuro that comes back to the address when you run ARJIS. Anyway, there's no way to look further into this right now and I've already got dispatch holding calls for me, so I'm going to have to clear."

"So nothing we can do with these two guys?" Jimmy asked.

"What have they done except park on the street? We didn't find any weapons on them." The officer looked at Jimmy and shrugged.

"Do me a favor?" Jimmy asked. "I know you guys are busy, but can you do a little extra patrol in the area for the next few days? Maybe pass this information on to the next shift as well?"

"I'll try, man. Be safe."

"You too."

The officer tore out the pages he'd filled in from his field interview pad and handed them over to Jimmy. Officer Brown then got back into his police unit and closed the door.

"I'll hang out for a minute until you clear," he said to Jimmy. Jimmy nodded, then walked over to the vehicle occupied by the two Tijuana police officers. He bent down just a little to look through the car window, handing back their identification documents.

"I know what you're doing over here, and it isn't waiting for grandma. I know who you are, and who you work for, and I'm putting you on notice. Stay in Mexico. Don't let me find you anywhere near this area again or I will have your immigration documents cancelled and I'll get word to Jose Leon that you guys are my informants. I know he's your boss so don't stare at me like you don't know what I'm talking about. *Comprende?*"

The men stared at Jimmy, expressionless.

"Go!" he said, turning and walking away.

Jimmy waived at Officer Brown who started his vehicle, nodded and drove away. Jimmy got into the Expedition and backed out of the way. The Crown Vic drove past him and headed out of the area. Jimmy followed it from a distance until it got onto the 805 freeway and headed south. As he neared the border, his cell phone rang.

"Agent Maxwell? This is Carmen Beltran. Are you going to come by and see me?"

"Yes. I'm finishing something up right now, but I'll be over in about ten minutes."

"Is everything all right? Why did you let those men go? No matter what they told you, they were here either watching me, or waiting for Angel."

"I know. Look, relax and I'll be over in about ten minutes. They won't be back today. Okay?"

Jimmy disconnected his call and moved over the number one lane as he neared the border. The Crown Victoria drove into Mexico and Jimmy made the U-turn and headed back towards Chula Vista. As he drove, he called Sector Communications.

"Hey, Sector. This is Alpha 353. I need you to put in a lookout for me."

Jimmy provided the Baja California, Mexico, license number on the Crown Victoria to his dispatch center.

"Have the vehicle searched, the occupants identified and put in the remarks to call me with the information prior to releasing the car."

Jimmy thanked the dispatcher and exited Orange Avenue, heading back to the Ravenwood address.

Carmen met him at the door. Jimmy could see Raul playing with a toy truck in the background.

"Come in," she said, looking nervously down the street.

Jimmy walked into the living room and closed the door behind him. He followed Carmen into the kitchen and sat down with her at a small table in a breakfast nook area.

"Everything is all right. The men have been identified and warned not to return to this neighborhood. If you see them, call 911 and then call me. Call in that order, okay?"

Carmen nodded, staring into Jimmy's eyes.

"Do you think they'll be back?"

"Well, I don't really expect those particular men to return, but yes, I think someone will be back. But listen carefully to me. The men aren't after you. They really aren't. If they were, they'd have just come inside and taken you. They're waiting for Angel. To do him harm or just to pick him up and talk to him, I don't really know, although I have my suspicions."

"He must really be in trouble," she said, almost to herself.

"Listen, Carmen. Whoever wants him, really wants him bad. What I told you is true, to a point. The cartel doesn't want you, they want Angel. But, if they don't find him soon, there is the possibility that they could come for you. They might try to hold you and Raul to force Angel to trade himself for you. Do you think he'd trade himself for you?"

Jimmy paused a moment to let Carmen think about what he'd told her.

"Carmen, I'm asking you again. Do you know how I can find him? I know you don't know me very well, and I do intend to arrest him and put him in prison where he belongs, but honestly, he will continue to bring a lot of trouble to you. Do you and Raul really need that?"

Carmen said nothing for a minute. She stared blankly into Jimmy's eyes, then finally turned and looked at her son.

"He called yesterday. He sounded okay. I didn't detect any stress in his voice, and he didn't mention any trouble."

"Did you talk to him about what's been going on over here?"

"I mentioned that there were people looking for him and that I was scared."

"What did he say?"

"He told me not to worry, that it would all blow over soon."

"Carmen, you can't believe that. Even if by some miracle he averts this particular crisis in his life, there will be others. And if he continues to come over here it will eventually spill over into your life. I'm being totally honest with you. There are going to be both cartel people and police watching this house. Best-case scenario, he's here and about a dozen police officers or federal agents dressed in black will knock very loud and several seconds later your door will be broken down and those men will come storming through your house, pointing submachine guns at you and Raul. There'll probably be one or two loud explosions from flash-bangs going off in back rooms, and you'll be put down on the floor and handcuffed. It's very scary. Once the chaos settles, Angel will be in custody and you'll have a mess to clean up. And that's the best-case scenario. Do you or Raul need that?"

"He's coming over to see Raul next weekend. I don't know which day or what time, but that's what he said."

"What number did he call you from?"

Carmen got up and walked over to a kitchen counter. She picked up a notepad and wrote down a telephone number, then walked back to where Jimmy was sitting. She stood in front of him and held the piece of paper out to him.

"He told me if there was an emergency I could call him at that number."

Jimmy looked at the paper. It was a Tijuana number. He folded it and put it in his shirt pocket. Carmen looked at him with unease. He reached out and took Carmen's left hand in both of his hands. She did nothing to pull away, but after a few seconds Jimmy sensed her starting to relax.

"I will do my best to make sure you and Raul stay safe. If you can call me and let me know precisely when Angel is here, I'll make sure we take him into custody with a very minimal amount of presence and commotion. There won't be any doors broken down or any of that other stuff. In the meantime, I'm asking you again, if there's someone not involved in this that you could stay with this next week, or if you can afford to stay in a motel, do it."

"I'll think about it, Agent Maxwell,"

"Jimmy. My name is Jimmy. I'm calling you by your first name, I think you can use mine."

Jimmy got up, releasing Carmen's hand. He smiled at her, then headed for the front door. When he got there, he turned and looked back at her.

"You did the right thing." He walked out of the house, got into his Expedition and drove to his in-laws house.

CHAPTER . . .

13

Sunday morning Jimmy took his family to church. On the drive there, Shirley seemed quiet, staring out the window. The weather was perfect, clear blue skies, sunny and about seventy-five degrees with a gentle sea breeze. Jimmy reached over and turned on the radio to a classic rock station. Shirley immediately reached over and turned the radio off.

"I don't want to listen to that," she said. Jimmy looked over at her questioningly. She turned away without saying anything and went back to staring out the window. He was starting to get used to her moods and didn't say anything.

They drove in silence with Nikki asleep in the back seat. As they drove, Jimmy looked over at Shirley several times, but she seemed to be trying to ignore him. Finally he said something.

"So, what's bothering you this morning?"

Shirley turned and looked at him.

"Why don't you ever want to talk to me about anything?"

"I think we've had this discussion before," he said with a sigh. He paused a moment, waiting for her to respond. Shirley stared out the window saying nothing. When he saw the lack of response, he continued.

"I do talk to you, but you make it difficult to want to start a conversation with you when I know it will turn into an argument."

"It doesn't always turn into an argument."

"What do you want to talk about?" he said, sighing again.

"We never talk about anything. Seriously, we don't talk because you don't want to talk. You'd rather listen to the radio or watch television. I think you'd do almost anything to avoid talking to me. You don't tell me what you'd like to do away from work, what you want to do when you retire someday, where you want to go on vacation, even about what kind of car you want to buy next year. Nothing."

"Which topic would you like to discuss?"

"I don't want to choose. I want you to talk to me about what you want to talk about."

"I've got a pretty good case going right now. We've seized a bunch of dope from this guy . . ."

"I don't want to hear about your job and dope," Shirley said, cutting him off in mid-sentence.

Jimmy was getting irritated but said nothing, driving in silence for another minute. *Okay, I'll try again*, he thought.

"I'm really looking forward to my hunting trip this year."

"So you can get away from me for two weeks, right?"

"No. No. I like hunting. It's relaxing to get away from the city, to get out where my cell phone doesn't work and the bosses and informants can't reach me. I can wander off into the mountains and sit and relax."

"Uh huh," came the disgusted reply.

They sat in silence again for a minute. Finally, Shirley spoke.

"So, if you want to talk about work, tell me about your visit to that woman yesterday."

"Not much to tell really. A couple of drug traffickers were parked on her street, probably waiting for her husband to get home so they could snatch him. They're Tijuana cops in their spare time," he said smiling. "This guy Angel Garcia owes the cartel money and they want him to answer someway or another." He paused for a moment. "At least that's what I think they want him for. We have seized quite a bit of dope lately that was being protected by him."

"Did you see her?"

"The woman? Yeah, I saw her for a couple of minutes."

"Did you go in her house?"

"Yeah, for a couple of minutes."

"Who was with you?"

"No one. There was a Chula Vista Police officer assisting when we initially contacted the guys watching the house, but he left."

"Not very smart of you to go in her house alone. She could make all kinds of accusations and where would you be? In trouble."

"Why would she do that? I'm trying to help her."

"You're trying to arrest her husband, right? She doesn't know you. Maybe she wants to get you in a compromising position to get you thrown off the case."

"I don't think so. Not all women think like you."

As soon as Jimmy said it, he regretted it and wished he'd kept his mouth shut.

"You know what, Jimmy? Fuck you. I'm trying to help you and you insult me. Fuck you. You think you know everything and that I don't know shit because I stay home and take care of our little girl. I do know things."

"I know you do. Look, I'm sorry. I shouldn't have said that. But, you know what? You're a very difficult woman to talk to. It isn't that I don't want to talk to you, but everything you say is contentious."

"You don't know shit. You work all day, come home and drink until you fall asleep on the sofa. The only time you get excited is when your cell phone is going off or when you get called out so you don't have to be with me."

"You know, I used to love being with you, but listen to yourself. You're so full of anger. I haven't done anything wrong. I know I work a lot. I don't talk to you that much anymore because you don't want to hear about my work. You're jealous to the point of, of, I don't know what. I don't talk to you because it always ends up in an argument. I really think you need some counseling."

"And where did you get your psychology degree from? I need a husband to be home with me, to want to have a life with me that isn't centered around drug traffickers and informants."

"Well, you should have married someone else then."

"I need to have a husband who doesn't sit around and drink in excess, use profanity, and then try and convince people that he's a Christian because he goes to church. You're the biggest hypocrite I've ever seen."

"I'm guilty of it all. That's why I go to church and read my Bible. That's what Christianity is all about. We're all flawed, especially me. But I try to be a good person, a good husband, a good father and a good criminal investigator. I acknowledge my weaknesses and failures, and I'm sorry I haven't been a good husband."

Jimmy paused a moment then continued.

"One thing I've learned in my studies of the Bible is that Jesus is a forgiver."

"Yeah, well he didn't have to live with your sorry ass."

The rest of the drive was made in silence. After church, Shirley decided to take the car and go visit her parents again. Jimmy offered to go along, but Shirley asked him to stay home with Nikki. He figured that it would probably be a good thing for her to get away from the house for a bit and decided to take care of some yard work and laundry.

By mid-afternoon, Jimmy and Nikki started watching a John Wayne western together but Nikki couldn't stay focused. She wanted to play in her room. Halfway through the movie she returned, climbed in Jimmy's lap and fell asleep.

Shirley came home around five o'clock and Jimmy barbecued some *pollo asado*, making beans and a salad to go with it for dinner. During much of their evening together little was said, but the couple avoided fighting with each other. After dinner Jimmy did the dishes while Shirley took care of putting Nikki to bed.

Once the kitchen was clean, Jimmy found Shirley watching a news program in their bedroom. Shirley looked up at Jimmy as he entered the room but said nothing.

"Don't you want to watch your show in the living room?"

"You don't want to watch this."

"I will watch whatever you want to watch."

"But you really don't want to watch this show, do you?"

Jimmy thought for a moment before answering then said, "It wouldn't be my first choice, but I'd watch it to be with you."

"Jimmy, you don't have to kiss my ass. I'll watch my show, you go watch whatever you want in the living room."

Jimmy shook his head, standing there a moment before leaving.

"Close the door on the way out. And keep the volume down so I can hear my show," she said as Jimmy walked away.

By ten o'clock, Jimmy decided to call it a day. He'd decided not to drink that evening, as he was the duty agent starting at midnight. He also hoped that his wife would come join him at some point. Going into the bedroom, he found Shirley asleep. He got into bed as quietly as he could and lay next to his wife. Jimmy tossed and turned for a while, his mind jumping around from thoughts about his marriage, his daughter, Carmen Beltran, and Angel Garcia.

Twenty minutes later, he found himself wishing that he would have had a few drinks so he could have fallen asleep without the mental aggravation. He finally fell asleep after about thirty minutes of tossing and turning.

A little after midnight the telephone rang.

"Hello," Jimmy said, half-asleep.

"Sorry to wake you, Jimmy. This is Angie at Sector. You're the duty agent today and I've got a call for you from headquarters."

Jimmy sat up in bed. He'd never been called from headquarters before.

"Okay, go ahead."

"Agent Maxwell. This is Peter Wong. I'm the fugitive coordinator here in D.C. and I got some information from a confidential source that indicates Steven Allen is down at the Harbor Island Yacht Club staying on the 'Molly Madison'."

"I assume the Molly Madison is a boat?"

"Yes. I don't know if you recognize the name Steven Allen, but he's on our top ten most wanted list. He is responsible for breaking into one of our drug storage vaults outside Detroit last year and stealing hundreds of pounds of assorted drugs. He used to be one of our seized property custodians, so he knew how to beat the alarm systems. Several months after the theft, he killed a cop near Toledo, Ohio, during a traffic stop. He's considered armed and dangerous. The source providing this information has helped us catch several other important fugitives during the past few years. Anyway, I'll stay in touch. Let me know if there's anything else I can do, and good luck."

Jimmy hung up the telephone. *Shit*, he thought. He lay back down for a minute, and then got up as quietly as he could. Shirley stirred slightly, but never seemed to wake. Once showered, he left a note for his wife, looked briefly in on Nikki, then left his house and headed towards Shelter Island.

"Sector, Jimmy. Hey, can you patch me through to Tom Phillips' residence," Jimmy said.

"Sure, Jimmy."

Jimmy put his cell phone on speaker and waited patiently. When nothing happened, he looked down to notice the phone had dropped the call.

"Piece of shit phone," he said aloud. "Well I guess you can't expect your damned phone to work in the middle of a city."

Jimmy recalled and was finally patched to Tom's residence.

"Hey, Jefe. Sorry to wake you but I just got a very unusual duty call."

The call from headquarters was explained as Jimmy headed towards Harbor Island at eighty-five miles per hour.

"I'll make some calls and get a surveillance team out there as soon as possible. How many people do you think you'll need to do this right?"

"Well, I don't see the need to try and rush this. To try and do an entry on a boat with someone who's considered armed and dangerous seems unnecessary. I'm thinking we put some people in discreet locations around the boat and just wait for him to leave. Grab him on the dock walking up to his car or something."

"I agree. We'll take it slow and wait him out. Shouldn't take that long."

"Good. So we'll probably need six or seven agents per shift. I'm thinking twelve-hour shifts so we don't have to tie up too many agents."

"Okay. So go scout out the marina, find the boat and I'll start calling people. I'm going to have Sal stop at the office and pull a flyer on Steve Allen. I'll have him print out a dozen or so for you to pass around with the troops."

"Good. That'll save me from having to go by on my way over to the marina."

Jimmy hung up the phone, looked in his rearview mirror and noticed the police car running code coming up behind him fast. *Shit*, he thought.

Jimmy headed for the shoulder of the road and waited as the CHP Officer exited his car and walked up to the passenger side of his Expedition. Jimmy rolled down the window as the officer neared and cautiously peeked into the vehicle.

"License and registration please," the CHP officer said.

Jimmy pulled out his credential's wallet and then handed over the registration document that showed the Expedition being registered to U.S. Customs.

"Hey, is this a G-ride?" the officer asked.

"Yeah. I'm on my way over to Harbor Island to try to find a fugitive I got a tip on," Jimmy said.

"Cool. I didn't know you guys had SUVs. Is it a seizure, or are they buying these for you guys now?"

"They bought this one. We don't drive many seizures anymore. Used to. Man, when I was first hired we had guys driving Mercedes, Jags, and Corvettes. My boss used to drive a Lincoln Town Car. But some asshole in Washington decided we couldn't drive seized vehicles anymore if they were worth more than thirty grand."

"Well, hey, sorry I stopped you." The CHP officer handed Jimmy back his creds and the registration.

"No need to apologize for doing your job. I know that this is that time of night when you guys try to target all the deuces heading home from the bars. Besides, I was speeding. I'll slow it down a bit."

"We do get a lot of DUIs this time of night. You'd think people would learn after awhile. Hey, be safe out there," the Chippy said. He turned and walked back to his car.

Jimmy shook his head, smiled, and put the Expedition in drive. *Too bad there aren't more Chippy's as cool as that guy,* he thought.

It was almost 1:30 a.m. when Jimmy parked at the Harbor Island Yacht Club. The dock master's office was dark. Jimmy got out of his vehicle and wandered down to a locked security gate that led out onto the docks. He thought about trying to climb around the gate, but didn't really want to draw attention to himself if there was a security officer watching the area, either from a distance or on some security camera. He waited.

It took about forty-five minutes but finally someone came up the ramp to the gate. Jimmy started walking towards the gate when he figured he was about as far from it as the approaching man. The man opened the gate to exit. Jimmy grabbed the open gate and nodded and smiled, stepping to the side to allow the man to pass him.

"Forgot my key card on my boat," he said to the man. "I'm sure glad someone was leaving this time of the morning or I'd have had to sleep in my car."

The man looked like he was going to say something, then just nodded and walked away.

Jimmy spent the next ten minutes walking the docks, looking for the Molly Madison. He finally found it on D Dock, Space 17. The Molly Madison turned out to be a forty-one-foot motor sail. It was located near the bay side of the marina, just about in the middle of several hundred other vessels. Not an ideal situation should things turn to shit while trying to make an arrest of someone considered armed and dangerous.

The boat looked dark but Jimmy thought nothing of it since it was almost 2:30 a.m.

"Well, nothing I can do until the cavalry arrives," he said softly to himself.

Jimmy returned to the parking lot and the comfort of his vehicle. He repositioned his car in the parking lot in order to keep an eye on the main gate to the marina in the off chance someone would leave. He really couldn't remember what Steven Allen looked like, despite having glanced at the 'Ten Most

Wanted' board in the SAC office numerous times while visiting the office on business. Jimmy just figured that if someone did leave that looked like a possible, he'd identify the vehicle for follow up and then they'd at least have a target to watch for if it returned.

No one ended up coming or going during the next several hours. Sal and Mitch Corrick showed up just before five a.m. and gave Jimmy a copy of the wanted flyer. Steven Allen was forty-five years old, balding, pudgy, not someone who looked armed and dangerous. *More like a banker*, Jimmy thought.

"You guys have any idea how many agents Tom called out on this?" Jimmy asked.

"No. But we're it from our group," Mitch said. "Since our group has duty today most of the group will be down at the port. We're the unassigned floaters, so since we aren't officially on the schedule, you get us."

"Good thing we weren't on the schedule. This way you get the A team," Sal said with a smile.

"Yeah, good thing," Jimmy said. He paused a moment then continued. "I wonder who else is going to show up, and when?"

"I wouldn't expect anyone for a while. Tom is going to have to reach out to some other groups for help with this one."

"On second thought, I think I'd have rather been on the duty schedule than to have to hang out down here watching the seagulls," Sal said.

"Oh, come on," Jimmy said. "The weather is good. There might be some bikini clad honeys down here to gawk at a little later in the day."

"If we get a chance for any of that," Mitch said.

The guys got into Jimmy's Expedition and kicked back, waiting for the arrival of more agents and for the sun to come up.

By 5:45 a.m. the sun was up. By 6:45 a.m., no one else had arrived and Jimmy was beginning to wonder how they were going to deal with Allen if he came off the boat.

"I think I saw someone go into the dock master's office. I'm going to go over and see if I can get some general information about our vessel and schmooze a card key to the docks," Jimmy said.

"Get a key for the head, too," Mitch said. "It's getting about that time for the morning constitutional."

"Thanks for sharing," Jimmy said, smiling and shaking his head as he walked to the office.

Once in the office, Jimmy took out his credentials and identified himself to a young woman who was just finishing up with making a pot of coffee.

"What would I have to do to talk you out of a cup of that coffee?"

"Just wait for it to finish brewing. What can I help you with?"

"Have you folks had any new boats show up in the last few days, or have you had any unusual guests reported to you in the last few days?" Jimmy asked.

"I don't think so. Is there someone in particular that you're looking for? Perhaps I could help."

She walked over to a file drawer, opened it partially and then looked over at him.

"Well, we are looking for someone, but I'd just as soon keep our visit as discreet as possible. I don't want to trouble any of your tenants or guests. But is it possible I could get, say, two of your card keys to the docks. I'm trusting you to be discreet and not say anything to anyone, except, of course, the dock master. You have my word that we'll try and be as discreet as possible ourselves. I will tell you that we have some information that there might be someone we're looking for down on one of your boats."

"Really? Like a criminal or something?"

"Or something," Jimmy said smiling, trying to downplay the matter so as to not worry the woman.

"How bad a guy are you talking about here? I mean, is there anything to worry about?"

"No, no. We're not even sure this person is here. If he is, there's still nothing much to worry about. Might be someone down here selling a little pot, but those folks really aren't worth worrying about. Still, if we find him we'll probably have to arrest him."

"Well, we're really not supposed to let these keys go out to anyone, but I guess you guys don't count," the young woman said, looking at Jimmy and giving him a little smile.

Jimmy thanked the woman and promised he'd return the keys at the end of their stay. Then he wandered back to the Expedition. As he approached the vehicle, Mitch jumped out and waddled up to him.

"Dude, did you get a key?"

"Yeah. Relax. The bathrooms are over there behind the office," he said, pointing.

"Come on, hurry up man," Mitch said, grimacing, "It's crowning!"

Jimmy and Sal broke out laughing as Mitch snatched a card key and waddled off towards the restroom at a brisk pace.

CHAPTER . . .

14

By the end of the day on Monday, agents had made friends with the Dock Master. He turned out to be a retired Coast Guard Captain who'd worked with Tom Phillips in his younger days when Tom was an agent in the marine smuggling group. The Dock Master, Wayne Simmons, had a friend who was a retired naval officer who was doing some consulting work in the Middle East and his boat, the 'Never Free But Easy,' was sitting empty. His boat was also on D dock, seven spaces inboard of the Molly Madison. Anyone leaving the Molly Madison would have to walk right by the Never Free But Easy.

Jimmy had received a list of agents who'd been assigned to the surveillance, and was sitting on the transom of the Never Free But Easy, working out a schedule. He and Tom had agreed that they'd be patient and wait for Allen to leave the boat rather than try an entry. That meant a round-the-clock surveillance schedule. Jimmy hated making surveillance schedules because it meant someone would be pissed off at him for assigning them to a night shift. He wished Tom would make the assignments, but Tom was tied up getting a San Diego Police SWAT Team assigned to assist in the surveillance. Jimmy didn't feel that the SWAT Team was necessary, especially with no entry plans, but he was just the worker bee case agent.

As he sat working on the schedule, his cell phone rang.

"Maxwell."

"Jimmy? This is Carmen."

"Is everything alright?" Jimmy asked with concern.

"Yes, we're fine. I just wanted to talk to you."

Jimmy relaxed, feeling a sense of relief. That was all he needed now. Trying to set up this surveillance, being committed to the new case, and then having to deal with a problem in the Angel Garcia investigation.

"What's on your mind?"

"I know I told you that Angel isn't supposed to show up until the weekend, but what if he comes early?"

"I thought we talked about this? You have my number, so if he comes by, call me when you can. But make sure you're alone when you call. Just act naturally. You don't expect any problems with him, do you?"

"No. But I'm still afraid of how this is all going to work out. I'm also afraid for him, even though we've been separated for a long time. You're sure you're not going to hurt him or anything?"

"No. I don't expect anything bad to happen unless he initiates it."

"I know you'll do your best, and this may seem strange coming from me, so please don't take it the wrong way, but I really do trust you. What's more, I really appreciate your being in my life right now." The comment struck Jimmy as being a little strange. It didn't seem like the thing a beautiful woman would say to him. A woman he'd envisioned as being strong; a woman who'd initially seemed so distant. He pondered the comment for a moment before continuing.

"Jimmy, are you still there?"

"I'm still here . . . Carmen, I have a question for you. Do you still love him?"

"No. But I care what happens to him. I did love him once, and he is the father of Raul."

"I appreciate your concern. Just know that I'll do my best to make sure nothing bad happens to him."

"What if those people who are after him get to him before the weekend and do something terrible to him?"

"Carmen. I think both of you knew what business he was in before this trouble started. Bad things happen to people every day in his business. Tijuana seems to be rapidly turning into the murder capital of the world and it's almost all drug trafficking related."

"I guess I just never thought much about it before."

"Listen to me. Angel has taken care of himself this long. I think he'll be fine for a few more days. And Carmen, I need you to know that there's other cases I'm responsible for, so if you call, I'll do my best to respond right away, but I can't guarantee that I'll be able to break free instantly. That said, I want you to try not to worry. You have my number, and don't forget to call 911 if any other men show up outside. Then you call me. I'll check in at least once a day. Okay?"

"I'm sorry to have bothered you. I am bothering you now, aren't I?"

"No. I'm at work, but it's all right. I actually kind of like hearing from you. Speaking of work, where are you?"

"I went to work, but I'm on my lunch break. It's so hard to concentrate on what I'm doing lately. My boss has noticed something is wrong and has tried talking to me several times."

"Just be careful and don't give him, or her, any specifics about what's going on, okay?"

"No, I won't."

"Okay, I'll try to give you a call this evening."

"That would be nice."

Jimmy ended the call, pausing to think about the conversation. It wasn't what was talked about that was on his mind, but the fact that Carmen seemed so emotionally vulnerable. He knew she was reaching out to him for strength and support—at least he hoped that was what she was reaching out for.

As the day turned into the early evening, the sun sinking into the western Pacific, the breeze turned cool. The smell of the salt air off the ocean reminded Jimmy of his days at sea in the Navy. He sat on the Never Free But Easy and watched the Molly Madison. It bothered him that they'd watched the boat all day and no one had seen any hint of activity, and now that it was getting dark, there was no light visible inside the boat.

Tom Phillips came by about 7:30 to check in with Jimmy.

"Any sign of your guy?" Tom asked.

"No sign of anything. Personally, I don't think anyone is on that boat."

"Hey, if Headquarters says they think someone is there, whether there's anyone there or not, we've got to act like there is. But, you're probably right. You need to let the other agents know that even if they don't think this guy's here, he may show up here. What if he's out somewhere and he comes back to the boat?"

"Yeah, I suppose that's a possibility."

"Who's coming out for the shift tonight?"

"Margie Gray, Ed Winestock and Sal."

"Good. I'm glad the SAC sent those agents from the Fraud Group to support this goat rope. It's not like any of them are working any overtime."

Tom and Jimmy talked a few more minutes. Jimmy thought about filling him in on the conversation with Carmen Beltran, but then changed his mind, deciding against giving Tom something else to worry about. Just before eight p.m. Tom left, advising Jimmy not to stay out all night, and to call him if it looked like they were going to have any activity. A few minutes after he left, Margie and Ed arrived.

Jimmy hadn't worked with either Margie or Ed before but knew them and their reputations from others he'd worked with in the office. Ed was in his early thirties, thin, athletic, bald, and clean-shaven. From what he'd heard, Ed was competent but not overly motivated to work hard unless it was something that really interested him.

Margie was in her late twenties, very good looking, with big green eyes and long brown hair. Jimmy knew she didn't have much experience but had always been a little impressed with her because she was smart and self-confident, good traits to have in a law enforcement profession.

"Well, who wants to sit on the boat with Sal and who wants to sit in the parking lot in their car to watch for our badass fugitive? It doesn't look like anyone is onboard this bucket at the present time, but maybe he's out doing evil things and will be returning later on tonight."

"I'll take the parking lot for a few hours," Ed said.

As Ed was leaving, Jimmy's cell phone rang.

"Maxwell."

"Jimmy, this is Sal. Dude, I'm sorry but I have a family emergency and can't get in for a few hours. I'll probably make it between ten and eleven. My son has a fever and is throwing up. The wife and I are taking him down to urgent care."

"Hey, do what you need to do. Family comes first. I'll just stay here and cover for you until you show up. Call me in a couple of hours though if it looks like you won't make it here so I can call and get someone else to cover the after-midnight portion of your shift."

"No problem, man. Thanks."

Jimmy looked over at Margie, smiled and shook his head.

"Looks like you're stuck with me for a while."

"Good. I've been wanting to get to know you better," Margie stated with a wink.

Jimmy ignored the remark and the two settled into the surveillance. As they sat and made idle conversation, Jimmy couldn't help but notice how attractive Margie was. She looked to be in very good shape, with skin darkened by a lot of time in the sun. Her clothes fit her perfectly, hugging all of her curves in all the right places.

As they sat at the back of the boat, they both looked up at the deep orange disc of the moon. Seagulls flew overhead, diving into the bay to feed.

"Nice moon," Jimmy said.

"A lover's moon," Margie replied with a wink.

Jimmy smiled and said nothing, suddenly realizing how tired he was. He began to yawn and ended up having to stand and move around a little to stay alert.

"You okay?" Margie asked.

"Just tired. I've been up since midnight last night. Guess it's catching up with me."

"Here. Sit down in front of me."

Jimmy sat down facing Margie, wondering what she wanted him to do.

"No. Turn away from me. I'm going to rub your shoulders."

Jimmy hesitated a moment, looking into Margie's eyes. She smiled and stared at him. *What the hell*, he thought as he turned away and slid down onto the deck in front of Margie.

She wrapped her legs around him and began to massage his shoulders and neck.

"Man, you've got talent there," Jimmy said with a groan. "Maybe you should have been a masseuse."

"I used to give my dad shoulder rubs. He loved them too."

"I can see why."

"Are you feeling any better?"

"It feels wonderful. But if you're not careful, I'll fall asleep right here."

"That's fine. I'm watching the boat. Besides, don't you think it would be nice to wake up to me?"

Jimmy started realizing that Margie was hinting at something more than friendship. He didn't need any more complications in his life but he let her continue with the massage without saying anything.

"Come back up here next to me," she said.

Jimmy sat up on the edge of the seat. Margie stood, got behind him and then sat again with her legs wrapped around his torso. She then pulled him back to her, and again began rubbing his shoulders. Jimmy could feel the softness of her breasts against the back of his neck.

"If you keep that up, you're going to get us both in trouble," Jimmy said after a few minutes.

"Promises, promises," she replied.

After several more minutes, her hands moved down around his waist. Jimmy stood up and was going to say something but Margie spoke first.

"It's my turn. Hope you know how to give a good shoulder rub."

Margie stood and Jimmy sat down. Margie then sat between his legs and pushed herself back into him. Jimmy began to massage her shoulders.

"You can rub harder than that. I won't break."

Jimmy increased the pressure. Several minutes into the massage, Margie turned, pushed herself up between his legs, kissing him full on the lips. Jimmy returned the kiss, cupping a breast with one of his hands. When the kiss ended, Margie smiled.

"Wow. That one hand is really good at massaging."

Jimmy paused and swallowed before answering.

"I shouldn't have done that. It's just a habit with me, one I shouldn't have. When I kiss, I go for the breasts. But that shouldn't have happened. I'm married and have a daughter."

"I'm not here to steal you from your wife. But if you want to come by my place sometime for a little recreational fun with no commitment, I think it would be fun. No one has to know."

"Margie, I'm flattered, really. And you look awesome. It's very tempting because I know you'd be great, but honestly, I can't."

"Why?"

"I just don't work like that. I took my marriage vows seriously. I made a commitment to love, honor and be faithful. I don't want to disappoint God, but as much as anything else, I don't want to disappoint myself. Besides, my wife is very jealous and I'm a terrible liar."

"I've heard that your marriage is a little rocky. But again, I'm not trying to take you from your wife."

Jimmy wondered who had been talking about him, especially about his personal life. It was something he really didn't really talk about.

"Well whoever told you that should probably have their ass kicked, he said."

"They weren't bad mouthing you or even gossiping. I asked about you. My source actually told me that I had a slim to none chance with you, but I thought I'd try. Still, you could just come try me once." Margie winked at him with a smile.

"Margie, you have no idea how tempting your offer is, but I can't. Matter of fact, I can't even stand up now if you know what I mean," he said with a little laugh. "But please don't ask again. I'd like to be friends with you, but it can't go any further."

"Well Jimmy Maxwell, you're a better man than most."

"I don't know about that. Believe me, it's hard not to take you up on your offer. Hey, if I call you back in a week and tell you I want to come over, you have to tell me no. Okay?"

Margie laughed. "Maybe. I'd have to think about it." She rose and then sat down next to him, the two not saying anything for a few minutes while they looked at the moon.

"Sorry to tempt you and come across like some wanton slut," Margie finally said. "It's just that I've always thought you were a good-looking guy that I'd like to get to know better. I figured it wouldn't hurt to give it a try." Margie turned to him and gave him a little kiss, grabbing his hands and holding them to his side. "Just making sure you kept check on those hands," she said with a smile as she stepped away from him.

The conversation quickly returned to work-related issues with Jimmy yawning every few minutes as they talked.

"You want to catch a little catnap while you wait for Sal to arrive? Margie asked.

"If I went to sleep now, I'd be here all night. Plus, I snore. I think I'd better just tough it out," Jimmy answered.

Sal showed up about midnight. Once Sal came aboard the boat, Jimmy grabbed his binoculars and portable radio and prepared to leave.

"So is your son all right?" Jimmy asked.

"He'll be fine. Hey, how long we gonna give this goat rope before we call it off? There's no one on board that piece of shit we're watching."

"First of all, that piece of shit is a quarter million-dollar yacht. Secondly, even though no one seems to be aboard our target vessel, he could drive into the parking lot and walk down to it at any time. So get with Ed Winestock up in the parking lot and relieve him so he can come down here and take a little break. And don't fall asleep up there."

During the drive home, Jimmy's thoughts bounced around like a pinball. This really was a strange surveillance. He needed to call this headquarters fugitive coordinator and get some more information about this alleged fugitive. It sure didn't seem like there was anyone on the yacht, or that there ever was.

Then there was Carmen. Jimmy had a strange attraction to her that was more than just physical. He felt a bond of some sort. He felt like she was someone he'd known for years, not five or six weeks. He really didn't want to be involved in this fugitive case right now. If only the office wasn't so incredibly busy. He wanted time to focus on the Angel Garcia case. That seemed like the priority to him, but again, there was only so much the office could do with new issues to deal with daily, not to mention the duty calls that came flooding in from the ports of entry.

He was tired, but his thoughts kept him awake as he drove home. What the hell was he thinking? He's supposed to be on surveillance and next thing he knows he's kissing a co-worker, grabbing her breast, thinking about taking her right there on the deck of the boat. That's all he needed with everything else in his life as chaotic as it was. Having a fling with her could be disastrous . . . but boy did she have a great set of . . . *Jimmy, you've got to quit thinking with your little head,* he told himself.

The next two days were uneventful, and Jimmy was beginning to get irate. He really needed to be focused on the Angel Garcia case. The weekend was coming up and he really hadn't had a chance to go to the office and do an operations plan for the arrest of Garcia when he visited Carmen's house.

"Tom? Hey, it's Jimmy. Got a minute to talk?"

Jimmy was in his usual position, on the fantail of the Never Free But Easy and had decided to call Tom and talk about this seemingly never-ending, nothing surveillance.

"What's up?" Tom asked.

"Look, I don't mind being out here if there's a good reason to be, but it seems as though this headquarters source information is pretty thin, and believe me, I'm trying to be nice. I'm going to push in a call to that fugitive coordinator and see if he'll hook me up with the source. I mean, this is crazy, tying us all up on a big nothing."

"Sure. Give him a call and see what he says. I'm having my doubts about this as well."

"Okay. I'll let you know how it goes."

Jimmy called Sector Communications and asked to be connected to the fugitive coordinator. He held for about a minute and was then connected.

"Hello, this is Peter."

"Mr. Wong, Jimmy Maxwell. We need to talk."

"Did you arrest Allen?"

"No."

"So what's on your mind?"

"I need some more information about your source. We've been out here all week, round the clock, and we haven't seen one hint of activity on this vessel. So, can you tell me who your source is on this information?"

"I really don't like giving up source information, especially the identity of a source to someone who really doesn't need to know," Agent Wong replied.

"Well, I do need to know. So here's the deal. You have until tomorrow to let me talk to your source or we're pulling the plug on this mess and getting back to some real work. I'd suggest getting hold of your source, and see how they feel about talking to me. Maybe they can convince me that there's some real reason to be out here. You know, we've been tying up a San Diego Police SWAT team for most of the last three days, as well as about fifteen or sixteen agents."

"You know, we can order you to stay out there as long as we feel it's needed."

"The SAC can. So if you think you've got a good argument, give him a call and then, if he orders me to stay, I'll stay. Otherwise, this is over. Look, I'm not trying to be a prick, but honestly, there's absolutely no hint of this guy being here. Not to mention that we've all got better things to do."

"I can tell you this, our source works for the probation department up in southern Oregon. He's provided information that has led to three prior fugitive arrests. I don't know what's going on out there in San Diego, but his information has been good in the past."

"Good for him . . . or her. I still want to talk to him," Jimmy said bluntly. Without waiting for a reply, he hung up the phone and walked back down to the boat.

The following morning, Jimmy called Agent Wong again.

"Agent Wong, Jimmy Maxwell. No change to report here. What's the deal with your source?"

Agent Wong sighed in seeming resignation. Apparently things hadn't worked out too well when he'd talked to his bosses about calling the San Diego SAC. "I'll have him call your cell phone within the hour."

"Thanks. I appreciate it," Jimmy said.

About twenty minutes later, Jimmy's cell phone rang.

"Maxwell."

"Agent Maxwell, this is Carl Howard. I've been directed to touch bases with you by Agent Wong."

"Are you the source on this Steve Allen fugitive information?" Jimmy asked.

"Well, sort of. I have a sub-source who's given me fairly reliable information in the past, and the sub-source told me about Allen. I called Agent Wong and passed on the information I received."

"Okay. Tell me about your sub-source."

"Like what?"

"Where did he get the information?"

"I'm really not sure. But I know his information is usually pretty reliable."

"Well let me tell you why I ask," Jimmy said rather sarcastically. "I've had two full groups, plus a San Diego Police SWAT team sitting out here at the San Diego Yacht Club for the last four days, watching a boat that no one's on, with no sign that anyone is coming. If we're going to continue to this operation, I'm going to need to debrief your source. What's the source's background? Does he run around with Allen? Does he talk to the guy on the telephone? Give me something, because unless I get something really, really solid, we're packing it in."

"How about if the source and I fly into Lindburgh Field tomorrow so you can talk to him? Will you keep your surveillance up and running until you get a chance to meet with him?"

"If you fly in tomorrow morning to see me, I promise I'll keep the surveillance up and running until you get here."

"Okay, okay. I think there's a Southwest flight in from Eugene that arrives at 10:05 a.m. We'll be on it."

"I'll be there to pick you up."

Jimmy hung up and gave Tom a call, bringing him up to speed on the plans.

"Good," Tom said. "Something needs to happen here soon. We have duty again tomorrow and I've got to figure out how we're going to pull it off with this nonsense going on."

"Hey, take Mitch, Sal and Shirley. I can cut back at least one agent per shift, and fill in for the third, even though I've been kind of floating between both shifts."

"Okay. I guess I'll have to reach out to one of the other groups if things get crazy."

"Get the proactive group to fill in. They don't seem to be doing much these days anyway."

"Don't tell them that," Tom said with a chuckle. "They sure try to sell upper management with the notion that they're busy."

"Look at their numbers. They haven't done shit for months," Jimmy snapped back with an edge to his voice.

Tom could tell he was beginning to get a little spun up.

"Jimmy, you're preaching to the choir. Chill. It's a good idea. I'll reach out to them if things get busy."

Jimmy got to the airport at 9:45 a.m. He was normally five to ten minutes late to almost everything he did that wasn't crucially important, but with another night of nothing happening on the yacht, Jimmy had just about had it. He was exhausted. What had given him a little boost of energy was the fact that he would finally get a chance to talk to this source. Maybe this probation officer just wasn't a good interviewer and he'd somehow missed something in the information he'd been provided.

Maybe Steve Allen was going to be on the boat next week, or had been on the boat the week prior to their arrival. Maybe there was another boat with a similar name that was located in a nearby marina. Jimmy's mind raced through the questions he was going to ask, and hoped this source personally knew Allen. Maybe he could get a tip on an associate in the area, or find a hangout he frequented when he was in the area. In any event, something had to have been missed.

The two men came walking out of the terminal gate, spotted Jimmy from the clothing description he'd given. They walked over to him. Carl Howard offered his hand, and Jimmy shook it. Howard looked nervous.

"Agent Maxwell, this is Sergio Pinal." Jimmy offered his hand to Pinal.

"Can we go somewhere close by to talk for a few minutes?"

"Sure, let's just go climb in my car and head to our office. It's only about a ten-minute ride."

"Agent Maxwell," Howard said in a whisper, moving in close to Jimmy. Jimmy backed away a step as Howard moved into a space where his mouth was almost against his ear.

"What's going on?" Jimmy asked.

"I just need a minute or two to talk to you alone."

"Well, walk with me over towards those payphones."

"Sergio, hold tight here a minute," Howard told him as he and Jimmy walked away. Pinal nodded, looking at Jimmy with big brown eyes that reminded Jimmy of a deer staring at him as he centered the crosshairs from his riflescope at its torso.

When they had moved about fifty feet, Howard slowed the pace a little. He turned and smiled at Sergio, giving him a little wave. Jimmy turned to look in time to notice the wave back. Pinal now looked somewhat fragile, and a little innocent. Jimmy looked at Howard, noticing the look he was giving Pinal. he looked almost like a parent sending their kid to school for the first time, waving goodbye to them just before the bus left. As they took a few more steps, Jimmy suddenly realized there was something more to their relationship than met the eye—maybe something personal. Jimmy didn't want to jump to any conclusions and waited for Howard to speak.

"Agent Maxwell, what I've got to preface this debrief with is to ask you to be open minded, and not jump to any conclusions without giving Sergio the benefit of the doubt."

"Mr. Howard, we've been giving your source the benefit of the doubt all week, based on your say-so and because our fugitive coordinator in headquarters says you've provided reliable information in the past. Let me ask you this: Was Mr. Pinal a sub-source for you on your previous information provided to us?"

"Well, no. I met Sergio, Mr. Pinal, about six months ago and he's helped me with some of my cases."

"Well, we need to go somewhere where I can find out a little more about his relationship with our target, Allen. Maybe then we can refocus our search because, quite truthfully, Allen isn't on a yacht in the San Diego Yacht Club, and I don't think he ever has been," Jimmy said with mild frustration showing through.

Jimmy turned and started to walk back towards Pinal.

"Agent Maxwell," Howard said loud enough to get Jimmy's attention.

Jimmy turned back towards Howard.

"I said we needed to talk and we still do."

"Yeah, so talk. Let's go get . . ."

"Agent Maxwell, Sergio doesn't know Allen. He's never met the man."

Jimmy walked back up to Howard, staring into his eyes, refusing to blink.

"I'm listening." He paused a moment and raised his eyebrows. "So does he have a sub-source that knows Allen?"

"I told you it was important to keep an open mind, and I'm asking you again for the same consideration."

"What the hell is going on? Spit it out."

"Sergio is a psychic."

Jimmy paused a second before answering. "You're kidding, right?"

"Law enforcement uses psychics fairly regularly now, you know, to find lost kids, to . . ."

"You've got to be kidding me!?" Jimmy said. "Tell me you're joking."

Howard just stared at Jimmy, his mouth hanging about half-open. A few seconds later, he moved in closer to Jimmy to explain further.

"Dude, back off!" Jimmy said, stepping away. "Tell me there's something more to this goat rope than your boy having a vision of Allen being in San Diego on a boat."

"Sergio is a true psychic; he can see things. He can tell where people are by using the spirit world. He's never met Allen, or ever been to San Diego before in his life, except in the spirit world."

"Are you friggin kidding me? You've been wasting our time on a stupid psychic? I should call your supervisor in Eugene, or wherever you allegedly work and report this total waste of law enforcement resources. As far as I'm concerned, what you've had us doing is criminal. We've been out in force for a week based on your cockamamie—no—your bullshit information. Man, you're supposed to be a professional law enforcement officer! Do you do any real law enforcement work in your job, or is it all this kind of stupid shit!"

"Agent Maxwell, give this a chance. Listen to Sergio."

"Why? Tell me why I should listen to him. For that matter, why should I listen to you? As far as I'm concerned, you lied to us, and have misappropriated government resources for whatever your screwed up reasons were. And I'm being nice about this. So go get your boyfriend, hop back on an airplane, and hope you never see me again."

Jimmy turned and walked away. He was as angry as he could ever remember being. As he walked away, he turned and looked back over his shoulder. Howard had his arm around Sergio's shoulder. It almost looked like Howard was trying to comfort Sergio. *Unbelievable*, Jimmy thought to himself. *Unbelievable and really weird.*

The anger faded quickly, turning into stunned disbelief that bordered on humor. Jimmy walked and pulled his cell phone off his belt clip. As he dialed Tom Phillip's number, he almost started laughing—almost.

"Tom, hey it's Jimmy. You won't believe what I found out about our case." He paused a moment. "This bozo I just met, he's a psychic."

"Okay. So Allen runs around with nuts. Does Mr. Psychic know Allen, did they used to do dope deals together, or what?" Tom replied.

"Boss, listen to me. The psychic doesn't know shit from shinola. He's a psychic who had a vision that Allen was here. He's never met Allen; he's never been to San Diego; he doesn't know anyone that knows Allen. He says he's seen him through some sort of vision."

There was a moment of stunned silence on the phone.

"Tom, I'm calling the guys and putting this thing down immediately. Can you call that idiot in headquarters and tell him to never call us again, at least with information from either of those two freaks that I just left?"

"You're not kidding? A psychic? A fucking psychic! I sure hope the San Diego Police don't find out we were out here based on a psychic. They'll never want to work with us again," Tom said, as much to himself as to Jimmy.

"Call me if you need help with duty. I'm going home and getting some sleep. When I wake up maybe I can do some real law enforcement work this week," Jimmy said. "I'm sending everyone else home. I can't believe it."

Jimmy disconnected his call with Tom and started dialing Mitch to have him put down the surveillance.

Driving home, Jimmy suddenly remembered that his group was going to have to roll back out the next morning on the Angel Garcia case. Jimmy groaned inwardly as he thought about having to call in his group on a Saturday. Then he realized that he hadn't called Carmen for the past few days after telling her earlier in the week that he was going to check in daily.

Well, hope she's the forgiving type, he thought as he as he dialed the number to her cell phone. *And hopefully there haven't been any changes in Angel's plans or her decision to work with us.*

"This is Carmen," she stated as they connected.

Jimmy's heart seemed to melt a little when he heard her voice.

"Hi Carmen, it's Jimmy. I'm calling to tell you I'm sorry about not calling the past few days. It's been crazy here."

"I'm glad you called. I've been wondering about you."

"I should have called like I said I would. I hope you'll forgive me."

"I understand. You're busy."

"Yeah, but that's no excuse. Anyway, I need to know if you've heard from Angel. Is he still coming over tomorrow?"

"I haven't heard anything for a week, but that's really not that unusual. If he said he was going to be here this weekend, he'll be here. He'd only call if something came up where he had to cancel."

Or if he was dead, or being held kidnapped, Jimmy thought to himself.

"Okay. Well we'll be out and ready to go early. Are you all right? Any last minute nerves, regrets, anything like that you need to talk about?" Jimmy asked.

"I always get nervous when he comes by. You know, it's been almost eight years since we lived together as husband and wife and yet, well, he comes by and sort of moves into my house for a weekend. It's a little uncomfortable. But, no, I'm not too nervous about having you folks come and pick him up. I will be glad when this is over though."

"So will I."

"Jimmy?"

Wow, she actually addressed me as Jimmy, he thought.

"I really appreciate what you're trying to do for me and Raul," Carmen said.

"It's really no big thing. I'm doing my job. Law enforcement officers are supposed to provide a service to the public," Jimmy said with a little laugh, trying to lighten the conversation.

"I know you've been busy, but I've missed hearing from you this week," Carmen said softly.

"I really am sorry I didn't call every day like I said I would. We've been working this round-the-clock surveillance and it's been a little distracting."

"I understand."

"Well, hopefully we'll get to see each other a bit tomorrow. If we pick up Angel I'll give you a call later in the day and see if we can't schedule a time when I can come by so we can talk a little more."

"I'll be looking forward to that," Carmen said.

There was a moment of silence on the line.

"I'd better let you go so I can call the troops and remind them of our operation tomorrow morning."

"Okay. I'll see you in the morning,"

"Don't hesitate to call, at any time of the day or night, if there are any changes or issues you need to discuss," Jimmy said.

"I don't want to disturb you, or your wife," Carmen said, seemingly trying to get a response of some sort.

"Just call if you need me."

The call ended and Jimmy drove for a while in silence.

Keep focused on work. It's just work, he kept telling himself. But he knew it was becoming a little more than work. Maybe his wife was right, he thought. He needed to cut back a little on his hours and spend more time at home with his wife and daughter. But Jimmy actually almost cringed when he thought about having to spend more time at home. He loved his wife, but the pressure he felt around her and her constant unhappiness was actually worse than the pressures he felt at work.

Still, he had a lot going for him. He was married, he had a beautiful daughter, and he had a nice home. On top of all that, this whole Angel Garcia case was just work. She's a sweet, beautiful lady, but it's just work. Yet he found himself thinking repeatedly that if the two of them had met before Shirley and before Angel . . . they'd be together and they'd be happy.

Jimmy realized he'd better place calls to the agents in his group to remind them of the Saturday-morning operation. He started down the speed dial list in his phone.

"Hey, Barbara, I'm calling to ask you not to forget that we have to be out early on Ravenwood. Hopefully we'll get to hook up Angel Garcia."

"Oh no! Jimmy, I got four cases today. I'm still at the port. It's crazy down here today. Is there any chance it won't go tomorrow?"

"A chance, but I think it's going to go. I'd call another group, but I know I won't have any luck getting anyone on a Saturday without the RAC interceding. And you know that's pretty damned unlikely."

"Oh, all right. I probably won't be home until midnight, but I'll be there. But you owe me. Hey, you get your guy on the boat or you turning it over to another agent?"

"We didn't get our guy and we're not likely to. The case is over. I'll tell you about it later, after a twelve-pack."

"That bad, huh?"

"Yeah. You need any help right now with cleaning up any of those duty cases?"

"You could come down and transport some of these folks to jail if you're willing. We're starting to run out of holding cells."

"I'm on my way."

Jimmy decided to have Sector Communications make the rest of the calls to his group. He really didn't need to hear any more complaints.

CHAPTER . . .

15

Jimmy woke with a start. He slapped the alarm clock in his effort to quiet it before it woke his wife nearly knocking over the lamp on his nightstand. It was five a.m. and still dark outside. Jimmy had a headache and a dry mouth. He stretched and then pulled back the shade to look outside. A thick fog hung in the air, reducing the visibility to mid-street, despite the streetlights being on. Jimmy climbed out of bed and stumbled off to the bathroom for a quick shower.

This really sucks, he thought. *Saturday morning and I should be sleeping in, especially after all the hours I put in on that cluster last week.*

He still couldn't believe that someone at the headquarters level would have hooked him up with what they termed, 'a credible and reliable source' that was a psychic. What was that idiot thinking?

The shower felt good. It was hard not to want to stay in it for another five or ten minutes, but if the whole crew was going to meet him at the staging location, he'd better not be late or he'd never hear the end of it.

Thirty minutes later, Jimmy pulled into the Von's shopping center where five of the eight agents in his group that were coming were waiting for him. Most of the fog had burned off but there was still a bit of a chill in the air.

"Dude," Mitch said, "You better have brought donuts."

"Bagels. They're in a box on the back seat."

Mitch grabbed the box and sat it on the hood of Jimmy's Expedition.

"Is Tom coming?" Shirley asked.

"Are you kidding? It's Saturday. I'm supposed to give him a call though and let him know what's going on every couple of hours."

"Every couple of hours? If he wants to know what's going on he needs to have his ass out here with the rest of us," Shirley said.

"Well, when you make supervisor we'll see if you come out on these gigs," Jimmy replied with a smile and a wink. Shirley returned the smile without further comment.

"All I know is it better not take a couple of hours," Sal stated, taking a bite of bagel and cream cheese. "I've got shit to do today."

"Yeah, yeah," Jimmy said. "Who we missing?"

"Deron, Greg and Barbara," Shirley replied. "Deron called a couple minutes ago and said he'd be here shortly."

Ten minutes later, with everyone assembled in a semi-circle, Jimmy began the briefing.

"Look, everyone. I want this to be low key. Angel is supposed to show up sometime this morning, hopefully very soon if he isn't already there. He's there to spend a few hours with his kid. His wife—I'm sorry, ex-wife—Carmen, is going to give me a call after he arrives. Sal and Mitch, you guys take the backyard. Deron, Shirley and I are going to knock on the front door and wait for an answer."

"And if no one answers?" Bill Anderson asked.

"Someone will answer. If it's Angel I'll just take him by the wrist and drag his ass out onto the front porch. We'll cuff him up and we're gone. If it's Carmen, we'll step inside and call him out. He may be armed so we're going to use caution. I want everyone suited up. Deron, that means in your vest. I know you don't like wearing the thing, but you will." Deron smiled and nodded. "That said, I don't believe he's going to get crazy around his own kid," Jimmy told the group.

"And the rest of us?" Barbara Burke asked.

"Stand by near the front door in case things do go to shit. I really don't think they will, but do what you have to do to go home safe and sound. But please remember, Carmen set this up. She may have married this idiot, but today she's one of the good guys. Okay?" Jimmy looked around at everyone. No one said anything.

"And there's a kid in the house that we don't want to hurt or traumatize, okay? Also bear this in mind. If Angel does head for a back room or grab the kid, or anything like that, we're not going in the house after him. We'll fall back to our vehicles on the street, call the P.D. and request a SWAT team. In other words, we'll wait him out. I've got the phone number to the house, and despite anything bad that might happen, Sal, we'll wait. Got it?" Sal was a good agent but had a reputation of being a bit of a hothead at times. Sal just looked at Jimmy and shook his head in resignation.

"By way of reminder, have a flashlight, no fingers on triggers, and if you have to use your weapon, be mindful of your background."

"Are we tossing the place after we have our boy in custody?" Mitch asked.

"No. For those of you who don't know, Carmen has let us search the house before. She's been very cooperative throughout this investigation. I have every reason to believe that if Angel has anything worth anything at her place, she'll let us know."

"Right. Like if he's got a stack of cash, she'll let us know and give it up to us," Jesus Sanchez said sarcastically.

"Yeah, Jesus, she will," Jimmy snapped back, staring at Jesus for a few seconds.

"What makes you think that he'll even show up?" Shirley asked. "The cartel has been watching his house on and off for a while now."

"Yeah, I know. So those of you on the street, keep your eyes open for counter." Jimmy paused a moment before continuing. "Look, I've got a daughter that I would dearly miss not seeing regularly. I think this guy is smarter than we're giving him credit for. He probably has someone in the cartel that has some loyalty to him, you know, who feeds him information about when and where they're looking for him. He comes in at night and leaves in a similar fashion." Jimmy paused a moment then continued. "Look, if I had all the answers . . ."

"You'd still be a street agent out here on a Saturday morning with the rest of us," Mitch cut in.

Everyone laughed.

"Yeah, you're probably right. There's really no appeal to being the guy who signs off on the discipline packages for the office, right?"

"I don't know, I can think of a few people I'd like to spank," Shirley said.

"I'm your man, for the spanking, that is," Sal shot back.

"You wish," Shirley said, turning and walking to her car.

The agents finished suiting up in their raid gear and then headed over to the Ravenwood address. Sal and Greg sped ahead of the others in order to take a good look around the neighborhood for any unwanted or suspicious activities. Jimmy called the NIN and advised them of the impending contact at the residence. Nothing out of the ordinary was reported and the agents quietly pulled over and parked several blocks away.

About ten minutes later, Jimmy's cell phone rang.

"Maxwell," he answered.

"Jimmy, he's here. I can't talk but he got here several hours ago. I'm sorry, I fell back asleep."

"It's okay. I'm glad you quit calling me Agent Maxwell. Anyway, we're close by. We'll be over shortly. Remember, act surprised but just cooperate with our requests. Okay?"

"Okay."

Carmen hung up before Jimmy could say anything else.

"Surveillance from Alpha 353. The target is home. Let's roll on over and get him. Any change at the residence?" Jimmy put out on the radio.

"Negative."

The agents quickly drove over to the Ravenwood address, parking about one hundred yards north of the residence. They exited their cars quietly, careful not to slam doors or do any unnecessary talking. Weapons were drawn as the agents began to assemble quickly.

Jimmy took the lead, walking about a quarter of the way to the residence, then turning and waiting for everyone to stack up on him. When the last agent arrived, Jimmy began a slow walk to the residence. It was getting lighter, but there was still a little concealment in the semi-darkness. Jimmy thought it a little unusual that there wasn't anyone up and about despite the fact that it was Saturday. Not even a dog was barking.

As the perimeter agents began to disperse to their assigned locations around the residence, Jimmy walked up to the door and knocked.

"I'm not hearing anything from inside," Deron said.

Jimmy knocked again, a little louder and longer. It was 6:45 a.m. according to his watch. *She's really playing the part well,* he thought to himself, *but I wonder why Raul isn't up yet?*

On the third knock, Jimmy heard steps coming down the stairs. A moment later, Carmen opened the door, then stepped back. She tightened the belt around her robe as Jimmy, Shirley and Deron stepped in.

"Is he still here?" Jimmy asked.

"He's in the bathroom."

"Where?"

"Top of the stairs, left, then second door on the left."

"Does he know what's going on? And does he have a weapon, a gun?"

"I don't think so. He may have a gun in his room."

"Where's Raul?" Jimmy asked quietly.

"He's asleep in his room."

"All right. Shirley, as soon as we get Angel in custody, I'll let you know and you bring Carmen upstairs to get Raul. No excess talking, and don't use Carmen's first name when you speak with her. I want Angel to think we just met her."

Jimmy headed up the stairs with Deron right behind him. Shirley stayed with Carmen.

The door to the bathroom was closed, but the bathroom light could be seen at the base of the door. Jimmy waited patiently for a minute until the door opened. He grabbed Angel as he stepped out into the hall wearing a pair of white briefs.

"Federal agents. Angel Garcia, I assume?" Jimmy said as he put Angel in a wristlock, forcing him to the floor. Jimmy holstered his handgun and drew a set of handcuffs, as Deron covered him from a few steps back.

Angel initially didn't say a word, and offered no real resistance. He seemed to be shocked that someone was actually placing him in handcuffs.

Once handcuffed, Jimmy stood him up.

"You speak English?" Jimmy asked.

"Some. I understand you, but I don't speak so good," he said with an accent.

"Where's your room. We need to get you some clothes."

"Right there," Angel said, nodding and looking towards a door across the hall.

"Do you have any weapons in there?" Deron asked.

"A handgun. It's only for self-defense."

"I knew he'd be an asshole," Deron stated.

The agents walked Angel into the room, but Deron stood by him just inside the doorway.

"Where's the gun?"

"Top shelf of the closet. What am I being arrested for?"

"There's a warrant for your arrest. We can talk more about that in a little bit," Jimmy said as he grabbed a Heckler and Koch P7 off the closet shelf and stuck it in his waistband. Jimmy spent a few moments looking around the closet.

"Do you have a search warrant?" Angel asked.

"Don't need one. This is part of what we call a protective sweep. I'm making sure there's nothing else in this immediate area that would pose a threat to me or my fellow agents."

Just as Jimmy finished talking he noticed some bills sticking out of the pocket of a jacket in front of him. He reached into the pocket and pulled out a small bundle of cash.

"This yours?"

Angel said nothing.

"I asked you a question, Mr. Garcia. I know you don't live here. You visit your son on a semi-regular basis, but this isn't your home. So, let me ask you again, is this yours?

Jimmy stared into Angel's eyes. Both men refused to blink or give in to the other in this minor test of will.

"Well, if it isn't yours I guess the lady of the house will have some explaining to do. Maybe she's involved in drug trafficking too."

"Look man, it's mine," Angel said. "I always keep a little cash on hand when I'm away from home."

"So how little cash is this?" Jimmy asked.

"It's not so much. Maybe nine or ten thousand."

"A little something in case of emergency," Deron said sarcastically.

Jimmy pulled a pair of pants off a hanger along with a matching shirt and set them on the bed next to Angel. Then he returned to the closet to finish a cursory search and to get a pair of shoes for Angel. Once finished, he walked a few steps out of the room and motioned to Shirley that it was all right to bring Carmen upstairs.

"If we take off the cuffs long enough for you to put on your clothes are you going to give us any problems?" Jimmy asked.

"What can I do?"

"You could give us a problem. That's not to say I won't shoot you, or kick the shit out of you if you try, but it's still early and I really don't need the exercise this early. I haven't stretched yet."

Jimmy smiled at Angel, waiting for his response.

"I'm not going to try anything."

"Good. Deron, please take Mr. Garcia's cuffs off."

Deron gave Jimmy a questioning look for a second, then pulled out his cuff key and removed the handcuffs.

"Get dressed, Mr. Garcia."

Angel began dressing.

"You're a brave man, coming here when everyone you use to know and trust and most of law enforcement is looking for you," Jimmy said.

"Not so brave. I just wanted to see my boy."

"I figured as much. You know, we've been watching this place on and off ever since you ran out of that house we hit over off Main Street nine or ten weeks ago."

Angel didn't respond to the comment.

"You know, the house where we got all that marijuana and cocaine and cash," Jimmy said after a brief pause.

Angel continued to dress but didn't respond to the probe.

"Man, I'll bet someone was sure pissed off after that loss," Jimmy continued.

Angel tucked his shirttail into his pants, then sat down on the edge of his bed to put on his shoes.

"So what is it that you're arresting me for?" Angel finally asked.

"Oh, there're plenty of charges. I'm sure we'll have the opportunity to talk about them, probably a few times over the next few months. Do you want me to arrange solitary accommodations for you at MCC?" Jimmy asked.

"What's MCC?"

"You know, federal jail. It's the Metropolitan Correctional Center. Come on Angel, you've been there before. Anyway, I'm just asking because I'm sure there are other cartel members being lodged there that may get orders concerning your safety and well-being. The question, of course, is what orders concerning your safety and well-being might they get?"

Angel stood up and turned around, backing up to Deron with his hands together, turned palms outward in the standard handcuffing position.

"You know, I think he's done this before," Deron said.

"He has," Jimmy said.

Shirley stuck her head in the bedroom door.

"The rest of the house is clear. The boy wants to see his father. What do you think?"

"Hang on just a minute," Jimmy said.

Jimmy got on the radio to the outside perimeter team.

"Any activity outside at all?"

"All clear out here Jimmy," Sal replied.

"You guys keep a sharp eye out. We have our suspect in custody. Let me know about anything suspicious. I want to get this guy transported to a secure location as soon as possible. I'm guessing we'll be out in about ten minutes."

Jimmy looked at Angel.

"You expecting anyone, anyone at all this morning?"

"No, it's Saturday and we all like our weekends off," Angel said with a smile.

"Wow, just like us," Deron said. Jimmy shot a scowl at his partner. Deron shrugged and Jimmy shook his head in disbelief at the comment. There was no sense telling the crooks when law enforcement worked and didn't, even if they had already figured it out.

"You're taking this pretty well considering the fact that you're looking at spending most of the rest of your life in prison," Jimmy said.

"Yeah, and have you noticed that his English seems to keep improving," Deron remarked.

"What can I do? Can I see my son for a few minutes?"

"I might consider that if you're going to be cooperative. Don't upset him, okay?" Jimmy said.

"Don't presume that just because I'm in handcuffs that you have the right to tell me about how to act around my son."

"I'm doing just that!" Jimmy snapped. "If you want to see him you will not upset him or I will not let you see him. *Comprende?*

Angel lifted an eyebrow and stared hard at Jimmy, the look more a desire to read Jimmy's mind than a challenge of wills. Jimmy stared back realizing that somehow he might be betraying some hidden feelings he had for Carmen and Raul. Angel studied Jimmy's face for another few seconds, then a slight smile began to appear as the realization struck him that Jimmy probably had some sort of relationship with his ex-wife and son. A relationship that likely had led to his betrayal and arrest.

Jimmy looked away before his expression could give away anymore secrets.

"You can bring the boy over for a minute," he said to Shirley.

Thirty seconds later, Raul walked into the room in a pair of pajamas. He was wiping a tear from his eye.

"Hey there *mijo*, what's wrong?" Angel asked his son.

"Poppi," the boy said, throwing his arms around his father's neck.

"It's okay *mijo*. Everything will be fine."

Angel looked over at Jimmy again, trying to read the look on his face.

"You'd better take good care of them while I'm gone," he said to Jimmy.

Deron and Shirley looked at each other, and then both looked at Jimmy, a little surprised at the remark and its implication. If they hadn't known any better they might have reason to believe Jimmy and Angel had known each other for some time.

"I'm sure they'll be fine, especially since you won't be here to draw trouble to them," Jimmy stated matter-of-factly.

"Are we still going to play some baseball later?" Raul asked his father.

"No, *mijo*. Not today. These people need me to spend some time with them. I know you don't understand this now, but I will explain it all to you some day."

"I'd like to hear that one," Deron said with a smirk.

Jimmy gave Deron another sharp look and shook his head no. The smile faded from Deron's face as he looked away from Jimmy.

Raul gave his father a long hug, not wanting to let go. Jimmy waited patiently for several minutes, noticing tears running down Raul's cheeks. The boy made no sound, just clung to his father. Angel sat still, seemingly emotionless, yet Jimmy knew better.

"Time to go," Jimmy finally said. "We need to get you out of here before someone shows up that neither of us needs to deal with today."

The agents walked Angel downstairs. Shirley held the evidence bags containing the money and the gun, and Jimmy and Deron each grabbed one of Angel's arms. Jimmy took his free hand and pulled his portable radio out of his back pocket.

"Agents coming out," he said over the air.

"Let's take him down to the Port of Entry to interview him," he said to Deron as they walked outside.

CHAPTER . . .

16

"Honey, can you go in a little late today? I have an appointment to get my hair done. I shouldn't be more than two hours."

"Why does it take two hours to get your haircut if you have an appointment, and why did you schedule a haircutting appointment during the week?" Jimmy asked.

"I scheduled it for last Saturday, but someone decided they had to work on Saturday, so I had to change it."

"Can't you just take Nikki with you?"

"No, I can't. I'll try to hurry, but I have to stop at Nordstrom's on my way home and get some makeup."

"I've really got a lot to do today, babe," Jimmy said in exasperation. He'd already realized he'd have to spend the morning at home in order to keep peace in the family but his frustration spilled out in his comments.

"Well have someone else do it," Shirley replied. "God, Jimmy! You do everything in that group. Make someone else do something for a change."

"I do not do everything in the group. Everyone is busy. I know I have this crazy case going right now, but it all works out in the long run. Everyone is busy. Plus I'm getting a lot of help and support from the group and I feel kinda guilty asking them to help me as much as they do, especially if I'm not there with them."

Shirley looked at Jimmy with a mixture of anger, frustration and disbelief. The stare continued for a few seconds, then she picked up her purse and headed for the front door.

"Please try to get back as soon as you can," Jimmy pleaded.

"I'll be back when I get back," Shirley said, slamming the door on her way out.

"Great!"

Jimmy called Tom and asked for four hours leave, explaining his situation. "Ahh, marital bliss," "Tom remarked sarcastically.

"You don't have these situations come up at your house?" Jimmy asked.

"Yeah, sometimes. I don't think my wife is quite as fiery as yours. Still, someday you'll be promoted to a group supervisor, and you'll find out the same as I, that you're only the boss at work."

Jimmy laughed and advised he'd be available on the phone if some question came up. Following the phone call he went to check on Nikki. She was playing quietly in her room so Jimmy headed to his computer thinking he'd work on a report. Just as the computer powered up, his cell phone rang.

"Maxwell."

"Jimmy, this is Carmen Beltran. I'm sorry to bother you."

"It's no bother, Carmen. What's going on?"

"I wanted to thank you so much for how you and your team handled yourselves when you were here on Saturday. I mean, I know you could have come into my house with force, yelling and pointing guns at us all. I know Raul would have been really scared. It was really nice that you cared about us enough to handle the situation with Angel the way you did."

"Don't mention it. And really, you shouldn't call my partners 'my team.' I'm just an investigator that gets help when he needs it from some very competent co-workers. When they have investigations, I help them."

"Well, thank them for me for their professionalism."

"I will."

"Do you suppose you'd have time to come by later. I found an address book that belonged to Angel in the closet he was using. I thought you might want it."

"Sure, what time is good for you?"

"I'll be home about six."

"Okay, see you a little after six."

Jimmy hung up the telephone, but thought about the call for a minute before starting on his report. There was something incredibly attractive about Carmen that transcended physical beauty, although she was incredibly good looking as well. Still, beautiful women aren't that rare, yet Carmen was more than that. She oozed sensuality, charm, intelligence, and something else that Jimmy found incredibly attractive to him personally. Need. Carmen seemed to have everything except a man, and she really seemed to be in need of someone during this time of change in her life.

I'm definitely taking another agent with me tonight, he thought to himself before changing his focus back to his report.

Several hours later, Shirley returned home. She'd cut her hair and had some highlights added. Jimmy noticed the difference in her appearance, but didn't immediately say anything as he focused on getting ready to leave for work.

"Do you like my haircut?" Shirley asked.

"Yeah, hon, it looks really nice. I like the highlights too."

He paused for a second, stepping in front of her and grabbing her face lightly with his hands. He looked into her eyes and kissed her tenderly on the lips.

"I'm sorry I gave you a hard time this morning about going. I know that you need time to get away sometimes and do things for yourself."

Shirley looked at him for a moment, a hint of a smile on her face that slowly faded to a slight frown.

"Why do I have to prompt you to say nice things to me?"

Jimmy looked at her in stunned silence. Her response was unexpected and antagonistic.

"Honey, I apologized . . ."

"Yeah, but I had to prompt you to say something about my haircut. You could have told me you like it before I brought it up."

"I'm sorry. I'm trying to get ready for work and I was a little distracted, but I did notice. You could have given me another minute or so to say something."

"I should be the foremost thing of importance to you. I understand work is necessary, but it shouldn't be as important as me or your family."

"Do we have to do this now? Why can't you just rest assured that I love you? Why is everything a competition between you and my work?"

"I guess because I feel like I just can't compete with your precious work. It's all you talk about. It's certainly more important than your family."

"Look. You're very wrong."

"Am I?"

"Yes. But I'm not getting into this with you right now. I'm already late for work and I need to go. We'll talk later, when I get home."

"See, my point exactly. Work is more important than me."

Jimmy was starting to get angry. He really hadn't expected his wife's return to lead almost immediately to a fight. He was also angry because he knew she had a point; not a good point, but one that he couldn't easily make an argument against.

"I'm sorry you feel the way you do, but you need to get over it and move on. I have a job that just happens to be one I enjoy. It's not my family, it's a job, but I'm not going to feel bad that I don't hate it and can't wait to get home every day. I'm also not going to have some long, drawn-out dramatic discussion with you because you feel neglected, or whatever. You let your feelings control you instead of common sense."

Jimmy immediately regretted the words he had just spoken to his wife, not because they weren't true, but because he knew they were inflammatory. There was nothing he could do about it now so he turned away and headed towards the door.

"Fuck you! Fuck you, Jimmy! You fucking hypocrite! Feelings are what people have to guide them. Feelings are what people have to let them know they're loved, and that they're in love."

Jimmy turned abruptly and walked back to his wife. He stood facing her, trying to show as little emotion as he could.

"Well there's something else we disagree about. Feelings are feelings. I will concede with you that they are important, but they're not the tell-all that someone loves you or that you're in love. Take a look at I Corinthians Chapter 13. That's what love is really all about. Love is patient, love is kind, love doesn't insist on its own way. It says love isn't jealous or irritable or resentful. It bears all things, believes all things and hopes all things. That's what love is."

"Well, well. A lesson from the guy that sits around all night and drinks until he falls asleep on the couch. The guy who swears and stares at half the pretty women he sees in public walking down the street, undressing them in his mind."

"You have no idea what I think, Shirley. You see, that's the problem with you. You think you know what goes on inside me, and you have no idea."

"I know you. I do know you, and like I said, you're a fucking hypocrite."

Jimmy knew things would only get uglier if he stayed to debate Shirley while she was angry. He turned and walked out of the house.

"God," he prayed as he drove away. "I need you to do something here. I'm trying to make this work. I want this to work. Please don't let me lose my family and give me guidance to know how to deal with that woman."

His prayers were cut short as his cell phone rang.

"Maxwell."

"Hey, Jimmy. It's Greg. I'm down here at the port meeting with one of my sources. He says his brother can show us a house with six hundred pounds of weed. How about coming with us while my guy shows us where it's at."

"Sure, I'll be there in ten minutes."

Jimmy pulled into the west side of the secondary inspection area at the San Ysidro Port of Entry and parked after spending a minute looking for an open space. As he went to step out of the Expedition, Greg and a Hispanic male in his early thirties opened his back door and got in.

"I guess we're going in my ride," Jimmy said as he got back into his vehicle.

"Dude, let's get out of here. Luis is going to show us a house in Spring Valley where this dope is located."

"Nice to meet you Luis," Jimmy said, turning and shaking Luis' hand over the top of his bucket seat.

Jimmy drove up to the north booth. The inspector recognized him and waived him north without an I.D. check.

"So Luis, how do you know there is six hundred pounds of marijuana in this house we're going to?" Jimmy asked.

"Cause I dropped it off there last night," he responded matter-of-factly.

"Nice," Jimmy said half under his breath as he shook his head in semi-amazement.

"Look Jimmy, Luis is pretty new to working with law enforcement. I've talked to him a little about how we do things, problems we have with prosecuting some of these cases, but maybe you could talk to him a little about what to do on future cases like this," Greg asked. Greg had been on the job a few years, but he'd never really worked with confidential sources before, at least from what Jimmy could remember. As a matter of fact, Jimmy wondered how Greg had recruited this source.

"So how long have you been working with Greg?" Jimmy asked.

"He arrested me six months ago. I got out of jail last month and the guys I'd been smuggling for got hold of me last week and told me that I owed them for losing their dope. I tried to tell them I didn't want to work anymore, but they kept pressuring me. I really don't want to go back to jail, so I thought I'd give Agent Thompson a call and do what I had to do for these guys to get them off my back."

Jimmy continued driving up the freeway, but he really wanted to pull over so the three of them could talk.

"You know that if you work with us, you can't just drive loads of drugs across the border without our advanced permission, right?"

"Jimmy, I told him, but I guess he felt like he had no choice," Greg said in a somewhat remorseful and guilty tone of voice. Jimmy figured Greg was afraid he was going to bring his lack of control or clear direction of his source up to management.

"Luis. We used to be able to work with confidential sources and let them drive loads of drugs across the border. I mean, we really didn't encourage it because we have no way to protect you down south if something goes wrong, either with the traffickers or the cops. But after Clinton took office, that all changed. He had the state department institute rule changes that now force us to get advanced permission from our country ambassador and the DEA and the Customs Attaché in Mexico City. The theory is that if you work with us, you become an agent of the government. Agents of our government are not authorized to break the laws of a sovereign government, namely Mexico. What our government really wants us to do is work with Mexican law enforcement on these types of cases."

Jimmy turned momentarily to look at Luis. His eyes were open wide in disbelief and he looked like he was going to say something.

"Relax. Look, you and I both know that there's no one in the Mexican government, and no Mexican cops in Tijuana, or probably elsewhere in Mexico, that you can trust. Even if I trusted them enough that they wouldn't have you killed, we'd see the same dope they seized while working with us smuggled across the border a few days later by their people."

"*Si*. I won't work with those guys," Luis said, now a little afraid.

"No one is asking you to. Still, we have to do things our way. If you'd been caught yesterday, you'd be on your way to prison. So here's the deal for anything we do in the future. If someone recruits you to bring dope across the border, you tell them you'll think about it and get back to them. Then you give Greg a call and we'll meet and figure out how we can help them without breaking the rules."

"Greg, have you explained to him the different scenarios we use on these cases?"

"No. I hadn't really had time. Luis only called me yesterday and I set up this meeting for today not knowing he was going to be doing what he did."

"Water under the bridge, man, don't worry about it. Why don't you explain the rules?"

Jimmy got off the freeway and headed east on Sweetwater Road.

"Okay, Luis, here's the deal. If we do one of these things in the future, you need to suggest to these guys that you really can't afford to get arrested so you won't drive in Mexico. Why don't you tell them that you know an inspector that might be willing to take money to let a vehicle containing drugs come through his lane without inspection."

Jimmy interrupted and said, "Yeah, tell them you have a cousin or sister that used to date an inspector. Tell them that you know the guy is in need of cash and that you overheard him saying he might be willing to let some illegal aliens come through the border for money. Tell them that you're willing to approach him and see if he's still interested in making a little money."

"That might work, but how much money do you think the inspector would be asking for?" Luis asked.

"Tell them that for twenty thousand dollars for each vehicle, they can put in the vehicle whatever they want, and as much as they want," Jimmy said. "But tell them you want half the money up front."

Then Greg jumped into the conversation.

"Or another thing you can do is to tell them you don't want to be arrested in Mexico. Tell them you've seen how bad the jails are down there and that it's not worth the risk for a few hundred bucks to spend months or years in a Mexican jail. Tell them . . ."

"Greg, let's not go there quite yet," Jimmy said. Greg nodded in acknowledgement.

"So, where to from here?" Jimmy asked as he drove past the animal shelter and stopped at the light at the South Bay Parkway.

"Go straight across the parkway and turn right at the second street."

Jimmy followed the directions and turned down a short cul-de-sac lined with smaller, older houses that were likely built in the 1950s and 1960s. A few homes were still well kept, but most had yards that were brown from lack of water, badly in need of mowing and overgrown with weeds. The target house located at the end of the street looked quiet, with no cars parked in the driveway or even on the street in front of the residence.

"That's the house you dropped off the dope at?" Jimmy asked.

"Yeah, Jefe. That's it."

"What time was it when you left?" Greg asked.

"Like 5:30, 5:45 this morning."

"Who lives there?"

"Shit man, I don't know. There's a lady that I think is hooked up with my friend Nacho. Nacho stays there some of the time, but I don't know if he really lives there. There was some other guy they called Gordo."

"A big boy?" Jimmy asked.

"A whale!" Luis said with a sneer. "And he's mean."

"I'm surprised they didn't call him Tiny if he was that big," Jimmy remarked.

"See any guns or anything like that?" Greg asked.

"No. But I know that Nacho carries a piece some of the time. Sleeps with it, I've heard."

"Okay. Greg, you got the numbers and a description? Jimmy asked.

"Yeah, got it."

Jimmy flipped a quick u-turn and headed back south.

"So, Luis, you need to go back to the port or what?" Jimmy asked.

"You got a car today?" Greg asked.

"Can you guys drop me off at 18th and Highland? I came down on the trolley, but I have a friend I want to go see in National City."

"What's her name?" Greg asked with a smile.

"Martha," Luis said with a smile. "Hey, how much money do you think I'll get from this information I gave you guys?"

"Like maybe six . . ."

Jimmy cut Greg off and said, "Luis, until we get in there and see what's there, it's going to be hard to say. We base our source payments on the amount of drugs we seize, the number of people we arrest, and all that stuff. We might get in there and find a bedroom closet full of cash, in which case you're going to be very well off. On the other hand, if they already sold or moved the dope and there's nothing there, you probably won't get anything. If the owner of the dope is the owner of the house and there's dope there, you might get a chunk of what the house is worth when it gets forfeited to the government. So, long story short, you're going to have to wait and see."

Jimmy drove Luis to National City and dropped him off, then he and Greg drove back to the port of entry.

"Sorry to have cut you off on that payment question, but believe me, you don't want to quote any prices to snitches. They'll try to hold you to it, and things don't always work out the way we think. Then you're the asshole who lied to them and isn't reliable. On top of that, if you get them excited over a large number or at least a large number to them, they'll bug you about it every day wondering where it's at."

"I never thought about that. See, now you know why I had you come meet that guy with me."

Jimmy smiled. Greg was a nice guy who would turn into a good agent with a little more experience. Jimmy sometimes worried a little about him that he was too nice a guy. If you were too nice, people would take advantage of you, something you had to be careful of when you were out running around with drug traffickers.

"So, did that guy tell you he was going to be bringing dope across the border?" he asked.

"He said he'd been asked to bring dope across the border for someone who works for Jose Leon."

"Yeah, everyone works for the cartel. I have to laugh when I think of at all the forty- or fifty-pound weed cases I've done where the crook tells me he works for Alberto Ruiz or Jose Leon."

"I guess I've heard it more than a few times myself. But who knows, someone's working for and with those guys," Greg said. "Anyway, Luis and I were supposed to get together this morning to talk about it, but he wasn't answering his phone. I didn't hear from him until around noon. I had no idea he was going to bring a load across the border before we met."

"He probably didn't answer because he was running around with crooks. The more you work with these guys the more you'll hear that one. And as frustrating an excuse as that is, it's probably true and will just be something you have to deal with."

"Actually he said he didn't have any minutes on his phone. Hadn't had time or money to go buy more minutes."

"And that's one of the other good excuses these idiots have when you're trying to reach them. When you finally track them down they always have some excuse."

"How did you get all the sources you have, Jimmy?"

"Geez man, I don't know. I pitch most of the guys I arrest to come back and see me after they get out of jail. You know most of them smuggle dope as a way to make easy money. If they find out they can still run around with shitheads and make money, well, some of them figure it's better than taking the chance of going to jail. Some of them are referred by other agencies or by the inspectors because of the relationships I've developed with folks over the years. Then there's my wife's theory."

"What's that?"

"I'm a piece of shit and a source is like a fly. They're just little annoyances that gravitate towards what feeds them."

Greg busted up laughing.

It was nearing three p.m. when they got back down to the port.

"So what are we doing?" Greg asked.

"Dude, it's your case. You decide. But I can tell you this. You need to do something today. If there's dope there now, there's a good chance there won't be tomorrow. It'll probably be sold or moved to L.A. in the near future."

"Are you free?"

"I've got a million things to do, but if you need me, I guess the least I can do is try and help you with this. We're going to need a few more people though."

"You think I have enough to get a warrant?"

"Not with just the say-so of an untested source. You need to call the Narcotics Information Network guys and find out if anyone is investigating that address. If they are, the NIN folks can hook you up with whoever has the investigation going. If not, well we don't really have time to work up a real investigation. Not in a few hours. I think what I'd do is set up a loose surveillance, hope we see another car show up, go in the garage and then leave. We'll have a black and white pull it over on a traffic ruse, toss the car or run a canine unit on it and hope we find some dope. Then we can roll back on the place with a warrant."

"Sounds like a plan. Let me call a couple of the guys. Can you call Tom and let him know what we're doing?"

"Yeah, I guess. Hope he doesn't want an ops plan. See you back over there shortly," Jimmy said as Greg got out of the Expedition and walked off towards his car.

Jimmy drove back to the Spring Valley residence, placing the call to Tom Phillips on the way to advise him they were going to conduct surveillance on a possible stash location. Then Jimmy called Carmen Beltran. All he got was her voicemail, but he left a message stating he didn't think he was going to be able to make their six o'clock appointment.

Setting up at the entrance to the cul-de-sac, Jimmy parked with the nose of his vehicle showing. He had a good view of the front of the house from about 150 yards. He was in position to see cars arriving and leaving the garage, and even a person leaving the front of the residence, but he knew he'd have trouble seeing any significant detail of someone leaving the house on foot if they walked to a car parked on the street.

As he sat and watched the residence, Jimmy smiled as he started thinking about all the cop movies he'd seen in his life. Watching cops do surveillances in the movies was so absurd as to be ridiculous. The movies liked to portray surveillance as something the cops did from several car lengths away. Like no one was going to notice you. You watched a house from across the street. Then there were the idiot directors who had their actor cops chamber a round into their weapon before using it. Maybe they thought it looked cool. Jimmy wondered how many times a bad guy could shoot you while you were chambering a round in your pistol. A man with a knife could cover twenty-one feet and stab you before you had time to take your weapon from its holster.

Greg arrived about twenty minutes later, parking at the opposite end of the cul-de-sac.

"Let's use TAC 2, coded, for comms," Jimmy said on the Customs common channel.

"So who's coming out?" Jimmy asked over the radio after the switch to the car-to-car channel.

"Jesus, Barbara and Deron. Shirley a little later maybe."

"Good. Glad you thought about asking a Spanish speaker," Jimmy said.

"Well, to be honest with you, I didn't. Those three were the only agents in the group available. Shirley is in court, and Sal and Mitch are doing a dope reweigh for some defense attorney."

The mid-afternoon sun beat down on the vehicles, making it impossible to sit and watch the house without the car running and the air conditioning on. Chatter on the radio was kept to a minimum so that when something started happening, whoever noticed it would be able to let the others know immediately.

At about five p.m. Greg keyed his mike and asked, "So how long do you want to give this?"

Jimmy knew the question was for him. He was the senior agent in the group. Still, it bugged him a little that after several years on the job some of his partners didn't want to make a decision on their own.

"You tell me, it's your case."

"Anyone out here have any significant plans for the evening that I'm interrupting?" Greg asked.

Based on the fight with his wife at around noon, Jimmy knew he really shouldn't work late, whether it was justified or not. His wife would view it as a planned attempt to avoid her.

"Well, I'm not hearing any response so let's give it until seven p.m.," Greg put out on the air.

The next two hours seemed to drag on. Traffic on the cul-de-sac had picked up some as people got home from work. Kids were out playing in the street, riding bicycles and skateboarding. Several had gone by Jimmy's car, staring in at him as he sat watching the target location. At about 6:30 p.m. a kid, probably eleven or twelve years old, stopped next to Jimmy's door and stared at him for a moment.

"Hey, mister. Who you watching?" the kid asked.

"Just waiting for my girlfriend to get home from work," Jimmy responded with a smile.

"Oh? Where's she live?" the kid asked.

"Your parents ever tell you that you really shouldn't be talking to strangers? You never know what kind of person you might meet on the street. What if I'm a bad guy?" Jimmy asked.

The kid pedaled away as fast as he could without saying another word.

Great, Jimmy thought. *Now I'm going to have some pissed off parent come out, or they'll call the cops on me.*

"You did run NIN, right?" Jimmy asked Greg over the air.

"Yeah, nothing came back."

"Well, we can't just leave here with six hundred pounds of weed in the house. I was really hoping to see some activity, but it just ain't happening. Let's go do a knock and talk and see if we can get consent to come in," Jimmy said. "I just had contact with a little kid who's probably going to have his parents call the cops on me or something."

"You're such a charmer, Jimmy," Barbara said.

Jimmy put his car in drive and started slowly drifting down the street towards their target location.

"Greg and I will go up to the door. Jesus, you follow us up, but peel off to the side of the house with the gate to the backyard. Watch for any activity out the back when we knock on the door. Barbara and Deron, park in front of the house, but stay in your car until we motion for you to come up. I don't want to be overly intimidating during the initial contact."

Once everyone was in position, Jimmy, Greg and Jesus got out of their cars and headed towards the front door.

"You do the talking," Greg said to Jimmy as they got to the door. Jimmy reached down into his shirt and pulled out his badge, letting it hang from the chain he kept it on around his neck. Greg looked over and followed Jimmy's lead, taking his badge out as well.

"Someday you're going to have to try this yourself, you know," Jimmy said in a hushed voice as he knocked on the door.

A Hispanic woman in her mid-thirties answered the door. She stared at the two men without saying anything. It was a look Jimmy had seen before, a look of, 'Oh shit! What am I going to do now?' Jimmy tried to look past her into the house in order to determine whether or not anyone else was at home.

"Federal agents, ma'am. Can we come in and talk to you for a minute?" Jimmy asked.

"What's this about, officer?" she asked after a moment's hesitation.

"Oh, I'm glad you speak English. We'd just like to talk to you for a minute about . . ."

"Lady, we're looking for a fugitive," Greg said, cutting into Jimmy's canned speech that he used, usually very successfully, to get people to consent to letting him come in and take a look around. "We've been tracking a man for several hours who is wanted on a variety of charges. We lost him in this neighborhood." Greg paused for a second, looking into the woman's eyes. "He could be dangerous. He's probably hiding in someone's backyard or he may even be hiding in someone's house."

Jimmy looked over at his partner in disbelief, wondering what was going to be the next piece of absurdity that came out of his mouth. *So much for a consent search*, he thought.

To his surprise, the woman opened the door wider, stepped back and motioned for the agents to come in.

Just keep your mouth shut, Jimmy thought to himself as he stared at Greg momentarily.

"Is anyone else at home?" Jimmy asked, motioning to Barbara and Deron.

"My brother and two of his friends," the woman replied.

"Can you ask them to come out here?" Jimmy asked.

The woman started towards the back of the house, Jimmy following closely. When the woman noticed Jimmy following, she stopped.

"We all want to go home to our families tonight," Jimmy said. "You don't have any weapons in the house, do you?"

"No." The woman turned again and started to yell out, but caught herself as three men in their mid to late twenties emerged from the garage. The door closed quickly behind them. The three looked at Jimmy, paused a moment, then walked towards him. Jimmy looked behind him, seeing Barbara and Deron coming into the living room. He felt a little better after feeling a bit outnumbered momentarily.

The woman spoke to the three men in Spanish for about thirty seconds. Jimmy tried to cut in but the woman continued with one of the men responding to her dialogue.

"I'd appreciate it if you folks kept your conversations to English while we're here," Jimmy said.

"It's okay," Jesus said from the doorway. "The woman told these guys that she allowed us to have a quick look around to make sure a dangerous fugitive wasn't hiding on the property. The brother told her she shouldn't have done that."

"Why wouldn't you want us to try and find a dangerous criminal, sir?" Jimmy asked, walking up to the man. He got no response.

"May I see some identification please?" Jimmy asked.

"He's my brother," the woman said to Jimmy.

"Can I see some identification from you, ma'am? I want to see if your last name matches his. This man could have asked you to lie for him."

The woman started rattling away in Spanish again, directing her verbal assault against her brother.

"Whoa, settle down! What's going on?" Jimmy asked in a loud voice, cutting into the conversation.

"She's upset that her brother has said things that are causing you to find out she's an illegal. She's afraid you're going to have her removed to Mexico," Jesus said.

"Lady. Lady! Look at me. I'm not the *migra*. I'm not here to deport you. Look, we'd like to take a quick look through the house, see if our guy is here, then we'll be on our way. Okay?" Jimmy asked.

"Okay," she responded.

"But I'd still like to see some identification. I need to know I'm not talking with our fugitive, or someone wanted for murder or something. Jesus, Barbara, check under the sofa cushions. Let's make sure there's nothing more dangerous there than some lost coins, and then get some I.D from these folks. They can take a seat while Greg and I do a quick walk through the place.

The four subjects were escorted over to the living room sofa, and after a quick check under the cushions, they were allowed to sit down. Jimmy watched until they were seated, then nodded at Greg as the two turned and headed into the back of the house.

Entering the master bedroom, Greg opened a closet door, looked around, and then went over to a dresser drawer, opening it. Jimmy walked over and pushed the drawer closed.

"Greg, your boy told us he dropped off six hundred pounds of marijuana. It isn't going to be in this dresser drawer. Let's find the dope if it's here. I don't like having only three agents out there with four potential bad guys, and I don't want any allegations of impropriety on our part if there's no dope here."

"Yeah, you're right. Sorry man."

They made a quick sweep through the three bedrooms and two bathrooms, finding nothing. Walking out of the last room at the end of the hall, Jimmy caught the faint odor of marijuana. He stopped and sniffed the air. It was coming from the area around the door leading into the garage. He walked to the door and opened it.

"Cha-ching!" he said, looking into the garage.

"Sweet!" Greg said as he came in behind Jimmy.

There were stacks of marijuana bricks laying everywhere, and about a dozen large, black, plastic lawn trash bags filled with what looked like lumpy packages. Jimmy walked over to one, opened the top and saw that it was filled with marijuana bricks.

"Definitely more than six hundred pounds," he said.

The two men walked quickly back to the living room. Once there, Jimmy walked over to the subject he believed to be the brother of the woman who'd let them in.

"Sir, stand up."

The man stood up and suddenly made a move around Jimmy, attempting to run around him towards the front door. Jimmy tried to reach out and grab him, causing the man to lunge further away from him. This movement caused the man to run directly into a coffee table, the low profile of which the man had failed to notice. The man fell across the table, breaking it into several pieces, landing with a crash and loud gasp as the wind was knocked out of him.

Jimmy reacted quickly to the man who was laying face down on pieces of broken coffee table. Standing over him, he took hold of the stunned man's arm and moved it behind his back, at the same time extracting a set of handcuffs from his rear pocket. He had the man handcuffed in a matter of seconds. He nodded at his partners who each, in turn, removed handcuffs, but just stood and watched the subjects on the sofa. Jimmy moved over to the sofa and took each subject one by one, stood them up and handcuffed them with cuffs provided by his partners. When the last was cuffed, Jimmy began doing a pat down on each of the men for weapons.

As the last person was being patted down, Greg spoke. "You'd think that with all the money people make selling drugs they'd buy decent furniture rather than this cheap K-Mart crap."

Jimmy suppressed a smile and moved over in front of the woman who'd let them into the house. "Looks like we have some weed in the garage." The woman said nothing.

Jimmy turned and walked towards the front door.

"I'm going to get my cell phone and call Tom for some help. Looks like we're going to be here awhile," he said.

Greg followed him out the door and walked with him to his Expedition. Jimmy was shaking his head in feigned disbelief, knowing that Greg was following him.

"What? What is it, man?"

"We're looking for a dangerous fugitive," he mocked in Greg's voice. "Dude, when I told you that you were going to have to start doing the talking someday, I didn't think you were going to start by pulling some bullshit like that out of your ass. On the other hand, maybe I should have you start doing the talking on every knock and talk," Jimmy said laughing.

CHAPTER . . .

17

Several days passed uneventfully, with Jimmy helping Greg complete his follow-up investigation related to the four arrests made at the Spring Valley stash house. Greg worked on the arrest reports while Jimmy ran down the owner of the residence and got a copy of the rental agreement. Greg was hoping that one of the defendants owned the house so they could seize it.

Jimmy offered to do the lab report. Agents had seized 1,465 pounds of marijuana at the residence. Not a bad score considering they had expected to find six hundred pounds. Finishing the DEA lab request report, Jimmy walked into Tom's office for a signature.

"Got the lab report done, Jefe. How about a quick signature?"

"I've got to get a signature stamp or something," Tom complained. "I can't believe how many times a day I have to sign something. Don't you know how to sign my name yet?" he asked, looking up and giving Jimmy a grin.

Jimmy plopped down in a chair opposite Tom's desk and waited while Tom gave the form a quick once over before signing. Once signed, he reached across his desk and handed back the form.

"Hey, good job, in case I didn't mention it. I'd like to scold you a little, but can't bring myself to it, what with the outcome and all," Tom said.

Jimmy looked at his supervisor questioningly.

"You know," Tom paused. "You told me you were going to be out on surveillance on a stash location, try and see someone leaving the place, do a traffic stop and work back with a warrant. What you did was conduct a consent search without giving me a call. If something would have gone to shit out there, we'd all be in trouble, especially me, since I didn't have an ops plan from you and didn't know what you were doing." Tom paused a moment to let it sink in.

"Sorry," Jimmy said. "You're right. I should have given you a call. Guess I've been getting used to making decisions out in the field lately and just took it upon myself to decide on the knock and talk. I should have called first."

"Well consider this your scolding. You're the senior agent in the group and I do let you run the group most of the time in the field, but I don't want the others learning bad habits. Give me a call next time."

Tom paused again, then smiled and winked at Jimmy. Jimmy got up and turned to leave but almost ran into Arlene Romero, the resident agent in charge of the office.

"Excuse me, ma'am," Jimmy said as he tried to sidestep his way around her.

"Maxwell, come back in and close the door," she said in a flat, matter-of-fact voice.

Jimmy turned and closed the door.

"Sit down," she ordered.

Jimmy sat back in the chair he'd left moments earlier and looked up at Arlene as she hovered over him.

"I want to talk to you about your consent search on Monday," she said stiffly.

Jimmy said nothing but waited for her to continue.

"What the hell did you think you were doing out there?" she asked sternly.

"My job, ma'am," Jimmy said.

"Don't get smart with me. I asked a question."

Jimmy again waited for her response a bit confused about where the exchange was going.

"You are a federal agent. You're not a cop anymore. Yeah, I know your reputation. You run loose and wild, but it's just a matter of time until you get someone hurt with your bullshit," she continued.

"Jimmy . . ." Tom started to say.

"Mr. Phillips, let me continue," the RAC snapped at him.

"I do not want my agents conducting these types of investigations."

"What kind of investigations do you want?" Jimmy asked. "We're a narcotics task force, not the Mickey Mouse Club."

"Do not be sarcastic with me." She paused for a moment, then lowered the tone of her voice, regained some of her composure and continued. "As I started to say, you're a federal agent. We conduct real investigations. If you think that you've identified a stash house what you should be doing is getting a subpoena for the utilities of the residence and finding out who lives there. You subpoena the telephone number and subscriber to the residence. You can do a mail cover and see who is receiving mail and you can subpoena their bank records. In other words, I want you to work up a complete profile on the residents, then plan some surveillance of your targets and eventually develop the probable cause you need to get a search warrant into the place."

"No disrespect intended, ma'am, but where did you work before you got to San Diego?" Jimmy asked.

The RAC looked like she was starting to get angry again. "Chicago. But investigations are investigations. They're done the same everywhere."

"Ms. Romero, let me explain something to you. If I was working five or six investigations a year, especially some white-collar crime like fraud, I might be inclined to try working an investigation the way you're suggesting, although in this instance I still would have done the knock and talk. I work sixty or seventy cases a year on average, as do most of the other agents here. I don't have the time to try working up what you'd call a real investigation. I get information about drug traffickers coming into me several times a week. I have to let half of what I get just slip between the cracks and disappear because I don't have the time to work it. San Diego is what we call out here a 'target rich environment.'"

The RAC stared angrily at Jimmy but let him continue.

"We got the information on the Spring Valley house on Monday around lunchtime. We tried surveillance for most of the afternoon but got nowhere with it. We could have gone home at the end of the day and started an investigation the following morning, but what would have happened is that the dope we knew was in the house would have likely gone up the road. In the time it takes to work up a real investigation, literally thousands of pounds of dope will likely hit the streets and at the end of what you are calling a real investigation, who knows where we'd be. The crooks may have moved by then. The source may not be available anymore. Some other agency could have moved in, arrested our target or done something that caused those folks to shut down operations for a bit until things cooled down. In the meantime, we're out there wasting man-hours and ignoring all of the other traffickers we could have arrested while we're examining someone's bank records. And by the way, most of these guys deal in cash, and when they get a little ahead, they drive it south and put it into a Mexican bank account."

"I want you to start doing more real investigations. Do you understand me?" the RAC said.

"Yes, ma'am!" Jimmy replied.

Ms. Romero turned and exited the office. Jimmy turned and looked at Tom in frustration.

"Well, that was fun," he said sarcastically.

"Close the door," Tom said to Jimmy. Jimmy closed the door and sat down.

"Look, I think she's over her head here and is running a little afraid of downtown management. If something does go wrong out there, she's the one on the hot seat. She wants to be an SAC someday."

"Tom, you and I both know she got promoted into her position because she checks two boxes."

"Maxwell, I would expect a comment like that from a few agents I know, but not you."

Jimmy paused a moment trying to cool down. "Look Tom, I'm not even slightly prejudice, you know that. But you were right when you said she's in over her head here. She might even be a good supervisor over a fraud or money-laundering group.

But she doesn't know what she's doing here trying to supervise drug groups. Some idiot in headquarters put her here for the wrong reasons. Now I don't want to create any problems for you, I really don't, but I will not work investigations like she wants. You've got to educate her on what we do here. Please."

"I'll try. But let me tell you something. I'm going to need an ops plan, in advance, when you go out on deals like you had Monday, and if something goes to shit, it better be the crook's fault."

"Sometimes there isn't time to come back here and put together an ops plan," Jimmy said.

"I'm telling you that while I'm on your side, I will not be responsible for anything that goes to shit out in the field if I do not know, in advance, what it is you're doing. Enough said?"

"Yeah, I got it," Jimmy said. "Sure was nice to get that 'atta boy from the boss on that good case," Jimmy said sarcastically as he turned and left the office.

"'Atta boy!" Tom yelled at Jimmy as he walked away.

Jimmy turned back towards the office as he walked away and momentarily thought about flashing Tom an obscene gesture with a middle finger. He rarely if ever did that sort of thing so he refrained and instead smiled and shook his head, then turned away again, frowning as he headed to his desk.

Boy, some people sure knew how to motivate the troops to go out and make good cases, he thought, still angry at his undeserved scolding. *Now I know why some people don't want to go do anything.*

Sitting down at his desk, he noticed his message light on. He dialed and heard Carmen's voice.

"Jimmy. I tried your cell phone and got your voice mail. Thought I'd try this number. I really need to see you. Something's come up and I'm scared again. Please call me on my cell phone."

What now? Jimmy thought as he started dialing. She answered almost immediately.

"Hey. Got your message. What's going on?"

"I walked out my front door this morning to go to work and there was a man waiting in my driveway. It startled me and I almost went back in the house. As I stood there staring at him for a moment, he walked up to me. I didn't know what to do so I just stood there."

"So what did he want?"

"He said his name was Jose Leon."

"Jose Leon-Gamboa?" Jimmy asked incredulously.

"I don't know? Who is that?"

"Describe him for me?" Jimmy asked.

"Mexican, about forty years old, dark complexion, looks like he had a broken nose that didn't heal right."

"Carmen, what did he want?"

"Who is he?"

"He's the guy your husband used to work for."

"That's what I was afraid of," Carmen said, trying not to sound upset.

"He didn't hurt you or anything, did he?"

"Jimmy, what am I going to do?"

"Take a few deep breaths and try to relax. He obviously didn't hurt you or anything or you wouldn't be calling me. So take a minute and collect yourself and tell me what he wanted."

"He'd been drinking. I could smell the alcohol on his breath." She paused for a moment then continued. "He was looking for Angel. He asked if he'd been here recently. I told him he was here a few weeks ago and that the police had come to the house and arrested him. I told him I didn't know where he was now." She paused again as Jimmy tried to digest the information.

"He stood there staring at me with those black eyes of his. I felt like he was looking right through me. Jimmy, I was really afraid."

"Do you want me to come meet you somewhere?"

"There's more. He asked if I'd seen Vera?"

"Vera? Who's Vera? Vera who?" Jimmy asked.

"He said it was his wife."

"Do you know any Vera's? Jimmy asked.

"No."

"So, then what?"

"I told him I didn't know anyone named Vera. Then he turned around and left. I don't understand what this is all about," Carmen remarked.

"I don't either," Jimmy said. "Did you happen to get a license number of the car he left in?

"No. I didn't even think about it. Jimmy, I was scared. I'm still scared. What if he comes back?"

"It's okay. What kind of car was it?"

"It was black. It was a Ford I think. I don't know for sure. It only had two doors and was kind of new."

"Did he say anything to indicate he'd be back, or that he didn't believe you or anything?

"All I can tell you is he didn't seem satisfied with not getting the answer he was looking for."

"Maybe he was just pissed off because he found out Angel was in jail," Jimmy suggested.

"He didn't seem that surprised about it. I think the only reason he was looking for Angel was to ask him where Vera was. He didn't ask me anything about the circumstances of Angel's arrest, or anything about his business."

"Are you going to be okay or do you want me to come see you?" Jimmy asked.

"I think I'll be fine. I sure wish I could have reached you this morning on your cell phone though. I wasn't sure I was going to be able to make it to work."

"I'm so sorry, Carmen. I don't know what happened." Jimmy took the cell phone off his belt and looked down at it. It didn't show a missed call, but there was a message in his queue. When he looked at his recent calls list it did show the call from Carmen.

"I do have a message from you. It must have come in while I was in a dead zone. I guess with my phone being unusually quiet this morning I didn't even think to check it for messages. I'm really sorry."

"It's all right."

"Well, since you're at work, why don't I just come by on my way home this evening and check on you. What time do you think you'll be getting home?"

"About six."

"Can I stop by?"

"That would be nice. Are you sure I'm not causing you too much trouble?"

"Carmen, I don't want you to ever think that. It's my job to look into these kinds of things anyway. Especially where Jose Leon is concerned."

The call ended with Jimmy sitting at his desk, wondering what else was going to happen in the Angel Garcia saga. Most of the original defendants in the case were still in MCC waiting to be indicted or work out a plea deal. From what he'd been told by the U.S. Attorney's office, it didn't look like anyone was going to trial except Angel. That in itself was somewhat surprising based on the amount of dope seized and the fact that every one of the defendants was looking at at least ten years in the bucket.

Obviously Angel would likely want to go to trial as he was looking at a thirty to life sentence based on his indictment. Of course, there was always hope that he might want to deal and come in and talk about Jose Leon or Alberto Ruiz. Not likely, but a possibility. A plea bargain might even be worked out to get him down in the ten-year range if he was lucky.

Jimmy wondered if he could get a message to Angel to ask him why Jose Leon was over asking Carmen questions. Something was going on but Jimmy wasn't sure what it was.

The day passed quickly. Still, Jimmy was glad to shut down his computer, escape from his cubicle and hit the road.

He checked the area as he approached Carmen's house but saw nothing unusual. He parked under a tree in the shade several houses away and looked the street over for a few minutes. Carmen's car was in the driveway. He decided it would be a good idea to take his handgun from his ankle holster and move it up to his waistband and to have an extra magazine in his pocket in the off chance he ran into Jose Leon or one of his lackeys. Once situated, Jimmy exited his vehicle and walked up to Carmen's house.

The thought crossed his mind that this was now the second time he'd contacted Carmen without being in the company of another agent. He'd been so busy working on reports that he hadn't really thought about getting someone else to go with him. Maybe subconsciously he wanted to be alone with her. As he stood at the door, he suddenly felt uncomfortable about visiting her without a witness. The first visit had gone okay, but his feelings for her kept getting stronger. He worried about what he'd do or say by himself.

Carmen opened the door wearing a pair of shorts and an open-collared blouse that revealed an abundance of cleavage. It was difficult not to stare, but he forced himself to look into her eyes as he entered her residence.

"I'm glad you were able to come by," Carmen said.

"Is everything all right?"

"Yes. Come in."

He stepped into her home. "You haven't had any other calls or visitors since we spoke this morning?"

"No, and I'm sorry. Maybe I overreacted by calling you."

"No, you didn't. Don't even go there. Jose Leon is a pretty bad dude. I just hope that now that he knows Angel is in jail he won't bother you anymore."

"What do I do if he comes back?"

"Dial 911, then call me. But hopefully he won't be back. Still, we don't know for sure. Have you ever used a handgun?"

"Once or twice at a range, but I don't want any guns in the house, especially with Raul here. I don't think I could shoot anyone anyway . . . I'm sorry, would you like to sit down?"

Jimmy had been standing in the foyer during their exchange. He smiled and nodded and followed Carmen into her kitchen.

"Have a seat at the table if you like," she offered.

"Where's Raul?"

"Upstairs playing on his Game Boy most likely. He'll occupy himself with it until I call him for dinner."

Jimmy sat and watched as Carmen worked on dinner. Jimmy became engrossed in her air of femininity, watching her move and listening to her as she made small talk. She asked about his job and what it was like working investigations and meeting people like her. Jimmy didn't tell her that he'd never worked a case like this before, nor had he ever met anyone like her.

Twenty minutes later, as she was finishing dinner preparations and beginning to set the table, Jimmy rose and started to leave.

"I don't want to intrude any longer. I need to get home to my family and let you and Raul have your dinner."

"You could stay and eat with us if you like," she offered.

"Thanks anyway, but I really need to get home."

Carmen walked over to him and stood inches from him, looking up into his eyes.

"I really appreciate you," she said. "I don't know what I'd do without you in my life right now." She then stood on her tiptoes and kissed him on the cheek.

Jimmy felt uncomfortable, but winked and smiled. "Well that made it all worthwhile," he said.

Jimmy walked to the front door, looked over his shoulder at Carmen who stood watching him. She looked sad to Jimmy. He turned and left before he had a chance to think about it too long.

"Call me if you need anything," he said as he walked away from her front door.

CHAPTER . . .

18

The next few days went by uneventfully with Jimmy spending most of his time in the office catching up on reports and administrative paperwork. Unlike what the public often saw on television, the life of a federal agent was filled with hours and hours of writing. There were initial arrest reports used in the criminal complaints filed with the courts, followed by investigative reports, surveillance reports, and lab reports. Customs agents also spent a great deal of time creating computer records on suspects, defendants and the vehicles used or suspected of involvement in smuggling.

There were also reports done to document confidential sources, along with the numerous background checks done on them, reports documenting travel, reports to document the destruction of evidence, chain of custody documents that had to be created and maintained, and reports used to justify payments to sources or for the purchase of evidence. There were also administrative subpoenas put together by the agents used as a method of getting subscriber information on things like unlisted telephone numbers or subscribers information on utilities at a residence under investigation. The more active an agent was in the field, the more paper he created for himself at the office.

Of course, every year headquarters asked for more documentation for almost everything, a wonderful way to entice investigators to really get out there and try to find the bad guys.

Still, there was a lot of work being done. But Jimmy was tired of sitting in the office and looked forward to getting back out in the field. It was a duty day tomorrow. Some of the agents dreaded another day at the port of entry but to Jimmy it offered the prospect of something new. At least he wouldn't have to sit in front of a computer all day.

Carmen had been calling to check in almost daily, usually on her way home from work. There hadn't been anymore visits from Jose Leon and Carmen seemed to be more relaxed and less worried with each passing day.

Things seemed to be a little more peaceful at home as well, mostly due to the fact that Jimmy spent much of the evening alone. Jimmy would have dinner with Shirley and Nikki, and then Jimmy would retire to the family room to watch television while Shirley would go off to their bedroom to watch her programs. Their intimacy level was at an all-time low, but Jimmy was willing not to press the issue in order to maintain peace.

Duty started early with Jimmy getting a 5:30 a.m. call from Sector.

"Hello," Jimmy said in an effort to sound awake after the telephone on his nightstand rang once and startled him from a sound sleep.

"Sorry to wake you, Jimmy, but an Inspector Simons wants you to call him about some wannabe source that they have in Pedestrian. Do you need the number?"

"No thanks, I've got it. Simons, you said?'

"That's what he said."

Jimmy got up and started a pot of coffee before calling. After being connected, he was put on hold for a minute before Inspector Simons came to the telephone.

"Agent Maxwell? Are you the duty agent?"

"Unfortunately . . . Hey, just kidding. What can I do for you?"

"Hey, I would have called you anyway, but I'm glad you're on duty. I've heard you're a good agent to work with from some of my *compadres* down here."

"I'm always happy to work with you guys and I appreciate the vote of confidence," Jimmy responded.

Inspector Simons changed his tone and lowered his voice a bit then continued. "You know, some of your agents are just dicks."

"Yeah, I know," Jimmy said with a smile that only he could see. He knew it was true. "Referring to anyone in particular, or just most of us?" he asked with a little chuckle. As he said it, the thought crossed his mind to tell him that some of the inspectors he knew were of a like kind, but he kept quiet and listened.

"Oh, there's a couple of guys I could tell you about, but that's not why I called. There's a guy down here. Don't know what to make of him. He's pretty jumpy and fidgety so I'm guessing his info is good. He says he's been recruited to drive a load of weed across the border today. Says he can give you all the information about the car and where it's going. He said he's been arrested before. He got out of jail a few months ago. I'm just starting to run up some information on him in the computer."

"What's his name?"

"Miguel Fonseca."

"Don't know the name. How about sitting on the guy until I get there. I've got to jump in the shower so I'm guessing about forty-five minutes, but I'll try and hurry."

"What if he wants to leave?"

"Don't let him. I'll take the responsibility if he pitches a bitch," Jimmy said.

Jimmy sucked down a cup of coffee while taking care of his shower and shaving. He looked in on Nikki and gave her a kiss as she slept, then went back to his room to finish dressing.

"I sure wish you'd sleep in the spare bedroom on duty days," Shirley said sleepily.

Jimmy gave no response, but shook his head and continued to dress with his back to his wife. When he finished, he turned to kiss his wife goodbye. She reluctantly gave him a peck.

"Can you at least turn the volume down as low as possible on the ringer?" she asked as he headed out the house.

"Have a nice day. I don't know exactly what time I'll be home, but hopefully it won't be too late," he replied without answering her question.

Jimmy got down to the port and found Fonseca sitting in the security office on a steel bench in the pedestrian secondary inspection office. The office was a drab place, old faded cream-colored paint, chipping in places, a few initials scratched into the steel bench, and old tile flooring that reminded him of the floors of a Navy ship. The incandescent lighting in the place gave everything a dreary, tired look.

There were four other subjects seated in the office. Two white males, each about twenty years old based on their looks, a hard-looking white male covered in prison tattoos and a Hispanic male in his late twenties.

Inspector Simons was seated at the computer behind the pat-down counter. Jimmy looked at Fonseca, nodded and gave a little smile, bypassing the four subjects as he walked over to the pat-down counter.

"Inspector Simons?"

"Hey. You must be Agent Maxwell," the inspector said, getting up and taking the two or three steps to the opposite side of the counter.

"Call me Jimmy. Thanks for calling me. I assume the Hispanic male must be Mr. Fonseca?"

"Yeah. I started running the checks on him but got sidetracked. Our two young gentlemen were referred in after one of my partners found a baggie of weed in the pocket of one, and several ecstasy tablets in the pocket of the other. I figured you guys would just defer prosecution on a case like this, but while running the wants and warrants and criminal history I discovered that one is on probation for criminal torture," Inspector Simons said, pointing to the heavier set of the two, a brown-haired youth wearing faded jeans and a dirty white tee shirt.

"No shit?" Jimmy replied. "I've never met anyone that's been prosecuted for torture before. What about his *compadre*?" His friend was taller and thinner with dirty blonde hair that kept falling across his eyes. He had bad skin and wore a faded pair of jeans and cowboy boots along with a denim jacket.

"Nothing on him. Probably hasn't been caught yet as an adult."

Jimmy nodded in understanding and glanced over at the other man sitting across from the two young men. "Your other visitor, why's he here?" he asked.

"Parole violator. We've been targeting parolees. None of them have permission to be in Mexico. We're trying to get hold of his parole officer to see what they want us to do with him."

Jimmy walked over to the parolee.

"Where'd you do your time?"

"Folsom," he responded.

"What for, if you don't mind my asking?"

"Voluntary manslaughter."

Jimmy had wondered if it was for narcotics-related violations, in which case the man was probably down south making arrangements for more dope to come north.

"Never been convicted of any narcotics-related offenses?"

"No."

"So, why were you in Mexico?" Jimmy asked.

"Went down to see my lady. She can't come up here anymore."

"Okay. Sounds reasonable to me," Jimmy responded, walking over to the two younger men.

"So, I guess you two drug smugglers think it's all right to bring dope into the U.S.? You know you committed a federal felony. This isn't just a ticket for the weed like a cop would give you. You know that, right?"

The two young men stared at Jimmy but said nothing. Jimmy walked closer to the man who'd been convicted of torture.

"Tell me about your torture conviction there, hero."

"I was just there. Some fifteen-year-old kid owed my friend Steve some money for a little weed and kept not paying. Steve caught up with him one day and asked him for the money, and when the kid didn't have it he grabbed his arm and held his lighter under it for a minute. But I didn't do it, I was just there."

Jimmy turned to the parolee.

"Excuse me," Jimmy said, getting the parolee's attention. "What do you think would happen to this fine upstanding citizen if he showed up in Folsom and the general population discovered he'd been convicted of torturing some kid?"

"We'd take him up to the top of the fifth level in Cellblock D and fuck him until he started to like it, then we'd throw him off," the parolee stated in a calm, matter-of-fact tone while staring with unblinking eyes into the young man's face.

Jimmy fought to keep an expressionless face, but was thrilled that the parolee had worked with him, whether he meant to or not, in making an impression on the two young men.

Jimmy gave the parolee a little head nod of acknowledgement. The parolee gave him a slight nod in return, turned away, and continued an expressionless wait. Jimmy turned his attention back to the two young men, looking hard into their eyes for their responses. The fear in their expressions was apparent.

"I'm going to defer prosecution on you two this one time because I've got more important business to attend to. But let me explain something to you. Inspector Simons has input all your information into the computer. That means that the next time you cross the border and get referred to us on any kind of criminal matter you get arrested and go to jail. As a matter of fact, since all the judges in this area know me, I think I'll ask them to have you housed in Folsom after you get convicted. So my suggestion, quit smuggling drugs. You're not very good at it anyway."

Jimmy walked over to whispering distance from Inspector Simons.

"Dude, how long's it been since you called for that guys parole officer?"

"I called and left a message on the guy's cell phone an hour ago."

"I'll take the heat, but how about letting him go. They know where to find the guy anyway if they're going to violate him. The guy just went down to see a girl."

"Okay," Inspector Simons said in a whisper, "I liked his response too."

Jimmy walked over to Fonseca, now able to focus his attention on him.

"Mr. Fonseca, come with me please."

Fonseca got up and followed Jimmy through a small doorway that led behind the pat-down counter, and out into a hallway behind the security office. There was a row of temporary holding cells located on one side of the hall. Fonseca was ushered into one of the cells where he sat down on a bench.

Jimmy looked down at the man, giving him a quick study prior to saying anything. Fonseca was a little man, probably 5'5" and 140 pounds. He wore jeans and a cowboy shirt, both of which looked like they hadn't seen a washing machine in a week. Jimmy detected the odor of sweat and dirt but was unsure if it was Fonseca or residual odor from the holding cell. Fonseca's greasy black hair was combed straight back, but longer stands had fallen across his face. He said nothing initially, waiting nervously for Jimmy to speak.

"First of all, Miguel, I appreciate your patience in waiting for me to take care of those other matters out there. Sometimes it gets pretty busy here." Fonseca said nothing but sat looking up at Jimmy impatiently.

"So, Mr. Fonseca, tell me about these people who want you to drive a load of marijuana across the border."

"It's the same people I was working for last time. They came to me after I got out of jail and told me I owed them money for what I lost. Since I don't have any money they told me I could work it off driving marijuana loads. I tried telling them that I don't want to do that anymore but they keep coming over. Now they're threatening my wife. So, I have to drive the car."

"What're the names of the people that want you to smuggle for them?" Jimmy asked.

"I know one guy is called 'Suavacito' and another guy goes by Rigo," Fonseca answered.

"You have any telephone numbers for them, or maybe an address in the U.S. where they live?" Jimmy asked.

"No."

"It figures," Jimmy said, mostly to himself. "Okay, Mr. Fonseca. We can talk about a few options available if you want to work with us, but first, let's go over a few ground rules. First, you can't drive loads of drugs out of Mexico. President Clinton's state department changed the rules on us a few years back. The philosophy behind the changes has to do with agents of the U.S. government not having the authority to authorize anyone to break the laws of a sovereign nation. So if you decide you want to drive a load of drugs out of Tijuana, we have to submit an operations plan to our headquarters and bring the Mexican police into the picture."

"You can't tell the Mexican police. The police work with the smugglers," Miguel said with a look of horror and tone of incredulity in his voice.

"Yeah, I know. Look, we all know the Mexican cops are corrupt, but those are the rules. That's why we should talk about some other ways we can get the dope across the border. There are some other things we can do that should work."

"Mr. Agent man, you don't understand. The car is already loaded and ready to go."

"It's Jimmy. Look, Mr. Fonseca, we don't have any way to protect you if you get caught with a load of drugs in Mexico. We can't authorize you to break the laws of Mexico and it's against our rules to work with you if you break the rules, even if we wanted to. I know the rules are stupid, but that's what we're stuck with. Just don't go pick up the car. How about telling the guys pressuring you to do this that you . . ."

"Mr. Jimmy. You still don't understand. I already took the car. It's loaded with marijuana and it's parked a hundred yards south of the border. I'm going to drive it across the border. I don't want to be arrested, I want to work with you guys, but I have to bring the car across the border. I have the car and I've already been here too long. I don't know what those guys will do to my wife if I don't." Fonseca was beginning to sound a little panicky and was definitely getting impatient.

Jimmy hadn't realized that Fonseca had the loaded vehicle with him. That certainly added a wrinkle to how things would have to be handled.

"Hang on," Jimmy said, reaching for his cell phone.

"Tom, hey it's Jimmy." Jimmy explained the situation to his supervisor. "I know the rules but this guy is going to bring the car whether we want him to or not," Jimmy said.

"The guy's wife is potentially at risk if we just seize the dope here at the port. Any chance of bending the rules on this one occasion?"

Tom sighed and said nothing for a moment, thinking about the situation.

"You know that Arlene is probably going to have my ass, but yeah, tell him we'll try to work this with him. But make it clear to him that this is a one-time deal," Tom said.

Jimmy was actually a little surprised that Tom had agreed to let Fonseca bring the dope through the border.

"Okay. Let me go so I can get things moving on this end," Jimmy said.

"How many more agents are you going to need to do the follow-out?" Tom asked.

"Five or six should be enough. I saw a couple of our guys when I first got down here, but we'll have to leave a few behind to take care of any duty loads that may come in."

"Okay, I'll have people start reaching out to you."

"Thanks, boss," Jimmy said, starting to hang up his phone.

"Jimmy, Jimmy, you still there?"

"Yeah, go ahead."

"Seriously, your idiot there needs to know that this is a one-time deal."

"Yeah, you said that already."

"Just making sure. And I don't want you guys rolling out with him until you at least have six or seven agents available."

"Got it."

Fonseca advised that the car he had parked near the border contained between ninety and one hundred pounds of marijuana. He described it as a late 80s maroon Chevrolet Celebrity with California license plates. The marijuana was supposed to be hidden behind the dash in a non-factory compartment.

It was nearly an hour before there were enough agents present at the port to allow Fonseca to leave to go get the car. He was advised to re-enter through lane five, and not take too long about it. The agents set up in and around the port and waited.

Twelve minutes after walking south, Alex Rojas, one of the agents Tom had recruited from another group, spotted Fonseca.

"Got him coming up in lane four," he said over the radio.

"I see him. Hey, he came close to following directions," Jimmy replied.

Jimmy ran to the 'Fish Bowl,' an office space so named because the supervisory inspectors were able to see the approach of vehicles in all twenty-four lanes of incoming traffic from Mexico through a long series of windows that looked south. Once there, he put in a quick call to the inspector on lane four.

"Hey, this is Jimmy Maxwell, one of the agents. We're doing a controlled delivery involving a maroon Celebrity that's about six or seven cars back in your lane. We have a friendly driving the car. He was supposed to come through lane five but as usual our sources can't follow directions or maybe he got confused or something. Looks like he'll be coming through your lane in another minute. Can you please just send him up the road? We have a whole team out here to follow him away."

"You got it cleared through the Watch Commander?"

"Yes. He just got in the wrong lane."

"Okay. What's his name?"

"Fonseca."

"Got it."

A minute later, the Chevrolet was through the primary inspection station. It exited San Ysidro Boulevard and drove west a few blocks parking in a pay parking lot near the port. Agents set up around the vehicle and watched Fonseca exit the car and walk back into Mexico.

The wait began. It was late morning by now and warm enough that agents let their cars idle in order to keep their air conditioners running. As time ticked away, the agents cycled through lunch breaks, restroom breaks and fuel fill ups.

By late afternoon, Jimmy was beginning to get worried because no one had attempted to pick up the load vehicle. Jimmy had given his cell phone number to Fonseca, but since Fonseca didn't have a telephone he had no way to reach him.

Shit, Jimmy thought to himself. *I should have told him to check in every few hours.* He hadn't planned on the pickup of the load vehicle taking this long. Tom had called to check on the status of the surveillance a few times. He didn't seem too concerned with the delay in someone picking up the load vehicle.

At 7:00 p.m., Jimmy put in a call to Tom.

"Jefe, I think we need to start calling in more agents. This could go all night and some of the troops are getting restless. I don't mind staying if I have to, but we should at least get the non-duty group agents relieved."

Tom agreed and by nine p.m. most of the agents who'd been out all day were replaced, albeit with other agents who'd been up working all day on other things.

Jimmy called home to advise Shirley of his status. She was, of course, unhappy but seemed to accept the situation, telling him to be safe. Nikki talked to him on the phone for a few minutes telling him about her day. As Jimmy listened to her, he was able to forget the leg cramps and boredom of the ongoing surveillance temporarily. He felt he was with her, sitting on the edge of her bed as she talked to him while adjusting her pillow and situating her stuffed animals around her for the night.

The night passed slowly with Jimmy catching a few catnaps in his Expedition. He felt sorry for the agents who had to do the same in a Mustang, Camaro or some other car designed for smaller-framed people.

The sun slowly rose to a new day. Jimmy sipped his 7-Eleven coffee, wondering if they'd been compromised and were wasting their time watching a hundred pounds of weed. He decided to give the surveillance until lunchtime, then put it down and have the Celebrity towed back to the port of entry.

At 9:15 a.m., Jimmy's cell phone rang.

"Maxwell."

"Mr. Jimmy. I've got another car to bring to you guys," Fonseca said in an excited tone.

"No, no, no. Hey, I told you yesterday that this was a one-time deal. We stretched the rules to the breaking point helping you out yesterday. Don't even think about bringing another load across the border."

"Sorry, Mr. Jimmy. I'm in line already. I'm going to be at the border in a few minutes," Fonseca said apologetically.

"What the hell were you thinking? Did I not make myself perfectly clear yesterday?" Jimmy said, clearly irate.

"I was with Rigo and he gave me another car. There was nothing I could do."

"What lane are you in?"

"I think I'm in the same lane as yesterday. The car I'm driving is the same."

"What? The same make and model or the same color?" Jimmy asked.

"Both. It's just like the one yesterday. What do I do? I'll be to the booth in about fifteen cars."

"Why are you just now calling me if you're that close?"

"One of the guys was with me in the car. He just got out to walk across the border. I'm supposed to pick him up at the Jack in the Box."

"Stay in the line and call me back in one minute."

Jimmy called the fish bowl and talked to Nick Charles, the Watch Commander, explaining the situation.

"Mr. Charles, I apologize," Jimmy explained. "I didn't know this knuckle-head was going to be bringing another load across. I can have some agents there in a few minutes to make sure our idiot doesn't go up the road."

"Have one of your guys come see me to sign a chain of custody form," Mr. Charles said.

"No problem, and I really do appreciate your help."

Ten minutes later, Fonseca parked a maroon Chevrolet Celebrity, identical to the one he'd delivered the day before, next to the one he'd driven across the border the previous day. As he exited the car, Jimmy motioned to him. Fonseca looked around suspiciously, and then slowly walked over to Jimmy's Expedition.

"Get in," Jimmy ordered.

Fonseca again looked all around, and then got into the Expedition.

"I shouldn't be here," he said.

"No shit! So why did you decide to bring another load across the border?"

"I told you. I went back to let those guys know I made it okay and they wanted me to bring another car. I told them I didn't want to, but hey, they didn't want to hear it. They gave me a Boost phone, told me to go home and stay with my wife and that they'd call. They called me this morning and told me to come meet them. When I went over, they gave me that car. There wasn't anything I could do."

"Sure there was. They gave you a phone yesterday, right? You couldn't call me?"

"What if they looked at the phone and saw the number?" Fonseca asked.

Jimmy took the cell phone from Fonseca and began scrolling through the numbers stored in the memory as he continued to talk. Finding the personal information in the phone, he wrote down the direct connect number.

"So you couldn't go find a public telephone and call? I don't think you're telling me the truth, and if I find out you've lied to me, I will put your ass in jail. Got it!?"

Fonseca stared at Jimmy wide-eyed without responding. Jimmy stared at him for a minute waiting for a response, and then handed back the Boost phone. Jimmy then called Tom on his cell phone.

"Tom, Jimmy. You're going to love this," he said, explaining the situation.

"And you wondered why I reminded you twice about explaining to him that this was a one-time deal. Jesus! Oh well, what's done is done. Don't let it bother you too much. Sources do stupid, unexpected things, you should know that by now," Tom said, mitigating the issue.

"You're not the one who's been up all night," Jimmy complained.

Tom ignored the complaint and asked, "So what's the plan? Who's supposed to pick up the cars and when?"

"Hang on a minute." Jimmy looked over at Fonseca. "What's next? And your answer better be that someone is coming to pick up these cars in the next few hours or we're shutting this whole thing down." Jimmy asked the question loud enough so that Tom could hear.

"Some lady and I are supposed to deliver the cars to L.A. I have to go meet her and bring her over here."

"Where in L.A.? They give you an address or a telephone number to call when you get there?" Jimmy asked.

"Rigo gave me this number to call," Fonseca said, pulling a scrap of paper from his dirty pants' pocket. Jimmy recognized the number as being a Tijuana cell phone number. "He'll call someone and tell them where to find me," Fonseca explained.

"You catch that, Jefe?" Jimmy asked Tom.

"Most of it. He calls T.J. when he gets there and they tell him where to go."

"Close enough. I'm going to send Mr. Fonseca south, then I'll brief up the rest of the guys out here on the game plan," Jimmy said. "Can you call L.A. and let them know we're coming up into their neck of the woods?"

"Sure. Let me know when you get up to Oceanside so I can let Border Patrol know you'll be coming through their checkpoint."

"Will do."

Jimmy sent Fonseca back to Mexico and then gave the surveillance crew the update via radio. When he was finished, he grabbed some fast food from a nearby Burger King, then sat back to wait for Fonseca's return.

Just after one p.m., Fonseca and a Hispanic female in her mid-thirties showed up at the load vehicles. The female looked like she'd been rode hard and put away wet once too often but she was dressed fairly well with what appeared to be clean clothes, although they were a bit wrinkled.

Fonseca opened the car door for the woman, then handed her the car keys. Jimmy couldn't tell what was being said, but it looked like he was giving her some sort of directions. Once her car door was closed, Fonseca walked over and entered the second Celebrity. Jimmy started to reach for his radio mike but Greg Thompson put out the information over the air before he got a chance to.

As expected, the two load cars headed north in tandem up Interstate 5. The agents spent the next two hours leapfrogging each other as they called out exits. As the surveillance neared the Interstate 405 interchange, a Los Angeles Customs' agent joined them in their surveillance.

"When is the 'wall team' going to join us?" Jimmy asked the agent over the air.

"Sorry, I'm not sure. I'm pretty new at this and my group supervisor just sent me out to meet you guys. Actually, I think he figured you guys were going to handle this yourselves," the agent said.

Shit, Jimmy thought to himself. *I should have told Tom that we needed a wall team.*

Jimmy spent a moment trying to decide what to do. Getting a wall team out would take at least an hour, maybe longer, and who knew where they'd be and what would happen by then. He was just about to call Tom when his phone rang.

"Hey, this is Max Dryer, the L.A. agent with you. I didn't want to tie up the air but, what's a wall team?"

"How long have you been out of the academy?" Jimmy asked.

"Almost a month."

Great, this just keeps getting better, Jimmy thought.

"Max, is anyone else coming from your group?"

"I don't think so. Most of the rest of the guys are doing a search warrant with Torrance Police Dept. on some money-laundering case."

"Well, real quick, a wall team is usually another city police narcotics team, like the Torrance P.D. narcotics team. What happens is when we bring up a load of dope like this from the border we turn over the surveillance and subsequent search warrants to a local police team. It creates a wall between us, the feds that would investigate and prosecute the case, and the owners of the dope. It helps protect the confidential source or cooperating defendant because the owners of the dope don't make the connection to the border with their losses. They think someone must have been watching their stash house, or maybe they think there's a snitch up here somewhere."

"Why not just seal the affidavit you use when you apply for the warrant?"

"Two reasons. The bad guys would still see Customs agents at their house, and because the U.S. Attorney's office almost always unseals the affidavit pretty shortly into the prosecution process. Unlike the feds, the state has laws in place to protect confidential sources. They can keep the portions of the affidavit that speaks to the involvement of the source sealed indefinitely."

"Oh . . . you want me to make some calls and see if I can get one of the L.A. Police Dept. Impact Teams to come out?" Max asked.

"I don't think we're going to have enough time. You can call if you want, but I think we're going to have to handle this ourselves unfortunately."

The surveillance continued as the traffic became increasingly more congested. The vehicle that had point had to close the gap on the female driver to the point that Jimmy began to worry about the surveillance being compromised. It would have been easier if Fonseca was the follow car instead of the lead car, as he knew they were being followed and agents could practically bumper lock him. But with the female following, agents had to be cognizant of the fact that she may be watching traffic behind her.

Max called Jimmy back fifteen minutes after their last conversation and advised that he was unsuccessful in getting a wall team to be available in the immediate future.

Jimmy wasn't very familiar with the area, but somewhere in the city of Bell, Fonseca exited the freeway and pulled into a shopping center parking area. The female followed and parked next to Fonseca. Jimmy wanted to call Fonseca but decided against it as the female was with him. The two walked over to a Denny's restaurant and went inside.

"What now?" Jimmy said to himself.

"Shirley, find someone and go get a seat in there where you can watch that knuckle-head," Jimmy transmitted to her.

"Ten-four."

"I'll go with you, I've got to piss like a race-horse," Greg said over the air.

"Oh, well thank you for sharing with all of us," Shirley answered.

"Greg, see if you can give our friend some kind of discreet sign and get him to follow you to the head. Then find out what the hell he's doing," Jimmy transmitted.

"Got it."

Jimmy sat back in his Expedition and tried to relax. As he sat, he spent a few minutes thinking. It bothered him that he was irritated, something he rarely indulged his emotions with. It bothered him that he didn't have better control of this source. It was starting to bother him that he was using swear words, something else he rarely did. He knew he was tired, but it bothered him that he was feeling a little mean. For some reason he felt like he wanted to smack Fonseca upside his head.

He started thinking about how much distance he'd let come between he and his wife. He even gave a little thought to the fact that he was drinking more than he should. As he sat thinking about all these things, starting to relax a little and getting sleepy, his cell phone rang.

"Maxwell."

"Jimmy, it's Greg. I talked to this dipshit in the men's room. Where did you find this guy?"

"Duty referral. What's he telling you?"

"The short version is that he said he got a call to get off the freeway here and wait. Someone is supposed to show up in the next little bit to get the load cars."

"Okay, I'll let the rest of the troops know. I figured that's what was happening, but you never know with some of these idiots. I wanted to make sure he wasn't just taking a break."

"Shirley and I will be out in another five or so. I was starving so I ordered a piece of pie."

"Just stay in there and wait. You can follow him out. But pay now in case our crooks get here early. We're going to need everyone in this commute traffic. Hope this gets put down somewhere before it gets dark."

It was another forty minutes before anyone arrived. Two Hispanic males came into the parking lot and drove by the two Celebrities slowly, looking the parking lot over closely. Mitch Corrick was the first to notice them.

"Hey, guys. Heads up. There's a green Dodge sedan that's been by our target vehicles about three times. It's got a California plate that ends in 247. Can't make out the rest," he said.

"Yeah, he's checking me out pretty good. I think I'll leave and circle the block," Barbara said.

"Quit wearing those low-cut tops and you won't draw so much attention to yourself," Sal transmitted.

"Bite me, Sal!" Barbara replied.

"Give me a call sometime and I will."

"Guys! Knock it off. Where did our two *chongos* go?" Jimmy asked.

"They're coming back. Your source is walking over to them . . . Okay, we have contact," Mitch said.

"Okay, they're parking. Both subjects are out of their cars. Looks like our boy is exchanging keys with them. Okay, the female is walking over from the restaurant and, hold on; no she's going over to the Dodge. We've got both subjects in our two target vehicles. I have backup lights. Is anyone staying with the source?"

"Surveillance from Jimmy," he said, getting everyone's attention. "Let the source go for the moment. We know who he is. Let's stay with the two target vehicles. Hopefully they'll stay together, but if they separate, Barbara, Bill, Mitch and Max, you guys go with the lead car. Shirley, Sal, Gary, Jesus and I will take the follow vehicle."

It was starting to get a little dark as they followed the two load vehicles through the surface streets of Bell. Neither Jimmy nor any of the other agents really had any idea of where they were, and it was becoming more difficult to follow as they got further back into the suburbs.

Ten minutes or so after they had began this phase of the surveillance, the two vehicles turned a corner and disappeared. Greg turned behind them, with Jimmy coming around the corner twenty seconds after Greg.

"Jimmy, I've lost them. I think they went into this apartment complex, but I'm not sure."

Jimmy turned into the complex. It was a huge mega-complex with several hundred units. Most of the units were built on top of garages. Jimmy turned a second corner in the complex and looked down a row of garage units, probably thirty or so on each side of the wide driveway. It was getting dark and Jimmy could see light shining out around the closed garage doors on only three of the units.

"Dude, I've lost them out here on the street. They almost had to have gone into that complex," Greg transmitted.

Jimmy turned down his radio volume to as low a volume as he could, then rolled his window down to listen. Sal came around a corner behind him, creeping along slowly, looking.

"Greg, Jesus, head into the complex and start looking," Jimmy said.

Jimmy parked in the middle of the driveway and quietly exited his Expedition, careful not to shut his door too loudly. Sal parked behind him and came up quietly.

"They have to be in here somewhere. I'll go down this side; you take the other side. Listen and see if you notice anything through the garage doors."

Sal nodded and started to walk away. Jimmy walked over to a garage door where there was light shining out and started to peek through the crack between the door and the wall. Just as he did so, the door started opening, the sound of the garage door opener startling Jimmy who jumped back a few steps from the door. As it came up, Jimmy saw the two Celebrities parked side by side, with three Hispanic males looking out at him, all as surprised as he was.

Jimmy immediately drew his handgun, bringing his front sight up at the middle of the three men.

"Don't you move! Hands up!"

Sal had heard the garage door opening as he'd started moving away, but quickly returned to the door drawing his sidearm. He came up alongside Jimmy as Jimmy began yelling his commands.

The three men froze momentarily, and then one of them turned and ran up a flight of stairs located at the back of the garage. Jimmy yelled to Sal as he began to chase the fleeing suspect.

"Stay with these two!"

Jimmy flew by the two suspects who were still compliant, bumping one of them with a slightly glancing blow. As he ran by he noticed several cardboard boxes full of marijuana bricks. Not paying attention to the drugs, he raced up the stairs after the third suspect. Opening a door at the top of the stairs, he entered a living room area and gave it a quick visual sweep, proceeding a bit slower and more cautiously.

The kitchen was on his left. It appeared to be empty. On the right was a semi-dark hallway. Jimmy moved to the entrance of the hallway.

"Police! Come out!" he commanded. "You have nowhere to go! Come out! It's only marijuana, man, don't make it any worse."

There was no response. Jimmy moved up to the first door and gave a quick peek inside. Nothing. He moved down to the next doorway and again gave a quick peek into the room. He noticed movement.

"Get up! I see you, man, get up!"

The suspect appeared to be attempting to get something out from under the bed. A horrible feeling hit Jimmy telling him he needed to act. He ran into the room, jumped up on the bed and then kicked the suspect in the back. The man fell forward, holding onto an object he'd been trying to retrieve from under the bed. Jimmy jumped down on the man, wrapping his non-gun arm around the subject's neck and bringing his handgun up to the man's temple.

"Let it go! Let it go, numb nuts!" he yelled.

The suspect was not immediately responsive so Jimmy tightened the pressure on his neck. Fifteen seconds passed. He felt the man starting to relax, passing out as the blood flow to his brain was being squeezed off. Jimmy continued to hold onto the suspect, his eyes adjusting to the low-light conditions of the room. As he continued holding onto the man, he was able to make out the object being held by the suspect. It was an AK-47 assault rifle.

After a few more seconds, the suspect passed out completely and the weapon slipped from his hand. Jimmy relaxed and was able to roll off the man. He kicked the assault rifle a short distance away and removed a set of handcuffs from his rear jeans' pocket. He rolled the suspect over and handcuffed him behind his back, palms out. Jimmy stood for a moment, removed his cell phone from his belt clip, and then sat down on the edge of the bed to catch his breath.

"Sal, you got any help yet?" he asked via the direct connect.

"It's close. I'm still covering these two but they're being good so far. You Code Four?"

"Yeah. I'll be down in a minute."

Jimmy sat still for another few seconds, contemplating what might have been. The suspect stirred, then opened his eyes and looked up at Jimmy.

"You speak English, asshole?" Jimmy asked.

The suspect shook his head no.

"Well, whether you understand me or not, that was one of the stupidest things you could have done. You are damned lucky I didn't just shoot your ass."

Jimmy stood up. The suspect rolled over and attempted to rise. Jimmy pushed him back down with his foot.

"Just stay put, YOU FUCK!" he said, anger starting to overcome the adrenaline.

He finished yelling the obscenity and looked up to see Jesus coming through the door into the room.

"You okay, man?" Jesus asked.

Jesus looked over at the weapon on the floor. Jimmy still hadn't re-holstered, but did so now that Jesus was there.

"Did he have the gun?" Jesus asked.

"Yeah. He ran when he saw us. I chased him up here. He was pulling it out from under the bed when I came in the room."

"You should have just capped his ass," Jesus said, shaking his head in wonder.

"I thought about it. Come on, let's get this idiot up and take him downstairs. I'm tired and I want to get out of here as soon as possible."

Jesus and Jimmy got the suspect to his feet, then walked him back down to the garage. The two other suspects were in cuffs and were being escorted to the backseats of two of the parked G-rides. Agents were still arriving, the driveway area filling up rapidly with cars.

"Don't park there," Jimmy told Bill as he started to get out of his car. "Come on you guys!" Jimmy said loudly, trying to get everyone's attention. "We're Code Four here. Whoever's parked out here blocking the drive area needs to move their car."

Jimmy immediately refocused his attention, looking around the garage. There had to be at least a dozen cardboard boxes, half of them with the tops open, bricks of marijuana wrapped in duct tape visible.

"You guys have been busy," he said to the suspect he still held by the elbow.

Barbara came over and took the prisoner from him, staring at him. She could see he was still a little out of breath and disheveled looking.

"You all right?" she asked Jimmy.

"He just had to fight this guy for a gun he was going for," Jesus told her.

"Go sit down for a few minutes," Barbara told him, a concerned look on her face.

Jimmy sat on the bumper of one of the cars and began looking around.

"Where's Max?" he asked.

"Right here, sir," Max said, walking over.

"You need to get on the horn to your group supervisor and let him know what we have here. Tell him you're going to need a search warrant. Looks like you got yourself a pretty good case."

Max gave a worried smile but said nothing. He began dialing his supervisor on his phone. Max walked a short distance away as he began speaking to someone. Following a short conversation, Max returned to talk to Jimmy.

"Hey, I'm sorry, Agent Maxwell, but we're not interested in this case."

"Your team still tied up?"

"I don't think so. My G.S. said to tell you that the federal guidelines for criminal prosecution on a marijuana case is a minimum of a ton of marijuana, and that they'd need some sort of additional special circumstances even then to get the U.S. Attorney's office to take it."

"You mean like guns or something," Jimmy said, more as a statement than a question that he all ready knew the answer to.

He looked around the garage, silently counting the boxes to himself. He knew he didn't have a ton of marijuana. He thought for a minute while most of other agents looked at him, waiting for direction.

"Jesus," Jimmy said, getting his attention. "Talk to our new friends and see if you can figure out which of them is the renter of this apartment. Let's try to get consent to search. Tell them that they're already screwed with this much dope visible. I don't want to be here all night."

A few minutes, later Jesus had a 'Consent To Search' form signed. Jimmy assigned agents to search and start processing the residence. He called Tom and updated him on their status. Fortunately the three defendants signed 'Waiver of Venue' forms, agreeing to be returned to the federal jail in San Diego instead of being booked into the federal lockup in downtown Los Angeles. Jimmy had Jesus tell them that if they were willing to waive their right to be brought before the nearest magistrate judge, it would speed up their ability to make bond. It was true enough although he didn't tell them he was going to have an immigration hold placed on them to prevent their release.

At about two a.m., the agents began their convoy back to San Diego. Using an electronic scale found in the garage, the marijuana had been weighed at 519 pounds. Not quite as much as Jimmy had first thought when he looked around, but not too bad. Then there was the loaded AK-47, a handgun, and a little over $12,000 in cash.

By the time they were in the Oceanside area, Jimmy had his windows rolled down and was slapping himself to stay awake. Just when he thought he was going to have to pull over for a few minutes and get out and walk around to wake up, his cell phone rang.

"Maxwell," he said, yawning.

"Agent Maxwell, this is Miguel Fonseca. Hey, I'm in line at San Ysidro waiting to cross the border. Rigo gave me another car," he said excitedly.

"Are you out of your mind! Does your brain do anything besides send electronic impulses to your heart to keep you alive? Turn around and take it back!"

"I'm only about ten cars away from the booth," Fonseca said.

"Fonseca, listen to me. We just arrested three guys up here in Bell and we're on our way back to the border. We seized a whole bunch of weed and a little money. When those idiots who hired you find out, they're going to be pissed. Listen. Are you listening?"

"Yeah."

"When you get to the inspector, tell him you're declaring a load of marijuana and have them send you into the secondary inspection area. Tell them you're working for me and that I'm on my way there. I'll be there in about an hour."

The call had helped wake Jimmy up. He drove south thinking about how stupid Fonseca was, wondering just how much longer it was going to be before Fonseca got killed. He also started wondering just how much longer it was going to be before he could get home and into his bed.

Once at the port, Jimmy contacted the inspectors and asked them to put Fonseca in a holding cell. He didn't want to talk to him until he calmed down a little more. The inspectors were asked to process the vehicle that Fonseca had brought. The vehicle contained ninety pounds of marijuana.

The luckier agents in the group had dropped off the prisoners at the Metropolitan Correctional Center in downtown San Diego and then went home from there. The rest of the group chipped in and helped out by processing the marijuana seized in Bell.

Jimmy dummied up some paperwork showing that Fonseca had been arrested at the border but released on a Notice to Appear. Retrieving Fonseca from the holding cell, he sat him down and gave him the NTA.

"Do you not understand that when I tell you that you can't drive any more loads of marijuana across the border, that you can't drive any more loads of marijuana across the border?"

"Yeah, I understand."

"So?"

"Well, they gave me another car," he said innocently.

"And you can't say no, I'm not going to drive another car?"

Fonseca just stared at Jimmy. Jimmy stared back for a moment.

"Look, maybe you should just get lost for awhile. If you don't know how to say no, go somewhere where they can't find you. Your friends down there just took a pretty good loss. They've got to know there was someone talking to us. They're going to wonder why you're not in jail. So disappear and then look me up in a week or so and I'll give you an update on the case. And understand this, if you show up at the border with another load of dope, I don't care what the reason, I'm arresting you and putting you in jail. Got it?"

Fonseca seemed unhappy that he hadn't pleased Jimmy, but said little more.

Jimmy drove home as the sun rose on a new day.

CHAPTER...

19

Jimmy climbed into bed after forcing himself to shower first, despite how tired he was. It was Saturday morning and he lay in bed thinking about his week, a little disappointed that he would be wasting one of his weekend days catching up on his sleep. He was so tired that it took fifteen or twenty minutes to fall asleep, something unusual for him as it usually only took about a minute. Several hours later, he woke to the sound of a vacuum cleaner running in his room. He rubbed his eyes as he sat up, looking over at his wife in stunned disbelief.

"Hey, I'm trying to get some sleep here."

"I've got a lot to do today and I need to get this done. I'll be out of here in a minute."

"Shirley! How do you feel when I wake you up? I haven't slept in over two days."

Shirley turned off the vacuum and looked over at her husband angrily.

"Just because you decide not to come home for days on end so you can avoid your family responsibilities, running around with god knows who, doesn't mean that I have to cater to you when you decide to come home," she said, suddenly starting to sniffle.

"I was working," Jimmy started to say.

"With who? What was her name?"

Jimmy was so tired he didn't even know to respond. He really didn't want to start a conversation that he knew was going to end badly, even if for the fact it would keep him up for several hours talking.

"I was working," he said quietly. "What is wrong with you? Shirley, look at me."

Her sniffles had now turned into tears.

Jimmy yawned and did his best to force himself awake enough to have a coherent conversation. It took him about ten seconds to sit up and focus. His body ached and his head pounded. He hadn't touched a drop of liquor for three days but he felt hung over.

"Babe, you know I have never cheated on you. There is no reason for you to be acting this way," he finally said, his voice getting a little stronger.

"Jimmy, don't lie to me. You never come home and when you're here, you ignore me. You sure act like there's someone else in your life. Just tell me."

"For god's sake. There's no one else. What is wrong with you? Who hides from whom at night?" he asked. "You're the one who exiles herself to the bedroom."

"Well I know you don't want to talk to me. You won't share any of your feelings with me or talk to me about, well, anything."

"Come sit down here," Jimmy said, patting the edge of the bed nearest him.

Shirley came over and sat down, a tear rolling down her cheek.

"You know, you're not an easy woman to talk to." He paused a moment then continued. "I've tried talking to you before, but there's so many things we don't see the same way. It seems to me that most of the time we try to have a conversation it ends up in an argument. But despite all that, I do love you and I want things to be better between us."

"I find that hard to believe. You know that you never talk to me about your hopes and dreams. You know, things like what you want to do when you retire, or places you want to see on vacation, or where you want our daughter to go to college. You know, our shared dreams."

"Maybe because you don't want to compromise about anything. I try to talk to you about things like where I want to vacation and . . ."

"Yeah, you just want to go hunting or take long motorcycle rides. That's not a vacation," she said, cutting him off.

Jimmy exhaled a little loud in his frustration.

"See! You don't want to talk to me even now," she said angrily, starting to get up. Jimmy grabbed her arm, stopping her.

"Shirley, hang on. I'm just really, really tired. He paused again to compose his thoughts. "You know, I'll talk to you about anything you want, but retirement, well that's years away and I really haven't given much thought to what I'll do then."

Shirley turned to look into his eyes as he continued. "I want Nikki to be able to choose whatever college she wants, but don't you think she needs to be a little older, maybe think about what career she wants before we have to start worrying about what school she's going to attend?"

"But, we could still just talk about it," Shirley said.

"Okay. You're right. We can. I'll try to do better about talking to you."

I don't know how we're going to be able to talk when she locks herself up in the bedroom most nights, he thought.

"I'll believe it when I see it," Shirley said.

Jimmy sat up further and placed his arms around his wife. Pulling her to him, he pushed the hair back from her face and kissed her. She responded and leaned against him, pushing him down onto the bed. Her hand went under the covers to find him. She stroked him for a minute then stood and started to undress.

"What about Nikki?" Jimmy asked.

"It's Saturday morning; she's watching cartoons."

The rest of the weekend passed without a call from work but by Sunday evening, Shirley had again retired to their bedroom, refusing to sit with Jimmy in the living room. Jimmy had hoped for some peace at home, at least for a while, after a pretty good day on Saturday. He had spent time talking to her Saturday evening after he woke just before dinner. But as the evening progressed, his conversations would tend to gravitate towards his work. At one point in the evening, in the middle of telling her about his ordeal with Fonseca, Shirley just got up and walked away.

Jimmy had spent much of the day Sunday doing yard work. He was hot and tired and now irritated that Shirley was back to her same uncompromising, angry self. He opened a cold beer, then another, then another. By late afternoon, Shirley was again complaining that he didn't do enough around the house. Jimmy said nothing but opened another Bohemia.

"How many of those have you had?" she asked.

"Four or five."

She got up and went to her room for the rest of the evening.

Monday morning was spent writing reports and filing complaints. By late morning, Jimmy was hungry and thinking about lunch when Barbara and Deron came by his cubicle.

"Come on, let's go get some lunch," Deron said.

"Good, I'm starving," he replied, logging off his computer.

As they were walking down to the parking garage, his cell phone rang.

"Hey, Mr. Jimmy. This is Miguel. Hey, I got another car. I'm in line at the Otay Mesa border crossing. What do you want me to do?"

"I want you to tell me that this a joke."

"No. No, it's not. Rigo gave me another car and told me to try crossing at the Otay Mesa Port. What could I do?"

"Are you crazy or just stupid? Why can't you seem to get it that we can't work with you like this. Why don't you understand that agreeing to smuggle dope for those idiots is going to get you killed. Now listen to me. If you can't turn around and go back, then you're going to have to tell the inspector that you have drugs in the car and have them send you to secondary," Jimmy said, looking at Deron and Barbara, shaking his head in frustration and shrugging.

"Can't you put a team together and try and deliver this like last week?"

"No! Miguel, we tried to help you out of a mess last week but I told you we have rules. They may be stupid rules, but they're rules. We're going to just seize the dope in the car and you're going to have to explain to whoever those idiots are that keep giving you dope that you lost their dope again . . . after you get out of jail."

"Dude, is that guy nuts or what?" Deron said after Jimmy filled him in on the call. "You need to cut your ties with that idiot. I guarantee someone is going to whack him."

"Yeah, and it's going to be me if he doesn't knock off his nonsense. I've never met anyone so friggin stupid."

Jimmy sent Deron and Barbara to lunch without him, but asked them to bring him a sandwich. He called Tom and advised him of the call, getting pretty much the same response from him that he'd gotten from Deron. Jimmy then called ahead to the Port of Entry and advised the watch commander of the impending arrival.

Fonseca showed up twenty minutes later and declared the marijuana. Jimmy wondered what it must have been like to be the inspector on the line who took the declaration. 'Sir, do you have anything to declare?' the Inspector probably asked. 'Yeah, I have a car full of marijuana.' The inspector probably didn't hear that very often.

The vehicle that Fonseca had been given was searched and another ninety pounds of marijuana was seized.

On his way home that evening, Jimmy got a call from Carmen.

"I haven't heard from you for a few days. How are you?" Jimmy asked.

"I'm okay. I'm on my way home from work and thought I'd give you a call. I didn't want to bother you over the weekend. Things are going all right I guess. Just thought I'd check in and let you know that I haven't had any more visits."

"Good. If you do, don't hesitate to call me."

"I still worry some. Raul has been asking about his father, wondering why he hasn't been by."

"Does he call? You know there's phones at the jail and he can call almost whenever he wants," Jimmy said.

"He hasn't called. I don't know why. Maybe I should go visit him or something."

Jimmy wondered if Angel was calling his other family, Maria and the little girl.

"Are you still there?" Carmen asked, interrupting his thoughts.

"I'm sorry, I'm still here. I don't know that it's such a good idea to visit him yet."

"Why?" Carmen asked.

"Well, why would you, other than for Raul? It seems to me that he was off in his own world, one you weren't part of, and maybe it would be better if you cut the ties to ensure you stay separated from that world. His world brings men like Jose Leon over to your home."

"I know. I guess I just want to know what's going on with him. I mean, I don't want anything bad to happen to him."

"Carmen, we need to talk about some things," Jimmy said. He was leaning towards telling her about Angel's other family.

"Okay. Is it about something bad?"

"No. Well not real bad. There're just some things I feel I should tell you."

When do you want to get together?" Carmen asked.

"How about tomorrow evening?"

"I'll be home at my usual time," she said.

Finishing their conversation, Jimmy drove silently, thinking about the pros and cons of telling Carmen about Angel's other family. By the time he pulled up into his driveway, he had just about convinced himself that it was a bad idea to tell her. He walked into the house, greeted by Nikki who ran into his arms.

"Daddy!"

"Hi, sweetie," he said, sweeping her off her feet and twirling her around.

Nikki giggled and gave Jimmy a kiss as he pulled her close to him.

"Where's mommy?" Jimmy asked, walking to the kitchen with her in his arms.

"She's making dinner."

Jimmy walked into the kitchen and walked up to Shirley who was holding a glass of wine. She held it out to him in a mock toast, nodding slightly but not smiling. Jimmy hesitated momentarily, then leaned forward and gave his wife a kiss.

"Well, well. What's the occasion?"

"No occasion. I just thought that I'd join you in a few drinks tonight. You know, if you can't beat 'em, join 'em."

Shirley turned and began stirring a small pot of corn that was simmering on the stove. Jimmy said nothing, sat Nikki down and gave her a wink, then walked up behind his wife and placed his hands on her hips.

"Careful. Don't mess with me while I'm stirring something hot."

Jimmy backed up a few inches, then leaned over and kissed his wife's neck.

"Honey, you don't have to drink just because I like to have a few."

Shirley ignored the remark and took another drink from her glass. Looking over, Jimmy noticed that Shirley had already consumed about half the bottle.

"Come on, sit down and I'll bring you a plate," she said. "Nikki honey, grab your daddy a beer from the fridge."

Jimmy sat, wondering what was going on with his wife. As they ate together Jimmy tried to converse with his wife, asking her about her day. As time passed though, his thoughts began to wander back to the issue of telling Carmen about Angel's other family. Shirley noticed the lack of focus on their conversation.

"What are you thinking about?" she asked.

"Oh, I'm sorry. Just some work stuff. Hey, want to go out and get some ice cream after dinner?" Jimmy asked.

"Ice cream! Ice cream!" Nikki shouted with glee.

Shirley shot him a glance of disgust. "I try to lose weight and you purposely sabotage me."

"Sorry."

"Well, I guess you'll have to take Nikki. I was hoping to spend the evening with you, but there you go again," she said.

"It won't take very long. Come with us."

"No, you two go. I need a little peace and quiet anyway."

Jimmy and Nikki drove to Baskin Robbins, Nikki talking non-stop about her day. Jimmy tried to listen, catching some of her one-sided conversation, but mostly thinking about how he kept screwing things up with his wife.

When they got home, Shirley was working on a second bottle of Chablis.

"Have a good time?" she said with a slight slur.

"Nikki did," Jimmy answered. "I'm going to go get her ready for bed."

"You do that."

Thirty minutes later, Jimmy grabbed a beer from the kitchen then returned to the living room. Shirley was watching a chick flick on television. He sat down next to his wife and popped open the beer. Shirley looked over at the beer, and then looked back at the television, saying nothing.

They watched the movie in silence for a while. Shirley continued working on the second bottle of wine.

"Honey? You going to be okay, drinking that much?"

"I'm fine," she slurred. "Don't worry about it."

"Well you normally don't drink, and when you do, it's usually a glass or two of wine, not a bottle or two."

"I said I'm fine."

They sat together in silence a little longer. Jimmy reached over and put his arm around his wife. She gave no indication of either liking or disliking the attention, but as time passed she began to lean into her husband.

Maybe I'll get lucky again, he thought to himself.

A few more minutes passed, the movie ending.

"Are you ready for bed yet, hon?" he said. Looking down at his wife, he realized she was out.

"Honey, wake up," he said, pushing her gently away and removing his arm from around her shoulder. "Wake up."

"Huh," she groaned.

Jimmy helped her to her feet and guided her to the bedroom. She fell onto the bed and was immediately asleep again. Jimmy pulled off her shoes and pants, but after unbuttoning her blouse he realized he'd have no success in getting it off without significant effort.

"Oh well, guess she'll just have to sleep like that," he said, covering her with the bedspread. Rookies shouldn't be drinking like trained professionals," he said aloud to himself, smiling at his little joke. He stood watching her for a minute while he undressed, then gave her a little peck on the cheek and headed to the guest bedroom.

CHAPTER . . .

20

Tuesday passed quickly with Jimmy getting a call from Carmen at lunchtime confirming that he was going to stop by on his way home. He thought about taking an agent with him but kept getting distracted by a number of errands and projects that popped up throughout the day. By the time he got ready to leave the office, most of the agents in his group had already gone home, most sneaking out a little early to avoid the late afternoon traffic.

Sitting at his desk, he vacillated as to whether he should call someone who lived in the south bay area to meet him at Carmen's house, but he was hesitant to call anyone at home to accompany him on what could be construed as less than official business, especially considering how busy they'd all been lately, most of which was working on his cases.

Shortly after leaving the office his cell phone rang.

"Maxwell," he answered.

"Jimmy. Hey, it's Chuey. I need to see you. I got some information for you."

Jimmy looked at his watch and decided that arriving a little late at Carmen's house wouldn't be that big of a deal. Chuey was one of those confidential sources that seemed to check in about every six months. Jimmy paid his sources pretty well and he figured Chuey was a little more responsible than most of his other sources so he'd probably make his money last a little longer. When he needed money, he'd come around and make a case, then disappear again for a while. Apparently he needed money.

"I don't have much time Chuey, but I can meet you at the Starbucks on Palm for a few minutes."

"Okay, man. See you in a bit."

"Hey, hey, Chuey, you still there?"

"Yeah, what?"

"I'll see you there at six o'clock. If you're more than ten minutes late, I'm leaving. I really do have someplace to be," Jimmy
said, knowing that Chuey was famous for keeping him waiting.

It was a trait that most agents didn't put up with in a confidential source. They just didn't have the patience to deal with
sources that didn't revolve around their little universes. Jimmy
understood the rationale to some degree, but reasoned that if
the person wasn't a cooperating defendant, they really didn't
have to meet with you in the first place, let alone give you information. Besides, Chuey had proven himself time and again
by coming up with credible, useful information that usually
led to a seizure or arrests.

Chuey was waiting for him by the time he got to the Starbucks.

"Hey, Jimmy," Chuey said, offering a sweaty palm to shake.

"What's up, dude?"

"Got a license plate for you. This car should be crossing
sometime in the next twenty-four to thirty-six hours with a
load of meth." Chuey handed him a matchbook that had the
license plate written on the inside cover.

"You could have just given me the plate over the phone,"
Jimmy said.

"Yeah, but then I wouldn't have been able to see you,"
Chuey said with a smile. "Shit man, I haven't seen you in a few
months."

Jimmy looked around. Everything looked normal, people
sitting with each other talking, some reading, others standing
in line to order their foo-foo drinks.

Okay, the guy just needed some coddling or something, Jimmy
thought.

"I also wanted to talk to you about something else," Chuey
continued. "I'm hearing that Jose Leon is running around
looking for his old lady. Word is that she's split with one of his
bodyguards, their two kids and a couple million in cash."

"No shit? How long has she been gone?"

"A month, maybe longer. I heard that Jose suspected she was
having an affair with someone for a while. He's been spending

a lot of time and energy trying to figure out who it was that was banging his wife, but never figured it out until she split. I think he suspected Angel for a while, but then I heard that Angel got arrested. I think he talked to one of Angel's people who convinced him that Angel wouldn't have done something like that."

"Well, things are beginning to make a little more sense. Thanks, Chuey. Hey, I'll get this plate on lookout and hopefully it'll pan out with some dope. I'll try and make your payday on this one a little better than normal for the additional intel. And by the way, Angel did get arrested, by me."

"No shit. Wish I could have given you the info that led to that arrest," Chuey said, smiling. He reached out the clammy hand again as Jimmy rose to leave. Jimmy reluctantly shook it.

"Jimmy, do you think you could spot me like twenty bucks. I don't have much gas and I need to get across town to see a guy."

"Man, why do you do this to me?" Jimmy said, taking out his wallet and shaking his head as he opened it.

"All I have is ten. You'll have to make do with that," he said, handing it over to Chuey. "Learn to manage your money better, dude. You haven't done too bad with us this year so you should be in better shape."

"Yeah, well I . . ."

"I don't even want to know what you spend it on. I just don't want to have to start claiming you as a dependant on my income taxes. Be safe," he said, turning away and heading towards his Expedition.

On the drive to Carmen's, Jimmy called Sector Communications and gave them the vehicle license plate given to him by Chuey.

"Yeah, have the inspectors escort the vehicle into secondary inspection for an intensive search," Jimmy told Angie at Sector.

It was 7:15 p.m. when Jimmy reached Carmen's house. He did his usual look around, parking several houses away and watched for a minute or two before getting out and slowly walking up to her front door. As he stood waiting for her to answer, he heard Raul crying inside. Carmen opened the door, wiping tears from her eyes as well and threw her arms around Jimmy's neck, pulling him close to her.

"What's wrong?" Jimmy asked.

"I had just got home and started to change when that guy, Jose Leon, you know the guy Angel used to work for, came into my bedroom."

"What! How did he get in?"

"I don't know."

"Did he, do anything?" Jimmy asked while trying to process all the possibilities of what happened next.

Carmen released Jimmy and took him by the arm, almost pulling him into the living room as Jimmy turned and gave a quick look up and down the street. Jimmy pushed the door closed behind him. He sat on the sofa while Carmen scooped up Raul and held him for a minute. He calmed down almost immediately. Carmen spoke to him in Spanish in a hushed voice for a minute and then took him upstairs. When she came down a few minutes later, she sat on the loveseat opposite Jimmy.

"He'd been drinking. He sat down at the foot of my bed and just stared at me for a minute, and then he started talking. He told me he was looking for his wife. He seemed really, really angry, yeah angry and frustrated."

Carmen took a breath and paused a moment before continuing. "I hadn't remembered before, but I met his wife about five or six years ago. I went with Angel to Culiacan. You know, it's one of the bigger cities in Sinaloa. We went down to visit Angel's sister, Leonora. His sister is a friend of Jose's wife Elvira. I guess she goes by Vera, that's why I hadn't remembered the name. I called her Elvira. Anyway, while Angel was out doing whatever it was he was doing back then, Elvira, Leonora and I spent quite a bit of time together. I mean, we were only down there about a week, maybe eight or nine days, but I saw the two of them almost daily. By the time we were ready to come back to San Diego I wrote down Elvira's name, address and phone number in my address book, and I guess she wrote down my name, address and phone number in hers."

"So when Vera disappeared, I guess she must have left without her address book. Jose must have found it, and started calling or visiting those people he believed were her friends," Jimmy said, as much to himself as to Carmen.

"I guess," Carmen said.

"So what did Jose say to you?"

"He asked me if I knew who he was. I shook my head no. He said he was a man who had people killed if he wanted to. Then he asked me again if I'd seen Vera. I told him I hadn't. He said he knew I was lying and showed me her address book . . . Jimmy, I was so afraid I didn't know what to do."

"But he didn't hurt you, right?"

"No. When he showed me the address book, he got up, walked over to me, and showed me the entry. That's when I realized who she was. Jimmy, I could smell the alcohol on his breath. I kept hoping you were going to come through the door and save me."

A tear started to run down her cheek as she looked at Jimmy. He felt horrible at having diverted to talk to Chuey, realizing he just missed his chance of not only rescuing her, but at possibly arresting one of the most notorious drug lords in the area.

"I'm so sorry I wasn't there for you."

"Jimmy, I know this isn't your fault. I know you're a good man who would have been there for me if you'd only known. I don't mean to make you feel bad," she said crying even more. After a minute she wiped her eyes with her hands and looked at him. "You're here for me now," she said softly.

Jimmy got up, moving across the space between their seats. He sat next to her and put his arm around her shoulder. Carmen composed herself over the next minute or two, then continued.

"Jose told me that he was going to continue looking for his wife. He said that if he found out I had lied to him he'd come back here and kill Raul and me. He said he was going to kill whoever he found with his wife. Then he got up and left."

"So he didn't hurt you or Raul in any way?"

"He just scared me. After he left, I broke down and started crying. I don't think Raul even knew he was here, he just saw me crying and it upset him to the point where he became very upset and began crying." She paused again momentarily. "Jimmy, I have no idea how he got in. I thought I'd locked the door behind me when I got home, but he seemed to have just walked in the front door. I must have left it open."

"I didn't notice any sign of forced entry when I came in," Jimmy said, looking over at the door. "Maybe somehow he got a key. Maybe from Angel. If you can afford it, I want you to call a locksmith tomorrow and have your locks all changed."

"Okay. But what if he comes back tonight?"

"I think that's pretty unlikely, but nevertheless, why don't you pack a bag and I'll escort you to a motel. I know you won't get any rest here tonight if you stay. Come on, get up and put some things together."

Carmen got up and started up the stairs to her room. Jimmy followed a few steps behind. Towards the top of the stairs he began asking himself why he'd followed her, wondering if it was a good idea. His attraction to her was growing daily and he was beginning to have feelings for her he knew were unhealthy.

Once in her bedroom, she opened the closet and started taking out clothing and laying them on the bed. Jimmy looked at the bed, noting the wrinkled spot at the foot of the bed where Jose Leon must have been sitting forty-five minutes earlier. Jimmy stood looking at the nude photograph of Carmen hanging on the wall, realizing that Jose Leon must have taken note of it himself while he was talking to Carmen. As he thought about it he began to feel both jealous and angry.

Lost in his thoughts for a moment, Jimmy was brought back to the present as Carmen spoke.

"I had that picture taken when I was twenty-seven years old. I guess I was feeling a little alone and ignored, what with Angel never being around, and I needed to feel a little sensual about myself."

Jimmy felt a little embarrassed, having been caught staring. "So you didn't have it done for the man in your life?"

"No. I had it done for me. The only man who's ever been in my life is Angel, and he wasn't in my life for very long."

"You're very beautiful, Carmen. Why haven't you ever moved on? There're still a few good men out there."

"I stayed married to Angel for quite a while before filing for divorce. You know, it's that Catholic thing. He is the father of Raul and I figured he'd always be around for his son."

Carmen returned to putting her things together, then pulled out a medium-sized suitcase from the closet.

"I apologize for staring at the photo. Have you ever thought about taking it down and putting it away somewhere?"

"No. I like it."

"I like it too, but with guys like Jose Leon running around and coming into your house, not to mention federal agents and who knows who else at this point, it might not be a bad idea."

"Do you like it, Jimmy? Do you think I'm attractive?"

"I told you, you're beautiful," he said staring at the picture. He turned to look at Carmen who had stopped packing to stare at him. "I don't like the fact that Jose Leon got that good of a look at you today. You're lucky that he didn't decide to, well, you know. A man that powerful would think he can have whatever he wants for the taking."

"I guess you're right." She walked over and took the picture down, holding it with outstretched arms, looking at it for another few seconds, then she slid it under the bed. Carmen then turned and walked into her bathroom and started putting together her toiletries.

"So what were you going to talk to me about tonight before all this other stuff happened? she said from the bathroom.

"I'm not sure it's that important right now. You've already got way too much on your mind to have to deal with anymore issues."

Carmen came back out of the bathroom and stood looking at Jimmy. She then slowly walked to her bed, then crawled on her hands and knees to the middle of it and sat cross-legged. She patted her hand on the bed, indicating she wanted Jimmy to sit down.

"Tell me why you were coming to talk to me."

"Carmen, I'm really not sure that it's that important. I think it will wait a few days."

"Jimmy, my day is already as bad as it could be. I want the next few days, and preferably the rest of my life, to be better. If it's bad, let's get it over so I can begin to move on."

Jimmy sat silently for a moment, thinking about what she'd said.

"I came to tell you that Angel had, actually has, another family." Jimmy sat looking into Carmen's eyes. She looked back showing no emotion. "We did a search warrant on one of his homes a few weeks ago and arrested his wife, or whatever she was. She's a woman he's been living with. They have a little girl."

Carmen looked a little shocked but didn't respond immediately.

"Carmen, I'm sorry. I really don't want to hurt you. I don't like hurting people, especially people I care about. I thought it was important for you to know because I really didn't want you spending a lot of time, emotion, worry, or whatever on Angel. He just isn't worth it."

"What's her name?" she asked, sounding drained.

"Maria."

"And the little girl?"

"Guadalupe. She told me to call her Lupita."

"That was Angel's grandmother's name. He told me years ago that if we ever had a little girl that's what he wanted to name her."

"I'm sorry," Jimmy said, reaching out and taking one of Carmen's hands.

Carmen got up and walked back into her bathroom. She busied herself putting her things together. Within a few minutes she was placing all her items in the suitcase. She finished without saying a word while Jimmy watched her from his seated position at the foot of her bed. Carmen stood facing him for a few seconds while he looked into her eyes. She looked so drained and so sad that Jimmy felt sorry for her.

He stood and walked over to her. As he neared her she threw her arms around him and held him close to her. He tentatively put his arms around her, standing and holding her for a minute. As he looked down at her, she looked up, reached up and took hold of his face, then drew his head to hers. They kissed passionately, the kiss becoming even more passionate the longer it went. Without really thinking about where it was headed, Carmen reached down and began unbuckling Jimmy's belt. Once it was undone, she unbuttoned his jeans, pulled open the zipper and placed her hand into his shorts, wrapping her hand around him. Jimmy let it continue for a minute, but then took hold of her forearm and pulled her hand away. She looked into his eyes.

"Carmen, no one wants this more than me. You have no idea how much I want you right now. But I can't do this. For a bunch of reasons I can't do this." He adjusted himself, zipped up his jeans and refastened his belt.

"Come on, let's get you out of here and to a motel," he said.

There was an uneasy silence between them as she finished getting ready to leave for the motel. Jimmy helped her put two bags she'd packed into her car and then escorted Raul to the car while she locked up the house. Jimmy decided he'd follow Carmen and Raul to the motel. Jimmy drove in silence, his stomach in knots. As he drove he thought about how close he'd come to changing his life forever. Part of him regretted not finishing what she'd started. He realized he'd never known another woman, ever, that made him feel like she did. As he thought about it he suddenly started to become afraid of the feelings. He'd only known her a few months, and it seemed crazy to him that he would have these feelings towards someone like her.

After pulling into the motel, Jimmy walked over and escorted her into the lobby, carrying her two bags. They stood together at the counter, Jimmy watching her as she filled out the registration card. When she finished she looked over at him, staring for a moment, studying his face. He gave a faint smile that she returned. He escorted her to her room, saw her inside, and then turned to leave. Carmen followed him to the doorway, pulled the door most of the way closed and looked up at him.

"Jimmy, I'm sorry if I've made things awkward between us. I didn't mean to. I really appreciate all you've done for Raul and me and, well I've been alone so long . . . I've needed someone for so long that I guess I just got a little carried away."

"I'm sorry too, and don't apologize. Look, Carmen, I have to be honest with you. I've got a lot of issues at home with my wife. We aren't doing too well and I'm really trying to make it work, but at the same time, I'm incredibly attracted to you. You are one of the most beautiful women I've ever known and you drive me crazy with desire when I'm with you. So maybe, if I need to come see you again, I'll need to have another agent come with me. I want to help you, be there for you, but I need to keep things on a professional basis."

"It's okay. I understand," she said calmly. It seemed to Jimmy that Carmen had just turned off her emotions and had become the cool professional woman he'd first met several months earlier.

"Call me tomorrow, and especially before you decide to go home. I know you'll want to go get some other things, maybe get your mail and such. I think you should probably spend a few days here if you can. But when you need to go home, I want to follow you over there and make sure no one is waiting."

He reached out and took one of her hands, holding it for a moment, his heart beating rapidly, his stomach starting to knot up again. It was hard to leave but he finally turned and walked back to his truck.

"You will be back tomorrow then?" Carmen said as Jimmy began walking away.

"When you want me back, I'll be back."

Jimmy drove home in silence, kicking himself mentally for what had happened between them.

As if my problems at home aren't bad enough, I have to do this, and start to fall in love with the wife of a major crook. Just great Maxwell! he thought. He wondered why he could almost always make the right decisions at work, but rarely made the same quality decisions in his personal life.

Arriving home, Jimmy was still such a mess mentally that he was nervous about spending time with Shirley. He knew he wasn't a good liar, and that under pressure from his wife's interrogations he usually broke and told her whatever she wanted to know. He tried to reason with himself that he had done the right thing and not given in to temptation. He also knew that Shirley would not see things in that same light if she knew what had just happened. She would view it as having cheated on her.

Dinner was over by the time he'd got in so he gave his wife a kiss, picked up Nikki and swung her around a minute, giving her kisses and all his attention. He asked Shirley about her day and after a brief exchange he went into the kitchen to warm up some leftovers. Opening the refrigerator he grabbed a beer, popped the top and poured down most of the can in one long swallow. He finished it seconds later then opened another one. By the time he'd finished eating, he'd finished the third beer and decided to pour himself a double shot of tequila.

It was nearly ten p.m. by the time he returned to the living room carrying the highball glass of tequila.

"Typical Jimmy," Shirley said disgustedly, looking over at him as he walked over to the sofa. "Stay gone all day and half the night, then come home, ignore your family and start drinking."

Jimmy ignored the sarcasm and sat down.

"Where's Nikki?"

"I put her to bed while you were eating, or drinking, or whatever you were doing in there. In fact, I'm going to bed too."

"Hey, I'll be up in a few minutes," Jimmy said as Shirley walked away.

"Don't bother!"

Jimmy sat in silence for some time. He finished his drink and then poured another, thinking of his evening.

CHAPTER . . .

21

The next four or five weeks passed uneventfully. Jimmy saw Carmen almost every day, although their visits were usually only twenty or thirty minutes during the early evening. Jimmy had started asking Deron to come with him during his visits with Carmen. Deron had been filled in on the issue involving the threats from Jose Leon, but Jose had not attempted any further contact with Carmen. Whether or not it was because Carmen wasn't home to be bothered, or because there were agents with her when she was home was unknown.

Things at home were somewhat static, Shirley being her cool, distant self. When he was at work Jimmy was very focused on his investigations. When he had free time, which didn't seem to be very often, his thoughts were of Carmen. During the evening when he was at home his mind skipped around from thinking about Carmen, to thinking that he shouldn't be thinking about Carmen, to thinking that he should be focusing on a relationship with God and being a better husband, to thinking about what a bitch his wife was.

Jimmy had been cutting back on his drinking, but with all the thoughts bouncing around in his head he would still take a few drinks in the evening in order to not have to lay in bed and stare at the ceiling half the night thinking about all the things he should or shouldn't be doing.

It was almost six weeks after his meeting with Chuey at the Starbucks that the license plate he'd been given came across the border and was referred for inspection.

"Jimmy? This is Supervisor Jensen. Hey, got one of your lookouts down here. Looks like it's loaded. When can I expect you?"

"I can get there pretty quick, maybe ten minutes. What was in the car?"

"Meth. Don't know exactly how much, but it's a fairly decent sized compartment. Hey, we haven't torn the car up yet; you want us to hold off until you get here?"

"That'd be great. What about the occupants? How many in the car?"

"One white kid, maybe twenty years old."

"It's getting better all the time," Jimmy said, genuinely happy. I don't need to track down a Spanish speaker or deal with the immigration folks."

Jimmy ended the call with Supervisory Inspector Jensen and then put in a call to Tom.

"Tom, it's Jimmy. One of my lookouts hit and it looks like it's going to be a decent load of meth. Can you send four or five agents down to the port? I'd like to try and deliver it if I could."

"Yea, I'll send the group. Let me know the details if you're going to head up the road."

"No problem. I should know whether or not this will go within twenty or twenty-five minutes."

Once he arrived at the port, Jimmy found the car parked in the east secondary lot. Several inspectors and a canine enforcement officer and his drug detector dog were gathered around it. The dog and his handler were playing tug of war with a rolled-up towel.

Inspectors Brad Lawson and Sally Arkin looked up as Jimmy approached.

"Nice hit, Jimmy," Sally said.

"Thanks. So where's it hidden?" Jimmy asked.

"There's a compartment you can access under the back seat that rests on top of the gas tank. Looks like it goes all the way across the back of the car. Not too deep but I'll bet it still holds twenty or thirty pounds," Brad said.

Jimmy exchanged pleasantries for another minute then walked over to the security office. He found the young driver sitting on the bench inside the office. He looked over at Jimmy as he approached.

"Special Agent Maxwell," Jimmy said, showing his credentials. "You the driver of the white Audi?"

"I borrowed it from a friend, sir. I didn't know there was anything in it. Really."

"Kid, hold on a minute. Come with me." Jimmy motioned for the young man to follow him. Jimmy led him to a holding cell adjacent to the security office.

"Sit down," Jimmy said, pointing to the metal bench seat. The six-by-six cell was adorned with a stainless steel toilet with no toilet seat and the bench. The walls and the bench had been painted a cream color, worn and stained now, carved and notched with people's names and assorted graffiti. The cell had a noticeable smell of bad feet.

"What's your name?"

"Josh. Josh Barnett."

"You ever been arrested before, Josh?"

"No, sir."

"Well you have now. There's a first time for everything. And guess what? You're going to the federal jail today. Look around you. This is what you have to look forward to for a while." He stared at the young man for a moment, letting the surroundings sink in. "So, do you like what you see?"

Josh hung his head and shook his head no.

"So what I really want to know is whether or not you'd be interested in working with us in delivering the dope that's in your car to the people it belongs to? I know it's not yours. I also know you knew there was dope in the car."

Josh looked at him without saying anything, then finally spoke. "I didn't know there were drugs in the car, I told you, I just borrowed . . ."

"Josh. Shut up. I need you to listen to me. Most of the people that smuggle drugs through here get caught with marijuana. This is a fairly marijuana-friendly state. With no priors most of the people caught smuggling do about a day a pound. Usually. That said, you have methamphetamine in your car. A lot of methamphetamine. Neither the state nor the federal government are very friendly about people bringing meth into the country. On top of that, we knew you were coming."

Josh's mouth dropped open and his eyes got big as Jimmy spoke. Within moments, his eyes started to well up.

"You're the only one in the car, so guess what? You're responsible. Now I can get the guy who called me and told me that you were coming to come testify against you if I need to, but if that happens, well you won't like how that might affect your future. So you have one chance to help yourself here. I know the drugs don't belong to you. You're going to take them to someone else, maybe the person that hired you to smuggle them, right? That said, are you willing to help us deliver the drugs to whoever that person is?"

"They just told me it was thirty pounds of marijuana," Josh said.

"Josh, hold on. I need to read you your rights. I just want to know if you're willing to work with us."

"Will it help me? Do you think I'll be able to go home later if I help you?"

"It should help you, maybe a lot, but no, you're not going home today."

Josh sat looking at Jimmy, tears starting to run down his face. "They told me it was weed," he sobbed.

After composing himself, Josh agreed to assist in the controlled delivery. Jimmy advised him of his Miranda rights, and Josh waived them, agreeing to answer questions. Josh told Jimmy that he was supposed to take the car to the Fontana, California, area, a little over one hundred miles north of San Diego.

According to Josh, once he got in the Fontana area he was supposed to place a call to a man in Tijuana. Josh admitted to smuggling dope once before and that on that occasion he'd been directed to a Target store parking lot. Two Mexican males came and met him within thirty minutes of his arrival. They took the car and left him at the store to shop while it was unloaded. Josh said it took them about an hour to unload the vehicle on the prior trip.

Over the next thirty minutes, Deron, Bill, Shirley, Greg, Barbara, and Sal showed up at the port. Jimmy briefed them on the case and destination and asked Bill to drive the Audi load car to the drop-off location. He placed a handcuffed Josh in the front seat of his Expedition.

Jimmy signed the chain of custody forms for the inspectors and got everyone ready to roll from the port. Bill got into the Audi, started it, then turned it off and walked over to Jimmy who was sitting in his Expedition with the windows rolled down.

"Dude, why do I always get the fucked up cars?"

"Because you're still the rookie. Besides, what's wrong with it?" Jimmy asked.

"It smells like someone puked in it. And I don't think it has much gas."

"The gas gauge doesn't work, mister," Josh said, leaning over towards Jimmy's open window.

"So how much gas is in it?" Bill asked.

"Like, three quarters of a tank. I've got some money in my wallet if it looks like you guys will need to stop," Josh said. Most of his earlier distress had seemingly melted away and it seemed he now was trying to feel a part of the law enforcement team heading out to catch the bad guys.

"Thanks Josh, but we'll see. Come on, Bill, let's get going," Jimmy said a little impatiently.

"Dude, the friggin car still stinks," Bill said as he turned and walked away.

"Keep the windows down," Jimmy suggested, turning away with a little laugh.

The agents rolled up the freeway in relatively light traffic. Jimmy called Tom and advised him of their destination. He asked Tom if he'd put in a call to their Customs counterparts in the Riverside office and ask for some assistance. The plan was to allow the two men to come pick up the car, discreetly follow them to the residence where the car was going to be unloaded, and arrest them as they parked the car at that location. Agents would then go into the house and secure the occupants, and then apply for a search warrant.

As they neared the Temecula Border Patrol Checkpoint, Jimmy remembered that he hadn't yet called to get permission from them to bring drugs through the checkpoint. He called Sector Communications and asked them to connect him with the checkpoint.

"This is Special Agent Jimmy Maxwell with U.S. Customs. Is this the Temecula Border Patrol Station?"

"Yes."

"You guys open?"

"Not right now. Why?"

"I'm with a team of Customs agents doing a controlled delivery of an unknown quantity of meth to a crook in the Fontana area. But if you're closed, don't worry about it."

"Agent Maxwell. You can't come through the checkpoint without approval from our Chief Patrol Agent or his deputy."

"You're not even open."

"We could open. If we refer the car and there're drugs in it, we'll seize it. Whoever is driving may be arrested," the Patrol Agent stated.

"Look guy, it's an agent driving it. We're doing a controlled delivery."

"Doesn't matter. You've got to get approval from . . ."

"Yeah, yeah, yeah. Look, sorry to cut you off, but we're starting to get close. What's the number I need to call?"

The patrol agent gave Jimmy the number. Jimmy hung up and called the number he'd been given. The number rang five times then went to voicemail.

"This is Deputy Chief Patrol Agent William Smith. I'm not at my desk right now so please leave a message and I'll get back to you as soon as I can. If this is an emergency press zero three now and you can talk to my assistant."

Jimmy pushed the zero three and was connected to another answering machine.

"Screw this," he said, hanging up in frustration. Josh didn't say anything.

A few minutes later, Josh looked over at Jimmy. "Hey dude, can you like loosen these handcuffs? My hand is really starting to hurt."

"We're almost there so just hang on. I'm trying to hurry, Jimmy replied."

Jimmy put in a call to Tom to check on the status of the Riverside agents. Tom advised that they had been tied up on some warrants but that they'd try to break loose a couple of agents when the San Diego agents got close.

The agents continued through the checkpoint. It was still closed. Forty-five minutes later they were at the junction of Interstate 15 and Interstate 10. Jimmy took Josh's cell phone and found the number in the memory for his contact in Mexico. He dialed the number, hit send and put the call on speaker. Three rings later, a male answered the phone.

"Josh, everything all right?" the man asked.

"Yeah, everything is cool. Any changes for me?"

"No. Just take it over to the shopping center and I'll have Albert come get it. How far away are you?"

"Like ten minutes, maybe fifteen."

"Okay, man. Call me when you're there. Hey, I told you this was easy. Shit man, you made it through like twenty times now and still no problems. See, see."

"Yeah, man, easy," Josh said, looking at Jimmy and hanging his head shamefully.

"Second time, huh?" Jimmy said a little sarcastically. But he let it go and didn't give Josh a hard time about having lied. They all lie, Jimmy thought to himself, but at least this kid is doing the right thing.

"So where's this shopping center?"

"I told you. There's a Target store and some other businesses. It's like off the Mountain exit on the 210."

"That's more than ten or fifteen minutes, at least I think. And I'm pretty sure that's in the city of Upland."

"Oh yeah, I think you're right, it is Upland. I don't know this area all that good," Josh said.

"Yeah, well I don't either so please try to think about anything else you might have gotten wrong."

Jimmy updated the rest of the surveillance via radio and called Bill on the cell phone to direct him to the updated location.

As they exited on Mountain Jimmy's phone rang.

"Jimmy. Where you guys at?" Tom asked.

"Just exiting Mountain Avenue in Upland. Our guy is about to make a call to the crooks to have them come get the car."

"Okay. Let me call Riverside back and check on their status. Hey, I got a call from Border Patrol. You guys go through the checkpoint without getting permission?" Tom asked.

"Hey, I tried. I called and got voicemail. My feelings are if it's not important enough to leave a cell phone number or something it must not be that important."

"Well they're pissed. The RAC got a call and you'll probably hear about it tomorrow. I'll get back to you."

You know, sometimes it just isn't worth all the bureaucratic crap to even try and do a good job, Jimmy said aloud.

"Dude, one arm is numb and the other aches like you can't believe. Please man, I really need you to loosen the cuffs. Please, I'm beggin you," Josh said desperately.

"Okay, okay. Hang on." Jimmy pulled over and got out and went around to Josh's side of the car. He took the handcuffs completely off and put them in the back pocket of his jeans. He returned to the driver's seat of the Expedition and handed Josh the cell phone.

"Okay, man, put in the call."

Josh looked at him for a moment while he rubbed his wrists.

"So why do you now trust me without cuffs?"

"Josh, we're going to put you back in the Audi in a minute. We want the guys who're coming to pick up the car from you to see that things are normal. Here's the deal, and pay very close attention to this. We have you identified. You've cooperated and done a good job so far. If you try and split a felony warrant will be issued and then somewhere, sometime, a cop will pull you over for a ticket or something and you'll go to jail and all this cooperation will have been for nothing. So don't blow it."

"No, no. I won't." Josh picked up the cell phone and started to dial.

"Put it on speaker so I can hear," Jimmy said. He would have preferred to have waited on the Riverside agents, but Josh's contact in Mexico was expecting a call and Jimmy didn't feel he could wait any longer.

"Okay man, I'm here," Josh told his Mexican contact.

"Good. I'll have Albert there shortly," the man said.

"So who's Albert?" Jimmy asked.

"It's Alberto something. I heard his name once but I don't remember."

Jimmy was always amazed at how loose drug traffickers operated, at least at the lower levels. He'd interview countless mopes who'd been caught bringing drugs across the border and asked them where they were going to deliver their dope. It was rare that they were able to give you an address. Most of the time they couldn't even tell you what exit they were going to take. They'd say, 'I don't know the address, but I think I can find it again.' Or, 'I don't know, but I could take you there.'

Jimmy called Bill and had him drive over to his Expedition. A minute later, Bill was alongside him. Bill got out and walked up to Josh's door. He opened it and stood there looking at Josh.

"Get out, man. Go get in the Audi. The keys are in it."

Josh tentatively got out of the Expedition and walked to the Audi, looking over his shoulder at Jimmy.

"Don't forget what I told you. Don't screw this up. You've been doing the right thing so let's not change anything."

As Josh neared the Audi Jimmy yelled at him again.

"As soon as you give the car keys away, walk slowly towards the Target store. Someone will come pick you up."

Josh nodded in understanding.

Jimmy and Bill followed the Audi as it repositioned itself on the east side of the parking lot. The other agents positioned themselves around the parking area covering all the exits.

As they waited, Jimmy's phone rang.

"Maxwell."

"Jimmy, it's Tom. Hey dude, you're going to have to shut down your operation."

"What? What for?"

"Customs Riverside can't break free to come assist you and they apparently called DEA out there to see if they wanted to send someone. The DEA Assistant Special Agent in Charge advised that since there was no real notice given to them, and because no one knows who we're dealing with, they don't want us up there, as he put it, potentially screwing up one of their investigations or having something happen where someone might get hurt. Bottom line, it's too short of notice and it's their sandbox. So you're going to have to call it a nice try."

"Tom, the crooks are one their way. They could be rolling up here any minute."

"If you don't shut it down, there's going to be some pissed off managers in both agencies."

"You know what, fuck them! This is bullshit!"

"Hey, I'm just the messenger so don't take it out on me."

"Jimmy, we've got someone making contact with our boy," Sal put out over the air.

"Ten-four," Jimmy replied. "Tom, we've got bad guys making contact with our cooperator."

"Okay, okay," Tom said, sounding a little perplexed at the situation. "Just box them in and take them off in the parking lot. At least don't try the surveillance to the house. If you lost the load we'd all be up shit creek."

"This is such bullshit," Jimmy said angrily.

"Take the guys off there, Jimmy," Tom said sternly.

"Yeah, yeah. I got it. I'll call you back." Bill had been looking over at Jimmy during the conversation with Tom.

"Dude, we have to put it down?"

"You've got to be kidding," he said, shaking his head and picking up his radio mike. "Guys, when our bad guys get in the Audi, move in on them and box them in. We're going to arrest them here. I repeat, we're not tripping anywhere, we're taking them off here."

"Why?" Barbara asked over the air.

"DEA doesn't trust us to play nice in their sandbox," Jimmy said. "Just take these guys off when they get to the car."

"Ten-Four," came the responses from five puzzled agents.

"We've got one bad guy in the car . . . backup lights . . . standby, the passenger is standing there talking to our boy." The conversation ended and the passenger started getting in the car while Josh walked away. "Okay, GO! GO! GO!" Jimmy put out on the radio.

Within seconds the agents had converged on the Audi, boxing it in so it had nowhere to go. The two suspects stared in shock as agents ran to them with drawn guns. Before they had time to react, the doors of the Audi were pulled open and the men were grabbed and pulled out. Once proned out on the asphalt, they were handcuffed and then sat up. Passersby in the parking lot gave the agents a wide berth, staring at what would likely be one of their high points of the day to talk about over dinner.

Jimmy watched as the two men were patted down. He'd been watching Josh who was staring wide-eyed from about fifty yards away. He gave a palm-down gesture indicating that he wanted Josh to just wait there. Josh nodded in understanding. Jimmy was also watching the rest of the activity in the parking lot, making sure there was no counter-surveillance activity. Nothing appeared to be out of the ordinary. Once the subjects were patted down they were separated, one seated in the back seat of Sal's car, the other in the back seat of Barbara's car.

Jimmy motioned for Bill to come over to him. Bill walked over.

"What's up?"

"Hey, I'm going to go have a short chat with our two new friends. Here, take the keys to the Expedition," Jimmy said, dropping his keys in Bill's hand discreetly. "Do me a favor and go pick up Josh. Yell at him a little so these other two idiots hear you, then handcuff him so they see it. It'll probably freak out Josh a little, but it might make his stay at MCC a little better. Tell him that he needs to convince these guys that he didn't know he was being followed."

Bill nodded that he understood and then walked over to the defendant seated in Barbara's car.

"You guys see where that other guy went?" he asked loudly, looking around.

"Yeah, I think I saw him hiding over behind a car towards, yeah, there he is!" Barbara said loudly, giving Bill a hint of a smile.

Bill ran over to Jimmy's Expedition, started it and drove over to Josh. They were far enough away that while you couldn't make out the words, you could hear loud voices. Bill grabbed Josh and pushed him up against the Expedition, giving him a quick pat down. Josh was handcuffed and put in the back seat of the Expedition. It was a pretty good show.

Jimmy had walked over to the defendant in Barbara's car. He looked at the defendant and showed him his credentials.

"You speak English, bud?" he asked.

"No, no *habla* English," the heavyset man replied.

"Figures," Jimmy said walking over to Sal's car. Jimmy again took his credentials and showed the other seated Mexican male. This man was about thirty, much thinner and more neatly dressed.

"How about you, you speak English?"

"A little," the man said with a Mexican accent.

"Well, I'm a criminal investigator with U.S. Customs. I guess you know why you're sitting in handcuffs, but if you don't, I'll be happy to explain it."

Sal moved over to the defendant, standing close to him and staring at him, his menacing size and demeanor having the desired impact. The defendant looked up at Sal, then gave a slight nod but said nothing.

"You got some identification?"

"His wallet is with some other stuff we took from his pockets on the hood of my car," Sal said.

Jimmy walked to the front of the car and picked up the wallet. He opened it and took out a California identification card. He also noticed a large roll of bills amongst the personal property. Jimmy picked it up, removed the rubber band, unrolled it, and thumbed through it. There were a few hundreds, but it was mostly twenties and tens. Jimmy put the rubber band back around the roll and returned it to the hood.

"You were the driver, weren't you?" Jimmy asked.

"Yeah."

Jimmy looked at the identification card, comparing the photograph with the defendant. Then he read the name.

"Oswaldo, right? Oswaldo Ruvalcaba?" The man nodded his head. "Well Oswaldo, do you have a driver's license?"

"It's suspended."

"Why? You not paying your tickets or was it a DUI?"

"I got arrested for drunk driving last year."

"That's what I thought. Well, looks like we have another charge to arrest Oswaldo on," Jimmy said to Sal with a smile.

Sal took a few steps towards Jimmy, turned sideways away from Oswaldo and whispered, "Yeah, and he'll probably get more time on the DMV violation than for the dope charge."

Jimmy gave Sal a wink and then turned back to Oswaldo. "Oswaldo, I need you to listen closely, okay? Dude, you are in a lot of trouble. I know you know what's in the car, so here's the deal. You drive us over to the house where you were taking this, and I'll talk to the prosecutor and let them know you've been cooperative. Do you think you might be willing to work with us on something like that?"

"But I'm still going to jail?"

"You're still going to jail."

"Then why should I help you?" Oswaldo asked.

"Because it might help you not to be in jail for as long. Look, let's say that the judge looks at the amount of drugs we find in the car and decides to put you in prison for ten years. Now, I'm not saying you're going to get ten years. I really don't know what you'll get. But just to illustrate my point, let's say ten years. Then the judge finds out that we found drugs in the house where you were taking this car to be unloaded. He figures that you were remorseful. You know, sorry enough about being a drug dealer that you decided to help us take those drugs off the streets. So he knocks off five of the ten years. If you have to go to jail, wouldn't five years be better than ten?"

Oswaldo sat there for a moment pondering what Jimmy had told him.

"But I'd still have to go to jail, right?"

"Yeah, but the point is, if you help us it might shorten the amount of time you spend with us," Jimmy said slowly, trying to make himself understood.

Oswaldo just looked at Jimmy without saying anything. Jimmy stared at him silently for about thirty seconds wondering if he was not understanding his options or whether or not he could believe him.

"This guy is just stupid, I guess," Jimmy finally said to Sal. I think I'll go try working on the other guy." Jimmy turned and walked away. As he neared Barbara's car, he called Sector Communications and asked to be patched into Upland Police Department. Once connected, he asked if they had an available Spanish-speaking patrol officer who could come by their location.

While waiting for the officer to arrive, Jimmy identified his second defendant as Fausto Franco. He had no criminal history on record under that name and there were no warrants outstanding for his arrest.

It took about fifteen minutes for the officer to arrive. Jimmy explained the offer he wanted proposed. The message seemed to sink in with Fausto and he accepted the proposal. Jimmy had the officer advise Franco of his rights, then asked him to show them where they were going. The officer wrote down his name, badge number and contact information in case he was needed in court, then cleared for another call. Jimmy shook the officer's hand, thanking him for the help before he left.

Franco took Barbara and Jimmy to a residence about half a mile from the shopping center. They drove by, got the address and then returned to the parking lot. As they drove up to the other agents who were waiting, Sal came over to Barbara's car. Jimmy rolled down the window.

"Hey, Jimmy. Oswaldo says he'll show you the house where they were going."

"Too late. We've got it already. Hey, have him sign a waiver of venue form so we can get out of here, okay. I really don't want to have to take him to downtown L.A. to book him into custody. What you can do also is advise him of his rights and do a good interview of him while we drive back to San Diego. I'd like to get him to cop to knowing exactly what was in the car."

"Aren't we going to get a team of locals and go hit the stash house?" Sal asked. "You know we're missing an Alberto and who knows who else might be at the house."

"Yeah, I know, but no. We have our orders. We'll have to turn the whole thing over to our Riverside counterparts. We were ordered not to do anything. I've already stretched the envelope a little just going over to the house. You know, everyone thinks that being a fed gives you this national authority to enforce federal laws throughout the country. What a bunch of crap. I had more juice to enforce the law as a city cop than I do now," Jimmy said, getting into his Expedition and slamming the door.

During the drive back to San Diego, Jimmy called Tom and apprised him of their status. He found himself complaining, something he normally didn't do too much of, about the fact that they weren't allowed to conduct the enforcement action that should have been done. If anything was in the house he'd identified it would likely be gone in the next few hours.

Jimmy also complained about the lack of Spanish speakers being directed to Operation Alliance. It was going to be another late night due to the fact that they'd have to wait until they got to San Ysidro and could track down a Spanish-speaking Inspector to help do the interview of Fausto Franco.

Jimmy called his wife and advised her of his status. She sighed in resignation and put Nikki on the phone for a few minutes.

As they neared the Port of Entry, Jimmy's phone rang again.

"Jimmy, it's Carmen. Can I see you?"

"Is everything all right?"

"I got a call from San Francisco Police. Jose Leon's wife has been found up in San Francisco. Jimmy, she's dead. They want me to go identify her body."

"Why do they want you to go? How did they even know to contact you?"

"They found a phone number for Jose in her purse and called him. He apparently told them he was in Mexico on business and wasn't available and asked them to call me. He said I was her closest friend and that I could identify her. Jimmy, I don't want to go, but I don't know what else to do. Why would Jose have me go up there?"

"Carmen. Listen to me. You're not going. Do you hear me, I don't want you to go," Jimmy said. His intention was to be protective of her, but he realized he sounded much harsher than he'd wanted.

"Can you come see me so we can talk?" she asked pleadingly.

"I've got a prisoner to deal with, but I'll be there as soon as I can. It's nearly six o'clock now," he said looking at his watch. "It might be close to ten before I can get there. How about if I come by first thing in the morning before you leave for work?"

"No. Please come by tonight," she insisted.

"Carmen, I want to see you. I really do, but I have no one to bring with me at that hour. The guys have been out all day and if I ask someone to come they'll wonder why I couldn't put this off until tomorrow. You know I'm attracted to you and that we're flirting with trouble here. So do you really want me to come by tonight?"

"Yes. I really need to see you."

"I'll call you when I'm on my way."

Jimmy hung up the phone, thinking about what she'd told him. He wondered who had killed Jose's wife. He wondered why Jose would want Carmen to go identify her. It didn't seem to make a lot of sense. Then his thoughts drifted to Carmen.

He was in love with her. He wasn't sure how it happened, but it had and he didn't feel comfortable about meeting her, especially late at night and alone.

As he continued his drive to San Ysidro, he remained lost in his thoughts for several minutes. Something out of the corner of his eye caught his attention and he glanced over at Josh who was looking at him quizzically. Jimmy noticed the look. "So what? Your handcuffs too tight again?" he asked.

"I don't know. My arms are too numb to know anymore."

They drove another minute in silence.

"Is she good looking?" Josh asked in a sober tone. Jimmy looked at him without saying anything. "Cause those are the ones that will make big problems for you. I know what I'm talking about, man. Big problems and they'll break your heart."

"How do you know anything about anything? You're twenty-two years old," Jimmy said.

Jimmy drove in silence, remembering when he first met Carmen. She was beautiful, both in body and in spirit. She was so strong, silent, distant. She seemed to know exactly what she was doing and why. Sure she was upset about the issues surrounding Angel's business, his arrest, and the various threats to her based on her connection to him, but she had never pleaded for anything, had never sounded so broken down. She was a woman alone, but she'd never given Jimmy the impression that she was really alone. Now she was pleading for him to be there for her.

'Big problems.' Those words, even from a drug smuggling little weasel like Josh seemed to resonate in Jimmy's mind.

Chapter . . .

22

Jimmy knocked on Carmen's door at 10:40 p.m. She opened the door wearing a very sheer pair of pajamas. Carmen led him into the living room and as she moved Jimmy could make out her form moving behind the material. Jimmy followed her into the house and sat next to her on the sofa.

"So what's this all about? I mean, I really don't get why Leon would single you out like this. Surely there must be other people who know this woman better than you?"

"Jimmy, I don't know. I've been sitting here thinking about it myself. You know Angel was his trusted right-hand man for so long that, now that he's locked up, and since I'm his wife, maybe he thinks he can trust me too. Maybe there's just no one else. He's obviously not going to go to a police station, even for something like this."

"I don't want him using you like this. First of all, I don't want you to see ugliness like that. Secondly, well I just don't want you doing anything for him." Jimmy paused and looked at her as she put her hand on his knee. "All right?" Jimmy asked. "Look, Carmen. You're not part of this world. You weren't part of Angel's life. I don't want you even slightly involved in any of this, this crap."

"You've got nothing to worry about, Jimmy." Carmen said with a weak smile, a tear forming in her eyes.

As he talked to Carmen, he couldn't keep from suppressing the feelings that had been building, that he had been fighting for the past three or four months. It made talking with her more than a little uncomfortable. It was hard to concentrate on what she was saying at times. It felt like it was his wife, a wife he'd never known except in his fantasies, talking to him about a problem.

Work decisions were easy, but he found himself sitting with her now trying to make a decision about what to do and all he felt was uncertainty. He felt like he had to have her consensus or permission to suggest a course of action for her. It wasn't that she had ever given him a hard time about any of his suggestions. On the contrary, she seemed to always agree with him. Here though, the decisions that would be made could be life altering. He cared too much about her to want her to do anything that might jeopardize her safety or sense of security.

She was obviously looking to him for guidance. As she looked at him, touched him, his thoughts kept drifting back to her, how she looked, how she felt as she touched him. He should be thinking things through analytically. Instead, he sat resisting the temptation to hold her. He forced himself to focus.

"So what happened? Why do you think this woman ended up dead?"

"I called Leonora earlier this evening. I didn't know who else to call that might know. We talked about a lot of things including Angel's arrest. She was upset but I think she knew it was bound to happen. I even think she's a little relieved. Having him in jail is certainly better than him ending up dead, something that probably would have happened sooner or later if he stayed in his business."

Jimmy didn't really like hearing about Angel, or his family, but he politely listened despite the fact that she was taking so long to get to the point of what happened to Jose Leon's wife.

"You know, Jose went down and visited Leonora too—several times. He was there last week. He threatened her just like he did me."

"I wonder who's running his dope-trafficking business while he's been tied up looking for his wife?" Jimmy said sarcastically, regretting his tone as soon as the words came out of his mouth.

Carmen continued telling him about her conversation with her sister-in-law, seeming to ignore the sarcasm. "I think Elvira had been talking to her all the way up until just before she was killed. Leonora seemed to know a lot." Carmen paused again as a tear ran down her cheek.

"She'd been having an affair with this bodyguard for several months. He convinced her to take a bunch of money and run off with him. Elvira took a little over two million dollars and stashed most of it in a safety deposit box up in San Francisco. She kept a little bit and she and the kids met with her boyfriend down in a little town south of Mexico City. I guess that after they'd been down there a few months the boyfriend convinced her that they were going to live happily ever after, so she got on an airplane and flew up to San Francisco to pick up the cash. They were going to move to South America and live happily ever after. He followed her to San Francisco and sometime after she retrieved the money, he strangled her and left her body in the hotel room." Carmen started to cry. Jimmy just sat next to her, reaching over to hold her hand.

Once she composed herself, she looked up at Jimmy and with anger and hurt in her voice he'd never heard before she continued. "You know, it's bad enough to kill someone over money, someone you trusted and changed your whole life for, but do you know what that bastard did? He flew back south and murdered her two kids."

"How did Leonora get this story?"

"From Jose Leon himself. Jose had put the word to various Mexican law enforcement agencies that he was looking for this guy. When the man arrived back in Mexico City, someone in the Federal Protective Police noticed his name, ran some checks and decided to detain him. Jose flew down there and questioned him himself. He admitted everything he'd done."

Jimmy stared at a spot on the wall, imagining what that interrogation was like.

"I wonder why he told Leonora?" he finally said.

"He wanted her to call me and tell me the story so I would agree to go identify the body.

"Do you think the story is true?"

"Leonora says she just got the newspaper article this morning that details the murder of the children. He threw them off a cliff outside of the town where they were staying."

"How old were they?"

"One was four, the other seven." Carmen began crying again, putting her face in her hands. Jimmy moved closer to her and put his arms around her, pulling her to him.

"When is this all going to end?" she sobbed.

Jimmy held her as she cried. Several minutes passed with no other words. Jimmy let Carmen cry, her tears soaking the front of his shirt. His cell phone rang as she continued to sob. He took it from his belt clip and saw that it was from his wife. He ignored the call, letting it go to voicemail.

Carmen took her head from his chest and looked up at him. Even without makeup she was an incredibly beautiful woman. Her pajama top had opened enough that he could see most of her breasts as he looked down at her. He forced himself to look away and focus on the more important issues at hand.

"I'm sorry. Do you have to go?" she said.

"I can stay for a few more minutes. Are you going to be all right?"

"Yes. I'll be fine." She paused a moment then looked at him again. "I wish you could stay."

"Me too," he said softly.

"Jimmy, I have to go to San Francisco. I don't know why, but I have to go."

"I really wish you wouldn't. Why don't you have them fax a picture of her to you?"

"It might do me good to get out of here for a day or two, even if it is to go do that."

"Listen, I'm no one here. I know my vote doesn't count, but at least promise me that you won't call and talk to Jose Leon. Any information you need to get to him, give it to Leonora and let her talk to him. And tell her to tell him you want no further contact or involvement in his fucked up life."

Carmen nodded in agreement. Jimmy stood up, both angry and sad that he had to leave her. He walked to the front door and turned, finding Carmen right behind him.

"I really don't want to go," he said.

"I don't want you to go."

Jimmy wrapped his arms around her and kissed her passionately, his hands traveling down the small of her back, then back up along her sides. When he finished, he pushed back from her gently, staring into her eyes.

"I've got to go."

"I know," she said sadly.

Jimmy opened the door and stepped outside, closing the door behind him. He stood at the front entrance for a moment, looking around the quiet, dark neighborhood before finally deciding that he needed to go home.

As he drove his thoughts assaulted him. He was angry with himself for kissing her, looking at her the way he had, thinking of making love to her. He had resisted, but he didn't know how much longer he would be able to.

He thought about this woman Elvira, who had been alive a few days ago, trying to escape with her children from what must have been a difficult life with a very dangerous man, only to have it backfire and end up in her demise. She had traded one problem for another much worse. It was hard to image how cold and dead a living man must be to be able to brutally murder two small children.

He thought about his career and how negative an impact there would be on it if some of the people he worked with found out that he was thinking about having a relationship with Carmen. He was a federal agent, a man who was good at what he did. He had worked hard to get to this point in his life. He had the public's trust, and the trust of his bosses and his peers. If they had seen him tonight, how would they feel about trusting him or even working with him in the future?

He thought about his family. He had made a commitment to his wife that he would be there, for better or for worse, in sickness and in health, until death do you part. He realized he'd made a mistake marrying Shirley, but he had married her. He believed in the sanctity of marriage, the commitment of marriage, and in honoring his vows. He cared about his wife, and he loved his little girl more than he could even begin to express.

As he thought about his marriage, his mind went to God. There was never a day in his life that Jimmy doubted the existence of God. Throughout most of his life he had been pretty devout in his faith and in his relationship with God. The last few years had been much more difficult. He had become more and more busy, spending less time reading his Bible and praying.

The issues with his wife had become a major distraction from his devotions and prayer time. He had once been accustomed to having an occasional drink. Now he averaged four or five drinks nightly. Where he had once only occasionally let a swear word leave his mouth, they now flowed much more freely.

All of these thoughts bounced around inside him. Things were a mess. Jimmy was very unhappy, and very stressed at the state of affairs he found himself in. As he pulled into his driveway, he suddenly realized he hadn't called Shirley back. He needed a drink.

He walked into his house, noticing that the television was on in the living room. He walked into the kitchen and poured several fingers of bourbon, swallowing about half of it in gulp. He replenished the amount he'd drunk from the glass, put the bottle away, then walked into the living room. Shirley looked over at him from her position in the easy chair. She was wearing a robe.

Jimmy walked over to her, bent down and gave her a little kiss. He walked over to the sofa, sat down, and kicked off his shoes, putting his feet up on the coffee table.

"Honey, don't put your feet on the coffee table. You're going to scratch it."

"I took my shoes off so I wouldn't," he replied.

She frowned but let it go. "I tried to call you earlier."

"I'm sorry, I meant to call you back, but got distracted. I was in an interview." He paused for a moment while Shirley looked at him, waiting for him to continue. He felt like she was trying to probe his mind.

"It was a long day. We ended up trying to deliver a load of dope to the Riverside area, Upland actually, and after getting all the way up there we had DEA tell us that they didn't want us doing our job. They cut short our operation before we could get the dope delivered to a stash house."

"Why do you let them dictate to you how to do your job?"

"It's always been that way. It just seems to get worse every year. There's always been the issue of geographical jurisdiction. It's based on how the courts are set up. If you arrest someone they have the right to be taken before the nearest judge, so they break our offices down based on the court's jurisdictional areas. It really shouldn't make a difference to us, as long as the arresting officer knows where to take his arrestee. But this crap between DEA and Customs is ridiculous. We have the authority to enforce any federal law. Then the idiots in headquarters take our authority and give it away in an MOU."

"What's an M-O-U?" Shirley asked. "I've heard you mention that before I think."

"A memorandum of understanding. Representatives from the agencies involved get together and decide who's going to have primary jurisdiction over what type of cases. So somehow DEA gets given primary jurisdiction over all Title 21 narcotics cases. The idiots in charge of our agency just give our authority away. We get to work any narcotics cases that deal with smuggling of drugs into the U.S. They get the domestic drug cases and whatever else they want. We don't normally get to work the domestic drug cases, but they can work smuggling cases, and, in fact, invite themselves into our cases if they decide it's sexy enough. It's crazy. Like I've said many times before, this is a target rich environment, with more than enough work for all of us. It's no wonder we're losing the war on drugs. We get told not to do our job by other law enforcement agencies."

Jimmy paused, shook his head, and then another drink of his bourbon. Shirley started to get up.

"Tell me about your day. Why'd you call?" he asked.

Shirley sat back down. "Nikki was coming down the stairs and fell."

"Is she okay?" Jimmy asked.

"It was only a couple of steps. She cried for about five minutes. Once I calmed her down she wanted to talk to her daddy on the phone."

"Ohhh, I'm really sorry I couldn't answer. What was she doing up so late?"

"She had a bad dream. She heard the television on and came down to be with us. I just got her back to bed about ten minutes before you came in."

Jimmy got up. "I think I'll go look in on her," he said.

"Don't wake her up," Shirley said as Jimmy bounded up the stairs.

Nikki was sleeping peacefully when Jimmy looked in on her. He sat down on the bed next to her and just watched her sleep for a few minutes. She was so beautiful, so tender, so innocent. The look of her touched his heart and a single tear rolled down his cheek.

Jimmy knew she would always be a huge part of his life, but as he watched her, his thoughts drifted back to Carmen. He wanted her in his life. He momentarily let himself wonder if there was a way to have both, but then realized the thought was an exercise in futility and dismissed it. Sitting there looking at Nikki, he began to wonder how little Raul felt without having a father around. Life seemed to be getting far too complicated, far too unfair. He brushed back the hair from her face. Swallowing the last of his bourbon, he rose and decided to go pour one more.

You've got to quit torturing yourself with these stupid thoughts about Carmen, he told himself as he poured another drink. *What's wrong with you, Jimmy Maxwell? You have a family and a good life. You are not going to screw it up.*

He finished another drink, then went up stairs and brushed his teeth. Shirley was already asleep. He lay down next to her, looking over at her. She sometimes felt almost like a stranger to him. He lay on his back and stared at the ceiling for a moment, but mercifully fell asleep quickly before any new thoughts could torment him.

CHAPTER . . .

23

It was another typical day in San Diego. The skies were blue and the temperature in the mid seventies. The relative humidity was about forty percent. It would probably warm up into the mid eighties by mid-afternoon. Most people that spent any real time in San Diego agree that it has the best climate in the world.

Jimmy wasn't thinking about the climate or the beautiful day unfolding. The drive to work found Jimmy still consumed in his thoughts about Carmen and his personal life. But to add to his misery, he wasn't feeling well. His head hurt, his mouth was dry, and things seemed a little hazy. He'd had three cups of coffee, a glass of juice, and some water but was still feeling a little dehydrated. He didn't think he'd had that much to drink. Maybe it was time to start cutting back.

The traffic was getting heavy and Jimmy found himself cursing some of the idiots who didn't seem to know what they were doing behind the wheel. *There's no good reason for traffic to stop on a freeway*, he thought as he fought the urge to use his emergency lights to get a few of the knuckleheaded drivers out of his lane.

He honked his horn at the vehicle in front of him. The driver was going so slow in the fast lane that everyone was going around it, filling into the lengthy gap the driver allowed between herself and the car in front of her. Jimmy finally pulled out into a gap in the traffic and went around the woman to her right, noticing she was putting on her eyeliner. He looked over and shook his head in disapproval. She raised her middle finger at him as his cell phone rang. Looking at the display, Jimmy noticed it was Sector Communications.

"Top of the morning, Sector," Jimmy said, trying to sound far more cheerful than he really was.

"Hey Jimmy, it's Jason. I've got a Special Agent Larry Adams on the phone for you."

"Don't know the man. Who's he?"

"He's a Customs agent in Los Angeles."

"Uh, okay, put him through." Jimmy knew a few of the agents in Los Angeles but he'd never heard of this one.

"Hey, Agent Maxwell, Larry Adams. Am I catching you at a bad time?"

"You got me just before I started going postal. The traffic sucks this morning."

Larry laughed. "I know what you mean. You should try driving up here."

"I have, thanks. I'll keep San Diego. What can I do for you?"

"We're on our way down to Chula Vista. We've got a female source that is supposed to meet a crook, and then hopefully follow him to a house where she's supposed to pick up two hundred kilos of coke. I was told I needed to bring a San Diego agent on board who can work the stash house end of the investigation. I don't know any San Diego agents except Robert Flores who I went to the academy with. He's in the Fraud Group. I called him earlier and he said if I needed an agent to work with I should give you a call."

"That was kind of him. I'll beat him later." There was silence on the other end of Jimmy's phone. "Hey, I was kidding. I'd be happy to help. What's your ETA and where do you want to meet?"

"I have no idea. I really don't know the area. We're in Oceanside, so what, we're about forty minutes or so out?"

"More like an hour, if the traffic cooperates. It usually gets really bad around Del Mar. You might be longer than an hour."

"So where's a convenient place to meet when we do get there?"

"At the I-5, 805 split, take the 805. Go all the way to 'H' Street in Chula Vista, go east a block and I'll meet you in the little shopping center there just off the freeway," Jimmy suggested.

"Okay. I'll call you again when we're almost there."

"Shit," Jimmy said aloud. "Just when you thought you were going to get a little break."

Ninety minutes later Jimmy rendezvoused with half a dozen Los Angeles agents in the Terra Nova Shopping Center in Chula Vista.

"Agent Maxwell, this is Yesenia. She's our friendly who's supposed to meet a guy named Horacio Velasquez. At least that's the name he's using. Don't know much about the guy except he's in his early thirties."

Jimmy nodded politely to Yesenia as she slid down of the seat of a full-sized, brown Ford Bronco to the asphalt of the parking lot. The Bronco made her look even smaller than she was. Once standing next to him, Jimmy shook hands with her. She was a typical-looking Hispanic female, medium length brown hair and a medium brown skin tone. She was in her mid-twenties, a woman with average facial features but a great body. She wore a low-cut blouse that showed a lot of her assets. Jimmy guessed it was to distract whoever she might run into as to her business. She said something to him in Spanish that Jimmy didn't understand.

"*Mi Espanol es muy malo,*" Jimmy said, doing his best to tell her his Spanish was bad. She nodded and smiled.

"So what's the game plan?" Jimmy asked Larry.

"We're going to have her put in a call to him in a minute. I don't know if he's going to tell her to come to the house or if he'll come over here and meet her and take the car. After talking to her a little more on the drive down, I'm thinking that it's unlikely that she'll go to the stash house, but maybe. Yesenia does come highly recommended by the guy the dope's going to. I guess we'll make the call and see."

"Is there a tracker on the car?" Jimmy asked.

"No. We'll just have to put surveillance on the vehicle to get the stash house identified."

"Wish I would have known, I could have brought one," Jimmy said.

Yesenia made the call to Velasquez. He asked where she was, then advised her that he'd be there in fifteen minutes.

"Can you guys get me the number to this guy Velasquez?" Jimmy asked.

"I'll give you the number if you want, but it's one of those cell phones that you buy over the counter with no contract, you know, the ones you just buy minutes for," Larry said.

"Figures," Jimmy said. "Those throw-away phones are a crook's best friend these days."

"Come on guys, let's break up our little party here and get set up to follow Yesenia's car to the stash house," Larry said to his team members who were all standing around chatting with each other. The crew dispersed in short order, mingling with the rest of the several hundred cars in the parking lot.

Velasquez showed up nearly forty minutes later, typical for a trafficker. It was rare that anyone in the dope business was on time. Jimmy had always figured that if a drug trafficker was responsible enough to be on time to anything, he'd be responsible enough to have a real job. Velasquez took the keys from Yesenia, telling her to do some shopping and he'd be back in an hour.

The surveillance team followed Velasquez to 807 Hillcrest Street. The Bronco went into the garage, the garage door closing behind it. Agents set up around the area and waited.

Jimmy parked a block south of the residence. The residence was across the street from a high school. Jimmy noticed a few teens in gym wear walking around the track watching him. He ignored them and looked down the street at the target residence waiting for the Bronco to re-emerge. As he sat waiting, he wondered how many other homes in the San Diego area were full of illegal drugs. U.S. Customs alone burned thousands of pounds of drugs a month, and they were probably only seizing a small percentage of what was coming across the border.

Jimmy's phone rang as he sat waiting.

"Agent Maxwell, hey, if our guy just drops the vehicle with Yesenia and leaves, we're just going to take off with her back to L.A. and let her deliver the dope. I wanted to thank you for coming out and helping. I do need to ask you not to take any action on this residence until I call you and let you know it's cool. We really don't want to burn Yesenia or have the investigation taken down before we've done our thing. My guess is that a few weeks from now you can do something with the house, although utilizing a local law enforcement team would be better because it would wall off our agency's involvement in the loss they're going to have today."

"No problem. Hey, I appreciate you guys giving me a call. Let me know how it works out up there, and yeah, I know the Chula locals pretty well. I'm sure they'd love to come work this place with me."

"Good. I'm sure we'll talk soon."

The garage door opened about forty-five minutes later and the Bronco pulled out onto the street and turned north. Ten minutes later it was back at the shopping center. Jimmy stayed back but heard one of the surveillance agents advise that the driver had given Yesenia the keys to the Bronco. A minute later, the Bronco pulled out of the shopping center westbound. Jimmy pulled closer to the exchange point and was able to get the vehicle license plate on the vehicle driven by Velasquez as he left the area.

Back at the office, Jimmy advised Tom of his morning activities. Tom listened without emotion, seemingly preoccupied with something else.

"By the way, DEA called and apologized for cutting your stay short in Upland last week. I don't think they understood at the time that it was a controlled delivery from the port."

"How could they not know? What happened?"

"I'm not sure. I think they got to thinking about it and realized they shouldn't have taken such a hard-line stance. Maybe they realized that they might get similar treatment the next time they have to come down here."

"You mean they realized that they're dicks?" Tom didn't respond. "Did they go hit the house we gave them and get something good?" Jimmy asked.

"Yeah. I think they only got a few pounds of dope, but they got three hundred grand and arrested a couple of mopes."

"What a bunch of crap," Jimmy said with a sigh. "Sure wish they'd give us a kiss once in awhile before they fucked us."

"Arlene is unhappy with us again. She thinks it's your fault for not explaining to the Riverside agents the details of your controlled delivery."

"Are you kidding me? Explain what? I didn't talk to anyone up there, let alone explain anything. I called you and you did the coordinating."

"I know. And believe me, I explained to her what was going on. That said, she seems to be having selective memory when it comes to getting calls from the SAC and getting scolded. He thinks she didn't push hard enough on DEA and that we should have been the ones to have gone in the house and made the seizures and arrests."

"Good, because he's right, although the seizures would have belonged to the Riverside office anyway since they happened in their jurisdiction. And you have to wonder what might have been in the house had we hit it earlier."

Tom nodded in agreement, then continued. "This doesn't go anywhere, understand?" Tom said, looking at Jimmy.

He nodded. "She's had her ass chewed a few times in the last month, and it's usually following one of your cases."

"Hey, I'm just doing my job."

"Doesn't matter. I don't want you talking about this with the troops. You're in her sights, and my guess is she's going to look for some way to screw you. She can be a vindictive bitch, and right now she sees you as the enemy. You probably need to slow down a bit, pass off most of your good cases to other agents and stay out of the forefront of things for a while. Maybe she'll cool down and find someone else to focus on."

"Great, just great!" Jimmy sighed, then paused to reflect a moment. "What's wrong with people? You know what, I'm not going to change a thing. I'm not doing anything wrong, so if she wants to try to screw me somehow, let her."

"Okay, Jimmy. Be a hardhead and don't listen," Tom said, staring into Jimmy's eyes. Jimmy stared back, wondering momentarily if he wasn't being hardheaded. After a moment, Tom sighed. "I'll do my best to run interference for you, but no guarantees."

Jimmy rose and started for the door.

"So you're not doing anything with the coke stash house for a while, right?" Tom asked.

"No. It'll probably be a couple of weeks. I'll let you know."

The next few days passed uneventfully. Jimmy went by the Hillcrest residence on his way in every morning, and on his way home every evening, taking down license plate numbers of every car he saw at the residence. Several of them were crossing the border quite regularly.

Jimmy hadn't heard from Carmen since she'd left for the bay area, and he started getting a little anxious about her and what was going on. He tried to call her several times, but there was no answer. He left a message the first time he didn't hear from her, but then decided against the messages on his subsequent attempts to reach her.

After five or six days of not hearing from her, he was sitting home watching television one evening with Shirley when his cell phone rang. He picked it up and noticed the call was from Carmen. He silenced the ring and put the phone back on his belt clip.

"Why aren't you answering the phone?" Shirley asked, looking over at him quizzically.

"It's just one of my snitches," he lied. "They can wait until tomorrow." Jimmy went back to watching television.

"So what's going on, are you turning over a new leaf, or what?" she remarked. Jimmy looked over at her, rolled his eyes and sighed while shaking his head. He didn't reply.

Half an hour later, he excused himself to go to the bathroom. Hitting the message options button on his phone, he listened to the message. "Hi, Jimmy. I'm back to work. Just wanted you to know so you wouldn't worry. Call me when you can."

As he came out of the bathroom, he almost ran into his wife.

"So who was it that called you? I heard you dialing numbers on your phone. I knew you'd call and see who left you a message." She stood in front of him, waiting for an answer.

"It was bothering me, not knowing what the message was. It's a source who had to go up to San Francisco and identify a body. I wanted to make sure she was all right.One of her friends got murdered. As a matter of fact, this woman and both of her kids got murdered. I decided I'd see how she was doing."

"Naturally," Shirley said sarcastically. "So you going over to see her and hold her hand?"

"She's fine. What is wrong with you? You know, half the people of the world, maybe more, are women. And I have to work with a bunch of them, so get used to it." Jimmy walked past his wife, brushing against her as she continued to stand in his way.

"Jimmy, you piece of shit, why do you treat me like this? You're a prick! I just wanted to know who she was." Shirley turned and stormed off to the bedroom.

Jimmy sat down in the living room and tried to calm down. He normally didn't get angry, but he was beginning to reach the end of his fuse. He opened the liquor cabinet and poured several fingers of Knob Creek.

The next morning, Jimmy left for work, again deciding to drive by the Hillcrest residence. Just as he departed the residence, his cell phone rang.

"Maxwell."

"Hey, it's Larry Adams. Am I catching you at a bad time?"

"No, just on my way into the office. Matter of fact, I just went by your Chula Vista address."

"That's why I'm calling. Yesenia's in the wind. We haven't heard from her in several days. She's not answering her phone and no one's seen her."

"Wow, hope she's okay," Jimmy said.

"Me too. We ended up making several arrests following the delivery of the cocaine she picked up. I'm sure someone was not happy about losing two hundred kilos of cocaine, not to mention having several of their worker bees ending up in the bucket. In any event, I'm calling to let you know you can do whatever you want with that residence."

"Great. You sure though? We can give it a little longer if you want."

"No, go ahead and do what needs to be done. Just don't mention Yesenia or our office's involvement in any affidavits."

"No problem. I'll let you know how it works out."

Driving to the office, Jimmy decided he'd also call Carmen. She answered on the first ring.

"Hi, this is Carmen."

"Hey, I got your message last night, but couldn't call you back. I'm sorry. Are you all right? Did the trip go okay? I was getting kind of worried about you."

"I'm fine. It was a little hard, being up there by myself, but it's better now that I'm home."

"Did you take Raul with you?"

"No, he stayed with my mom. She likes it when he comes over, and I don't think it would have been good for him to be around me up there. He would have worried."

"Well I'm glad you're back. Can I stop and see you tonight on my way home?"

"Do you want to see me?" she asked tentatively.

"Of course. Why wouldn't I?" Jimmy asked.

"Are you going to bring another agent with you?"

"Do I need to?" Jimmy asked teasingly.

"Maybe," Carmen said flirtatiously.

"Good, then I'll be alone." Jimmy told her he'd be over around 6:30 p.m. and hung up with a smile. As he drove he began to get nervous about going over alone. He wondered if it was a mistake.

At the office, Jimmy looked at his list of license plates he'd seen at the residence. There were three that seemed to be pretty regular visitors. He decided to put them on lookout so they'd be stopped and searched when they crossed the border.

As Jimmy drove back to the office after lunch, he got a call from Sector Communications.

"Jimmy, hey it's Angie. Give Inspector Hawthorne at the Otay Mesa Port of Entry a call."

"Okay. Thanks, Angie. By the way, where have you been hiding? I haven't heard from you in a while."

"Midnights, darlin."

"Well it's good to have the A team back," Jimmy said.

"Ohhh, how sweet," she said. "When you coming to Florida to visit me?"

"As soon as you can get my wife to give me a hall pass," Jimmy said with a little laugh.

Jimmy called the Otay Mesa Port of Entry's Security Office.

"Hey, Agent Maxwell. This is Inspector Hawthorne. Got one of your lookouts down here. Congratulations. Looks like the gas tank is full of coke."

"No kidding. What's the plate?" Jimmy asked.

"It's a Plymouth van with Baja plates. Looks like you just put this on lookout this morning. I'll have to go find the paperwork to get you the plate."

"Never mind. I know which vehicle it is. Any chance of doing a delivery if I get down there quick?"

"I don't think so. We've already dropped the tank and I think the driver's in a cell. Sorry, man."

"Oh well. Hey, I'll be there in about thirty minutes."

"Anything else we could do for you?" Inspector Hawthorne asked. It sounded to Jimmy like he was trying to sound apologetic over the fact that the van was non-deliverable.

"Nope. Thanks."

Jimmy hung up, then called Tom and advised him about the lookout. He explained his mild frustration over the fact that the inspectors had jumped the gun a little, dismantling the vehicle to the point that a controlled delivery to the Hillcrest residence wasn't going to be possible. It was a common reoccurrence as the inspectors gloried in the seizure at the moment but usually gave little thought to the investigative or overall prosecutorial aspects of a case.

"Tom, can you send Deron and Bill down to give me a hand? And just so you know, I'm planning on heading over and doing a knock and talk on 807 Hillcrest when we're done processing this load. I have a feeling that if we wait, whoever's there is going to relocate. They lost two hundred kilos recently, and a bunch more today. They may be getting nervous."

"Deron's in the office. I'll send him over to the port," Tom said. "I'll put in a call to Bill. I'm not sure what he's doing."

Arriving at the port, Jimmy walked over to the van and watched as two inspectors unloaded bricks of cocaine from a gas tank compartment in the vehicle, handling the bricks with their bare hands.

"Guys, guys," Jimmy said. "How about putting some gloves on. I'm going to want to try and get prints from these packages." The inspectors stopped what they were doing and said nothing, giving Jimmy a little scowl. One of them found a box of surgical gloves and pulled a pair for himself and his partner. Once fitted with the gloves, they returned to unloading the gas tank.

The driver of the van was a skinny white male, twenty-two years old, his face covered in acne. He had a thin, patchy growth of whiskers on his chin that reminded Jimmy of Scooby Doo's owner in the cartoon series. Jimmy ran a series of computer checks not finding any records or criminal history. According to his driver's license, his name was James Cameron. He had an El Cajon address. Jimmy pulled up all the data he could on the young man and then walked him into an interview room. As he sat him down, Deron walked into the room, nodded at Jimmy and took a seat.

"James, this is Deron. He's going to join us," Jimmy paused and arranged his stack of paperwork before continuing. "My name is James Maxwell." Jimmy looked up at the young man. "So I guess you know why you're here." The young man nodded his head without looking up.

Jimmy filled out all the booking information on the driver, making small talk with him as he worked. As Jimmy wrote he remained friendly and James began to loosen up and talk a little.

"What a drag that the people that talked you into this mess put so much cocaine in the van," Jimmy said.

"Cocaine! Dude, they said it was going to be weed."

"Hold on there, James," Jimmy said, turning to Deron. "James is an excellent name, isn't it?" he asked Deron. Deron smirked but said nothing. "I need to read you your rights before we start talking about how you came to be in this fix today. Okay?" Jimmy pulled a DEA Form 13A card from his wallet.

"First, you have the right to remain silent. You understand? You don't have to talk to me. Second, anything you say can be used against you in court. That means that whatever it is we talk about, I'm going to put it in a report, and the prosecutor is going to do whatever he wants with it. You have the right to talk to a lawyer for advice before I ask you any questions and to have a lawyer with you during questioning if you want. If you cannot afford a lawyer, one will be appointed for you before any questioning. And James, I tell everyone I interview this. You can agree to talk to me and if there's something I ask that's too personal, or you just don't want to answer, don't answer. But how about listening to the questions first before you decide. I'd like to hear your side of the story, but I can't if you don't want to talk to me. Do you understand your rights?"

James nodded yes.

"James, we need to hear you say yes or no," Deron said.

"Yes. I understand and I'll talk to you guys. Dude, they told me it was going to be twenty pounds of weed. How much cocaine?" James asked.

"Like forty-five kilos."

"Oh no! It can't be. It can't be!" James said, starting to get very excited.

"Calm down. Listen to me. Did you watch the van get loaded?" Jimmy asked.

"No. I met this guy and he offered me two hundred dollars to drive twenty pounds of weed to the Costco store on Palomar. I really thought it was just weed."

"But you didn't, look did you? James, let me ask you something. You graduated high school, didn't you?" James nodded yes. "You're pretty smart, right?" James just looked at Jimmy.

"What if this guy, that I assume you'd never met before, put nerve gas in the van? What if he put a nuclear device in the van? What about a biological weapon? But you didn't look, did you? How smart was that? You know, you're going away for a while. But at least you don't have to live with the fact that you killed potentially tens of thousands of Americans. Think about that before you decide to smuggle something into the U.S. again."

"Better yet, don't ever smuggle anything again—you're not that good at it," Deron said.

The two agents finished their interview along with the booking paperwork and transported James to jail. Fortunately it only took about forty-five minutes to get a prison guard to come to the rear entrance and let them in, nearly a record for the normally understaffed and mismanaged federal jail system guards.

As they drove back south from downtown San Diego towards Chula Vista, Jimmy got on the phone with Chula Vista Police Detective Greg Keller.

"Greg, Jimmy. Hey bud, how you doing?" he asked.

"Good, Jimmy. How are you?"

"I'm good. We need to get together soon and knock off a few cold ones and howl at the moon."

"Just tell me when."

"Okay. It won't be long. In the meantime, what are you doing right now?"

"Getting ready to call it a day since it's almost seven. Hope you don't need anything tonight."

"Well, yeah, I do." Jimmy explained the whole history of the case surrounding 807 Hillcrest and told Greg he was hoping to get him and a few narcotics detectives to come with him to do the knock and talk at the address. Once Greg heard about the amount of cocaine involved, his attitude changed.

"There's a couple of us still here. Why don't I grab these guys and I'll meet you over there in about fifteen minutes," he said.

It was starting to get dark when they parked in front of the residence.

"Wow, this place is right across the street from Saint Paul's High School," Jimmy said.

"Guess maybe they should rename it Jesus Malverde High," Deron said with a laugh.

Jimmy looked at him questioningly. "You know, Malverde is the patron saint of drug traffickers, " Deron said.

"Ah, that's right."

"Dude, why don't you just keep working this address," Deron said to Jimmy. "You're probably not going to get anything here, even if you can schmoose your way in. You just took off the load that would have been here. If they're bringing cars here regularly to unload, just keep copping plates and putting them on lookout."

"I just have a feeling that if I do that, these guys will relocate in the middle of the night, or DEA or San Diego P.D. or someone else will knock them off first. Trust me though when I say that there will be something here. I don't know how much, but there'll be something. Besides, you know my motto. A bird in the hand," Jimmy winked at Deron and gave a little smile.

Jimmy parked his Expedition two houses down from the 807 residence. As they got out of the vehicle, Greg and several other units pulled up, a marked black and white parking right in front of the house.

"Guess there'll be no surprise when we knock on the door," Jimmy said softly to Deron.

The two agents walked up to the house, meeting with Greg on the sidewalk near the front of the residence as he stood by the open passenger door of his car. Greg pulled his badge out, and like Jimmy, let it hang from a chain around his neck. He then took a .45 Colt in a paddle holster from the car seat and tucked it into his waistband. Jimmy remembered when he'd been able to carry a .45, cocked and locked, and wished his agency wasn't so ridiculous in their conservative firearms policy.

"Thanks for coming, Greg. You remember Deron?" Greg nodded as the two men shook hands. Several other officers had gathered and walked over, forming up on Jimmy, Deron and Greg, waiting for the nod to go up to the door.

"Hey, let's not show up at the front door with six or seven guys. How about if Greg and I go up and make contact, then when we get consent, we'll wave the rest of you guys up," Jimmy suggested while keeping an eye on the front of the residence.

The officers nodded in understanding and Greg and Jimmy walked up the steps onto the front porch. Greg knocked as Jimmy stood off to the opposite side of the door from him. They waited about ten seconds then knocked again.

"I hear noise inside. Might be the television," Jimmy said in a low voice. Jimmy was positioned between the door and a window, but the curtains were drawn and you couldn't see into the house. Greg knocked again a little louder.

As the officers stood waiting for an answer, the curtains were pulled back an inch or two and a Mexican woman in what appeared to be her early thirties looked out at them.

"Hey, Greg," Jimmy said, bringing his attention to the window.

Greg moved over to his side of the door and stuck his badge up against the glass.

"Police, lady, come open the door."

She stood looking at the badge, staring without moving for a few more seconds.

"Open the door, police!" Greg said more loudly.

The curtains closed and a few seconds later the door was inched open. Jimmy pushed the door open further, feeling a little resistance from the woman. He wanted to see who might be inside, feeling it was an officer safety issue.

"Excuse me, ma'am," Jimmy said, showing his credentials. "We're following up on some information we received that there might be some narcotics activity going on here. We don't want to take up too much of your time, but can we come in and talk to you about it for a few minutes?" The woman gave no initial response but it was obvious by her expression and wide eyes that she was afraid.

"We get a lot of these types of calls and don't really have time to investigate them all so sometimes we just go contact the occupants of the houses we've been told about and try to get them to let us have a quick look around so we can clear the complaint."

"My husband is not home right now. Maybe you can come back later," she suggested in a thick accent, looking past Jimmy and Greg to the other officers at the street.

"Where is he?" Greg asked.

"He went out to pick up a car. He should be back in about thirty minutes. You come back then." She started to push the door closed but Greg put his hand out, stopping her and holding the door open.

"Okay," he said. "Hey, if he's coming back in thirty minutes, we'll wait here for him." The woman just looked at him, and then tried again to push closed the door. Greg again stopped her.

"Lady, since we don't know you, and since I have some concerns about our safety, I'd prefer that we keep the door open while we wait. I wouldn't want you going and getting a gun or something," he said, giving her a brief smile. As he finished talking, a little boy about five years old walked out of a back room. The woman spoke to the boy in Spanish, then turned and picked him up. She held him for a minute, whispering in his ear, then put him down and walked into the kitchen.

Over the next few minutes, Jimmy and Greg watched from the open front door as the woman busied herself with something cooking on the stove. A few more minutes passed and the woman turned the stove off, letting whatever was simmering in the pan sit where it was.

As they waited, the sun dropped below the horizon. It was getting a little cool and the woman walked over to a chair and picked up a sweater and put it on. Then the woman walked past the open door, glancing at Jimmy and Greg, going into the living room where she turned on a small television set. She changed the channel to what looked like a Mexican soap opera, then turned and headed back towards the kitchen. As she came back by the front door, Greg spoke.

"So, lady, how about we come in and wait in the living room so we can close the door. You know it's cooling off out here and we don't want your little boy getting cold. She hesitated for a minute then nodded, letting the men come in. Greg nodded to the men who were standing out on the sidewalk making small talk. Deron came up on the porch briefly to see what was going on. Jimmy explained that they were going to wait inside for a little while and asked him to keep an eye out for the husband.

Closing the door, he and Greg walked over and sat down on a sofa in the living room. The woman sat in an easy chair and began watching her show, occasionally glancing over at them.

As the three sat in the living room, the little boy played at their feet. After about five minutes, the little boy came over and started batting playfully at Greg's badge. Each time he'd take a swing at the badge he'd giggle and jump back a few steps. After about a dozen swipes at the badge, Greg took it from around his neck and handed it to the little guy. He seemed excited at the shiny new toy.

"What's his name?" Jimmy asked the woman.

"Pedro."

"What's your name?"

"Marcella. Marcella Limon."

"Marcella, I'm not from the INS, but are you here legally or illegally?" Jimmy asked.

"I don't have any papers."

"Is that why you didn't want to let us in?" Jimmy asked.

Marcella didn't respond.

"Okay. You don't have to answer, I was just curious."

They all finished the program and Marcella started to get up.

"Marcella, what are we going to do if your husband doesn't show up?" Greg asked.

"Do you think he's not going to show up?" she responded, looking first at Greg, then over at Jimmy.

"Marcella, we've been here about forty minutes now. There's police cars parked in front of your house. You said that your husband went to pick up a car, right?" Jimmy asked. She nodded. "Well we stopped a car at the border this afternoon that had a whole bunch of drugs in it. I'd guess that that was the car your husband went to pick up. I also think there's more drugs here in the house. So my guess is that if your husband comes back and sees all the police cars out front he's not going to stop."

Marcella walked over to a small table and sat down, hanging her head.

"All right. You can search," she said with a sigh.

Jimmy walked over to the front door, opened it and motioned to Deron who was standing out on the sidewalk talking to one of the uniformed officers. Deron paused then bounded up to the front of the house.

"Hey, go get a consent to search form out of my car," he said, handing Deron his car keys.

Deron hurried off, returning less than a minute later with the form. Jimmy went back in the house and sat down across from Marcella and began filling in the address on the form. When he finished a minute later, he slid the form across the table.

"Now you really don't have to do this if you don't want, but I do think you're doing the right thing. If there's drugs in the house, you really don't want your little boy being around them, do you?" he said.

Marcella said nothing as she signed the form. When she finished signing, she looked up and said, "The coke's in the back bedroom."

Jimmy nodded to Greg who walked over to the front door. Opening it, he motioned for the rest of the waiting officers to come into the residence. One officer remained out on the street in case the husband showed up.

As the men entered the house, they paired up and started moving methodically from room to room. Jimmy walked towards the back of the house, giving each room a quick look, more to ensure himself that there was no one else there than anything else. As he reached the end of the hall, he opened a closet door. There were steel mesh drying shelves in the closet, with heat lamps attached above them. One kilogram of what appeared to be cocaine was sitting on the top shelf. Jimmy smiled and called Greg. Greg walked back and joined him.

"Nice hit, dude," he said with a smile.

The two men then opened the last door at the right end of the hall. As the door opened, their mouths followed suit. There was a large pile of kilogram packages of cocaine lying on the bed. Stacked on the floor on a large piece of grease and oil-stained cardboard were many more packages. They were covered in what looked like axle grease. The men walked into the room, surveying their surroundings. Everything was covered in a white film. The dark drapes had a white powder residue. Jimmy walked over to the drapes, took his gun from his holster and tapped one of the drapes with the muzzle. A small cloud of white dust billowed out, settling at his feet. He stepped back, holding his breath for a moment while he holstered his weapon.

Greg walked over to a closet door. Sliding it open, he observed what appeared to be about a hundred kilograms of cocaine, neatly stacked in rows on the floor. There were also three five-gallon containers of acetone sitting on the floor next to the cocaine.

"Holy shit," he said to Jimmy.

Deron walked into the room and looked over at Jimmy wide eyed.

"Not going to be anything there, huh?" Jimmy said with a triumphant smile.

"I stand corrected," Deron said. He paused as he looked around then again said, "Holy shit!"

"You just said that," Greg said.

The three men reveled in the moment a little longer, asking one another things like how long did they think the stash house had been up and running, and how much dope did they think had moved through the place.

As they talked, they continued to poke and probe through the room. Opening the top drawer of the dresser, Jimmy found a stack of labels for the cocaine packages. One stack had the picture of a crown with the word 'Reina.'

"I guess this cocaine is fit for a queen," Jimmy said with a smile.

Another stack of labels just had a picture of a scorpion.

"Hey, look what I've got here," Deron said. In another closet he'd found some clothes hanging on hangers. He held up a handgun he'd just removed from a jacket pocket, gingerly holding it by the grip with two fingers.

"Cool. Let's try and preserve it for prints. I know we probably won't get any since it just came from a cloth pocket, but it's worth a try," Jimmy said.

"I'm with you, man," Deron replied. He walked back to the front room of the house, got a brown paper bag, and dropped the weapon in the bag.

As they continued to search, Jimmy's phone rang.

"Maxwell."

"Hi Jimmy. Are you coming over tonight?" Carmen asked.

"Hi gorgeous. I'm not sure. Is everything okay?"

"I just want to see you."

"I'd like that too, but I got caught up in a case and we're right in the middle of searching a house. I'd say that it's really not looking good for tonight. You sure you're okay?"

"I'm okay. I wish you were here, but I can wait until tomorrow," she said. It sounded like she was trying to sound more cheerful than she felt.

"I promise I'll be over tomorrow," Jimmy said.

"All right. Be safe, okay?"

"Thanks, I will. See you tomorrow. Hey, and seriously, if you need me for anything, call."

Jimmy hung up and looked over to see Deron giving him a strange look. He shrugged, knowing that he'd have to do some explaining later. He felt bad that he'd got so caught up in this case that he'd forgot to call Carmen and tell her he wasn't going to make it over. Then he thought about his wife. He hadn't called her either, yet somehow he didn't feel quite so bad about not calling her. Still, maybe he should call, he thought. He dialed his home number.

"Hi, babe. I'm going to be late," he started.

"Yeah, no shit, Jimmy. Dinner's been over for an hour. It's 8:30," Shirley said, cutting him off.

"Hey, we're in the middle of searching this place that's just full of cocaine. Remember when those L.A. agents . . ."

"Jimmy, I couldn't care less. Go finish whatever you're doing and stay out as late as you want. Never mind that your family sits home alone most nights. As long as you're having a good time, just go do your thing."

The euphoric feeling he'd had over the discovery of the drugs was immediately gone, replaced by anger and frustration. He didn't say anything else, just listened while his wife continued her tirade. A minute later, as she continued talking, he hung up the phone and put it back on his belt clip.

They finished the search, finding a car in the garage that had crossed the border the evening before. The gas tank was solid sounding when he tapped it with his flashlight, indicating it was probably full of cocaine.

It was midnight when Jimmy left the police department garage and headed home. He was still upset at the telephone call he'd received from Shirley. He knew she'd be asleep when he got home and as he drove he kept thinking of Carmen. His stomach started churning as he made a turn and headed towards Carmen's house. He knew he was going to do something he shouldn't but he just couldn't seem to resist.

Jimmy parked in her driveway and got out, walking to the door. He knocked softly at first. There was no immediate response so he knocked a little louder. He was about ready to knock a third time when Carmen opened the door wearing a sheer baby doll teddy. She looked up at him and without saying a word took him by the hand and pulled him into the house and wrapped her arms around him. As they kissed, Jimmy reveled in the taste of her.

Carmen walked him over to the sofa and sat him down. She unbuckled his jeans and opened the front of them. He did nothing to stop her as she reached in and pulled his hardening member from his boxers. She looked up briefly, pushed her hair aside and lowered her mouth to him.

Ten minutes later, licking her lips, she looked up at him.

"Are you okay?" she asked.

"No, not really. But I think I will be at some point. I hope so." Jimmy sat, staring at her for a minute. Neither of them spoke. Carmen snuggled up to him, pushing as much of herself as she could against his body.

"You are the most incredibly beautiful, sexy, wonderful woman I've ever known," Jimmy said softly, almost whispering it in her ear. He reached out and started to stroke the inside of her thighs. She let him touch her for a minute, then reached down and took hold of his hand.

"You don't have to do that. I know you're struggling with what's going on here. Get it straight in your mind before you do anything you're going to regret."

Jimmy already had some regrets, but he didn't say anything for the moment. Carmen didn't say anything else either, but pushed herself up against him even more. The minutes passed with Carmen falling asleep against Jimmy. He didn't want to wake her, but he needed to go home. He pushed gently on her shoulder, freeing his arm. He stood and fastened his jeans. Then he picked her up and carried her up to her room, laying her down on her bed. She woke and looked up at him.

"You could stay with me," she offered.

"Carmen, I can't. I'll call you tomorrow. He bent down and gave her a gentle kiss, then walked from the room.

"What have I done? What have I done?" he said to himself over and over as he drove home.

CHAPTER . . .

24

Jimmy had snuck into bed without waking his wife. As usual, he got up before she did and went into the bathroom to take his shower. Going into the kitchen to make some toast, he found Nikki sitting alone eating a bowl of Captain Crunch.

"Morning, sweetie," Jimmy said to her.

"Morning, daddy." Nikki was watching cartoons on a little television that sat on the kitchen counter. She kept eating, smiling at her father every so often between bites. Jimmy stared at her as he waited on the toaster. He felt a little sick as he thought about the previous evening. It had been terrible and wonderful at the same time. He felt torn in two. Here sat the love of his life while several miles away he thought of another love in his life, a love he shouldn't have.

As his toast popped, his cell phone rang. "Shit, just great," he said aloud. Figures."

"Daddy! No bad words," Nikki said. Jimmy smiled and mouthed, "I'm sorry," which caused Nikki to smile.

He tried to butter his toast while holding his cell phone against his ear with his shoulder.

"Jimmy, it's Greg. Hey, thanks for calling us last night."

"No problem, I appreciated the help. Matter of fact, I'm probably in trouble with my management. I didn't call them."

"Well, call and they'll get happy. The final weight is just a smidge over 416 kilos. That's the most dope I've ever got on a consent search. As a matter of fact, that's the most cocaine I've ever seized all at once."

The phone dropped into a stick of butter as Jimmy started to respond.

"Shit!" Jimmy said, picking it up and trying to wipe it off with a napkin.

"Daddy! No bad words," Nikki scolded again.

"I'm sorry, honey." He put the phone back to his ear.

"Sounds like you're having some issues this morning," Greg said, sounding cheerful despite the commotion.

"Dropped the damned phone, sorry, darned phone in the butter while I was trying to butter my toast," he said, looking over at Nikki and smiling.

"Okay, man, I'll let you eat your toast. What time you going to come by the P.D. and pick up this stuff? Our lab guy says we don't have room to store it."

"How about just after lunch. Let me get to the office and brief the bosses and let them scold me first. Then I've got to pull a seizure number."

"Okay man. See you around oneish."

Jimmy hung up and finished buttering his toast.

"Daddy, you shouldn't be saying those bad words. Remember what you've always told me."

"I know. You're right my little darlin. I shouldn't say bad words. You keep reminding me when I slip, okay?"

"Okay," Nikki said with a smile. She took another big bite of cereal, a trickle of milk running down onto her chin. She wiped it away with her pajama sleeve and went back to watching cartoons.

Jimmy ate his toast, drank a cup of coffee and then got up and kissed Nikki on the forehead. He gave her a butterfly kiss before he headed out the door.

"Be a good girl today. I love you," he said as he left the kitchen.

"I love you too, and I'll tell mommy you love her too," Nikki replied.

"Okay, pumpkin. Later potater."

Jimmy sighed at the thought of Nikki telling her mother that he loved her as he walked out the front door. He felt a mixture of gladness over the outcome of the case, and sadness and turmoil over what was happening to his personal life.

"God, I'm sorry," he prayed aloud as he drove to the office. "I really screwed up, but what do I do? I'm falling in love with her. I want my family, but I want to be happy." Jimmy drove, thinking about his predicament. He tried searching his heart for feelings for his wife. They seemed to be gone. *Where did our love go?* he wondered.

Just as he got to the office, his cell phone rang. It was Carmen.

"Hi, Jimmy. I'm on my way to work and I just wanted to give you a call and see how you were doing. Did you get any rest?"

"I'm not sure yet. I got a little sleep, but I don't feel very rested. Don't worry. Hey, I'm sorry to have called on you so late and, well I'm sorry about letting things get out of control."

"Are you? Because I'm not sure I am."

"Carmen. You're beautiful, and I'm falling in love with you. But I'm married. I believe in the sanctity of marriage and my vows. If I were married to you, how would you feel about me getting involved with another woman?"

Carmen didn't say anything as Jimmy waited for a response.

"Are you still there?" Jimmy asked.

"I'm here," Carmen said. Jimmy could tell she'd started crying. "Jimmy, I don't want to break up your marriage. I really don't. Maybe we should stop seeing each other."

"Maybe. Probably. Look, I don't want to hurt you. I'm making a mess of everyone's lives. Think about what I said. I'm going to stay away for a few days and think things out. You do the same and we'll talk in a few days. Okay?"

"Yeah, talk to you in a few days," Carmen said sniffling. She hung up.

"Great, just great. God, help me out of this mess!" Jimmy yelled as loud as he could.

Jimmy calmed back down over the rest of his drive, settling into what was becoming his normal state of unsettled worry about his personal life. The thought crossed his mind that he was fortunate to stay ass deep in work, something that kept him distracted from the rest of his life. He parked at his office and walked upstairs going directly to Tom's office.

"Hey, boss. I have some good news and some bad news," he said, sitting down opposite Tom's desk.

"Hang on a minute," Tom said, finishing something he had up on his computer screen. Thirty seconds later, he turned and looked at Jimmy with a smile.

"So, congratulations on last night's hit."

"Thanks," Jimmy said a little confused.

"So what's the good news and the bad news?"

"Well, how did you know about last night?"

"You told me you were going over to do the knock and talk. When I didn't hear from you I tried calling. I guess you were busy cause you didn't answer, so I called Deron. He filled me in. What'd you guys get there?"

"You tried calling me? I don't remember hearing the phone ring," Jimmy said, taking his phone out and scrolling through the call history. Tom's number showed up about five calls back. "Guess you did call. Sorry, I didn't even hear it ring."

"So, what'd you get? Then the good news and bad news." Tom said.

"Well, I came in here to apologize for not calling you last night. So, that said, I apologize for not calling you last night."

"Apology accepted. Now will you quit avoiding the issue and tell me what the hell you guys got? I've got work to do, as I'm sure you do if you got a bunch of dope last night."

"The Chula Vista lab folks weighed our cocaine seizure at 416 kilos."

"Nice. Good job. Have you taken care of the criminal complaints?"

"Not yet. I'll have them done by lunch."

"Good. Did the guy who lived at the residence ever come home?"

"You're kidding, right?"

"Hey, sometimes traffickers aren't so smart. Sometimes they even care about their wives or significant others enough to want to come take the hit for them so they don't have to go to jail."

"Well, no such luck. The wife went to jail and the kid went to the Polinski Center. No one else showed up. I've got to track down the owner of the house and get a copy of the rental contract, but quite honestly, I don't think I'll get to it until tomorrow. I'm hoping he used good identification because I can't identify anyone with the name and age the wife provided."

"So why didn't you guys get a warrant for the house. You'd have been up shit creek if that woman hadn't let you in," Tom remarked.

"Didn't have enough for a warrant without burning the L.A. informant. The van that we got at the port had Mexican tags. No connection to the residence other than me seeing it there every other day for the last few weeks since L.A. came down and made their pick up. I promised the L.A. case agent we wouldn't burn their source."

"Okay," Tom said. "I briefed Arlene this morning but didn't have any numbers for her. I'll give her a call and try to run interference for you. I know she's going to be unhappy about not getting a warrant. She'll probably be critical about hitting the place at all without verifying that the husband was home."

"She's a moron. What did she ever do as an agent?" Jimmy asked sarcastically.

"She worked smuggled artifacts and Persian rugs I think," Tom said with a smile. "But if you quote me, I'll deny it and hunt you down like a dog." He winked at Jimmy. "Now get out of my office and go do some work."

"Do some work? Do some work? Kiss my backside," Jimmy said, getting up.

Tom looked over his glasses smiling. "Hey, you haven't seized any dope today, have you?"

Jimmy started for the door. He stopped and turned around just before exiting. "Where do you get snitches with info on Persian rugs?"

"Swap meet? How should I know? Get out of here," Tom said, feigning that he was going to throw a stapler at Jimmy.

Jimmy left with a smile. He walked over to Deron's desk.

"Dude, hey why didn't you let me know you talked to Tom? I worried half the night and all morning that I was going to come in and get my ass reamed for not calling and giving him an update last night."

"How was I supposed to know you didn't talk to him, you shithead? And all morning? It's 9:30. Go away, I've got work to do?" he said, yawning.

"Thanks, dude. I owe you," he said as he walked away.

Sitting down at his desk, Jimmy started to slip back into depression, thinking about his personal issues. He forced himself to refocus and started working on his criminal complaints.

Just before lunch, his desk phone rang.

"Hi Jimmy. You busy or do you have a few minutes for me?" Shirley asked.

"I've got a few minutes. I'm just working on reports."

"I didn't hear you come in last night. I'm not trying to start a fight but a lookout at the border doesn't usually keep you out so late."

"I know. I should have called. I'm sorry. I got forty-five kilos of cocaine in a van that I've been seeing at that house I told you about that L.A. informant identified for us. We decided to go over and try to get consent from the residents of the house after we booked the driver into MCC. We ended up getting consent and 416 kilos of cocaine. Turned out pretty good."

"Huh, well, that's pretty good. No one got hurt or anything, right?" Shirley asked.

"No, everything went pretty smoothly." Jimmy began wondering why Shirley had called, and wondered even more about why she was acting as interested as she was.

"So I wanted to run something by you. One of my girlfriends that lives in Tucson called last night. We played softball together in college and I haven't seen her in a few years. She's on vacation next week and wants to know if I want to come out for a few days and spend some time with her. We could catch up with each other." She paused momentarily. "It also might give us a little break from each other. I'll bring Nikki with me. Anyway, you can work late, drink as much as you want, or whatever."

"Yeah, cause that's all I ever do, work late and drink too much, right?"

"Jimmy, don't start with me. I didn't call to fight. I called to ask you if it would be all right if I could take off for three or four days. If you don't want me to go, I won't."

"Honey, I'm sorry. You know you don't have to ask my permission for anything, and you know I would never say no. You should go and see your friend."

"So you don't mind?"

"No. Like you said, I can stay up late and drink whiskey."

Shirley started to say something but Jimmy cut her off.

"Hey, I was just kidding. I mean, I may drink some whiskey, and a few beers, but I wasn't making fun. Seriously, go. I think it'll do you some good."

"Okay. I think I'll put a few things together and take off this afternoon. I'm going to take the van. I'll give you a call when I get there so you know we made it in okay. I should be there by seven."

"When are you coming back?" Jimmy asked.

"Probably Sunday. Figure I'll stay four or five days."

"Okay. Hope you have fun."

"Do you? Do you really care whether I have fun or not?" Shirley asked in a serious tone.

"Of course I do. I don't understand how after being together all these years that you don't understand me."

"Jimmy, it's just that we never really talk so I really don't ever get to know you. You and I have such different views about life, about family and about what's important."

"I don't understand you saying that. I am home every day. We talk every day. I know my job bothers you, but it was my job when we met. It pays the bills and it's something I like. There's so many people stuck in jobs they hate. I think I'm fortunate."

"I know, it's my fault for marrying someone already married to their career. Look, I don't want to talk about this right now. I'm going to get ready and leave. Jimmy, I love you but I don't know how much more of this life I can take."

"What does that mean? Are you talking about a divorce or what?" Jimmy said, his stomach knotting up again.

"No, I didn't say that. Look, I don't know what I want right now. But I need a break. I'll call you later." Shirley hung up abruptly. Jimmy sat holding the phone for a minute before putting it back in its cradle.

It took a few minutes to refocus but Jimmy did manage to get going on his criminal complaints and after lunch, he went by Chula Vista Police Department. Sal Fierro had just been assigned a new G-ride, a Dodge pickup, so Jimmy asked him to meet him at the P.D. so that they could load the coke in his truck. Deron and Jesus also came by to provide escort duty for the trip to the DEA lab in National City.

It was a long day and Jimmy was hot, tired and glad to be home when he parked in his driveway just before six o'clock. He went in, kicked off his shoes, grabbed a beer and sat down in front of the television. One of his favorite shows, "The X-Files," was on.

By eight p.m. he still hadn't heard from Shirley so he gave her a call. She answered her cell phone on the third ring.

"Hi. Everything go okay on the drive?" he asked.

"Fine. Got here about an hour ago. Nikki says hello."

"Well I wish you'd have called and told me you made it in. I was getting a little concerned."

"Yes Jimmy, we made it in alright. We're just sitting down to dinner so let me go so I can visit. I'll check in tomorrow," Shirley said. Jimmy could hear the annoyance and impatience in her voice so he hung up without further comment.

"Well screw you too," he said aloud as he walked back to the refrigerator and got another beer. Following his fourth beer, Jimmy began to get hungry. He revisited the fridge and stood staring in, looking for something easy to prepare. There was nothing readily apparent.

He walked back to the living room and put his shoes on, deciding he'd go out and get something. As he drove, he started thinking about Carmen. He knew he shouldn't call her, but somehow he couldn't resist that temptation.

"Hi," he said when she answered her phone.

"Hi. What's wrong? Are you okay?" she asked.

"No, I'm not okay. I miss you. I know I told you I needed to stay away for awhile but I'm not sure I can." Carmen didn't respond. "I'm on my way out to get something to eat, although I haven't figured out what yet. Are you in the mood for anything in particular, or have you already eaten?"

"Why aren't you eating at home?" she asked softly.

"Shirley took Nikki and took off to Tucson today. They won't be back until Sunday. I'm batching it and since I couldn't find anything at home that I felt like fixing I decided to go out."

"Are you starving?" Carmen asked.

"A little, but I can wait for you if you have something to do."

"Let me go drop Raul off at my mom's. There's a good Italian restaurant on El Cajon Boulevard, just east of the 805. Want to meet me there in an hour?"

"Sure. Is that the one just a block or so east next to the paint store?"

"Yes."

"Okay, see you in an hour."

The hour seemed to take two. Jimmy started having second thoughts about having invited this incredibly sexy, beautiful woman to dinner. His plan to stay away for a few days and think things out hadn't worked. But he was happy that she'd accepted and would be with him soon. He didn't know where things were going, and at that moment didn't care. He couldn't see the future, but he should have known that the future was going to be a dangerous, troubled, painful place if he continued on his course.

"Hi Jimmy," Carmen said as she walked up to him and put her arms around him. He'd been standing in front of the restaurant, waiting by the door. He bent down and kissed her on the lips.

"Hi back," he said, opening one side of the double door, then taking her hand with his free hand and escorting her into the restaurant.

They ate without saying too much. Jimmy ordered a carafe of wine with the meal and by the time they'd finished he had a nice glow. Carmen seemed to be feeling pretty relaxed as well.

"Well, what now?" Carmen asked as they stood together near the front entrance.

"Spend the night with me," Jimmy said suddenly, looking into Carmen's eyes.

"Are you sure?" she asked.

"No. But I need you."

"I need you to."

There's a motel up the street. Come on," he said, taking her hand and walking her to his truck. She followed, leaving her car parked on the street.

Once in the motel office, Jimmy began filling out the registration card. He paused when he got to the line that asked for an address.

"Anything wrong, sir?" the clerk asked.

"No, no," Jimmy said, trying to think about what address to use. Carmen looked over, noticing where he was on the form.

"Honey, it's 1561 Ravenwood," she said to him. She looked over at the desk clerk. "We just moved there recently. He was having trouble remembering it earlier while filling out a credit application for some new furniture," she said. "It'll be nice when the paint dries and all those fumes are gone. We'd really rather be sleeping in our own bed."

Jimmy looked over at her and smiled. He gave her a little kiss. "I don't know what I'd do without you," he said.

As soon as they reached their room and the door closed behind them, Jimmy turned and kissed Carmen passionately, grabbing one of her breasts and squeezing it as he let his passions take over his actions. A minute later he released her and looked into her eyes.

"I'm going to have to really be careful around you," he said.

"Why's that?" she asked, starting to undress.

"That story you told for the desk clerk. It seemed so easy for you."

"I saw where you were stuck and, well, it just appeared out of nowhere so I went with it," she said as she removed her bra.

Jimmy stared at her as she began to unfasten her pants. Carmen looked over at him and smiled. "Come on, Jimmy, get undressed."

"I will. But I want to watch you for a minute first." Jimmy sat on the foot of the bed and watched, a slight smile on his face. The knot in his stomach was momentarily gone.

Carmen finished undressing, then walked over and stood inches from Jimmy, her breasts even with his face. She placed her hands on her hips, spread her legs a little and looked into his eyes.

"Like what you see?" she asked.

Jimmy stood, grabbed her and spun her around, the two falling onto the bed together in each other's arms.

CHAPTER . . .

25

Jimmy woke up with Carmen lying next to him. He smiled as he looked at her, but then felt a sudden panic attack. *What if Shirley had tried to call him at home during the night*, he thought. He rolled away and got up, immediately starting to dress. When he finished dressing he sat down next to Carmen and brushed the hair back from her face.

"Honey," he said softly. She opened her eyes and looked up at him. Giving him a little smile, she pushed herself up and wrapped her arms around his neck.

"Morning, baby," she said. Her scent, her touch, the hair covering his shoulder and cheek were the most fantastically feminine things he had ever known.

He didn't want it to end but he pushed her away a little and said, "Listen, I've got to run. I need to be to work in a couple of hours and I'm a little concerned that Shirley may have tried to call me at home."

"I understand. It's fine. I've got to go to work too," she said with a restrained yawn. "I probably should have called my mom last night and told her I wasn't coming back to get Raul, but I think she knew something like this was going to happen when I dropped him off."

"Does she know who it is you're seeing?" Jimmy asked.

"Yes. I've told her all about you."

"Even that I'm married?"

"Well, no. She knows your name, and that you're a Customs agent and that you helped me with the issues with Angel, but she doesn't know anything about your personal life. She doesn't need to know that."

"Well if I was your mother, or father, I'd be asking. I wouldn't want you doing the wrong thing, and I wouldn't want you hurt."

"Are you going to hurt me, Jimmy Maxwell?"

I might. Not on purpose, of course, but this is bound to end badly, don't you think?"

"We'll see."

"That's what I'm afraid of," Jimmy said, giving her a kiss. "I've got to go. Here's twenty bucks for a cab so you can get back to your car."

"Jimmy, I have money. Don't make me feel cheap by giving me twenty dollars."

"See, I'm a bonehead and I'm already screwing up and insulting you. I didn't mean to, but I did. Babe, I'm sorry . . . really, but I've got to go," he said, picking up the bill and pushing it down into the pocket of his jeans.

Jimmy turned and walked out the door, making it to his truck and then home in record time. There was no message on the answering machine and the phone didn't show any new calls. He breathed a sigh of relief as he stripped and headed to the bathroom to shower.

Letting the hot water run down his body relaxed him some, but as he washed himself he began worrying again, suddenly feeling a little sick. Again, his heart and head were at odds with each other. He didn't like what he'd let happen but he was smiling. He'd spent the night with the most incredible woman he'd ever known. He thought about the baggage her past brought to the table. She had been married to a major trafficker.

For someone not working in law enforcement her past wouldn't have mattered. But there was also the fact that he was married, and he had a beautiful little girl. His thoughts tormented him as he thought about being stuck with a woman he no longer felt any passion towards, a woman that made his life so difficult he didn't even want to come home at times. Then there was this incredible woman that loved him and wanted him, both smart and beautiful.

He knew that despite the fact that his relationship with God had been slipping over the past year it really didn't need to get any worse. Yet here he was, letting himself get involved in the biggest dilemma of his life. He'd been telling himself for days that he knew what was right and that he needed to break off his relationship, even the non-sexual one, from Carmen. He hadn't been able to do that. He had even begun to blame his marriage as the reason for getting involved with Carmen, and maybe it was partially to blame, but certainly his relationship with God should have pre-empted any reason for getting involved with someone while he was married. A part of him regretted ever getting married, but when he thought about Nikki he couldn't regret it too much. She at least was a wonderful reason for getting married. His mind continued to be flooded in a mishmash of these thoughts as he dressed and then drove to work.

"Morning, Jimmy," Tom said as he walked by Jimmy's desk just as he was sitting down.

"Morning, Jefe," Jimmy replied, yawning.

"Late night?" Tom asked.

"Yeah, in a manner of speaking it was." Jimmy smiled at the thought of having made love to Carmen half the night.

"You know, you might try beating the boss into the office sometime," Tom said as he walked away towards his office. "You know, just a thought."

Jimmy looked at his watch. It was 9:15. Yeah, the workday officially started at 8:30, but Jimmy didn't feel too bad about his tardiness. He knew the government always got their money's worth from him.

An hour after he sat down his phone rang.

"Maxwell."

"Hey, Jimmy, it's Chuey. I got some business for us. When can I see you?"

"How about right after lunch. Let me finish this report I'm working on and I'll meet you down at 'J' Street Marina, in the launch ramp parking lot about one."

"Okay, but make it the park just before the parking lot. Harbor Police just put a trailer office down there and I don't really want to meet around a cop parking lot."

"The park then, but don't keep me waiting."

"No, I'll be there. This might be a good one."

Jimmy hung up and went back to work on his report.

Most of the group ended up having lunch together at a Japanese restaurant in National City. Everyone was laughing and talking and generally having a good time. Deron noticed Jimmy was a little quieter than normal. When they finished lunch, Deron got a chance to corner his friend.

"What's up, man? You seem distracted. Everything going okay?"

"Yeah, fine. Hey, I've got to go meet with Chuey over near 'J' Street Marina. Can you come with me?"

"Sure."

As they drove over to the meet, Deron noted that Jimmy was definitely more subdued than normal.

"Dude, I've known you like five years now. What's up? I know something's bugging you."

Jimmy looked around, checking his mirrors, acting very un-Jimmy like.

"Let's get this meet with Chuey over with. We're almost there."

Chuey was late, a trait common with him. The two friends stood outside the Expedition, leaning up against the front quarter panel. Jimmy tried calling Chuey on his cell phone but got no answer.

"How long you want to wait for him?" Deron asked.

"Let's give it a little while. He said he might have a good one for us." Jimmy paused a moment then continued. "I know exactly what that idiot is going to say when he shows up. Hey, I couldn't answer, I was with the crooks."

"Yeah or, the border line was really, really long," Deron said, mimicking Chuey.

"Yeah or maybe like, hey man, I didn't have any more minutes on my phone. Can you spot me twenty bucks?"

The two laughed and tried to settle in for the wait.

"Looks like we have some time," Deron said. "So what's up with you?"

Jimmy hesitated, trying to study Deron's resolve in getting an answer. He wanted to talk to someone, but he felt uncomfortable confessing this particular sin to anyone, let alone someone he worked with. He trusted Deron but wasn't sure he should share this with anyone.

"Look man, if I tell you something, you've got to promise me your absolute silence. I mean, you can't say anything to anyone. Okay?"

"As long as it's nothing criminal."

"No, it's not criminal. Criminally stupid maybe, but not criminal."

"So, what?"

"I spent last night with Carmen in a motel. Made love half the night. It was incredible. What's worse, I think I'm in love with her," Jimmy said, ending with a big sigh.

Deron looked at Jimmy in stunned silence for a moment before he said anything. Despite the gravity of the issue, Jimmy smiled momentarily as the thought crossed his mind that Deron was trying to decide whether or not he was messing with him.

"Well, you're right. It was criminally stupid. Dude, what the fuck were you thinking? Her ex-husband is a major cartel crook who's only been in jail a few months. On top of that, you're married. And Jimmy, you have a kid. Jesus, do I have to friggin chaperone you everywhere you go to keep you out of trouble?"

The smile that had flickered across his face vanished as the thought now struck him that he had something new to worry about: Deron.

"Well, now you know why I didn't want to tell you. You know, if I needed another mother, I'd, I'd, I'd, well, let's put it this way, it wouldn't be you. I knew I shouldn't have told you."

Deron paused and looked at his friend. Jimmy sensed that he was going to say something to him, but before he found out what it was, Chuey rolled into the parking lot in a couple of year old black Suburban, squealing tires. Once in the parking lot he accelerated briefly, and then turned sharply, doing a short skid to a stop next to Jimmy's Expedition. He got out with a big smile on his face while Jimmy looked down at his watch.

"Who taught you how to drive?" Jimmy said sarcastically.

"You did, boss," Chuey said cheerfully.

"And where did you get that monstrosity?"

"How do you like it? My *tio* Jorge loaned it to me. I think I'm going to buy it from him."

"Your uncle probably wants to sell it to you because he can't afford the gas that thing guzzles. I know you can't." Chuey turned and gave the vehicle a thoughtful look for a second then turned and gave Jimmy a big smile. "I like it. We're going to make a lot of money on this case and then I won't have to worry about it."

"You're not going to make any money if you keep me waiting for you. I just won't be here when you show up. You're a half hour late. Guess I shouldn't let it bother me though, it could have been an hour," he said. Jimmy was aggravated, but he knew there was nothing he could do about it so he let it go.

"So what's the excuse this time?" he asked.

"That line at the border is really, really long," Chuey said.

Deron and Jimmy looked at each other, smiled and then gave each other a high five. Chuey looked puzzled but said nothing about their antics.

"So what's up? You said you had something good."

"I got this guy who wants me to help him get a ton of weed across the border day after tomorrow."

"What's his name?"

"Hilberto Palomares. He says he'll pay me one hundred dollars a kilo in advance."

"In advance? All of it?"

"That's what he said. He gave me five thousand dollars up front in good faith."

"You have it with you?"

A big smile spread across Chuey's face. "I know you, boss. Sure I got it." He reached down into the front of his pants and pulled out a large wad of bills. Jimmy and Deron gave each other a look of disgust.

"Dude, what are you doing?"

"What?"

"Why did you put the money down in your pants?"

"Look man, the guy gave me mostly tens and twenties. It wouldn't fit in my pocket and I didn't want this big wad of bills bulging out where someone would see it and maybe roll me. Besides, if I keep it down in the front of my pants the women will just think I got the big *chorizo* and maybe I'll get lucky." He laughed at his little joke. Jimmy shook his head and smiled.

"Dude, you're a twisted little shit," Deron said.

"Yeah, but the women who know me know it's true." He laughed again.

Jimmy took the wad of bills and went to his Expedition. Opening the back he found a plastic evidence envelope. He opened it and dropped the bills inside, sealed it and threw it under his jacket on the front passenger seat. Then he walked back to Chuey and Deron.

"So who's this Hilberto guy? How'd you meet him?" Jimmy asked.

"He used to be a Rosarito cop I think. I met him at an auto body shop in TJ where one of my *compadres* works. He was picking up a couple of cars that had compartments built in them."

"You get the license numbers of the cars he picked up?"

"The cars that get worked on in this place don't come or go with plates. Those people aren't stupid, you know. They do a lot of business and some of their customers know they do some side work for smugglers. They don't take chances by leaving license plates on the cars they work on."

"You can't find out what happens to the plates?"

"No. Why would I ask questions about something that doesn't concern me? If my friend knew I had an interest in the license plates, and especially if one got taken off at the border, I sure wouldn't be welcome back at the shop. They might even do worse to me." He shuddered, apparently thinking about what might happen to him.

"Yeah, probably not a good idea to ask about license plates," Jimmy said. "Oh well, it was a thought. Still, if you see one with a plate . . ."

"Jefe, what is wrong with you today? I know what to do."

"I'm just a little stressed out lately. Too much work I guess. Anyway, as for this ton of weed, it's going to be a little tight getting an I.C.D. approved by day after tomorrow. Think you can push it off until Friday?"

"I.C.D?" Chuey asked, looking questioningly at Jimmy."

"International Controlled Delivery. You do remember that we have to get everybody and their brother to give us their approval before we can let a load of dope through the border, right?"

"Yeah, I remember. Sure wish it was like the good old days when we first started working together. I remember you coming down to TJ and sitting in the bar with me while I met with all the little juniors that were trying to hire me to get dope across the border for them so they could make a name for themselves."

"Believe me, I wish it was still like that too. Unfortunately things change. That idiotic Brownsville Agreement that Janet Reno came up with forces us to get permission from the Mexican government to do anything in their country without notifying them. Then we have to notify and get the blessing of the U.S. Attorney's Office, DEA, Customs headquarters, our country attaché in Mexico City, and local office management. I wish the politicians would get a clue and realize that permission or not, agreements or not, dope is coming across the border. They may as well not tie our hands and let us deal with it. Oh well, what are you going to do? Things change. We'll shoot for Thursday, but no guarantees. You need to drag your feet a little and don't make any commitments until I tell you it's a go."

"I'm not a rookie, I know the rules." Chuey almost sounded a little hurt that Jimmy would remind him of the obvious.

"Sorry, Chuey. Bear with me. It just makes me feel better saying it to you, but I know you know. Besides, my boss will sometimes ask me if I told you the rules. I don't want to have to lie to him. By the way, is this Hilberto providing the load vehicle or do you have to come up with one?"

"They got me a van, Jefe. Only problem, if I hide the *mota* in the side panels like they want it's going to take me three or four trips to get a ton across the border. I can run a load every couple hours, but I don't know what else to do unless we can get something bigger with a better compartment."

"We'll have to start early," Deron said, looking to Jimmy for an approving response.

"Yeah, you're right. I hate early. Traffic sucks during the commute hours. Think you can get another truck?" Jimmy asked Chuey.

"I'll try, but I don't think so."

"Well, we'll have to run multiple loads then. I'll hit Tom up for some more bodies so we can have two teams available, one for the rolling surveillance and one to sit on a stash location. Guess we better wrap this up so I can go write the pass through request." Jimmy put away a small note pad he'd jotted down a few notes on and reached out to shake Chuey's hand. "Keep us informed on what's happening down south, man. Oh, and good job so far, even if you did keep us waiting," Jimmy said with a wink.

"Okay, man," Chuey said, cheering up a little. "Do you suppose I could keep like a couple hundred bucks for expenses out of that money?"

"What, you out of gas in that beast of yours already?" he said, walking over to his SUV.

"Yeah, and I got other expenses too."

"Well I wish you would have said something before I sealed the package."

Jimmy took a pocketknife from the pocket of his jeans and cut a slit in the top of the evidence bag. He pulled out two hundred dollars and then opened his briefcase and took out a chain of custody form. He walked over to Chuey holding the money in one hand and the form in the other. He started to hand over the money to Chuey but pulled it back quickly just before he took it.

"See, see, you don't know the rules. You know you have to sign the form first and you tried taking the money first." Jimmy gave a little laugh as he handed the money and a pen to Chuey. Chuey shook his head, laughing as he signed his name.

"Now don't forget to call me and let me know when good old Hilberto is ready to give you the money for this deal. As a matter of fact, try to get him to pay you on this side of the border. I'd like to have something to indict this guy on after we take off his dope."

"I don't think he's going to bring any cash across the border, Jefe. Why would he do that if I'm with him in Mexico and live in Mexico?"

"Maybe not, but at least ask. But whether he pays you here or in Mexico, I need to know right away. I have a feeling he'll change his mind and not want to pay you anything until he gets his dope over here to a buyer, but you need to push for the money up front. At least half, okay?"

"You got nothing to worry about, Jefe. I'm on this," Chuey said with a worry-free smile.

"Now you are starting to worry me," Jimmy said, teasing Chuey with a frown for a few seconds after he made his comment. When he noticed Chuey starting to look a little worried, Jimmy smiled at him and winked. "I'm just kidding you, Chuey.

"Come on now, I always come through for you," Chuey said, quickly slipping back into his cheerful mood.

Once gone, Jimmy walked to the back of his vehicle and pulled out another evidence bag. He'd gotten a little sulky again, but said nothing as he busied himself resealing the cash in another bag.

"Thanks for covering this with me. I appreciate you always being there for me," Jimmy said to Deron.

"No problem, dude. You ever notice that more than half of our deals seem to go on Friday? Why is that?"

"We're a 7/24 outfit, my friend. You get all that built-in overtime and the take home car just so you won't feel bad about having to work late on Friday."

"Yeah, right, and do reports over the weekend," Deron said sarcastically.

Jimmy smiled and turned to get in his Expedition. Deron walked around, opened the door and got up into the passenger seat. Deron looked over at Jimmy as he started the SUV and backed out of the parking space.

"Hey, Jimmy. Look, I'm sorry I reacted like I did when you told me about you and Carmen. I've never been in love. I've had a few girlfriends that I cared about, but I've never really been in love. Dude, I know you're a big boy and you know what's right and wrong. But I sure hope you know what you're doing. I hope you're ready to deal with all the consequences you might be facing if certain people find out about this." He paused a moment. "Least of which are any of the agents you work with. I'm thinking about your wife. I don't see her taking this well at all. I'm worried about you, man."

"Yeah, I know," he said, sounding downcast. "Sometimes I think it wouldn't be too bad losing my wife. We've had our share of issues over the years. But I don't want to lose my kid, or my sanity, not to mention my house and a lot of money."

"Yeah and you need to realize that you could lose even more. You could get yourself killed. Don't think for one minute that Angel Garcia still doesn't have a long arm from inside that jail cell. I'll bet that guy has more money stashed away than both of us will make in our lifetimes. You know as well as I do that all he has to do is make a call and some very bad things could happen to you."

Jimmy didn't respond and the two drove in silence. A few minutes later, Jimmy pulled up and parked next to Deron's G-Ride. Deron got out and had taken a step towards his car when Jimmy started to speak. He turned around and looked at his friend.

"You know what Angel said to me the day we arrested him? He told me I'd better take good care of them, his wife and Raul," Jimmy said.

"Dude, I don't think he meant he wanted you banging her!" Deron said loudly.

Jimmy felt himself starting to get pissed off. He turned away and looked over his shoulder, putting his vehicle in reverse.

"Jimmy, Jimmy! Hey, wait." Deron walked up to the passenger window. "Dude, I'm sorry." Jimmy stopped and looked over at him. "Seriously, I apologize. I guess I'm just worried about you, but I shouldn't have said that. Really, I'm sorry. It just slipped out."

Jimmy stared at his friend for a moment in silence before responding. "Apology accepted. Hey, I'll see you back at the office. I've got to get this I.C.D. request submitted today if we're going to have a prayer of getting this thing done on Thursday."

"Hey, if you ever need to talk to me about anything, I'll listen. And I promise I won't give you too hard a time. I may tell you the truth, which you may not want to hear, but I'll try and do it a little more tactfully."

"You, tactful? Don't change on my account." Jimmy smiled at his friend then backed out of the parking lot and headed off to the office.

Towards the end of the day, Jimmy's phone rang. It was Carmen.

"Hi gorgeous, how was your day?" Jimmy asked.

"Busy, and yours?"

"The same. I'm really beat. You wore me out last night," he said with a chuckle.

"Come over to my house. I'll make you dinner and rub your shoulders."

"Is that all?" Jimmy asked playfully.

"Depends. Come over, okay?"

"Okay. Give me about a half hour."

Jimmy hung up and then called his wife.

"Hey, having fun out there?" he asked.

"Yeah, it's nice. It's a little warm so we spent the day lying out by the pool. I got a little sunburned like usual, but it's been pretty relaxing. Here, talk to your daughter."

Jimmy didn't get a chance to further the conversation before being cut off.

"Daddy! Hey, I miss you."

"I miss you too, sweetie. Are you having fun?"

"I went swimming today for five hours," she said excitedly.

"So now you're my little prune girl?"

"Nooo. You're silly, daddy."

The conversation lasted only a few minutes but Jimmy hung up, fighting to minimize the amount of tears welling from his eyes. He looked around as he wiped his eyes with his shirt sleeves. There were only a few agents left in the office and fortunately no one was looking over at him.

During the drive over to Carmen's house Jimmy thought about breaking off the relationship again. He parked in Carmen's driveway, walked to the door, knocked once and opened the door slightly, sticking his head in.

"Hello. Anyone home?"

Carmen came out of the kitchen wearing only an apron. She smiled seductively and motioned for him to come in as she licked something off her fingers. Staring at her for a moment, she offered a finger for him to taste. He took her hand and sucked the sauce from the finger, staring into her eyes.

"Ummm. I take it your mother has Raul again?" Jimmy said, bending down and kissing her.

"Uh huh. Mmmm, this mole sauce is really good," she said, licking several more of her fingers. "You like chicken mole?"

"Sure. But I'm easy. I like almost any Mexican food. Especially when it's on you."

"So I'm finding out," she said with a smile. She turned and walked back towards the kitchen. Jimmy watched her naked backside. *Oh my good Lord, what a body*, he thought. Her hips had just the right amount of sway. As he watched her, any thoughts of breaking it off walked away with her into the kitchen.

CHAPTER . . .

26

"Typical," Deron said to Tom and Jimmy while standing in Tom's office. "Looks like another Friday deal, and all because of a stupid name on a signature form."

"You guys haven't figured out that upper management lives just to ensure that there's enough spaces between address lines in memos, and that the font type and letter size is correct?" Tom asked with a smile. "What else would they do to earn their $130,000.00 a year?"

"What I'm worried about is Chuey," Jimmy said. He's getting a lot of pressure from the trafficking organization to make this happen today. I'm concerned that when we take down this case it's going to put more heat on him due to the delay. I know it's only a day, but what the hell. You know a normal crook driver wouldn't be dragging their feet, they'd go when they were told." He paused a moment looking at Tom. He continued when he didn't get one.

"So we're held up a day because of a name on a form? I mean, how are we supposed to know every time some DEA Assistant Special Agent in Charge gets transferred and a new guy takes his place? It's just a name on a form. Have the new guy line out his name and write in his own."

"You know how anal bosses get," Tom said calmly. "It's just a day delay. Have Chuey tell the smugglers that he has to take his mom to the hospital or something. Shit, have him turn off his phone for the day. How about just once he tells the traffickers he ran out of minutes on his phone? He does it to you guys often enough."

"True. I just don't have a good feeling about this. What if the smugglers just grab another driver and cut Chuey out of the deal? We get nothing."

"Look, I know these cases mean a lot to you, but do you know how much dope crosses the border here every day?" Tom asked. It was a rhetorical question. Tom was aware that Jimmy was as much an expert as anyone in law enforcement about the amount of dope that came into the area. "Besides, you're not supposed to let the informant run the case. You control it."

"Tom, there's a difference between us controlling the case and having stupid management issues controlling the case."

"It's just like I've always said," Deron remarked before Tom could say anything else. "No one really cares about these cases."

"Least of all me today. I don't give a rat's ass about another load of weed coming across the border. I've got an important inventory to finish so get your whiny asses out of here," Tom said.

"Boss, you're not supposed to have this attitude about this very important job you're doing here on the border," Jimmy said, suddenly smiling. "I mean, you're supposed to be gung ho and tell us we're winning the war on drugs. Come on, get with the program, because goodness knows that doing a new inventory every few months will stem the flow of illegal drugs and put these traffickers in prison where they belong."

Deron and Tom started laughing.

"Well, you quote me on what I just said and I'll deny it." The guys kept laughing.

"Seriously though," Tom continued. "Someone else will be trying to hire Chuey next week if this does fall through. It's not like you don't have enough work already, for God's sake. Don't worry, it'll likely go tomorrow."

"Yeah, yeah. We'll see," Jimmy said, turning towards the door. "Of course, it still screws us. We just can't get a break on these Friday cases. We'll see you after awhile. We're going out to hook up with Chuey and give him the bad news."

Deron and Jimmy left. As they drove from the office, Jimmy called Chuey and asked him to meet with them at the 'J' Street Marina Park.

"How about we go do a knock and talk as soon as we finish with Chuey?" Jimmy suggested as they drove to the park. "I still need to do some follow up on that 807 Hillcrest case."

"Yeah, all right. Where we going and what are we doing?" Deron asked.

"Well, there were three cars I was seeing at that residence pretty regularly when I would drive by the place prior to us visiting it. One was seized at the border; one was in the garage when we did our search. The other car is a maroon Mazda registered to a Oscar Armenta who just happens to live around the corner from 807 Hillcrest in apartment 32 at the Cedar Hills Apartments."

"Did you run up Armenta?"

"Yeah, he's been stopped at the border a few times with illegal aliens in his car, but he's never been arrested."

"Graduated to the big time, huh?" Deron asked, a little distracted as they pulled up and parked next to Chuey's car. "I can't believe he's here and on time."

"Well, I do believe in miracles. Could be this is ours for the day." Both men got out of the Expedition and walked over to Chuey.

"We're ready to go, right?" Chuey asked anxiously.

"Tomorrow."

"Don't tell me that! Shit man, these guys are ready to go."

"Sorry man. I was really hoping we could do it today myself," Jimmy said.

"What do I tell em? I told them last night I'd be ready to go today."

"How long have you worked for us? Seriously. You know how we work."

"Well they don't. You guys are going to get me killed one of these days with your stupid rules."

"Chuey. If anyone gets you killed it'll be you doing it yourself. If you wouldn't make commitments and promises that you know might change there wouldn't be a problem. Look man, I've told you before. No one likes these stupid rules but we're stuck with them. We're not going to operate like the crooks or the Mexican cops."

Jimmy knew the reason for the delay was ridiculous, but there was nothing he could do about it. He also worried that what he'd told Chuey might someday come true. Most sources got in trouble after making commitments that seemed to change just in time for the trafficker's dope to get seized and people arrested. The traffickers weren't that stupid that they couldn't put two and two together.

"You guys better be ready tomorrow. Shit, shit, shit!" he said, walking away. He got in his Suburban, slammed the door and drove away.

"Well I guess we'll talk to him tomorrow morning, if we get the chance. I'd hoped we'd have the chance to work out where and how we'll hook up with him after he gets across the border. We sure need to get a tracking device on that car before he gives it back to the crooks," Jimmy said.

"Why do you put up with him?"

"Oh, he's a decent enough guy. A little high strung, a little flaky, but he's likeable enough."

"He's a crook and a moron," Deron said.

"Yeah, he's probably those things too," Jimmy said with a smile as they got back into his SUV. "Let's go over and do that knock and talk."

Ten minutes later they parked on the street in front of the Cedar Hills Apartments. They took a walk through the apartment complex looking for the Mazda but didn't find it. Jimmy thought about talking to the apartment manager about trying to get a copy of the rental contract for apartment thirty-two, but decided against it in case no one was home. There were times when apartment managers told tenants that the police were looking for them and then people disappeared.

It took several minutes to find apartment thirty-two. They walked up slowly, looking around the complex for anyone that might be watching them. Standing on the concrete pad that comprised the entry to the apartment, they could see that the living room blinds were closed. Neither of the men could hear anything inside. They listened for a minute and then knocked. Jimmy and Deron pulled their badges out from under their shirts, letting them hang on display from their necks. After waiting about twenty seconds, Jimmy knocked again. A few seconds later the door opened and the two agents stood looking at a Hispanic male in his mid-thirties.

"How you doing today?" Jimmy asked. The man stared at the agents without saying a word. "We're looking for Oscar Armenta. Is he home?"

"No," came the stiff reply.

"What's your name, sir?" Deron asked.

"Armando Arguelles."

"Can we see some identification, sir?" Jimmy asked the man.

The man reached into his back pocket, continuing to stare at the two agents. He removed his wallet and then retrieved a California driver's license from it, offering it to Jimmy. Jimmy looked down at the I.D. It showed the name Armando Arguelles but listed a San Diego address on Boston Avenue. Deron had pulled a small notepad from his pocket. He took a step closer to Jimmy, leaned towards the identification and jotted down the information from the license.

"So who lives here?" Jimmy asked, handing the driver's license back to Arguelles.

"Why?" Arguelles asked.

"We'd just like to ask Oscar a few questions. This is his apartment, isn't it?" Jimmy sensed that Arguelles either didn't like the police or he was hiding something.

"Look, does Oscar live here or not?" Deron asked, getting impatient.

"He did," Arguelles said soberly.

"So, what does that mean?" Jimmy asked. "Like I said, we just want to ask him a few questions."

"That's not going to be possible."

"Why?" Jimmy asked.

"He was killed yesterday morning. He and our cousin Francisco Sanchez Armenta."

Jimmy and Deron stared hard at Arguelles for a few seconds, trying to make a quick assessment as to whether or not they were being told the truth.

"What happened?" Jimmy asked.

"They were murdered. Rosarito police found them next to their car on the side of the toll road to Ensenada. They'd been beaten and shot to death. At least that's what the Rosarito police told me last night."

Jimmy believed he was being told the truth based on the circumstances. If someone blamed them for the losses at the Hillcrest address, it made perfect sense. Someone would really be pissed off after losing over six hundred kilos of cocaine and someone would have to pay. That much cocaine was worth a lot of money, over nine million dollars wholesale, and that translated to a good deal of blood.

"We'd like to come in and take a quick look around, Mr. Arguelles. We have some reason to believe that Oscar was involved in drug trafficking and we just need to make sure there is nothing illegal in here," Jimmy said matter-of-factly.

Arguelles stepped back from the door, sighed and motioned for the agents to come in. He didn't look happy about the intrusion but now that he'd told the agents what had happened to his cousin, he seemed to be a little more relaxed and at ease with their presence.

"We're not going to be very long, and we're not going to tear the place up or anything. There's no weapons or anything in here, are there?" Jimmy asked as he walked towards the back of the apartment.

"I don't think so," Arguelles called out to him. "I never spent much time here. I don't think Oscar spent much time at home either, maybe just to sleep."

"He sounds like he may know a little more than what he's told us so far," Deron whispered, leaning over to Jimmy as they walked to the bedroom.

The agents looked around the apartment, finding little of interest. There were a few small but important exceptions. The vehicle registration document for the Plymouth van used to smuggle the forty-five kilos of cocaine that was destined for the Hillcrest residence was in the top drawer of the nightstand. Right next to it was a small caliber semi-auto pistol, a .380 Llama.

"All the money these guys make doing this and they can't even afford to buy a decent gun," Deron said.

"I couldn't agree with you more," Jimmy said with a little shake of his head. The agents continued to look around the room for a few minutes, opening drawers and sorting through the closet shelves.

"You know, I've made some interesting observations over my years in law enforcement," Jimmy said to Deron as the continued to search the bedroom.

"And what would they be, oh sage of law enforcement? Please enlighten me," Deron intoned in a poor imitation of an Asian accent.

"Well, it's something I've reflected on a few times over the years. Your discovery of that cheap-ass gun reminded me of it. Why is it that the idiots that do armed robberies usually hit a convenience store or donut shop instead of, say a grocery store where there'd be so much more money. I mean, why risk six to eight years in the bucket over forty bucks? And the guys that are out stealing cars, those idiots steal almost as many old pieces of junk as they do nice cars. Again, why risk all that jail time for a friggin Ford Pinto or Chevy Citation? Yeah, I know, there's money in parts and all that, but still, if I'm stealing a car, it's going to be a nice one. My final observation for the moment is even more profound. Well probably not, but pretend it is."

Deron looked up at him, having satisfied himself that there was nothing else in the room worth looking for. Jimmy finished as well and walked over to within a few feet of Deron so he could lower his voice.

"Why is it that rapists seem, generally of course, to rape ugly women? I'm telling you, if I have to go to prison for rape, I'm going to rape the best-looking woman I can find. When I was with the P.D., we arrested a guy once for raping an eighty-year-old lady. I don't get it, and I'm not sure I buy that whole power trip theory.

"You're a sick puppy, thinking of shit like that," Deron said.

Jimmy looked over at his friend. "Yeah, I don't know why some of these things pop into my head, but you have to admit, they make sense. Seriously though, most of the crooks we arrest could have an additional charge of felony stupid added to whatever other charges they end up with."

"Dude, all I know is that the stupid crooks keep us in business. You'll never have to worry about getting laid off in this line of work," Deron said. The agents walked back out into the living room where Arguelles was waiting.

"Mr. Arguelles, I'd like to take this vehicle registration document with me. The vehicle isn't registered in your cousin's name, and we have information linking it to a seizure of narcotics at the port of entry a couple of days ago."

"Yeah, no problem. Oscar won't be around to complain about it, so why not? You guys didn't find anything illegal or anything, did you?"

Deron pulled the handgun from his pocket and held it up for Arguelles to see. "You mean, something like this? It was in the top drawer of his nightstand." Deron paused a moment. "I'm taking it out to my car but I'll be back in a minute with a receipt for the two items."

"Mr. Arguelles, what did Oscar do for a living?" Jimmy asked as Deron was leaving.

"I'm not sure. I know he bought and sold cars. You know, he'd go to an auction, buy a car, fix it up and re-sell it. I think he mostly did that."

"Are you aware of anything else he might have been into? Obviously he got himself killed over more than selling someone a car that they weren't happy with."

"I know he got stopped at the border with illegals in his car a time or two, but like I said earlier, we weren't that close."

"What you said was you didn't come over much. My memory is pretty good, Mr. Arguelles." Jimmy paused a moment, studying Arguelles' face. "We're investigating a group of men who have been smuggling a lot of cocaine into the country—a lot, Mr. Arguelles. Do you know what the owners of a lot of cocaine do to the people that lose large amounts of their prod-uct, especially if they think there's negligence, theft or coop-eration with law enforcement involved?" Jimmy continued to stare at Arguelles. "Your cousins found out. I can tell you this as well. If the owners of the dope are really, really pissed off, they sometimes go after the family members of those who be-trayed them; maybe even because the people who worked for them let them down by not doing a better job of protecting their interests. So you think about that and if you decide you want to talk to us about your cousins, you give me a call."

Jimmy wrote down his cell phone number on a sheet in a small pad, then tore it out and handed it to Arguelles. He took it without saying a word as Deron reentered the apartment.

"Got that receipt ready for Mr. Arguelles?" Jimmy asked, turning to Deron.

Deron was just finishing filling out the receipt form and was pulling off a carbon copy. "Yeah. Here you go, Mr. Arguelles. Good luck," he said, shaking his head and frowning.

The agents turned and left. Once on the road, Deron turned to Jimmy. "Think we laid it on a little thick with that guy?"

"No, not at all. Everything we told him was true. I doubt anyone will bother him, although it's possible, unless he really is involved with his cousins. If he is, maybe he'll call and talk to us. I think the thing to do now is get hold of our liaison agent in T.J. I'd really like to go meet with the state judicial cops about the murders, see if we can get any more intel."

Jimmy reached for his cell phone and called Sector Com-munications.

"Hey, it's Jimmy. Can you patch me through to Jaime Vasquez on his cell?"

Thirty seconds later, the call went through. "Jaime, it's Jimmy. Hey, I need a favor. We're working this cocaine traf-ficking case and it seems like a couple of our suspects may have been whacked in the Rosarito area yesterday. Can you see if you can verify that and try to set up a meet for me with the investigators sometime in the next few days? I think I'm going to be tied up tomorrow, but any other day after that should be fine . . . Okay, good. Thanks, man."

"Lunch at Jalisco's?" Jimmy asked.

"Sure."

By the time his workday ended, Jimmy was really tired. He called Carmen and told her he wasn't feeling well and that he thought he'd better go home and get some rest. She said she understood but Jimmy knew she sensed there was a little more to it than that.

Once home, Jimmy poured himself a shot of Knob Creek and after sitting down on the sofa, he put in a call to Shirley, speaking briefly to her and Nikki. She seemed distant and cold to him. He wondered if she could sense the same thing from him.

Finishing the call, Jimmy sat back on the sofa and tried thinking about his life. He looked around the room, taking in the familiar surroundings, finding comfort in the room. He took a sip of bourbon and felt the warmth of the liquid as it radiated relaxation to his body. When would he ever end the struggle for some peace in his life?

Part of the problems between them stemmed from the fact that Shirley was now a stay-at-home mom while Jimmy had a career. The problems had grown, now encompassing a myriad of other issues. As he sat thinking, he again wondered if some of the problems he had were due to him drifting away from his relationship with God.

What a mess he was in. He was in love, in a relationship that violated every principle he believed in, yet his principles seemed to pale in comparison to his feelings. But he had always had the philosophy that feelings weren't nearly as important as principles. He'd always believed real love should be the kind found in I Corinthians, Chapter 13. "Love is patient, kind; it's not arrogant or rude, not jealous, not irritable or resentful, not rejoicing in wrong, but rejoicing in the right. Not insistent on its own way, bearing all things, believing all things, enduring all things."

Yet here he was thinking about Carmen. If only he'd waited for her to come into his life. He was angry and frustrated over his plight. Should he continue to live in an unhappy marriage or move on? But then moving on violated his principles and values and the commitment he made to his wife and God. So, be unhappy but do the right thing, or be unhappy and still not necessarily do the right thing? Or be with the one you love and be happy some of the time but not all of the time because you'd always have regrets and know you were violating your beliefs and principles?

He took another drink of bourbon as he pondered this personal chaos. Nothing had become any clearer by the time he fell asleep on the sofa.

CHAPTER . . .

27

Jimmy was at the office at 8:30 the next morning. His ICD request had finally been approved and he hurried to complete his Ops Plan. The agents in his group were standing around talking amongst each other, laughing as they recounted those little bits of each other's personal lives that they'd experienced together or with others over the last few months. He paused for a moment as he wondered what it was in his personal life he had to laugh or joke about. He couldn't think of anything.

Once finished, Jimmy stood at the copy machine, making photocopies of the Ops Plan for the agents he'd be working with today. Halfway through, his cell phone rang.

"Maxwell."

"We're doing this today, right?" Chuey asked quietly.

"Yeah. What time?"

"Good thing. They're bringing me the van now. They think my sister's old boyfriend is going to let me through without inspection. If they're on time, I can be in line at Otay in about an hour."

"Otay? I thought we were going through San Ysidro?"

"They're loading the vehicle someplace out in one of the east *colonias*. La Mesa, I think. It doesn't make sense to drive it through San Ysidro. When we were talking yesterday and they mentioned the vicinity of the stash house, I mentioned my sister's old boyfriend was an inspector at Otay. They seemed to be better about the delay if I could talk to him and figure out when he'd be working and which lane he'd be on. I mean, they didn't actually suggest bribing him or any of that, they just felt like I'd have a better chance of getting sent up the road without inspection if I came through his lane."

"Chuey, if the van is going to have a ton of weed in it they've got to think someone's on the take. Any moron would be able to tell the van was loaded when it comes up with that much dope in it. On top of that, why the hell can't you give me a call and tell me what's going on before making plans? If you had this conversation yesterday, why am I hearing about it now?" Jimmy felt himself getting angry as he spoke.

"It's one of those utility vans, you know, with a cage and partial wall behind the two front seats. You can't see much back there unless you slide open the side door."

"But you can smell that much weed!"

"Yeah, you can smell it some, but not that much. I'm going to have it covered up with a tarp. If you can keep the dogs away, plus make sure the inspector just waves me through, it'll be just fine. Really, they just think my sister's ex-boyfriend trusts me."

"Well, the Ops Plan shows San Ysidro, but I guess I can line that out and write in Otay," Jimmy said, pausing a moment to think of how he was going to have to work out the wrinkles with the location change. "I just don't understand why after all the deals we've done, you can't call me and work this stuff out before you just change plans?" He was angry, but as he thought about it, he realized there were really no options at this point other than walking away from the entire case. The dope would still come across the border, maybe at a different time and place, but the smugglers would likely get it across.

"Sorry, Jimmy, but you changed plans from working yesterday to today, and when I heard them talking about picking up the stuff out east, I threw that story at em, hoping they'd feel better about the delay."

"You've got to do better about staying in touch with me," Jimmy said, the frustration evident in his tone.

"You know, the other good thing is that I can get everything across in one load instead of three or four. You guys don't have to be out here all day with me taking three or four trips to get everything across the border. Besides, I know you didn't want me waking you up at midnight to talk about it."

Chuey was right. Getting everything across in one shot was going to be easier on everyone than trying to maintain control of three or four hundred pounds crossing every four hours. The agents wouldn't have to have two teams, with one of them maintaining vigilance on the marijuana that crossed, wherever it was dropped off, while the other went back to the port of entry where they'd wait for the next load. Oftentimes maintaining control of the dope that crossed was such an impossibility that the agents would have to move in and effect an arrest, taking the case down prior to completing the smuggling of all the dope.

"Okay, okay. You know I don't like change, especially at the last minute, but we'll make the necessary adjustments on this end because you're right, getting everything across the border in one shot is better for all of us. I can't believe the owners of the weed are willing to take that kind of risk, but hey, who am I to second-guess their greed. You have the plate for the van?"

"It doesn't have a plate, but you can't miss it. It's a 1985 full-size Chevy van, white with a primer gray front left quarter panel. It says 'Jerry's Auto Glass' in big bold letters on both sides. By the way, I stuck to my guns and insisted on getting one hundred dollars per kilo as my transportation fee in advance. They agreed so everything is good, right?" Just as Jimmy was going to say something, Chuey cut him off with, "Hey, I gotta go."

"Son of a bitch!" Jimmy said when Chuey hung up. He knew one of the traffickers was probably coming over to talk to him but he'd wanted to tell Chuey to come through the easternmost lane. The fact that he didn't have enough time to tell him had really irritated him. Now he was going to have to set up surveillance, hoping to spot the van approaching and still have time to move an inspector into his lane that was willing to allow the van to go up the road without inspection.

Along with being irritated at Chuey, Jimmy was a little irritated at himself. He paused a moment, thinking, I never used to swear this much. *As a matter of fact, I was always pretty patient and could massage changes into place without giving it much of a thought. What's the matter with me? Am I losing it?*

Refocusing on the ICD, Jimmy realized he'd better get his act together. He had to advise Tom of the change so he could keep the Customs management up to speed. Then there were notifications he was going to have to make at the Otay Mesa Port of Entry. Besides getting the shift supervisors on board with the ICD, he realized he'd better get over to the port and find a willing inspector. Although most of the Customs and Immigration Inspectors were willing to work with the agents on pass-through operations, there was always a few that failed to see the overall law enforcement benefit of trying to make a delivery of the smuggled drugs in an effort to hopefully arrest either the sellers or the buyers of the drugs instead of just a delivery driver.

A controlled delivery of the drugs also gave you a 50/50 chance of being able to seize more drugs at the stash location. It was a shame that some of the inspectors were only concerned about the appearance of impropriety, not the reality of it. Jimmy always felt that those inspectors should be forced to get with the program, but unfortunately their union protected them from being forced to do much more than to show up to work on time.

"So guys and gals, gather round. It's about time to rock and roll," Jimmy said.

Jimmy dismissed the agents that would no longer be needed, although he did ask them to stay in standby mode in case there were further changes. Jimmy's entire group remained for the brief, plus Terry Smith, a Technical Enforcement Officer. Terry was going to assist in the operation by placing an electronic tracking device on the load vehicle. The tracking device transmitted its location via cell phone signal. Terry could monitor the location of the vehicle via laptop computer as long as he had a good signal and the batteries held out.

Just as he started briefing, his cell phone rang.

"Maxwell."

"Jimmy, is this a bad time?" Carmen asked.

"I'm just starting a briefing, but I have a second. Is everything okay?" he said. Most of the rest of his group looked at him, waiting for him to continue. He could see the questioning looks from several of them, wondering who he was talking to.

"Everything is fine. I was just calling to tell you I love you."

"Me too," he said.

"Oh. You really can't talk now, can you? It's all right. Call me later when you can." She hung up abruptly.

"That sounded interesting," Barbara said with a smile. "Anyone we know?" Jimmy ignored the question.

The briefing was over in ten minutes and everyone dispersed, heading off to the restrooms and then down to their vehicles. Jimmy called the air group, advising the surveillance aircraft of the change in location. He also confirmed that show time was close so they could do their pre-pass-through preparations. Internal Affairs was also called and advised of the operation. They would log it in as a sanctioned pass-through operation in the off chance that someone called in to allege that there was a corrupt official letting drugs go up the road.

The agents set up around the port of entry and then strung themselves out along State Highway 905, placing themselves in positions to drop into the surveillance as it moved, allowing someone who may need to pull off the highway the opportunity in case they'd been behind their target too long and were in jeopardy of being compromised.

Following Chuey wasn't going to be difficult. He was a controllable asset. The problems arose with the counter-surveillance vehicles. Traffickers would often have a security team in another car follow the larger loads of drugs. They were there to provide some protection of the load, as well as be able to ensure that the driver didn't either steal the load or try to make contact with the police. They could also report the progress of the delivery, or problems associated with it; things like law enforcement stops, referrals to secondary inspection and other problems that might occur.

One of the other routinely encountered problems that always amused most agents was the use of junk vehicles by the trafficking organizations. Drug smugglers would often risk tens of thousands of dollars worth of narcotics by using a vehicle that barely ran. It wasn't unusual to see a load vehicle break down. As was often quoted among law enforcement professionals, 'we only catch the dumb ones.' The agents knew it wasn't always true, but there were times that it certainly helped.

It was another typical morning at the border. The wait to get across the border varied, taking anywhere from twenty minutes if you were lucky, to several hours. The cars jockeyed for position, moving from lane to lane, hoping to get through inspection as quickly as possible. There were times when cars cut each other off, fights broke out or fender benders occurred due to the impatience of the commuters. This morning the traffic was heavy, but was moving fairly well with no apparent problems. The inspectors guesstimated that the border wait was just under an hour.

Jimmy and Bill went to the watch commander's office to check in with the shift supervisor and to wait and watch for Chuey's arrival. They filled out the request form for the ICD and waited while the supervisor called the Port Director to request authorization for the operation. The operation was blessed within twenty minutes.

Like the San Ysidro Port of Entry, the watch commander's office there was called the 'fish bowl' as well, again because from it you could look out into Mexico and see all the lanes of approaching traffic and all of the primary inspection stations, albeit some of them from a distance. The glass windows were bulletproof and tinted, making it a good observation point.

It was almost eleven a.m. before Bill Anderson spotted the van Chuey was driving approaching primary inspection. Naturally, it was in a western lane, difficult to see, as they were the farthest from the watch commander's office.

"Can we get word out to the inspector in lane twelve? We need to make sure that our van doesn't get referred," Jimmy asked.

"I'll walk out and talk to him myself," the shift supervisor said.

The supervisor came back quickly, talking on his radio.

"Keep the canine units away from the west side," Jimmy heard him put out over the air.

"Thanks," Jimmy said with a wink.

"No problem. The primary officer is good with letting your guy go."

"Cool. I really appreciate your help."

As Chuey neared the primary inspection booth, a space opened up in the lane immediately to his left. He hesitated briefly, then jumped into the spot. He was two cars away from the primary inspector.

"Did you see that?" Bill asked Jimmy excitedly.

"Yeah. Stupid idiot," Jimmy said, looking over at the supervisor.

"Let me see if I can call out there," the shift supervisor said, picking up a telephone.

Before there was an answer, Chuey reached the inspector. The inspector spoke briefly to him, taking a declaration, Jimmy guessed. Fifteen seconds into the contact, the inspector jumped back from the van and drew his sidearm, aiming it at Chuey who stared at him wide-eyed.

"Holy shit!" Bill said.

The shift supervisor ran from the office, across the traffic lanes, covering the 150 feet from the office door to the panicky inspector in record time. The supervisor placed a hand on the weapon held by the other officer, pushing it down to his side. The two spoke briefly and then the inspector holstered his weapon. Several vehicles stopped to watch briefly.

"Shit, that's all we need. A public audience," Jimmy said disgustedly. "I'm going to break that idiot's neck when I get the chance," he said, referring to Chuey.

Bill, who had initially been shocked at the occurrence, now became amused and started to laugh. "Dude, you better not. He's making you famous."

"I don't need that kind of fame. I can see it now. 'Everyone that was interviewed told us they were shocked and surprised. They still can't believe it. They are all still asking themselves why he snapped and put ten rounds in the chest of the, as yet, unidentified man.'" Jimmy did his best to mock one of the many idiotic news reporters that too often showed up at a police incident.

Bill laughed. Jimmy smiled as well, pleased that he was starting to snap out of a bit of the melancholy that he'd started the day with.

"Surveillance units from Jimmy. Our boy is up the road, passing the north end of the port."

Chuey had been released by the supervisory inspector seconds after he arrived at the primary inspection station. The inspector who had started to panic walked back to his inspection station and then stared angrily over into the fish bowl. Jimmy knew the look was for him, or whatever agent was behind what had happened to him.

Oh, well, shit happens, he thought to himself as he and Bill trotted quickly out to their cars.

Agents followed Chuey up State 905. No counter-surveillance vehicles were observed and nine miles later, Chuey parked the van in a shopping center parking lot located just off I-805 and Telegraph Canyon Road in Chula Vista. Jimmy drove around the parking lot looking for anyone that might appear to be waiting for Chuey. The other agents in his group set up in the lot and on the street, preparing themselves to be able to follow the van whatever direction it left as soon as it was picked up. Jimmy didn't see anything unusual in the lot so he cautiously approached Chuey.

"Nice job, butthead," he said to Chuey with a faint smile.

"What did I do?" Chuey asked, acting a little hurt.

"How many times have we done these pass throughs?" Chuey didn't answer but looked at Jimmy questioningly. "At least a dozen. Do I ever have you come through on the west side of the port? No, because it's the farthest away from where we can see you. And then you change lanes at the last minute and almost blow the whole damned thing. I should kick your ass." Jimmy stared at his source for a moment, then continued. "They don't know where you are now, right?"

"No. I told them I'd call them after I got across the border."

Chuey continued to stare at Jimmy without further comment. Jimmy stepped behind the driver's door and pulled on the sliding rear door handle. The door slid open several feet. Pulling down a brown canvas tarp, Jimmy looked at marijuana bricks stacked almost to the ceiling.

"I thought they were giving you a ton?" he commented. "This has to be closer to a ton and a half unless the bricks aren't compressed very well."

"They told me a ton."

"They're ripping you off, but that's okay. They are going to pay before they take delivery from you, right?"

"That's what they said."

Jimmy got on his phone and called Terry Smith.

"Terry, come on over."

Terry drove up a minute later and immediately began working on hiding the bug on the van. It was installed shortly and he nodded.

"Let me go see if I have a signal," he said as he walked away to his van.

"Call me as soon as you know," Jimmy said. Terry nodded.

"Chuey, come on and jump in with me. Lock this baby up. I've got people watching it. I'm going to drop you off about two blocks from here. That way when they show up to get their dope they don't just see the van and try taking it before they pay you. Once they pay you, you can have them drive you over to the van. Are they calling you or did they give you a number to call them?" Jimmy scanned the parking lot continuously as he spoke to Chuey, not really looking at him as they spoke.

"They're going to call me."

"Okay. Once you get the call, let me know. Try to get an ETA out of them and ask them what they're going to be driving." Chuey locked up the van and pocketed the keys.

"Jimmy, I know what to do," Chuey said as they walked over to Jimmy's Expedition.

"Yeah, well that's what I thought earlier when you showed up at the port of entry."

Chuey hung his head like a scolded stepchild. They got into the Expedition and drove west through the parking lot. Jimmy advised the surveillance team of the plan and ensured there were several units with eyes on the van containing the marijuana. Chuey didn't say a word as Jimmy drove him to a

7Eleven store several blocks away. Jimmy continued to carefully watch activity around him but also couldn't help but notice how hard Chuey had taken his admonishment.

As soon as Jimmy parked, Chuey opened the door and started to exit.

"Chuey," Jimmy said. Chuey turned around and looked back at Jimmy. "Hey, nice work on setting up this case and getting your smugglers to give you all that dope at once. It sure beats sitting out here all day." Jimmy gave his source a little wink and a smile. Chuey's face lit up.

"Boss, I'm going to do better next time," he said with a big smile.

"Yeah, yeah," Jimmy said to himself as he drove away.

It was a good thirty minutes before Jimmy heard from Chuey.

"Jefe, there's supposed to be two guys coming pretty soon. They said they were ten cars back in line at the border. They're driving a white Chevy pickup."

"Okay. Make sure you call me if you hear from them again," Jimmy reminded him.

Jimmy put out the information over the radio as the wait continued. Jimmy had parked across the street from Chuey at a gas station, in front of a water and air dispenser. It was a good location as long as some big vehicle that needed water or air didn't come park in front of him, blocking his view.

Another thirty minutes went by with no sign of anyone showing up. Jimmy decided to call Chuey.

"Hey, I know you don't have the number for the two *chongos* that are supposed to show up, but how about giving a call to Hilberto and see what's going on with those guys."

"I'll try."

Ten minutes later, Chuey called Jimmy back.

"They're in line at the border. They'll be here soon. That's all they told me."

"Figures," Jimmy said, more to himself than Chuey. "I sure wish these idiots could get their act together." Jimmy began to wonder if someone had sent the incident at the port of entry and had reported it to the owners of the dope.

An hour ticked by while everyone waited. Jimmy called Chuey again.

"Hey, you need to try calling again. If those idiots were ten cars back at the border they should have been here at least an hour ago. I'm going to call the port of entry and make sure they didn't get sent into secondary or something."

"Okay, Jefe," Chuey replied.

Jimmy called the port and asked the secondary lot senior inspector to look around for a white Chevrolet pickup. He was on hold for three or four minutes. When the inspector returned, he told Jimmy he hadn't found the vehicle. Jimmy hung up and his phone immediately rang.

"Jimmy," Chuey said excitedly, "I've been trying to call you back. As soon as we hung up I got a call. Those guys are right around the corner from here. They're going to be here any minute."

"Chuey, relax. We're on this. Take a deep breath and act normal. And don't forget to insist on your payment before you take them to the van. Got it?"

"Yeah, I got it."

It was still nearly ten minutes before a white GMC pickup pulled into the parking lot. Chuey walked over to the two men inside and bent down to talk to the passenger through his open window.

"Surveillance units from Alpha 353, we have a meet with our source," Jimmy put out over the air. Jimmy heard several clicks of the mike, indicating the transmission was received.

Following a short conversation, Chuey opened the door of the pickup and slid in next to the passenger. The pickup drove away eastbound towards the parked van.

"Surveillance units, our source is headed over to the van with at least one and possibly two Hispanic males in our white Chevy pickup."

"Ten four," came the reply from Bill who had the primary eye on the van.

Arriving at the van, Chuey and the other two men got out of the pickup. Chuey led them over to the side door and after looking around to make sure there were no police units converging on them, he opened the sliding side door and showed the men their merchandise. A few seconds later, the van door closed and the men walked back over to the pickup.

"Omaha 89, are you overhead?" Jimmy asked.

"We'll be on sight in about five minutes. We had to divert around inbound traffic for Lindbergh."

"Ten four. Let us know when you hit the area," Jimmy said.

"We have the passenger handing over a shoebox to the source," came the radio transmission from Bill. "Okay, the source is walking away towards the supermarket and the passenger is walking over to the van . . . He's looking around . . . Okay, he's opened the driver's door . . . We have backup lights . . . Standby, I think he's moving. Yep, he's moving southbound through the lot. Who's got him?"

"I have him coming by me," Greg responded. "He's signaling for a westbound back onto Telegraph Canyon Road . . . Okay, we're westbound Telegraph. I can stay with him to the freeway, then I'm going to have to go straight. Who can pick him up at the 805?"

"I'll pick him up," Shirley said.

"Okay, I'm by him. He got on the northbound 805. Units copy? Northbound 805," Greg said.

"Who's with me?" Shirley asked.

"I'm two cars behind you," Sal replied.

"Deron, Sal and I are trailing as well," Jimmy put out over the air.

"It's going to take me a while to get turned around and through the traffic," Jesus said. "I was set up east."

"Me too," Mitch added.

"Okay, Jesus, how about picking up the source? I think he has something in that shoebox for us," Jimmy said.

"Got it, I see him over by the pay phone at the front of the store."

"Alpha 353, this is Omaha 89. Where are you guys?"

"Northbound 805. Looks like we'll be exiting Bonita Road," Jimmy said.

"Roger. What's our target vehicle?"

"A mid-eighties, white, full-size Chevy van. Primer gray front left quarter panel. Says Jerry's Auto Glass on the side."

"Roger. Do you have a good reference vehicle for us?"

"Omaha 89, we're going by Bonita Car Wash. Then there's a flower store just east of there," Shirley said.

"Okay. I have the car wash . . . I think I have the van. Is it passing a blue Mustang?"

"Yeah, a blue Mustang is in the number two lane," Shirley responded.

"Got him," Omaha 89 transmitted.

The surveillance units all backed off a little once the surveillance aircraft locked onto the target. The surveillance continued eastbound on Bonita Road, then southbound on Otay Lakes Road, heading towards Southwestern College.

Jimmy didn't want to interrupt the surveillance being called by the aircraft so he decided to call Terry Smith and asked if there were any problems with the electronic tracking device.

"Terry, do you have a good track on the van?"

"Yeah, it's still southbound on Otay Lakes Road. Standby. It just turned east on Ridgecrest."

"Okay, as long as you have it," Jimmy said. "I'll call you if we lose it. Let me know if you have any trouble."

"No sweat."

The surveillance units all hung back as the van entered a residential area that had little through traffic. The streets off of Ridgecrest all led to cul-de-sacs, and nearly all of the traffic in the area consisted of residents. Several units went into the area while the remaining surveillance units stayed out on Otay Lakes Road.

"Who's got it?" Jimmy asked.

"It went eastbound on Ridgeview, then turned down the third street to the north. I lost it under some trees, but I believe it's either in the third or fourth house from the end of the street on the west side," said the voice from Omaha 89.

"Shit. Any ground units in the area?" Jimmy asked.

"I can go down the street and take a look," Deron suggested.

"Go ahead. All other units stay off that street," Jimmy put out over the air.

Jimmy's phone rang while he waited for Deron to get back to him.

"Maxwell."

"Jimmy, how's it going?" Tom asked.

"The van got picked up by two idiots and we're over off Otay Lakes and Ridgecrest. You coming out to join us?"

"Maybe in a bit. I just got out of a staff meeting with the other managers and I have to go to a short meeting with the inspectors at their Office of Field Operations."

"So your stupid meetings are more important than real operational issues ongoing in the field?" Jimmy asked, making the observation lightly, teasing his boss. It was also a little dig to his supervisor whom he believed should be out in the field with his troops.

"Don't start on me, Maxwell. You know I'd rather be out there. Sometimes I wish I hadn't ever put in for this stupid job."

Jimmy smiled, knowing Tom was telling him the truth. "I know. Remind me never to put in for supervisor. Hey, I've got to go. We've temporarily lost the van. I mean we know about where it is, but, well I'll tell you later, I have to go." Jimmy hung up before Tom had a chance to question him further about what was going on.

"Surveillance units from Deron, it's behind a tarp on the side of the third house from the end of the block. The numbers on the house are 2477. Yeah, it's going to be 2477 Ridgecrest Court."

Jimmy's phone rang again.

"Yeah."

"Jimmy, it's Shirley. Nikki and I just got home and . . ."

"I'm glad you made it home okay but I can't talk right now. I'll call you later." Jimmy hung up abruptly as he was driving to the 2477 address.

"Surveillance units from Jimmy. Let's move into the area and stage at the entrance to the cul-de-sac. I want everyone moving in on the residence at the same time. Sal and Greg, you take the south side of the residence and work your way to the backyard. Barbara and Gary, take the front door. The rest of us are going in on the north side of the residence where the van is located behind the tarp. There's probably an entrance on that side of the res. No one at the front goes in until one of us lets you in."

The agents staged at the entrance to the cul-de-sac and then slowly drove down the street, the lead car stopping about two houses before the 2477 residence. Agents exited their vehicles in their raid gear and formed in a line to approach the residence. Deron, Mitch, Jesus, Shirley, Bill and Jimmy drew their weapons and started walking towards the north side of the residence in a single line.

As they approached, they could hear voices and see two pairs of legs moving below the bottom of the hanging tarp. Jimmy moved up alongside the house and pulled back the side of the tarp. One person was inside the van. The other subject was coming out of the residence, moving towards the van. Jimmy stepped into the carport area and pointed his weapon at the man who'd exited the residence.

"Police, don't move!" The man turned and froze. Jimmy could see movement inside the van. "You in the van. Come out with your hands where I can see them! Do it now!"

As Jimmy spoke, the other agents with him flooded into the tent-like area of the carport. Deron approached the van on the opposite side of the open door trying to get a look through the front windshield area. Jimmy approached the man he could see and took hold of him by the arm, tucking his handgun well back, almost into his armpit. He pulled the man forward and dragged him to the ground.

"Someone get up here and cuff this guy!" he commanded, keeping an eye on the door of the van. Shirley and Bill came up and took custody of the man on the ground. Jimmy remained focused on the open van door. The man inside had yet to appear.

"You in the van. You're not going to like what happens next if you don't come out of there," Jimmy said loudly.

Just then, Jimmy caught sight of some movement from the open door of the house. He turned his attention momentarily to the open door as a large German Sheppard came running from the residence, growling, teeth bared, right towards him. The front sight of Jimmy's .40 caliber Sig Sauer moved to the dog, the muzzle of his weapon following the dog as it approached him. When the animal was about four feet from him he fired. A tuft of fur disappeared from the top of the dog's head and the dog yelped as it went down. A small puddle of urine ran from the animal as it lay twitching at Jimmy's feet.

"Okay, buddy, out of the van!" Jimmy commanded, his gun now coming to point at the subject in the van.

The man appeared at the door, wide eyed, his hands well up over his head. A wet spot was growing at the groin area of his jeans. He carefully jumped out of the van, never taking his eyes off the front of Jimmy's weapon. As Jimmy stepped over the dog it got up and ran off to the backyard. Jimmy ignored the dog and moved to the man, grabbing his arm and pulling him down while giving the inside of the van a quick look to ensure that no one else was inside.

Jimmy temporarily holstered his weapon and began handcuffing the man after having him lay down face first on the ground while the remaining agents with him passed him by and made entry into the side door of the residence. A minute later, the house was secure.

"Jesus, can you put this guy in your car?" Jimmy asked.

"Dude, he pissed himself. You put him in your car," Jesus replied, turning his nose up and walking by, ignoring the request.

Jimmy sighed and started walking the guy to his Expedition. Before he'd gone more than a step or two, Barbara came out of the house.

"Jimmy, there's two little kids asleep on a bed in the back. I don't know where their mother is." Jimmy nodded in understanding.

"Hey you, what's your name?" he asked the handcuffed man. The man just looked at him. "*Como se llama?*"

"Felipe. Felipe Calderon."

"*Donde esta la madre por la nino's?*" Jimmy asked in his poor Spanish.

"*Trabajo.*"

"She's at work? Is she coming home?"

"*Si. Un hora, mas or menos,*" Felipe responded.

"She'll be home in an hour, more or less," Jimmy said to Barbara. "We're going to be here another couple of hours anyway, I guess. The other guy is the guy who lives here, right?"

"That's what he said," Barbara replied.

"Did he sign the consent form?"

"Yeah. He's worried about the kids though."

"Good. We'll let him see them in a bit. I'm just happy he's saving us a few hours not having to get a search warrant."

"A few hours? It would take four or five hours if we were lucky!" Barbara said.

Jimmy let go of his prisoner for a moment and moved closer to Barbara so he could talk to her without being heard. "Yeah, but I wouldn't get a federal warrant. The U.S. Attorney's office would burn our source without even thinking about it. I'd get a state warrant. I know the penalties aren't as good, but at least I wouldn't have to worry about Chuey."

"Really? The U.S. Attorney's office would give him up?" Barbara asked.

"Yeah. They sure would. Federal law doesn't really protect sources worth a damn."

Barbara gave him a shake of her head, indicating her disgust at what she'd just learned. She turned and went back into the residence without further comment.

"Hey, Jimmy," Sal said. "That dog is hiding behind some bushes in the backyard. It won't come near us, but it seems to be all right."

"Geez. I'll bet it has a hell of a headache," Jimmy said, amazed that the animal was still alive. Let's give a call to Animal Control and have them come get it." He turned to Deron who was standing close by, keeping an eye on the van. "I guess I better call Tom back and let him know I popped a cap on that dog."

"You know, I wasn't sure you'd even fired a round. Sounded like a cap gun to me," Deron said.

"I didn't even feel the recoil," Jimmy said, dialing Tom's number.

The search of the residence produced nothing of interest except a few bricks of the marijuana that had been unloaded out of the van.

An hour later, the mother of the two children came home from her job as a housekeeper. She had a Border Crossing Card, so she was legal to be in the country as a visitor, but she wasn't legal to live or work here. Border Patrol was called and arrived an hour later. After discovering that there were children involved, they declined to take custody of the woman.

Jimmy talked Greg and Shirley into transporting the two prisoners to the San Ysidro Port of Entry for processing, although he had to give up his raid jacket for Felipe to sit on.

The search of the residence was slow. The house was disgustingly filthy, like most drug stash locations. Jimmy opened a kitchen cabinet, jumping back a step as about half a dozen roaches fell out onto the counter and scurried away.

"How do people live like this?" he said, mostly to himself.

The stove had several pans and a skillet on three of the four burners. They contained food that was half dried up and moldy. Clothes lay strewn everywhere, filthy, piled in corners and on chairs and the sofa. There were dirty diapers lying on furniture and on the floors in almost every room.

Tom arrived at the house about thirty minutes after the search started. He walked upstairs, stepping in a pile of dog shit at the top of the stairs.

"What the . . .! Jesus Crimeney! There's a big pile of dog shit here. Holy crap, I've got it all over my new shoes!"

Jimmy looked over at his boss and started to laugh. "That's what you get for showing up late. By the way, there're several more piles of dog shit strategically located throughout the place, and since I'm not going to tell you where they are, you'd better watch where you step." Jimmy continued to laugh as Tom tried wiping his shoe off on the carpet.

"Hey, hey, hey. People have to walk over that area to get up and down the stairs. Don't make it any worse. Go somewhere else." Tom continued to try to wipe off a shoe on the carpet. "Tom, go over to that bathroom and rinse your shoe off in the tub or something, if you can stand to be in there," Jimmy said, his voice trailing off as he made the last remark. Tom looked over at him.

"I think the toilet is plugged up and there's a load in it. The lid's down now, but it still smells pretty bad," Jimmy explained.

"Great! Just lovely! I knew I should have stayed at the office."

As the agents were getting their gear together and getting ready to leave, Jimmy's cell phone rang again.

"Maxwell."

"Still busy?" Carmen asked.

"A little. I can talk for a minute."

"Can you come over and stay with me tonight?"

"Carmen . . . My wife and daughter came home today. I need to go home."

"Oh . . . When will I be able to see you?" she asked, sounding a little disappointed.

"I'd come by tonight for a minute, but it's going to be really late by the time I get everything done here. We just arrested a couple of guys with a ton of marijuana. It would be better if I came by tomorrow evening for a bit."

"Okay," she said softly.

Jimmy lowered his voice a little. "Carmen . . . Look, I don't know what's going on with us . . . with me. I know I love you. I shouldn't have let myself fall in love with you, but I did. I don't know why I met you, but I did. I also know I'm married and although my wife and I are having serious issues, I've never even considered leaving her. I have a daughter that I dearly love and, and, well I don't know what to do. I need some time to think things through. Okay?"

"Jimmy, I love you too. Take all the time you need. I don't want to break up your marriage so if you decide that we can't see each other anymore, we won't. Maybe it's better that way. I've always felt that I'm destined to be alone anyway."

"I'll call you tomorrow, okay?"

"Okay. Be careful out there, Jimmy Maxwell."

The call ended with Jimmy thinking of how sexy Carmen sounded when she talked to him. It didn't even matter what she said. Her voice melted his heart with its femininity. No one had ever made him feel that way.

Driving home that evening, Jimmy felt almost sick to his stomach. He almost felt a sense of panic at having to talk to his wife. It was such a foreign feeling to him.

He walked into his living room at 8:45 and saw his wife sitting on the sofa. She looked over at him, giving him a hard, angry stare.

"You couldn't get off a little early? I mean, we just got back after being gone most of the week. We came home early to get back to you, and what, we interrupted something you were doing that was more important?" she said sarcastically.

"I thought you weren't coming home until this weekend?"

"We weren't, but I thought I'd surprise you. I called to let you know we were home and you hung up on me. Jesus, Jimmy, if you don't want a family, you're sure going about it the right way."

"It has nothing to do with not wanting you home. I have a job that . . ."

"Yeah, you have a job. Well fuck your job! You have a family. It's about time you started making them a priority in your life; that is, if you want to keep them."

"You have no idea what is or isn't a priority in my life. You never have. I've always tried to make you a priority, but my job is important and it dictates the hours I work. I can't just tell the damn smugglers to quit bringing dope across the border at five o'clock because I'm expected home for dinner. What the hell is wrong with you?"

Shirley softened a little. "I hate your job. I hate everything about it. But I do know you're good at it and I understand that you have to work late sometimes. I just wish you were as good at being a husband as you are at being a criminal investigator."

"I don't think I'll ever be that good," Jimmy said sadly as he walked off to the bedroom to take a shower.

When he emerged from the shower, he dried himself and then walked into the bedroom. Shirley was waiting for him in bed. The covers were thrown back enough that Jimmy could see her breasts. He knew she was naked and wanted to make love. He tried giving her a little smile, but was nervous at the thought of making love to her.

"What's for dinner?" he asked with a little smirk.

"Me."

"Let me go brush my teeth," he told her. She nodded, saying nothing.

While he brushed his teeth his mind raced. For the first time he could remember he didn't want to make love to his wife. It seemed wrong. It seemed like he was cheating on Carmen.

He walked from the bathroom and walked over to his wife. She reached up and grabbed him, pulling him down onto her. She reached down and took hold of him, manipulating him as they kissed until he was fully erect. With some hesitation, he pulled her hand away and worked his way down her body.

CHAPTER . . .

28

Jimmy woke with a start as his cell phone rang. He picked it up from the nightstand and answered it.

"Jimmy, this is Chuey. Hey, sorry I got to wake you, man, but I got a call from Hilberto. He said that the owner of the marijuana, some guy named Isidro, wants to talk to me. I have to go down to T.J. and see what they want. I just wanted you to know."

"Where are you now?" Jimmy asked, trying to wake up.

"I'm with this girl. Her name is Sylvia. I've been staying in the Easy 8 Motel over here off Broadway. Room 312."

"Why don't I come over so we can talk about what you need to say before you go down there?"

"No. I told them I'd be there in a little bit. It's fine. I got nothing to worry about cause you guys did it pretty clean, right?" Chuey asked with a little nervousness in his voice.

"Pretty clean. You're not in any of the paperwork. They're going to suspect that someone talked to us, but you need to convince them that it wasn't you. Understand? You don't tell too many lies and stick to your story of not knowing or suspecting anything unusual. Make sure."

"Okay, man, I'll call you when I get back. Should be before noon."

"Okay. See ya. Hey, make sure you call me as soon as you're back across the border." Jimmy wasn't sure he'd heard the last of his directions.

"Jimmy, go in the other room," Shirley said sleepily, rolling away from him.

Jimmy got up, looked at his wife and shook his head. It still didn't feel right being in the bedroom with her. The previous evening started coming back to him as he again started feeling guilty about having had sex with his wife. He felt just as guilty for having been with Carmen. He tried reasoning with himself that feelings were not to be trusted but somehow it wasn't making him feel any better. Part of him wanted to turn off his conscience, but he knew that wasn't the answer either.

As he drove to work, all he could think about was seeing Carmen later that evening. What would he tell her? What was he going to do? Where had all the love for his wife gone? What were his bosses and peers going to think of him getting involved with a trafficker's wife? He hoped he could trust Deron not to say anything. He knew she'd had no part of Angel's illegal activities, but the fact that she had been his wife would be enough to convict both of them in most of their minds.

Jimmy grabbed his briefcase from the back seat of the Expedition and let himself into his office. His thoughts continued to assail him as he made his way to his desk.

"Nice hit yesterday," Maggie Copeland said as he passed her in the hall.

"Thanks, Maggie."

"How much did you guys end up with?"

"I think it was right around 2,400 pounds, give or take a couple. Two arrests. We haven't counted the money yet but it'll probably be close to a hundred grand."

"Sweet. Hey, I'll talk to you later," she said, walking away towards her side of the office.

"Okay. See ya."

Jimmy walked over to his desk and sat down. He knew he had to focus on his work so he forced the thoughts surrounding his personal life from his mind as best he could. By lunchtime he had finished the immediate reports he needed to have done. His report of investigation would wait a day or two.

Halfway through lunch, his cell phone rang.

"Hey Jimmy, this is Jaime. I tracked down the State Judicial investigators handling the Armenta and Sanchez murders. You want to meet them?"

"Sure. When and where?"

"How about I pick you up at San Ysidro in forty-five minutes and I'll take you to a good restaurant in Tijuana. We can have lunch with them."

"Well, I just finished lunch, but I'll come down and have an iced tea or something while you guys eat."

"Okay. See you at the port in forty-five."

An hour later, Jimmy was sitting down to lunch with Jaime and two Baja California State Judicial Police Officers. He'd had to lock up his weapon at the port of entry, making him feel a little uncomfortable. The border was a good ten minutes away by car, and getting back into the port of entry might take awhile with traffic.

"Jimmy, this is Alberto Carrillo and Mario Fuentes," Jaime said, introducing the men. Jimmy smiled and shook their hands. Alberto was a big man, 5'9" and about 240 pounds, while Mario was much more slender, 5'7" and maybe 175 pounds.

"Nice to meet you, gentlemen. Hey, I appreciate you talking to me."

"No problems. Hey, sit down, order something. Jaime's paying," Alberto said with a big smile that showed a single, gold-capped tooth in the top row of his teeth.

Jimmy sat down and picked up a menu. He wasn't hungry but thought maybe he should order something to be polite. The two plain-clothes officers and Jaime were deep in discussion about something in Spanish. Jimmy was only picking up about every tenth word and couldn't follow the conversation.

As the conversation progressed, Jimmy started thinking about the fact that Tijuana was known for its extreme violence. Then he started thinking that U.S. agents were probably worth a pretty penny to some of the cartel members. On top of that, everyone knew that Mexican cops were corrupt.

I'm being ridiculous, he thought to himself. *God will watch over me.* Then he began thinking about how far out of God's will he'd let himself get over the last few months. Maybe God wouldn't take care of him. He hadn't even been to church in a month.

"You're very quiet over there, Agent Maxwell. I apologize. I just asked Jaime if you spoke Spanish and when he said you didn't, well I assumed you did. I'm sorry. We're talking about wives and girlfriends and the fine line needed to balance both relationships. What's your opinion?"

"Well, I've always felt that one woman is enough trouble in any man's life. Life is complicated enough without more problems."

The three men stared at him for a moment then broke out laughing.

"We have a philosopher among us. Still, I think a little variety isn't too bad."

"Are you Catholic?" Jimmy asked.

"*Si.*"

"What would your priest think?"

"How can you expect good advice about women from a man who takes none?" Oscar said, laughing again at his little joke. Jimmy decided to try to change the subject.

"So you guys handled the murders of Oscar Armenta and Francisco Sanchez?" he asked.

"Yes, but let's finish lunch before we talk of it," Mario said.

"Okay. So, you guys always have lunch at two o'clock?" Jimmy asked. He felt a little silly asking so mundane a question, but he really didn't know what to talk about.

"Usually about now. We work from nine a.m. to noon; then we're off between noon and three p.m., then we work until eight p.m. It's that noon to three time where we find time for the girlfriends," Alberto said, laughing again.

Well, I'm glad they're in good moods, Jimmy thought to himself as he smiled at their remarks.

"Guys," Jimmy said, getting their attention, "I apologize for asking this, and I don't mean to offend anyone, but being the curious jerk that I am, I have to ask. Those of us in law enforcement in the U.S. constantly hear about the corruption down here. What's your opinion about it? Is it as rampant as we hear?"

Alberto, who seemed to be the spokesman for his partner, likely because his English was considerably better, got a little more serious.

"By U.S. standards, we are all corrupt." He looked at Jimmy, letting it sink in a moment while he continued to eat. After chewing and swallowing what he had in his mouth, he continued. "I mean, we all take money. Once a month our boss calls us into his office and gives us an envelope that contains a certain amount of money, maybe a $1,000.00 or $1500.00." He smiled and winked. "For the money we get we know if we come across certain people, no matter what they're doing, we look the other way. There are certain houses where we don't go to; there are certain cars we don't stop. That's just the way it is." His face grew more serious as he looked into Jimmy's eyes. "Now we could refuse the money, but if we do, and if we try to arrest those certain people or go to those certain houses, or report the bribes, I'll tell you what will happen. We'll either get fired or we'll be killed."

Alberto continued to look hard into Jimmy's eyes, unflinching and unremorseful. Jimmy stared back, studying this cross-border counterpart, waiting for him to continue. A moment passed then Alberto broke eye contact and went back to eating.

"You know, Agent Maxwell, some of us want to be police officers," he said after another bite from his plate. "But our culture will never truly modernize as long as there is so much money to be made in drugs."

Francisco then said something in Spanish to his partner. Alberto replied in Spanish and then looked over at Jimmy. "My partner is asking me to tell you that the truly corrupt cops down here are those that seek employment with us in order to seek out bribes. Those are the men that need to be removed from our ranks and prosecuted."

"Well I appreciate your candor. It's just something I've wondered about and I prefer getting my information from those who know instead of second or third hand," Jimmy said.

"Life is for learning," Alberto said. Just then, a beautiful brunette waitress came to the table to refill everyone's drinks. She smiled at Alberto and then walked away. "And I'd like to learn a lot more about her." Alberto then looked at Jimmy and again started laughing. Everyone else laughed with him.

When lunch was finished, Jaime looked at his watch. It was a little after three o'clock.

"So, Alberto, what have you been able to determine about the murders of Oscar Armenta and Francisco Sanchez?" Jaime asked.

"Well, we know they were U.S. citizens and that their deaths were drug related."

"How do you know that?" Jimmy asked.

"There was a pickup parked within half a block of where their bodies were found. It was registered to Francisco Sanchez at an address in Chula Vista, I think the same one as Armenta's."

"They were both living off the 400 block of Amber Street in the Cedar Hills Apartments, Unit 32," Jimmy interjected.

"That sounds right. I didn't bring the report with me but I'm sure you're right. In any event, we searched the pickup and found almost sixty kilos of cocaine hidden in a compartment behind the seat. Whoever killed them left the cocaine. Probably didn't know it was there, or they were in a big hurry to leave. We also found two other bodies about a hundred meters west on the beach. They'd been shot in the back of the head as well so they were probably related. We haven't been able to identify them, and probably never will. After they were killed, someone covered their bodies with about a dozen car tires, doused them and the tires with gasoline, and started a nice bonfire. So someone was pretty pissed off at them it seems."

"Well, yeah. They just lost about seven hundred kilos of cocaine in the last month, and that's what we know about. Who knows what other losses they've suffered."

"Not aware of any big cocaine busts here in T.J. recently, but I'll try asking around. Anyway, that's really about all we have. I wish we had more, but there's nothing else for the moment. I could check the report and see if I've missed anything, but I don't think so. There're no prints from the bodies left on the beach. I could get you a bullet taken from one of the bodies left by the pickup, in case you find a gun to match it against; that is, if my boss would go for it," Alberto said.

"No thanks. Nothing else in the vehicle? Address books, any paperwork with anyone's name or address on it, anything like that?"

"Nothing. The truck was really clean. Just the dope. Right, Mario?"

"*Si. Nada mas.*"

Jimmy looked at Jaime and shrugged. "Well, guess that's it then. I appreciate your information and help. It was nice meeting you," Jimmy said as he stood. He reached over the table and shook both men's hands.

"Hey, we'll stay in touch. Maybe we can get together and philosophize again in the not too distant future," Alberto said with a smile. "Only this time with a bottle of good tequila."

"Sure. Sounds like fun. But as for this case, nothing much left to follow up on so it seems. One guy missing from the house we took off in Chula Vista, but who knows. He might have been one of the guys under the tires on the beach. Guess we'll have to be content with what we got and just move on to something else."

Jimmy started to pick up the check for lunch but Jaime grabbed it first.

"My treat," he said. "You can buy me lunch next time I come to San Diego."

"I'd rather get this one," Jimmy said. "The San Diego lunch is going to be twice as expensive."

Jaime laughed. "I know man, that's why I grabbed this check."

By the time they got back to San Diego, it was nearly four o'clock. Jimmy didn't want to go back to the office but it was too early to head over to Carmen's house. She wouldn't be home for another two hours. He decided to call Greg Keller, the Chula Vista detective who'd helped him on the case, and update him with the information he'd just received. He called him on his cell phone.

"Hey Jimmy, what's up?"

"Wanted to get together with you and give you an update on the 807 Hillcrest case. You at the station or out in the field?"

"Took the day off. I'm home. Why don't you come by? We'll have a cold one and we can talk."

"Okay. You still over in Bonita Long Canyon?"

"Yeah. Need the address?"

"No. I remember. See you in about fifteen minutes."

Greg and Jimmy sat out in the back patio of Greg's home and talked for the next two hours. Jimmy caught him up on the murders in short order then the two men moved on to less serious issues. Two hours later, Jimmy had put away four or five beers and was starting to feel pretty good.

"Hey, I appreciate your hospitality, my friend," Jimmy said with a slight slur. "Think I'd better hit the road."

"Just be sure you don't hit anything else, bubba. You're in the company car, you know. Want to hang here for a while longer until you burn off a little of the buzz?"

"Naw, I'm a trained professional. I'll be fine," Jimmy said. "But I appreciate the offer."

Jimmy drove over to Carmen's house with no problems, despite the fact that he was risking a thirty-day suspension for misuse of the government vehicle. Carmen's car was in the driveway but he decided to call her before he went to the door.

"This is Carmen," she answered.

"Hi gorgeous. Where you been all my life?"

"Waiting for you, Jimmy Maxwell. Where are you?"

"Right outside your house. Thought I'd call and make sure you didn't have any male callers that I'd be surprising, or something like that."

"Sounds like you've been drinking."

"A little. Can I come in? I need to use the restroom."

"Come in. I'm unlocking the front door. Make yourself at home. I'm going to go upstairs for a minute and check on Raul."

Jimmy entered the house, used the restroom and then went into the kitchen. Opening the refrigerator, he found a six-pack of Pacifico. He opened one, then sat down at the kitchen table and took a long drink.

Carmen came into the room a minute later and walked over to him. Without getting up Jimmy grabbed her and pulled her to him, wrapping his arms around her midsection, his head between her breasts.

"What's wrong, baby?" she asked.

"I don't know. I guess I don't know what to do about us. I've looked for you my whole life, I've loved you my whole life. I'd have waited for you but I didn't really think you existed. So what do I do, I get impatient and screw things up by not waiting for you, and now I'm with someone else."

"It's okay, Jimmy. It's okay." They held each other for several minutes before Jimmy let go and asked her to sit with him.

"How's Raul? Doing all right? Is he calling his dad?"

"He'll be fine. He's started talking to Angel about twice a week. I'm thinking about taking him down to see him on Saturday."

"You sure that's a good idea?"

"No. Angel isn't crazy about the idea either, but Raul wants to see him."

Jimmy took another swallow from the beer and stared at Carmen. She looked back at him, neither of them saying anything for a minute.

"What? What are you staring at, Jimmy?" Carmen said with a smile.

"You. I just want to study the face of the most beautiful woman I've ever known." He felt both elated and extremely sad at the same time.

"I want to make love to you," Carmen said.

"I'd like that too, but it's not going to happen tonight. You've got a little boy upstairs and I have to go home to the family." Jimmy said nothing for another minute, looking into Carmen's eyes. "Babe, please be patient with me while I try to figure out what to do about this dilemma we're in."

"I don't want you unhappy, Jimmy. I've been alone for a long time. Like I said before, maybe I'm supposed to be alone. I don't want to be the cause of your marriage failing."

"Carmen, my marriage has been failing for a long time. I haven't been happy for a long time. It's just that I never thought it would fail and maybe it's going to take me a little while to get used to the idea. I believe in marriage, you know; that's what's making this so hard. I guess I just have to figure out what's the most important thing to do—stay in a marriage where everyone is unhappy, or abandon my commitment and my vows of for better or for worse. I think I'm destined to be unhappy either way."

Jimmy finished his beer, kissed Carmen and headed to the front door. Once there, he turned to her. "I'll either call or see you tomorrow." She reached up and kissed him again, then let him slip into the evening, the door closing in her face.

Driving home, Jimmy realized he hadn't heard from Chuey all day. He reached for his cell phone and dialed his number. The phone immediately went into a Spanish recording indicating that it was turned off. He decided to go by his motel to see if he was there or if his girlfriend had heard from him.

Turning the corner near the motel, Jimmy noticed four or five marked police units. The parking lot entrance had yellow police tape up, preventing access into it. Jimmy found a place on the curb and parked, taking his badge out from under his shirt and hanging it around his neck.

"Oh no!" he said. "Oh, shit."

He walked up to a uniformed officer guarding the entrance to the crime scene. Showing his credentials, he asked, "What's going on?"

"Body got dumped in front of one of the rooms a couple of hours ago. A couple of whackos drove up in a van and slid open the side door, fired a couple of shots, dumped the body and drove off."

"I need to go see who it is. I have an informant that's staying in 312. He just helped us make a pretty good dope seizure. He went to Mexico to meet with some bad guys. I need to know whether it's him or not."

"Hang on." The officer got on his radio and had an exchange with someone. When he finished, he lifted the crime scene tape and Jimmy stepped under it. "Go ask for Sgt. Sanderson."

"Thanks, man."

Jimmy walked up to the motel, careful to avoid anything that looked like it might be part of the crime scene. There were several crime scene techs taking photographs of skid marks in the parking lot. Jimmy could see a body on the ground, his heart starting to sink as he got closer. Three detectives stood by it talking among themselves. It was Chuey. His hands were bound behind his back.

"Who's Sgt. Sanderson?" Jimmy asked.

The shortest of the three, a man about forty, stocky with a pale complexion and red hair cut in a crew cut answered. He was smoking a cigar. "That's me."

"Nice to meet you, Sarge," Jimmy said, extending his hand. He shook hands with the three detectives but tried not to breathe on them, keeping his head back so that no one noticed any smell of alcohol on his breath. "I'm Special Agent Jimmy Maxwell with the Customs Service. I know this man."

"Really? How so?"

"He's been a confidential source of mine off and on for about five years. His name is Jesus Fernandez-Zedillo but most of us know him as Chuey. I spoke with him this morning. We did a controlled delivery of a little over a ton of marijuana yesterday. Arrested a couple of guys and seized the dope and cash. Chuey set it up for us. He called this morning and said he was supposed to go talk with the owner of the dope in T.J."

"You let him go down there on his own, without anyone to cover the meet?"

"Yeah. We can't go down there for anything operational, and it's pretty normal after a trafficker loses a load to want to get his people together and talk about it. Chuey's gone down to Mexico dozens of times before and never had any issues."

The man standing next to the Sergeant had written down Chuey's name in a notepad. When he finished, he looked over at Jimmy. "I'm Detective John Matheson. So who was he meeting with?" he asked.

"Not really sure. He was initially dealing with a Hilberto Palomares. I don't have the guy fully identified yet. This morning Chuey got a call from Hilberto. Hilberto wanted him to come down and talk to the owner of the dope we seized yesterday. The guy's name was Isidro, but no last name."

The third detective who had yet to speak also had a notepad. It looked like he'd been sketching the parking lot. Sgt. Sanderson would glance over at his notepad occasionally. Jimmy figured he was making sure he was getting the important stuff.

Jimmy hadn't done more than take a cursory look at the body initially. He had tried to focus his attention on the detectives as he spoke with them. Now that he'd finished giving them what little he knew, he crouched down and looked at the body of his source more closely. *Chuey, what did you get yourself into?* he thought.

The face was swollen and it looked like his nose had been broken. Jimmy looked closer and noticed the mouth slightly open. Some semi-dried blood was visible.

"Anyone have a flashlight?" Jimmy asked. Detective Matheson took a small Stinger flashlight from his rear pants' pocket and handed it over to Jimmy. Jimmy turned it on and looked into the mouth without touching the body. It looked like a piece of his tongue had been cut out. Looking further, Jimmy noticed that one of his fingers had been cut off as well. Jimmy handed back the flashlight.

"Well, looks like they did figure out he was working as a snitch."

"Yeah, we noticed the missing finger," Sgt. Sanderson remarked.

"Notice the chunk of his tongue missing too?"

"No. Hadn't noticed. But I'm sure the coroner would have," Sgt. Sanderson said.

"Shit," Jimmy remarked, shaking his head. "He wasn't a bad guy." He paused, starting to get upset. "I never thought this would happen to anyone I ever worked with." Jimmy paused a moment as his thoughts started coming back together.

"You guys been up to 312?"

"What's in 312?" the detective who had yet to speak asked.

"That's his room. That's where he'd been staying for the last few days. He's been shacked up with a woman named Sylvia."

"George, get on that," Sgt. Sanderson said to the detective with the notepad. George turned and headed towards the motel office.

"George Flinn. Just came over from patrol," Sgt. Sanderson said offhanded. "So what's Sylvia's last name?"

Jimmy shook his head in disgust at not knowing. "Don't know, Sarge. Some woman he hooked up with last week. Women were one of his weaknesses. He loved them, but kind of changed them like his socks, you know, every few weeks."

The two detectives smiled at his little joke. Jimmy had made the remark trying to distract himself from some of the shock he was feeling at Chuey's loss.

"Hey, guys, I've got to call my boss and let him know what's going on. Excuse me for a minute," Jimmy said. He stepped away a few paces and started to dial Tom's number. As he did so, he started feeling nauseous. It took him a minute before he could hit the send button on the phone while he fought the urge to throw up.

"Tom, Jimmy. Sorry to bother you but you need to know this. Chuey's been killed. Went to Mexico this morning to meet with the owner of the weed we seized yesterday and someone whacked him. I'm down here in South Bay with some San Diego P.D. detectives standing over his body as we speak."

Jimmy spent the next few minutes explaining what was going on.

"You doing okay, Jimmy?" Tom asked.

"As well as can be expected. Man, I never thought this would ever happen. God, and over some stupid dope."

"It's over betrayal and it's over money," Tom said.

"It's a bunch of bullshit."

"Jimmy, Chuey knew the risks. Do not beat yourself up over this."

"Yeah, yeah."

"Seriously, let it go. You both know what happens in this business. It's the risk of doing business. Think about it." Jimmy listened without saying anything further.

"You coming in to start on the report?" Tom asked.

"Not tonight. Not unless you order me to. I've had a few beers and I need to hang here a bit and see what I can find out."

"Well, you'd better be in early, and I do mean early. We're going to have to call headquarters and report all we have to the Unit Chief for Confidential Sources. I'm sure he's going to want a timeline written up of everything that's occurred since the onset of this investigation. And you know Arlene is going to want to be briefed. I'll give her a call now and give her a head's up."

"Okay, see you about seven o'clock."

"No later than that, Jimmy. I want something ready to send off, even if it's just a preliminary report, by the time Arlene gets in."

"I'll be there." Jimmy hung up and walked back over to the two detectives.

George Flinn walked up to them before Jimmy had a chance to say anything else.

"Your Jesus Fernandez was registered in 312. Registered alone but showed he was driving a 1992 T-bird registered to none other than a Sylvia Castaneda. I wonder if old Sylvia knew that her car information got put on the registration card."

"I wonder where she is? Maybe she got scared after the body got dumped and decided to split," Jimmy remarked. "Where's the car registered?"

"A Tijuana address," Detective Flinn said.

"Figures. Good old DMV, they don't care where something is registered, real address or not, or who it's registered to, as long as they get their money. You know, we seize vehicles at the port that have changed ownership three or four times but are still currently registered to a very old owner. Someone goes in and pays the fees and they issue a new registration sticker without worrying who the real owner is," Jimmy said.

"You're preaching to the choir, Maxwell," Sergeant Sanderson said.

"Yeah, I figured. I guess I get a little frustrated with the roadblocks our own government puts in the way of our jobs.

Hey guys, I need to get home. Here's my card," Jimmy said, handing his business card over to Detective Matheson. "I'll be available if you need anything from me."

As he leaned over to Detective Matheson, he apparently got a little closer than he should have.

"You okay to drive home?" Matheson asked.

"Yeah, I'm fine. I had a couple of beers with a Chula Vista Detective before I got here. Didn't expect to be working. Anyway, I'm fine."

"Okay. Just making sure. We can give you a lift if you need it," Matheson offered.

"Seriously guys. I only live about five miles from here and I've only had a couple. It's cool." Jimmy turned and walked back to his Expedition. He could feel three sets of eyes on his back.

Shit, that's all I needed, he thought to himself. *Hope they don't call any of my management.* The thought was quickly dispelled as he drove, his thoughts quickly returning to the demise of his source.

CHAPTER...

29

Jimmy got home, a headache setting in as the alcohol had started to burn its way out of his system. He was depressed and angry at what had happened to Chuey. He wondered what he could have done, if anything, to prevent his demise. He wondered how the trafficking organization found out—what they found out.

Jimmy went into the restroom as soon as he got home. He washed his face and stood over the sink, again thinking about throwing up. Three or four minutes later, he decided he wasn't going to so he brushed his teeth and gargled with some mouthwash.

Shirley was sitting on the sofa watching television when he came in.

"So you can't even come in and say 'hi honey, I'm home,' before you have to disappear into the back?" she said sarcastically.

"Sorry, I needed to use the restroom."

"Where you been? It's almost 8:30."

"Work. Where's Nikki?"

"I just put her to bed." Jimmy started for her bedroom. "Jimmy Maxwell, do not go in there. Hopefully she's asleep, but if not, she's going to want to stay up for awhile to be with you. I just sat down and I need to relax."

"Jesus, Shirley, I'd like to see my daughter!" Jimmy said loudly.

"Then come home at a decent hour. And don't you raise your voice to me. Just because you had a long day doesn't mean you get to come home and take it out on me."

"Oh, I'm sorry," Jimmy said sarcastically. "I forgot. You're the only one who gets to snap at someone."

Jimmy turned and walked off to their bedroom. He sat in a chair beside the bed and turned on the television at the foot of the bed. Shirley walked in a minute later.

"So what's up? What's wrong?"

Jimmy looked at her for a moment. He didn't want to talk, but maybe it would help. "Chuey, the guy who called here this morning, got killed today."

Shirley took a second to answer, staring at her husband in what appeared to be mild shock. "I'm sorry. What happened?"

Jimmy continued to look at her. He heard the words coming from her mouth, but somehow they didn't seem sincere. It seemed more like she was going through the motions of asking about Chuey because it was her duty.

"He went down to meet with some traffickers who we seized about a ton of weed and a hundred grand from yesterday."

"Well he had to know what he was getting himself into, dealing with people like that, right? It's not your fault, is it?"

"Shirley, he was working for me. He's been working with me off and on for a long time. I knew him pretty well." He looked at her for a moment before continuing. "You know, I'm sure he knew the risks involved in working with us, just like a police officer knows there's risks associated with his job, but so what. It doesn't make me feel any less responsible and it still sucks. He was a human being and he's dead."

"Okay, okay, it is sad, it's a tragedy and I'm sorry. But maybe you shouldn't let yourself get so close to your informants."

"You know, I really don't need this. I don't need your lectures, your advice, or your motherly wisdom. You really don't understand what it is that I do, and I'm not sure you ever will. I get the feeling that you really don't even care about this; that you're just trying to act like a caring wife because somehow you think that's your job."

Shirley stared at him a moment. "You know, Jimmy, I used to care. But when your job, your informants, your stupid dope loads, when they all became more important than me, more important than your daughter, I quit caring."

"Well why didn't you just say so."

"Honestly, I don't know how much more of this I can take," Shirley said.

"Me either. So why don't we just get this over with." Jimmy got up and went to the closet and grabbed a suitcase. He laid it open on the bed and then turned and pulled open a dresser drawer. He began packing shirts, pants, underwear and socks.

"So you're leaving? You're just going to leave because I have an opinion? You're going to leave because I want a husband that wants to be home with me?"

Jimmy continued to pack without saying anything.

"I thought we had something that was worth fighting for. I thought I had a husband that loved me."

Jimmy turned and looked at her. "You did. But it goes both ways. I want a wife who loves me for who I am. I can't be the person you want me to be. I have a career that's provided pretty well for us, but it requires a lot from me. Sure, I could notch it back a little, but that's not me, and quite honestly, I think if I did, you'd just find something else to bitch about. You didn't like my job when I was a local cop, and I came home at the same time every evening. You know, I'm pretty good at what I do, and I think it's an important job."

He went back to packing.

"If you leave me, Jimmy, don't expect to come back."

"No worries," he said without looking up. Then he caught himself and looked at her. "I will be back to see Nikki. You make sure and tell her I'll be back and that I love her dearly."

"Jimmy, I've always known how much you love her. I just wish you'd have loved me as much." Shirley started to softly cry. Tears streamed down her cheeks.

Jimmy stopped again and looked again into Shirley's eyes unaffected by her tears. "You know the difference between Nikki and you? She loves me unconditionally. She's excited to see me whenever I get home. She loves her cartoons, riding her bike, ice cream, but she's almost as happy sitting on my lap watching the news."

"She doesn't know any better. That will all change when she gets a little older."

"Maybe, but I doubt it."

"Jimmy, you're a bastard. A son of a bitching bastard for doing this."

Jimmy closed his suitcase and picked it up. "You've wanted to be free of me for quite a while now. Well, your wish has been granted. Maybe you can find someone who'll work at a bank or drive a bus or something with regular hours that isn't law enforcement. I'll be back for my truck this weekend."

He walked out and got into his Expedition. He sat in the driveway for a minute then started to cry, his forehead resting against his steering wheel. Two minutes later, he wiped his face, started the vehicle and drove away. *Oh God, what have I done*, he thought. *Forgive me.*

He drove for a while just thinking. He knew what he wanted. He knew where he was going. Was it the right thing to do? There was so much that was both right and wrong about it. He parked in front of Carmen's house, then got out and stood at her front door for a minute. He knew it was something he had to try. He knocked softly. A few seconds later, she opened the door.

"Hi, babe," he said, giving a quick glance around the neighborhood, then looking at her face. She stood peeking out at him through a one-inch slit in the door opened to the length of the security chain. "Can I come in?"

"Jimmy, what are you doing? Why are you here?"

"I left Shirley. I . . ." Before he could finish she'd removed the chain, opened the door and had her arms around his neck, holding onto him as tight as she ever had.

"I need a place to stay," he said.

"Did you bring any clothes or anything with you?"

"I have a suitcase in the car."

"Go get it. I'll meet you in the bedroom. I'm going to go brush my teeth," she said excitedly.

Jimmy dragged himself into the office at 6:40 a.m. to work on the timeline related to the ICD and Chuey's murder. He was exhausted, not so much because he'd stayed up with Carmen, but because he hadn't slept well thinking about leaving his wife, and about Chuey's death. Maybe his wife was right. Maybe if he hadn't worked so hard or pushed so hard Chuey would still be alive. He didn't have to work so hard, or care so much, or have such a good time doing what he was doing, at least most of the time.

No one, certainly no one Jimmy knew in the government, really gave a rat's ass about taking dope off the street. Especially marijuana. Sure, the bosses would pat you on the back once in a while, tell you what a wonderful job you were doing, but at the same time they made it more and more difficult each passing year to accomplish anything. And God forbid if you made a mistake while you were out trying to do your job. They'd put your nuts in a blender without giving it a second thought.

Jimmy knew from experience that many agents had had successful careers not doing much of anything. He just couldn't bring himself to be like them. If he could have kicked back, not caused any problems for anyone, never voiced his opinion, he might already be a supervisor. Still, he had gone into law enforcement to arrest bad guys, not to conduct inventories, order pencils or be a disseminator of information from above.

There were so many supervisors and managers who'd never really done anything of significance in their careers, not that being a good investigator necessarily meant you were going to be a good supervisor. But it always kind of bothered Jimmy that someone could get promoted, usually within five or six years after having only worked one or two proactive cases in their career. The rest of the time they socialized with the bosses, politicking and building their wardrobes, because God knows the successful agent dressed well.

He fought to stay focused on his report. It wouldn't be long until Arlene and Tom showed up. Oh well, another ass chewing wouldn't end the world. After nearly ten years of marriage to Shirley, Jimmy knew there was no one who could verbally intimidate him anymore.

Thirty minutes later, Arlene came in. Jimmy saw her coming. He'd practiced what he was going to say in his head a few times. He'd explain that Chuey had gone down and met traffickers countless times before without having any issues. He'd tell her that Chuey understood the risks he was taking. He'd remind her that he'd got the affidavit for the warrant sealed in order to protect the identity of his source.

"Morning, Jimmy," she said, standing over him as he sat at his desk.

"Morning, Arlene."

"I'm really, really sorry to hear about your source," she said, sounding truly remorseful.

"Thanks. I'm really sorry too. I still can't believe it."

"You know, I met him once. Remember, I came out last year on one of your ICDs, well after really. Your group was finishing up a search of a self-storage unit over off Sweetwater. I think you got just under a thousand pounds of marijuana, after a short pursuit, as I remember."

"Yeah, I remember. One of the buyers of the dope showed up and when we moved in to arrest him he took off. Chase lasted about six or seven minutes, although it seemed longer. The guy hit the back of a van going through a red light at the intersection of Willow and Bonita Road."

"Yeah, that's right," she said looking at Jimmy, studying his face. "You all right?" she asked.

"I will be."

Arlene smiled and nodded. "Did Chuey have a family?"

"His mother's still alive, I think. She lives in Tijuana."

"I wonder if she's heard. That has to be horrible for a mother. Do you know if anyone's contacted her?"

"I don't know. Maybe I can go down later and hook up with Jaime, our Tijuana rep, and go talk to her," Jimmy said.

"I thought I heard he had a girlfriend too," she said questioningly.

Jimmy gave a weak smile. "Well, he's had a number of girlfriends since I first started working with him. I think they're the reason he's been so productive over the years. He needs to keep a good cash flow going in order to entertain them."

"Oh . . . Tom said something about a girlfriend who's disappeared. Was he staying with her?"

"He had recently met up with a woman named Sylvia Castaneda. We have a Tijuana address for her that I'm going to get Jaime to follow up on later today. I don't think he'd known her long, but she had spent the night with him prior to his demise."

"You think she's all right?" Arlene asked sounding concerned. The whole conversation with her was introducing a side of her Jimmy had never seen before.

"I would hope so. There's no reason for anyone to be pissed off at her. It's likely that he'd just had a short fling with her and then she went home. Or maybe she heard or saw what happened and took off, fearing for her own safety."

"Well, let me know what you find out about her."

"Sure."

Jimmy, are you sure you're okay?" Jimmy was a little confused and puzzled over the concern.

"I'm fine, at least I think. I'm tired, and I don't know whether to be angry or sad, or even whom I should be angry with. I'm actually very frustrated because I don't know what I can do at this point, but I'll be fine." As he spoke, he felt a tear well up in one of his eyes. He turned and let it drop to the floor. When he looked back, Arlene was watching him.

"Try and get that timeline done, then have Tom review it and fax it to headquarters. Then I want you to go home and get some rest." Arlene turned and headed off to her office.

Well that was unexpected, Jimmy thought to himself. *Life was sure getting weird*, he thought. *Oh well.* He continued typing.

Ten minutes later, Tom came in.

"How's it going? You get any sleep?" he asked.

"A few hours."

"Well, you've had a lot going on over the last forty-eight hours," he said.

"You have no idea," Jimmy replied.

Tom looked at him for a moment. "I thought I did have an idea. Is there something else going on that I've missed?"

Jimmy looked at Tom, regretting a little at having cracked the lid to a potential Pandora's box.

"Well, spit it out, Jimmy? What else?"

Jimmy stood and faced his supervisor. "Let's go into your office. I'd prefer that our conversation be private."

"Oh, shit. This doesn't sound good," Tom said as Jimmy followed him across the squad bay to his office. Once inside, he sat while Jimmy closed his door and then sat across from him.

"Shirley and I split up. I left her last night," Jimmy started.

"Really? I'm sorry. I knew you'd had issues with her over the years, but I didn't realize it was that bad. Is there anything I can do?"

"No, not really, but I appreciate your asking."

"Where'd you stay? Deron's place?"

"No."

"I thought he was your best friend," Tom remarked.

"Look, Tom, I need to run something by you, and I don't want you to overreact, but I also need a straight answer from you because I do value your advice and my career."

"There's more? Man, this sounds serious."

"It is, but probably not in the way that you think. I moved in with another woman . . . a woman with some baggage. Not personal baggage, but baggage that might spill over onto me and the agency." Jimmy hesitated again before continuing.

"Well come on, spit it out."

"Remember that good-looking woman that Angel Garcia was married to?"

"Which one? The good-looking one?" he said with a sudden smile. "I loved that picture of her over her bed. She was one hot mamma."

"Yeah, that one. And, before you open your mouth again, I'm living with her. I'm in love with her."

The color in Tom's face drained. He said nothing for a moment then cleared his throat.

"Holy moly, Jimmy. Well, I guess I should be embarrassed after my comments but shit man, I didn't know."

Jimmy stared at him for a moment, wondering why he wasn't yelling at him, or at least trying to lecture him about how stupid he was. He remained silent a little longer, waiting for Tom to say something. Finally he did.

"Look, Jimmy. You're right; the agency would probably be more than a little embarrassed if something like this got out. So you're going to have to be discreet. But from a personal point of view, I don't think there's that much of an issue there. I mean, if you're discreet, at least for a while. I mean, I guess you're right to be a little worried about what our management might think, or the folks in the group. Some of them probably wouldn't understand or approve. But, bottom line, it's not up to them. She's not a crook, right?"

"Not even a little."

"She didn't know what her husband was doing, or support him in any of his nonsense, right?"

"No."

"She wasn't a snitch, right?"

"No, not really. She did come to us early on, like maybe five or six months ago, and ask for some help after she started getting threatened by Jose Leon when his wife took off with one of her bodyguards."

"Yeah, but you never paid her, right?"

"No."

"Then she wasn't a snitch."

"Okay, so what should I do? Somehow it seems so wrong."

"Jimmy, I think the world of you so I'm going to give you some advice. Maybe you should let your conscience be your guide. But if you truly love her, despite the fact that she may not be the ideal match from a career point of view, I'd say, follow your heart. That said, your bigger issue for the moment is how you are going to deal with your divorce. Wives don't like you leaving them for other women, whether that's the case or not. On top of that, your wife is going to own a pretty big piece of you. You're going to be paying for a long time, and not be around your daughter as much as you'd like. What I'm saying is this: make damn sure this is what you really want to do. Think about your kid, and don't be offended by this, but make sure you're not getting involved with this woman because she's a good-looking piece of tail. There's a lot of hot women out there with a lot less issues."

"Yeah, I know. But Tom, honestly, I didn't want my marriage to fail; it just worked out that way. I just can't deal with all the mistrust, and hate and strife anymore."

"You know the other thing about hooking up with Ms. Sweet britches,"

"It's Carmen, you old goat."

"The other thing about hooking up with Carmen is that if Angel finds out, he might be pretty pissed off. He can still reach out a little from prison, you know."

"So I've been told." Both men said nothing for a minute, Jimmy looking down at the floor and Tom looking at Jimmy.

"Jimmy, you've got a timeline to finish. Once that's done, we're going to have to sit down and talk about what went wrong with your case that somehow cost Chuey his life." Jimmy shot a fiery glance up at Tom but said nothing. "I'm sorry, Jimmy. I didn't mean it that way. Nothing may have gone wrong with your case, or at least nothing that you did. It might have been something Chuey did that got him killed. Shit happens in case you haven't heard. But we'll talk about that later." Jimmy calmed down and started to stand.

"Headquarters is going to want that timeline soon. Have you talked to the unit chief there yet?" Tom asked.

"No. I haven't talked to anyone except Arlene. Couldn't believe it. She was actually pleasant with me when she came in this morning."

"Maybe she got laid last night," Tom said with a chuckle. Jimmy looked up at him."Jimmy, seriously, she's all right most of the time. She gets a little uptight with people because she's in over her head here. But her heart's in the right place. On your other issue, my advice is to keep the relationship thing quiet for a while and see what happens. I'm not going to say anything to anyone. If you need to talk later I'll be around, but for now, get out there and finish that timeline. I'll call headquarters and let them know you're working on it. When you get the timeline done, go home, or to what's her name's house, but get out of here. It's Saturday morning, and I don't want to see you until Monday."

CHAPTER . . .

30

The weekend with Carmen was incredible but bittersweet. Every moment with Carmen answered the question he'd had his entire adult life as to whether or not love between a man and a woman could really be good and beautiful if the two people really loved each other. It was; that is, as long as he wasn't thinking about his marriage to Shirley, his daughter or his belief system.

Jimmy had spoken with Nikki on the phone, and then picked her up on Sunday to spend a few hours with her. They cried together but Jimmy assured her that he would call every day and see her every weekend. She was so beautiful, so fragile and she had such a pure heart. It continued to nag at him as to whether he was doing the right thing. He kept thinking about how selfish he was, how he should just accept his fate and deal with his marriage, despite how unhappy he was. After all, he was an adult who'd made an adult decision to marry. It didn't seem right that his daughter should be affected by the jealousy, selfishness and overall lack of civility between the adults involved in his particular melodrama.

Saturday evening, Raul and Jimmy got to spend a little time together. As they got to know each other, Jimmy sensed that Raul really enjoyed having a man around. They talked about Nintendo games, sports, and school. Carmen watched from a distance without interfering, smiling at both of them any time they looked over at her.

Once Raul was in bed, Jimmy poured a drink while Carmen worked on her computer. Sitting in her house, watching her work, Jimmy thought about this new chapter in his life. His thoughts of whether being with her was right or wrong seemed to disappear when he was in her presence. A part of him felt so very comfortable in his love for this remarkable woman, but he also found himself wondering if he'd made his decision to be with her because of purely physical reasons.

As he sat relaxing and watching her, he found himself feeling a little uncomfortable being in her house, a house where Angel Garcia had lived, even if only briefly and later part-time; a house that other traffickers had just shown up at for various reasons.

"What are you thinking about?" Carmen asked him.

"All kinds of things. Mostly about us, and being here in Angel's house. And I'm still thinking about the death of my source. Wish I knew what happened that caused it."

"It was never Angel's house. As for what happened to your source, it will all become clear sooner or later. I know you're a good investigator and you'll figure it out," she said.

It was such a refreshing change to have someone in his life that was sweet and agreeable.

Early Sunday evening, Jimmy's phone rang. "Maxwell."

"Jimmy, it's Tom. How's it going?"

"Fine, what's up?"

"Hey, sorry to bother you but the duty agents are getting hammered with port cases tonight. The whole day has been busy but I've only got two agents on tonight. Can you go down and give them a hand?"

"Well, I guess. I thought I was supposed to take the weekend off?"

"I know. But I don't have anyone else to send."

"Okay, I guess I can head south. You should know though, I've had about six or seven beers in the last few hours."

"Drive real careful then," Tom said, surprising Jimmy. "I'll let Shirley and Bill know you're in route."

They must be getting hammered, he thought as he hung up. He had to smile at the 'drive careful then' remark.

Jimmy looked over at Carmen. "I guess it's really busy at the port. I have to go to work." The fact that she smiled, kissed him and told him to be careful seemed so foreign to him that he didn't know how to respond.

Arriving at the port of entry, he discovered that his group had already handled over twenty drug loads that day. Jimmy took two marijuana cases and went to work, running criminal history checks, TECS checks, completing the booking paperwork and then handling the interviews of the load drivers.

As he was wrapping things up, around midnight his phone rang again.

"Jimmy, I'm sorry to wake you up, man, but I got something cooking." It was his long-time source Beto.

"Why is it that I only hear from you twice a year, and at least one of those times it's in the middle of the night?"

"Hey, you want me to call you tomorrow? It might be too late, but no problem, man," he said.

Jimmy took a deep breath and sighed. "Look man, I'm up. You called already. What's up?"

"I've got this guy, names Felix Sandoval, he wants me to go up to L.A. with him in the morning and pick up a load of weed. We're going to leave around eight o'clock."

"In the morning?"

"Yeah, eight a.m."

"You're going to L.A. to pick up dope and bring it, where?" Jimmy asked.

"Back here to San Diego."

"Dude, you been smoking some of the stuff you're moving? Weed goes from San Diego to L.A., not the other direction."

"I know, but I'm telling you the truth, he said excitedly. "This guy Sandoval, he lives at 429 Montgomery Court, National City, and drives a 1990 tan Dodge pickup. It's over there now. So he's leaving his house at about quarter to eight, coming over and picking me up and I'm going to rent a van at one of the car rental places by Lindbergh Field. So all you have to do is follow us from my place in the morning and you'll find where the stash house is in L.A., then follow me back here to find out where I deliver it."

Jimmy sighed again. He was tired, really tired, and a little skeptical about the whole thing. Thinking about it for a moment, it occurred to him that Beto, despite his flakiness, had never given him bad information. He exaggerated once in awhile, like all sources, but he didn't make things up. The last information he'd received led him to Carmen.

"Where you been the last six months?" Jimmy asked.

"Guadalajara mostly. My mom is sick," he said. Jimmy didn't respond but continued to try to think. Despite how tired he was, he knew what he had to do.

"Okay, man. I'll be over at this Felix's house around six, but you be sure and call if something changes. Hey, before I let you go, what's old Felix famous for?"

"He and I used to smuggle weed together three or four years ago. He's still smuggling a little, but not like the old days. Works construction and is married with a kid. I think he just got offered a job he couldn't refuse."

"No guns or history of violence?"

"No, man. I told you. He's a family man."

Jimmy hung up and got the booking paperwork together for his two prisoners. *Shit, by the time I get these idiots booked into custody and get home it'll be after 2 a.m.* He'd call Tom in the morning, he told himself. It was way too late to wake him up on a dope deal that he didn't know much about and wasn't even sure was going to happen.

As predicted, he parked in Carmen's driveway at 2:15 a.m., barely able to keep his eyes open. He let himself into her house and thought about having a drink before he went up to bed. He decided against it, despite having a headache that was likely due to the fact that he'd had the drinks earlier and they were now about burnt off. *Damn, all this work is really cutting into my cocktail hours,* he thought to himself with a little smile as he trudged up the stairs to the bedroom.

Once in bed, Jimmy started thinking about the call from Beto. As he thought about Beto, his extended absence from the area, and what tomorrow might hold, he started to think about Chuey's death. What if something goes wrong with this case? I sure don't want to risk Beto's life over some dope. *I sure don't want to go through any of that crap again.* Jimmy lay there and tried thinking about what could possibly have gone wrong on the previous case, but he just couldn't put his finger on any one specific thing.

He knew he had to get up early and yet he was struggling with his thoughts and with sleep. Twenty minutes passed and his headache was getting worse and he still wasn't asleep. He decided to get up and go downstairs and pour himself a double shot of bourbon. Opening the cupboard, he realized he'd drank the last of the Knob Creek two nights earlier. Carmen had a bottle of Crown Royal next to a bottle of El Patron tequila. Tough choice. He decided on the Crown Royal. He sat down on the sofa and sipped it. Ten minutes later, he finished the drink and went to bed. He was asleep almost as soon as his head hit the pillow.

Six o'clock came much too quickly. Jimmy got up and left quietly, giving Carmen a kiss on her forehead on his way out. She smiled, stretched and kind of purred, then reached up and pulled him down onto her, never opening her eyes. He rolled to her side and lay next to her, holding her close, tired but very comfortable in her love.

"Honey, I've got to go to work," he said after a few minutes.

"I know. Just hold me another minute or two."

"Okay. I may be late tonight. I'm not sure. I'll call you later when I know more. Looks like I'm going to L.A. today."

"Just be safe for me. And know that I love you and need you."

"I love you too."

Jimmy got up and headed out the door, happier than he'd been in a long time despite how tired he was. As he drove over to the National City address, he tried focusing on the case at hand, but again found himself going over the pros and cons of being with this woman he'd fallen in love with.

Arriving at 429 Montgomery Court, he found Sandoval's truck parked across the street, just where Beto told him it would be. The registration check on the plate came back to Sandoval at the Montgomery Court address. Jimmy had Sector Communications run a criminal history check on Sandoval and had NIN run the address. Both checks were positive. Sandoval had been arrested several years earlier for possession of marijuana for sale and the DEA had investigated the address a little over a year earlier after they'd received information that he was involved in moving large amounts of marijuana. He hadn't been arrested as a result of the DEA investigation, but the information definitely indicated that Beto's information about this guy was probably accurate.

He called Sector back and asked them to call out the agents in his group, with the exception of the duty agents from the previous shift, and have them roll out to his location as soon as possible.

Jimmy decided to call Tom himself. He woke him and told him the story.

"Sounds pretty crazy to me, but if you think it's for real, I'll get my ass up and join you as quick as I can," Tom said.

"I know. Sounds a little weird to me as well, but I think it's probably true. Hey, can you call DEA and see if they have an agent that wants to join us? This is pretty domestic and I don't want anyone getting their panties in a bunch over us doing a domestic dope case without them."

"Yeah, I'll call George Webber and see if he wants to assign someone to be our babysitter." If they were lucky, DEA would blow them off and not accept the invitation. Marijuana cases held little interest to DEA. Of course, if this were a powder case it would be a whole different story.

Jimmy hung up and started his waiting game. As he sat watching the residence, it occurred to him that it would probably be better to have half of the agents waiting over at Beto's apartment. He went back to his phone and diverted Gary, Mitch and Barbara to the source's residence.

Twenty minutes later, he realized he'd better go find a restroom. Once the surveillance started rolling, there was no telling how long he'd have to hold it before he got a chance to go again. Like many agents, he almost always kept an empty Big Gulp cup with a lid in his car for those moments when you just couldn't find a restroom or didn't have time to use it even if it was close by. Even the Big Gulp cup was tough to use if you were driving down the freeway. It was possible, but difficult. He smiled as he thought about those times when you were out with a partner in the car and you had to go. And people wondered why partners were so close.

He left and drove a little over five minutes before he found a McDonald's, the only thing open in the area at that hour. He went in, ordered a breakfast sandwich and used the restroom. He had been gone less than fifteen minutes when he returned to the Montgomery Court residence. As he came around the corner, his heart sank. The pickup was gone.

Shit, the guy shouldn't have left so soon, he thought. *Well maybe he's getting breakfast first, stopping to visit someone else. I don't know.* Jimmy knew he'd better get over to Beto's place.

"Anyone in Group Five up on the air yet?" he asked over the primary radio channel.

"This is Alpha 357," Deron responded. "I'm on my way."

"What's your 10-20?"

"Northbound 805 at Telegraph Canyon."

"Hey, get off there if you can," Jimmy said. Deron made a wild right from the number one lane, cutting off only one car, rapidly decelerating and just made the exit.

"I'm off. What's up?"

"I had to take a leak. When I got back I noticed our target vehicle was gone. Can you head over to Beto's apartment and see if it shows up. Our guy left early so maybe things have changed."

"Great timing, Jimmy. Why didn't you just tie a knot in the thing until one of us got out here?"

"Hey, he wasn't supposed to be gone so early so screw you. You know where Beto lives?"

Yeah, I think. Which apartment is his in that rat hole of an apartment complex?"

"Bottom unit, second from the street."

"Got it. What's our target vehicle description?"

"Tan Dodge pickup, 1990, 2A98123."

"I'll call you when I get there."

Jimmy drove over to the residence as fast as he could but the morning commute was getting a little heavy. Several minutes passed as both agents headed towards Beto's apartment.

"Jimmy from Deron, bad news. I got here just in time to see the tan pickup leaving northbound on Fourth. I was stuck at a light several cars back and couldn't move. I don't have the vehicle anywhere. What's your 20?"

"Southbound on Third at 'G' Street. Let me cut over to Fourth and see if I can pick them up . . . Where is everyone?"

"A358 to Jimmy. I'm just getting off the 805 at 'E' Street," Sal responded. "I'll go west and see if I can spot them. Tan Dodge pickup occupied twice, right?"

"Yeah. Anyone else in the vicinity?" Jimmy asked over the air.

Barbara, Gary and Mitch were all five to ten minutes out. Tom was twenty minutes out. As it turned out, Jesus was filing the complaints from the duty day and wouldn't be available for at least an hour.

All of the agents drove around the north end of Chula Vista looking for the tan Dodge pickup but had no luck at all finding it. Thirty minutes later, Jimmy rallied everyone together and decided on a new plan of action. Andres Fernandez, one of the younger agents from DEA, showed up as they all got together for a mini-brief.

"Guys, I've been trying to call this idiot, but his cell phone's off. He said they were leaving here and going to rent a car over by the airport. Let's split up and check them all out and see if our tan Dodge is over at one of them. Deron, you take Hertz; Barbara gets Economy; Gary, you take Enterprise; I'll take Budget. What's left? I know, Alamo. Sal, you get that one. Whoever's left, head over there and find one I've forgotten. If you don't see our vehicle, go in and ask if they've just rented a vehicle to Alberto Calderon. That's Beto's real name."

"Jimmy, I'll go back and sit on this Felix Sandoval's res in National City. There's a chance that he might have forgotten something or that he'll swing by there again before they leave. You know to drop off the truck or something," Tom said.

"Thanks, Jefe, I appreciate it."

The agents dispersed and headed towards Lindbergh Field.

It was nearly an hour later when Barbara called Jimmy. "Jimmy. They were here. Left about twenty minutes ago. Rented a full-size Ford van, white. I've got the plate."

"Good. Well, his cell phone is still off, but I've got to believe he's going to try and call us at some point. Barbara, how about calling the San Clemente and Temecula check points and asking Border Patrol to keep an eye out for the van. If they find it have them refer it on an immigration ruse and call us. As a matter of fact, we may as well head up there and just hang out. I hate splitting our forces again, but I don't know what else to do."

Thirty minutes later, the agents were northbound, half of them up Interstate 5 and the other half up Interstate 15. As Jimmy was going through Del Mar, his cell phone rang.

"Jimmy, what happened to you? Shit man, Felix and I are taking off in a few minutes."

"Where are you?" Jimmy asked.

"We're over with this friend of his at his apartment. It's off Adams and the 15. We're going to take off shortly up the 15. We're going to someplace in Ontario."

"What's shortly, Beto?"

"Like ten or fifteen minutes."

"Okay, here's what you need to do. I'll have our guys up near Escondido. When you get to the 78 freeway, pretend you're calling your mom but call me and tell me when you're going to be home tonight," Jimmy instructed.

"Why would I do that? I'm a grown man. I wouldn't do that."

"Beto, I know you're a grown man. It's just like a code that lets us know to look for you. Now you've got to be a good actor and make the call. We don't want to miss you going by."

"Oh, I get it. Okay, that's a good idea. Listen, Jimmy," Beto said in a whisper, "I've got to go." With that he hung up. Jimmy got on the radio and cell phone and diverted everyone to the North County Fair shopping mall parking lot.

Forty minutes later, Jimmy had briefed everyone and had vehicles strung out at every onramp from mid-Escondido to halfway to Temecula. Now the wait began.

It was nearly an hour later when Jimmy's phone rang. He answered without saying anything. "Mom, mom, are you there?"

"Talk to me," Jimmy answered.

"Yeah, mom. I'm not going to be home until really late. I'll call you later."

"Okay boys and girls," Jimmy put out over the radio. "Our boy should be coming up the road any second."

Two minutes later, Deron got on the air. "He just went by me, first exit north of the 78. I'm trying to catch up."

Jimmy was at the next exit north. He started slowly rolling down the onramp, picking up speed. As he neared the bottom of the ramp and started to merge into traffic, he still hadn't seen the van.

"Dude, this guy is flying. I'm doing eighty-five and he's pulling ahead of me," Deron transmitted. Jimmy watched his rear-view mirror and started to accelerate.

"What's wrong with this asshole? I'm doing ninety and I still can't keep up."

Jimmy kicked it up to eighty, expecting to see the van any moment. There it was. It was coming up fast, moving between the number one and number two lanes, the two fastest lanes of traffic. The van was rapidly gaining on Jimmy as he accelerated further. Seconds later, the van passed Jimmy. There was only one occupant—Beto.

Jimmy was barely able to keep up with the van as Beto slipped in and out of traffic, traveling between ninety and ninety-five miles per hour. *What an asshole,* Jimmy thought. *I'm going to kick his ass later, if we survive this.* Jimmy had been getting sleepy waiting for Beto to go by. Now he was wide awake. Jimmy got on the cell phone to him.

"Yeah," Beto said calmly, answering the phone.

"What the hell are you doing?" Jimmy said, almost yelling in the phone.

"I'm driving to Ontario."

"Slow down, you shithead." Beto dropped his speed to about eighty-five.

"What's going on?" Jimmy asked.

"I told you. I'm on my way to Ontario."

"Yeah, but you're alone."

"Felix left about ten minutes ahead of me in another car that belongs to his friend that lives in that apartment we were at off Adams."

"Then why did you call me with the mom thing?" Jimmy asked.

"Because you told me to," Beto said, raising his voice a little.

"You're an idiot, you know that? Get off on the next exit so we can talk to you. We really need to find out what's going on."

"I can't, they're expecting me to arrive right after Felix and he left ten minutes ahead of me. I'm trying to catch up."

"So pull off at the next exit. We'll only keep you five minutes. We need to talk and I'd really feel better about things if we could slap a tele-track on your van."

"Jimmy, I just can't. I don't know who might be following and Felix drives almost as fast as me."

"Well, can you at least slow down a little so we can keep up? Jesus man, you're a friggin hazard. If I were a traffic cop I'd arrest you and impound your car," Jimmy said, frustrated that he wasn't getting anywhere with Beto.

"If you were a traffic cop, I'd outrun you," Beto said with a little laugh.

"Yeah, just like you did two years ago when you got arrested by the San Diego Police after that stupid pursuit. I still can't believe you tried to run just because you had expired registration. How long did you spend in jail?"

"Seven months. But it wasn't fair, them having a helicopter. I'd have lost the black and whites easy."

"Like I said, you're an idiot. Not that I don't like you some of the time, but you're still an idiot."

"Why am I the only person I've ever heard you call names?" Beto asked with a little sadness in his voice.

"Because you do stupid things and don't follow directions, and you know it pisses me off. And I'm not an easy person to piss off. You're like that puppy that you try to get to mind you, lovable and all that, but no matter how many times you take him outside, he still pisses on the carpet."

"Really, I'm like a puppy?" Beto asked, sounding a little cheerier.

"Just slow down."

"I did, as soon as you asked."

"Beto, going from ninety-five to ninety isn't slowing down much. Nothing over seventy-five, okay?"

"Okay. But you know I hate driving that slow." Beto terminated his cell phone conversation with Jimmy, slowing down to about seventy-five momentarily. A mile later, he was doing eighty and a mile after that he was nudging eighty-five again. Jimmy dialed his number and hit send. The phone rang, but no one answered.

Fortunately the drive between Escondido and Temecula was open and easy, with most of the traffic doing between eighty and eighty-five mph. Jimmy tried to reach Beto several more times as they traveled north but got no answer. The traffic tightened a little between Temecula and Ontario but the agents were able to keep up without too much difficulty.

Exiting at the Vineyard exit off Interstate 10, the agents followed the van back through the suburbs and watched as it headed down an alley and into the backyard of a house. There was a gate off the alley that a Mexican male had opened as the van approached. Obviously Beto had turned on his phone again or he'd been to the residence on some prior occasion.

Riverside agents had been called during the drive north and several met with Jimmy and Tom in the residential area near where the van had parked about an hour after they'd arrived. Jimmy briefed them on the case and advised them that he thought a search warrant should be sought for the residence where the van was parked. Tom agreed with him.

"Agent Maxwell, I know you folks down in San Diego do things a little differently than most of the rest of the country, but this is a purely domestic dope case. We want to help you folks out but we're going to have to call in a local narcotics team to write any warrant. Even if we got DEA to come out on this and help with a warrant, unless they found the place filled to the rafters in cocaine or heroin, no one in the U.S. Attorney's office will touch this. So we'll call Ontario P.D. and ask them to come out, but understand that the case is going to become theirs," Group Supervisor Chad Rothchild said.

"Yeah, I know, Chad. We've been up here before. Shit, we got sent home a few months back because DEA didn't get enough advanced warning that we were coming and didn't trust us to play nice in their sandbox."

"You have a DEA agent with you to preclude that problem this time though, right?"

"He has one," Tom replied.

"Thought I might need one, knowing how crazy the bosses get, especially when you're out of district," Jimmy answered, giving Tom a little smile.

Jimmy and Chad continued talking and after a few minutes, Chad put in a call to an Ontario Police Department narcotics team buddy and asked if they could respond. They advised that they'd be there within an hour.

It was about an hour later when Barbara chirped Jimmy on his Nextel. "Jimmy, the van's moving."

"Thanks Barbara. Call it out," he replied to her. "Chad, the van's moving. Get on the phone to your Ontario team and see how far out they are," Jimmy said as he trotted to his Expedition.

The van pulled out of the backyard. A male driver got out and closed the gate, then got back into the van.

"The van is westbound down the alley at about five miles per hour," Barbara put out over the air on her radio.

The surveillance team followed the van out onto the street. Several of the units were a little closer than Jimmy wanted, but late afternoon traffic was heavy enough to warrant following closely as they didn't want to lose whatever was in the van. Jimmy hadn't heard from Beto and he didn't want to risk a call to him while he was with bad guys.

Several blocks from the load house, the van pulled over on a residential street lined with trees, thick with leaves, branches hanging down almost to the top of the van. It was starting to get dark. The driver of the van got out and walked away.

"Jimmy, should we take this guy or let him go?" Greg asked.

"Let him go. Let's stay with the van. He'll probably be back."

The agents stayed with the van, one hour, then two, then three. Jimmy had Barbara get out of her car and walk by the van so she could look inside.

"There's a bunch of big black trash bags inside. I don't know what's in the trash bags but I can guess," she transmitted once she was back to her car.

At approximately 9:30 p.m., Ontario P.D. executed a state search warrant at the residence where the van had been loaded. No one was home but one of the bedrooms was filled with packages of marijuana.

"What do you think, boss?" Jimmy asked Tom via Nextel radio.

"I'd say someone burned your surveillance."

"I think so too."

"So you decide. It's your case. Obviously we're not leaving the van. We can call a tow truck and just take it, or give it a little longer and see who shows up for it."

"Well, it's pushing 9:30 and I'm fading. Let's give it an hour. No one shows, we'll call for a tow truck."

"Fair enough," Tom said.

The Riverside agents had joined the Ontario P.D. detectives to help process the residence while the San Ysidro agents had spread out to cover the van's departure, if it was ever to occur.

Jimmy decided to give Carmen a call while he sat waiting. "Hi, babe," he said when she answered.

"Hi yourself, handsome. Working late I guess?"

"Yeah, but I'd rather be with you."

"Well that's the nicest thing anyone's said to me all day," she said sweetly.

"Hey, we're up in the Riverside area. I'm hoping to be on my way home within the hour. Just wanted to check in before you went to bed. Don't wait up. I may be late."

"Okay, Jimmy. Thanks for the call and be careful."

"Just call me Special Agent Careful. Love you." He hung up with a smile on his face, something he wasn't used to doing after a call home.

Jimmy decided to try to reach Beto but got no answer on his cell phone.

At a little after ten, Andres Fernandez got on the air. "Hey, guys. Got a lone male walking down the sidewalk towards the van."

Everyone perked up a bit, waiting to see what would happen.

"Okay, he's nearing the van, looking around. Ladies and gentlemen, we have a winner. He's getting in. Stand by. Okay, we're rolling southbound."

Everyone involved in the surveillance immediately stopped what they were doing and began to focus on following the van. Jimmy started the Expedition and turned around in the dark, having been set up to go north. Once he was headed south, he turned on his lights.

"This idiot is flying," Mitch transmitted. "He's back to Vineyard and if he doesn't kill someone first he'll be on the freeway in about thirty seconds."

"He had to be going about sixty when he passed me," Gary said. "Speed limit over here is thirty-five."

"I know. Never a cop when you need one," Jimmy said.

Once the agents were southbound on Interstate 15, the van accelerated and was soon lost to all the agents. It had taken the driver less than five minutes to lose Jimmy's entire group.

Jimmy tried to reach Beto again but the phone went to voicemail after the first ring. He called Tom and advised that his source still wasn't available. He hoped Beto was okay, then wondered if it wasn't him in the van based on how the van was being driven. If that was the case, he'd kill Beto later himself.

"Hey, guys. Thanks for playing today. Riverside just called me and advised they got approximately 650 pounds of weed out of the house. No one was home but I'm sure they'll track down whoever lived there. Let's call it a day. See you tomorrow," Tom transmitted to the group.

Jimmy had his windows rolled down during the drive south and was doing everything he could to stay awake behind the wheel. He'd tuned his radio to a hard rock station and turned it up as loud as he could stand. Even with the loud music and cold air blowing in, it wasn't long before he was slapping himself as hard as he could to keep his eyes open. He made it home by the grace of God, having just enough energy to get upstairs, brush his teeth, undress and fall into bed. It was a few minutes after one a.m. A minute later, Jimmy's cell phone rang.

"No, it can't be," he said as he picked up his cell phone and looked at the number.

"Beto, where are you?"

"Hey, Jimmy," he said in a hushed tone. "I'm home, but I know where the van's parked. Come over and pick me up and I'll take you over to it. It's getting picked up at seven a.m."

"Where is it?"

"It's over at that apartment complex where we stopped earlier, over off Adams and 15."

"How do you know?"

"Cause I drove it there."

"Were you the guy who picked it up in Ontario?"

"Yeah, why?"

"Cause you're an asshole. What in the hell is wrong with you? I should come over and kick your stupid ass, you . . ." Jimmy cut himself off as Carmen started to stir beside him. "Why do you drive like such a dick?" he said in a much quieter tone.

"I just drive like normal," he replied.

"If I was still a cop, I'd suspend your license, forever if I could. But then you'd just drive without one, wouldn't you?"

"Yeah."

"And you couldn't call me on the drive back to San Diego? I don't think I'm going to pay you for this case, what do you think about that?"

"I do a good job for you and you wouldn't pay me? How am I going to get back to Guadalajara to see my mother?"

"Maybe I'll pay you a little just to get you out of my hair for awhile."

"Come on, man. I do good work for you. Don't be that way."

Jimmy threw the covers back and sat up. He thought for a moment, sighed and got up, knowing that if he didn't go now, he'd never see the van again.

"Okay, stay awake. I'll be over in a half hour."

"I'll be awake," he said, sounding alert.

Jimmy put in a call through Sector Communications to Tom's residence to advise him of what was going on. He got the answering machine. Trying his cell phone he again got no answer. He left a message on his voicemail. Then Jimmy went down the list of agents in the group. No answer with Bill, Barbara, Shirley, Greg or Jesus. When he reached Deron, he got an answer.

"Yeah, Jimmy, what's up?" Deron answered sleepily.

"That idiot Beto just called. He wants me to pick him up so he can show me where the van we lost is parked. I should have just called you first after the luck I've had getting someone to answer their phone."

"Guess I should have turned mine off too," Deron said.

"Sorry dude. I'll owe you."

"There's a surprise. I'm kidding . . . sort of. I'll get dressed. And you don't owe me. I've written them all off cause I know I'll never get paid back for all the times you've used and abused me."

Jimmy smiled. "I know. You do it because you love me."

"Let's not get carried away, you sick bastard. Where you want to meet?"

"Head towards the Adams Avenue exit off the 15 north."

Jimmy continued sitting on the edge of the bed, trying to get enough energy to get dressed. He looked over at Carmen sleeping next to him. He smiled as he watched her. *How did I get lucky enough to end up with someone like her?* he thought.

Thirty minutes later, Jimmy pulled up in front of Beto's apartment. He started to dial him on the cell phone when Beto appeared at his door and headed over to him. He opened the car door and jumped in next to Jimmy.

"Come on, man, let's go," Beto said.

Jimmy put the Expedition in drive and pulled out without saying anything.

A mile down the road, Beto looked over at him. "What? Why aren't you talking to me?" he asked.

"I'm trying to get over wanting to kick your ass," Jimmy said without looking over at Beto.

"Why? I brought you this good case and everything is working out, right?"

Jimmy looked over at Beto. "You willing to testify against Felix?"

Beto said nothing.

"You willing to testify against the people from the house in Ontario?"

"You don't want me to get killed or anything, do you?"

"Beto, what I got today was no sleep and a bunch of weed, which, quite frankly no one except maybe me gives a rat's ass about. You risk everyone's life, including yours, driving up and back from Ontario at speeds that should have got you arrested at least. You're going to get yourself or someone else killed eventually driving like you do. You drive like an idiot." Jimmy paused a moment before continuing. "We're trying to work a case and you don't have the good sense to leave your cell phone on or give me a call and let me know what's going on," he said, finally looking over at him.

"Yeah, I'm sorry about that. I'd turned it off when we were loading the van cause I didn't want you calling while I was with Felix and his friends. Guess I forgot to turn it back on."

"Or to call me during the two-hour drive home," Jimmy said angrily.

"Sorry."

"Beto, I hardly ever get angry, but you've got me really pissed off. I'm telling you, if it wasn't for our past history and some of the other good cases you've done over the years, I'd wash my hands of you, blackball you from ever working with any other agent and probably put your stupid ass in jail. You know I had a whole team out a few hours ago, and now it's just Deron and I. If you'd have called and told us you were in the van, we could have followed you over to where we're going. Now it's just the two of us."

"You've got me too," he said.

"You don't count. In fact, you complicate things for me."

The two drove on in silence until they got over to the Adams' exit.

"Deron, I'm getting off on the exit. Go west two blocks and then turn left again. There should be an apartment complex about a block and a half down the street on the east side."

The agents found the complex and located the van. It was parked under a carport in the center of the complex. The van still had the black plastic trash bags visible through the windows. Jimmy tried Tom again at his residence. There was still no answer.

"Well, it's almost two a.m. and I can't reach Tom so I guess I'll have to make an executive decision," Jimmy said. "We can't sit out here all night with Beto and we can't just leave this here."

Jimmy got on the cell phone again. "Sector, it's Jimmy. Need you to hook me up with San Diego Police, the non-emergency line and then do me a favor and call our contract towing service and have them send me a tow truck." Jimmy gave them his location and then waited to be connected to the P.D. Once connected, he asked for a unit to respond to his location.

Twenty minutes later, a two-man unit showed up. Jimmy pulled out his badge as he walked up to the unit.

"Hey, guys. Customs. Can you guys hang out with us until a tow truck shows up? We've got a van full of weed parked over there and we'd sure appreciate your company until we can get it out of here, you know, just in case someone decides to show up wanting it," Jimmy said.

"And we don't want anyone calling you guys and reporting us for stealing a car," Deron said.

"How much weed's in the van?" the driver of the patrol unit asked.

"Don't really know for sure but it looks like a lot. Probably three or four hundred pounds at least," Jimmy said.

"Cool. I've never seen that much dope before. Mind if I go take a look?" the officer asked, getting out of his unit.

"Go ahead. It's parked over there."

The officer walked over to the van and tried the door. It was locked. He took his flashlight and illuminated the interior, then walked back to Jimmy and Deron.

"Got the keys?" he asked.

"Beto, you have the keys?" Jimmy asked.

"Nope."

"I've got a slim jim in my car. Want me to open it?"

"Sure."

The officer got out his slim jim and within a minute, had the door open. Once open, he put on a pair of gloves and opened a bag. It was full of marijuana bricks. He then hefted the bag, trying to sense the weight. He closed the bag and then closed up the van, leaving it unlocked.

"Jeez man, I think you're closer to five hundred pounds. Those bags weigh about thirty-five or forty pounds and I counted fifteen of them."

"Well, the more the merrier, I guess," Jimmy said.

Jimmy, Deron, Beto and the officers stood around talking for about twenty minutes until the tow truck arrived. Jimmy directed the driver to the van and a short time later, it was hooked up to the tow truck. Jimmy thanked the officers for hanging out with them and everyone cleared, with Jimmy and Deron following the tow truck.

Jimmy had directed the driver to take the van to his office. It had an underground parking garage, no public access and an armed security guard that stayed on the premises twenty-four hours a day. He was so tired that he even engaged in conversation with Beto in order to stay awake. Once at the office, he confirmed the bag count, then had the tow truck driver place the van in a seized vehicle space. The security guard came out of his office while the van was being dropped and inquired about the late-night visit. Jimmy locked the van and asked the officer to keep an eye on it, giving him the short version of the events that led up to the seizure. It was 3:30 a.m.

"Can you log the time I dropped the van here in your log book and write in that there are fifteen black trash bags in the van?" he asked the officer.

"Sure."

"Thanks. I'll be back to pick it up by 8:30 a.m."

Chapter . . .

31

Jimmy was on his way to the office at 8:30 a.m. when his cell phone rang.

"Jimmy, where are you?" Tom asked.

"About ten minutes from the office."

"Did you leave a van loaded with marijuana parked in our parking garage?"

"Yeah. When I got home last night, Beto called and told me where that van was that we lost leaving Ontario. Deron and I had to roll out. I tried to reach you several times, but you didn't answer."

"Arlene came in this morning and saw it parked in the garage. When she inquired with the security officer and found out it was loaded with weed, she freaked out. What the hell were you thinking? You can't leave drugs in the garage. They're going to have your ass."

"What was I supposed to do? I couldn't get hold of anyone except Deron and I was too tired to process it. Plus I had Beto with me. If I'd have stayed up to process it I'd probably just be getting home now."

"Well get down there and deal with it as quickly as you can. I'll have some of the group come help you, but get it out of there. Then you're going to have to go up and write a memo explaining why you violated policy, and then we're going to have to go see Arlene and get our asses chewed."

"Okay."

Jimmy was still tired. He really didn't need this crap.

He finished processing the marijuana around eleven a.m. and headed up to his desk to start on his memo. He passed Group Supervisor Angelo Brown on his way. Angelo started shaking his head as Jimmy neared.

"What the hell were you thinking, man? I always figured you for being a lot smarter than that," he said.

"Well, now you know. I'm not perfect, I guess." He kept walking as Angelo stared at him, making no further comment.

It only took about fifteen minutes to write the memo and once printed, he walked over to Tom's office. Tom looked up from his desk but said nothing as Jimmy came in and sat down.

Tom finished writing something on his desk calendar and then pushed his chair back from his desk. "I swear, Jimmy. Does that woman you're staying with really have your head that screwed up?"

"I can't believe you would say that. I was tired. You called me in to work late and I get a couple hours sleep and then spend almost another twenty-four hours up."

"Okay, okay. Are you ready? It's time to go get our asses reamed."

"Whatever." The two started walking up to Arlene's office as they continued to talk. "By the way, it weighed 504 pounds. The Riverside agents called and told me their total from the house was 650 pounds even. Sure is great. I get 1,154 pounds of marijuana in a one-day case and then get in trouble for it. Makes you wonder why an agent would want to do proactive investigations. Nothing in them but trouble."

"Oh, quit your whining. You know you wouldn't be happy sitting on your ass like some of these slugs around here. You fucked up. So take your medicine and move on."

Jimmy said nothing for a moment. "Sorry, Tom. I'm tired and I just don't get why Arlene worries about all this stupid crap. She doesn't have to be such a—well—the way she is."

"Jimmy, the security officer doesn't have any authority to guard our dope. You know that, and you know the parking garage isn't an authorized drug storage area. No matter how tired you were you knew that. "

"The guard wasn't guarding the dope. He was just there as a deterrent, more or less."

Tom stopped walking and looked at Jimmy. "I'm telling you flat out, you fucked up. My advice to you is to be apologetic and don't try making a bunch of excuses." They started walking again.

"I'll try." •

A minute later, they walked into Arlene's office and sat down on the opposite side of her desk.

"Let's see the memo," she asked. Jimmy handed it over and both men sat watching her for a minute as she read.

"I really don't understand you, Jimmy. Just when I was starting to like you a little you pull a boneheaded stunt like this. What were you thinking?"

"It's in the memo. I was very tired, couldn't reach my supervisor or anyone else in my group. I had an informant I had to get rid of and just thought that it wouldn't be a big deal to leave the van for a few hours."

"Is this an authorized drug storage facility?" she asked.

"Well, DEA has a vault upstairs, but obviously there was no one available to let us into it," Jimmy said with a little sarcasm.

"No! No, it isn't an authorized drug storage facility. That is the answer that should be coming out of your mouth. This violation will be forwarded to the SAC for him to decide what punishment is fitting, and I'd guess you're looking at a few days off at the very least."

"Great. So what was I supposed to do last night?"

"If you can't get hold of your supervisor, you call someone else. You could have called me. I'd have got you some help."

"Well, now I know." Jimmy looked over at Tom. "I realize I screwed up. I'm sorry and it won't happen again."

Following another minute of admonishment, Jimmy was excused. Tom stayed behind, closing the door behind Jimmy as he walked away. Jimmy guessed it was his turn to get chewed out.

Jimmy walked back to his desk and pulled a case number on his case. He sat a few minutes, fuming about his situation. Yeah, he hadn't followed the protocols in place, so technically management was right, but it was hard to figure why people would spend so much time, energy and emotion over something so easily explained and innocent in nature. People were human, with human failings, fatigue being the primary one at play in this circumstance.

He tried to work on the report for a little while but was so wound up that he decided to get out of the office. Once on the road, his mind began to work overtime again. He began to wonder what was happening to his life. Where things had once been pretty smooth, they were getting to be pretty rocky.

He started thinking about Chuey. He shouldn't have been murdered over dope. Jimmy wondered if God had somehow removed his protection because of his screw-ups, yet he knew that really wasn't the way God worked. But maybe his actions had moved him out of God's protection. He pondered this as he drove, finally ending up at 'Las Quatro Milpas.' It was farther from the office than he really liked going at lunchtime, but he loved their food and the drive gave him time to think. As he sat eating, his cell phone rang.

"Maxwell."

"Jimmy, this is Angelo." Jimmy sighed, waiting for another condescending remark about his screw up with the van. "Hey, I talked to Tom and got his blessing to call you. You interested in doing some undercover for our group tomorrow?"

"Tell me about it."

"Miguel Martinez is working this heroin trafficker that lives in that older area just east of downtown. He's got a source into him. According to the source, he's got thirty pieces of tar for sale, but the source doesn't want to do the buy because he doesn't want to testify. I thought maybe we could introduce an undercover. After all, two kilos of heroin is a pretty good case."

"Actually, it's a little over 1.6 kilos. Remember a piece is twenty-five grams."

"I know, but it sounds better when I round it up."

Jimmy laughed. "But a white guy?" he asked.

"Sure."

"Why not use one of the guys in your group?"

"I thought about it, but I really don't think they're experienced enough. I know you've worked a lot of sources and you've been in the area a long time. I also know you've seen a lot more heroin up close. I'd just feel better about having you do it."

"Angelo, I'll do it, but I think introducing a white guy to make a heroin buy around this area is a mistake. Not only that, but your source is going to get burned when the reports show him introducing a cop. You know, I've got another source: Tony Rivera, a Puerto Rican who used to live in New York. I think he'd be ideal for something like this."

"Well an undercover is a better observer and testifier."

"I agree, but Tony has been around for a long time and has testified in both state and federal court. He's the smartest source I've ever dealt with and he's really easy to control."

"Well, ideally I'd rather use you, but if you think this Tony guy can do a good job, I'll be open to it. Can you have him in the office tomorrow morning so I can talk to him?"

"Yeah, I think so. Let me give him a call and I'll let you know shortly."

Jimmy hung up and decided to finish his meal in peace before calling Tony. Twenty minutes later, after walking out to his Expedition, he made the call.

"Tony, Jimmy. What's up?"

"Nothing man. Just hanging out with the family. What's up with you?"

"Feel like driving down to San Diego in the morning? I might have some work for you."

"It's about time. I haven't been doing much lately. I finished a case for the money-laundering group last month, but no one else seems to be calling. It's been almost a year I think since we did anything together. It was that heroin case up in Poway. Remember?"

"Dude, how can I forget? You were negotiating with that guy for the three kilos of heroin when he had a visitor. When he excused himself for a moment to go talk to the guy, you walked over to the window and looked out, memorized his plate and gave it to me after the meet. Still don't know how you remembered it. You were in with the guy for another twenty or thirty minutes before leaving."

"I'm not sure how I remembered it either. But I remember you putting it on lookout. When it came across the border a few weeks later, you guys found eighteen pounds of heroin hidden in a rear bumper compartment. But the best part was that you got me ten grand in three days. No one else has ever matched you in getting me paid so quickly."

"Hey, you get a good source, you have to take care of them," Jimmy said.

"By the way, Jimmy. I heard about Chuey. I only met him a couple of times, but he seemed like an okay guy. I'm sorry, man."

"Yeah, thanks. Me too."

"What's the gig tomorrow?" Tony asked.

"Meet and negotiate a thirty-piece heroin deal."

"Only thirty? Must not be one of your cases," Tony said with a chuckle.

"Actually, it's a guy in another group in our office. He's a good guy, a little inexperienced still, but he's on his way to being a star. You know, they wanted me to do the undercover on this deal instead of using another source."

"So is the dealer a white guy?"

"No, Hispanic, I'm pretty sure."

"So why would they want to screw it up by using you?" Tony asked.

Jimmy laughed. He had grown to realize that Tony was a man who spoke his mind, never holding back on giving you his opinion of the way he viewed everything in life. Jimmy guessed that he was probably self-confident because he was a good-looking guy, Puerto Rican, mid-thirties, intelligent, dressed well, articulate, well spoken in both English and Spanish. He'd also had a lot of luck in most of what he'd done working for Jimmy and other agents. Still, a lot of his personality stemmed just from being a New Yorker.

"They don't know any better. I mean, it might have worked, but it would have been a long shot."

"Man, you did the right thing calling me. No sense in getting yourself killed, or at least screwing up the case using you. No offense."

"None taken. So how about being at the office around 9:30?"

"The wife has to take the kids to school. When she gets back I'll have a car. Make it around ten," Tony said.

"Okay, see you."

"Late."

Jimmy started his G-ride and headed back to the office. His call to Tony had cheered him up a little, taking his mind off his day, reminiscing over good cases during less complicated times. Driving back to the office, he decided he'd rather go to the range and burn some government ammunition. He usually tried to get to the range about once a month, but it was pushing three months and he was scheduled for his quarterly range qualification the following week He figured the practice would do him good.

He spent nearly two hours at the San Diego Police range. By the time he was finished, he was shooting a lot better than when he'd started.

That night he spent a quiet, relaxing evening with Carmen and Raul. During dinner very little was said. Jimmy noticed Carmen watching him a little, but dismissed it. As time passed, he started feeling a little uncomfortable about not having much to say. He had asked her about her day, but he'd offered nothing about his. It just seemed like too much work to open himself up and talk. As he sat slowly eating, he began feeling so drained that he almost felt like crying. There was really no good reason for it. It was just one of those things that hit him every once in a while.

"So why don't you tell me what's on your mind?" she suggested.

"I'm just tired, I guess. Sorry I haven't been very good company tonight," he said, a tear welling up in his eyes.

"Is that all it is?"

"Yeah. I didn't have the best of mornings, but then again, it could have been worse."

"What happened?"

"I screwed up a little on that case we worked day before yesterday. I left some dope in a van overnight. No big deal really, but I might get a couple of days off for it."

"I'm sorry, babe."

"Hey, I'm not really worried about it. I don't know what it is that's bothering me. I really think I'm just overly tired. I just need some sleep, maybe a few days off."

"You sure that's all it is?"

Jimmy looked up at her. "That's all it is. I don't want you to worry about anything else. Seriously. It's work. I love you."

Carmen looked into Jimmy's eyes, searching his thoughts. Slowly, a smile started and she seemed to relax. "You know what?"

"What?"

"I saw an attorney today and checked on his fees for a divorce for you. The guy is pretty reasonable."

"Good. That's really a good thing. I guess if you give me his number I can give him a call in a few months. "

"A few months? Why do you want to wait?"

"I just don't want to rush into it. I think Shirley is more than a little pissed off at me, and I'd like her to cool down some and get used to the idea of divorce. I really don't want her to try and poison Nikki against me."

"Oh." She looked at him briefly without saying anything else.

"It will all work out. I have no intentions of being with anyone else but you for the rest of my life," Jimmy said.

"I know," she responded, letting it go for the time being. "So what else did you do today?"

"I got offered the chance to do some undercover work. I don't think I'm going to do it, but it was nice to have the offer."

"What kind of undercover work did they offer you?"

"To buy some dope from a guy. It turns out that the guy is Mexican. If he'd have been a white guy, maybe even a black guy, I'd have been tempted to do it, but my Spanish is terrible and I just don't fit the mold of a drug dealer to a Mexican."

"It sounds dangerous. I'm glad you're not doing it."

"Well it would be more dangerous for the confidential source. Once we arrested the guy trying to sell me the dope, he'd find out I'm in law enforcement. Anyone who had anything to do with the bad guy would know that the source introduced a cop. Traffickers don't like snitches."

"Well then I'm doubly glad you're not doing the undercover work."

"Yeah, well I guess I agree with you. Still, I like doing undercover work it's just that I don't have much of a chance to do any in this area." Jimmy paused a moment and stared in the other direction, not really focused on anything except his thoughts. "It's probably time to notch things back a little anyway. Everything I've done lately seems to have gone wrong. Yeah, it may be time to slow things down and take a good hard look at what I'm doing."

"If you're talking about work, that doesn't sound like you. If you're talking about us, well, you're scaring me."

Jimmy turned and looked at her again. "All I'm saying is that, well, maybe I need to change a little. When I was with my wife I was always in trouble with her for working as much as I did. Now that I'm with you, I'm in trouble with work. And, I don't want my work to come between us."

"It was your work that brought us together. That was a good thing, right? Of course, you might find some other woman on another case. I wouldn't like to see that," she said, giving him a little smile.

Jimmy continued to look into her eyes as he spoke. "No worries, honey. One woman is enough trouble for any man. Besides that, there's no one out there any better or more beautiful than you, so you have nothing to worry about."

Later that evening, after making love, they lay in bed together, holding each other, but saying little.

"Are you okay?" Carmen asked Jimmy.

"Yeah. I still wonder sometimes if I'm doing the right thing, you know, being here with you. I've been in love with you, or some fantasy woman that I didn't know even existed just like you for as long as I can remember. I just didn't know you were real. I'm happy with you in so many ways. Yet I feel guilty in some regards, and I worry about my daughter. I sure wish I'd have met you before I met Shirley, and before you met Angel. What a life we would have had."

"Jimmy, we're both still young. We can have a happy life. You're going to have to let go of your past."

"You know that's impossible. There's way too much of it and we'll both have our children to constantly remind us of it."

"I know. That was a stupid thing for me to say. Our pasts are what made us who we are. Well at least our children are the best part of our pasts. Still, we can plan for a future, can't we?"

Jimmy turned and looked at the woman who had changed his life. "I so much want you to always be my future. I'll love no one else but you."

"Then make love to me again," she said with a smile.

"I don't know if I'm that young. But okay, let's find out," he said as he rolled over and put his arms around her.

CHAPTER . . .

32

The following morning, Jimmy met Tony at the office and took him over to meet Angelo. Once their meeting was over, Jimmy had Tony go get some lunch so he could talk to Angelo about the upcoming case.

"So when did you guys want to set up this buy?" Jimmy asked.

"Well, I kind of wanted to do it this afternoon, but I have to tell you, I have some trust issues with your Tony."

Jimmy was a little taken back. "Why?" he asked, wondering why there were sudden issues.

"I met him once before a few years ago. Ron reminded me when we were talking this morning. I'd forgotten his name, but he worked on a ten-kilo cocaine buy-bust that one of my guys who's since transferred to headquarters set up."

"Yeah, and did it go?"

"Oh, yeah. It went, but Tony kept wanting to change things. He was very manipulative of the agents. It just didn't feel right and the agents weren't sure what his motives were. By the way, whose source is he, really?"

"I signed him up about a year after I got hired. Initially he was working off a beef, but he wanted to keep working after his problems were behind him. We started targeting all the folks he used to work with. It only took a year or so and we'd arrested them all. But he was really good at schmoozing other traffickers so we kept plugging him into deals, usually in place of undercover agents."

"Why would you want to use him instead of an under-cover?"

"For a couple of reasons. He was smarter, more experienced at dealing with traffickers and he provided a good level of insulation for other sources. You know as well as I that having a source introduce an u/c burns the source. The minute the organization finds out that someone, namely your source, introduced a cop to do a deal, he's got serious problems." Angelo listened.

"Once we'd run out of targets to plug him from this office, I started farming him out to other groups to get work. I can tell you this: traffickers seem to trust him, and he's never let me down. And just so you know, he's signed up with DEA, FBI, San Diego P.D., L.A. Sheriff's, ATF and us. He's done work with some other task force groups as well. So far I haven't had any serious complaints from anyone else about him."

"Well, I can tell he's been around. Still, I don't really trust him. Someone who tries changing things, manipulating the agents, well, it doesn't sit well with me. I talked it over with the DEA group supervisor who's bringing out some of his guys on this deal today. He's not overly enamored with your guy either."

Jimmy gave a little laugh. "Who, Ray? He doesn't trust anybody, not even his own agents most of the time. You know Tony's biggest problem is that he thinks of himself as one of us at times. But let me assure you that if Tony is trying to change things, he's doing it for a good reason. I don't think there's any ulterior motives other than the good of the investigation."

"Well, the problem is, he's not an agent and most of my guys are too inexperienced to know what his motives are. If we use him, you're going to have to stay involved and monitor everything he does."

"As long as Tom doesn't have any issues with that, I'm good with it."

"I'll clear it with Tom. Let me have our source make a call to his crook and see if we can get this thing set up for today or tomorrow."

Jimmy left the office and went across the street to a little deli restaurant where Tony was having lunch. He'd just ordered a sandwich and fries. Jimmy walked up to the counter as Tony reached for his wallet.

"I got it," he said, throwing down a bill to cover the meal.

"Jimmy, you don't have to do that," Tony said.

"I know, but you better let me pay now. I'm going to have to start paying child support pretty soon and then I won't have any money. Next time we work together you may have to pay for my lunch. But don't tell anyone, it's against the rules, as you know. " Jimmy smiled and gave Tony a wink.

Tony smiled back. "Yeah, I'll just file it away with all the other dirt I have on you." Jimmy placed his order then the two men sat down at a table.

"So, Jimmy, is there any truth to the rumor that you're living with Angel Garcia's old lady?"

Jimmy looked at Tony and sighed. "I don't know how information like that gets around, but it shouldn't," he said. He looked at Tony, trying to decide whether or not to talk to him about the relationship.

"Hey, you don't have to confirm or deny anything, my friend. I heard a rumor and just wondered if it was true."

"You know, Carmen has officially been around Angel for about ten years, but they were really only together as husband and wife for about eighteen months. He came around to visit their kid once in a while, but it's not like they were really married. And it's not like she's going to be around him any longer now, is it? I've been living with her for a few weeks now, but no one needs to know this, so I'm asking you to keep it to yourself, okay?"

"Sure, man." Tony paused a minute and took a few bites from his sandwich. "So, what's up with this heroin deal?"

"The group sup had a few reservations about using you, but I vouched for you. They're trying to get hold of the crook and set something up for this afternoon. You're good to stick around for awhile, right?"

"Sure man, but tell me, why would anyone have an issue using me?"

"He mentioned something about a cocaine deal you helped his group with where you tried changing things a few times."

"Yeah, I remember. His rookies didn't know what they were doing. I just helped point them in the right direction. I don't get it. Why wouldn't they take the advice of the more experienced agent."

Jimmy laughed. "That's the problem, my man. I knew I had you pegged." Jimmy took a sip from his drink then continued. "You're more experienced, but you're not an agent. Now I don't have a problem with treating you like an agent because the law says you're an agent of the government if you're working with us. However, most agents do have a problem with putting you on a par with us. The great majority of our sources are crooks so almost everyone looks at the sources we use like they're crooks. Even the few reformed ones who work with us don't have the law enforcement training and experience necessary to make decisions on our investigations. We have egos to deal with, trust issues, issues with prosecuting cases because of the public perception. On top of that, no one wants to take responsibility for anyone or anything unless they're totally within guidelines and they're sure that nothing will go wrong."

"Yeah, but I have a very good record of achievements with law enforcement over the last—what's it been—like seven or eight years."

"I know you do, but you have to understand that not everyone knows you as well as I do. So be patient with those who don't know you because, well, let's put it this way, you don't face the same sanctions we face if you make a bad decision. And remember that the average time an alliance agent's been on the job is about three or four years. But no worries man, I trust you."

Following lunch, Jimmy and Tony walked back over to the office. Jimmy called Angelo and was told to head up to the conference room.

"Looks like we're a go for about three o'clock. Let's do our brief then gear up and head out," Angelo said.

Tony was introduced as the friendly to Angelo's group and was then excused to go wait in his car.

Miguel passed out ops plans to everyone and started the brief. Jimmy thumbed through the pages, stopping at the suspect page. The suspect listed was a man named Alfredo Saenz. He knew the name.

"Hey, Miguel, excuse me for interrupting. This guy Saenz, you run him in NADDIS and TECS?"

"I ran him in TECS but not NADDIS."

"Nothing?"

"Didn't see anything, why?"

"I think I know this guy. He's the half-brother of Angel Garcia, unless there's another guy named Alfredo Saenz that's in his late twenties slinging dope. Tijuana and San Diego are big cities, so maybe, but I'd be a little surprised."

The briefing continued, the plan being pretty straightforward and simple. Tony and Miguel's source, a man named Francisco, would meet Alfredo in the parking lot of the Palomar Trolley Station. Francisco, who went by Frank, would introduce Tony to Alfredo to make the buy. Tony would tell Alfredo that he didn't have any money with him, not wanting to be robbed, but he'd explain that the money was close. He'd tell Alfredo that once he saw the dope he'd make a call to have someone drive into the lot with the money. Once he saw the heroin, he'd walk away to make the call. If he saw the heroin he'd let the agents know by pulling a handkerchief from his pocket and wiping his nose. The agents would then move in and take everyone into custody, including the two sources. Of course, they'd find reason later to release the two sources because they were never found with any narcotics.

Once the briefing was finished, the agents began to prepare for the deal. Tony walked down to Jimmy's G-ride with him, standing around while he prepared his gear. Jimmy took a bulletproof vest from the back of the Expedition and placed it in a backrest position on the driver's seat of the vehicle. He then fully loaded a magazine for his AR-15 and set the weapon muzzle down on the front seat, passenger side floor of the vehicle.

Returning to the back of his Expedition, Jimmy put on a tactical belt that held handcuffs, pepper spray, and extra magazines for his Sig. As he readied himself he listened to Tony make small talk. He was having trouble staying focused on what Tony was telling him, having a sense of something not being right with the upcoming deal. He couldn't put his finger on it, but it nagged at him.

Reaching for a small flashlight, Jimmy noticed a thin, level II vest under a box of supplies. It was the vest he used to wear when he was a cop, one that fit under his uniform shirt. It wasn't as bulky as the vests issued by the feds, and it only offered protection from handguns, but it was a vest. It had expired a few years earlier, but since it wasn't being manipulated every day, and wasn't being sweat on regularly, he figured it was probably still effective. He pulled it out from under the box.

"Tony. Hey dude, I want you to take your shirt off and put this on for me."

"No, no thanks. Don't need it," he said, dismissing the gesture. "I've never used one of those."

Jimmy tossed it to him. "Do it for me. What's more, do it for your wife and kids." He looked at Tony for a moment. "I lost a source not too long ago. I don't need to lose another one."

"Whoa. Now you're starting to freak me out. Maybe I should just go home," Tony said with a weak smile. "What do you know about this guy that you're not telling me?"

"I think he's the half-brother of Angel Garcia. I don't know for sure, but it could be. But that aside, I just have a weird feeling about this, so humor me and put on the vest."

Tony slowly unbuttoned his shirt and donned the vest. Once his shirt was back on, you couldn't tell he was wearing the vest except for a very thin line of blue showing above the top-most buttoned button on Tony's shirt.

"Button up one more button on your shirt," Jimmy directed Tony. Tony sighed and reluctantly buttoned another button on his shirt.

Jimmy was surprised at how well it was hidden by the top button. You really couldn't even tell Tony was wearing the vest.

"So, if you're this worried about something going wrong, are you going to give me one of your guns?"

"No," Jimmy said curtly without even looking up from what he was doing.

"Doesn't hurt to ask," Tony said with a smile.

"Yes it does. Don't make me lump you into the gaggle of other knuckleheaded sources that I have," Jimmy said, looking up and giving Tony a wink. He closed the back of his Expedition and walked over to his driver's door. "All right. I'll follow you over, but don't drive too fast," Jimmy said.

"I never drive fast, you know that."

"Yeah, I know, but humor me and let me say it. It makes me feel better. I've also had bad experiences with sources behind the wheel lately."

Tony shook his head and rolled his eyes, wondering what he was talking about as he walked over to his Camaro.

Jimmy saw Frank talking to Miguel and walked over to them. "Hey, we're going to have Frank here ride with Tony, aren't we?" Jimmy asked.

"You good with that, Frank?" Miguel asked.

"Yeah, sure." He walked over to Tony's Camaro.

Jimmy followed as the two men drove over to the area of the Palomar Trolley Station, pulling in front of them a few blocks from their destination. He pulled over to the curb about a block away. Jimmy got on the air and made sure everyone was set up before he called Tony and Frank and sent them in to meet Alfredo.

Typical of most dope deals, Alfredo wasn't there yet when the sources arrived. The waiting game began. Twenty minutes into the wait, Jimmy called Tony and had him put Frank on the phone.

"Hey, you got a number for Alfredo?"

"Yeah, but I just spoke with him and he says he'll be here in about ten minutes."

The wait continued and about fifteen minutes later, a tan Dodge van pulled into the parking lot. Jimmy noticed a Hispanic male driving and looking around. Jimmy maneuvered to the east where he could watch from a supermarket parking lot about forty yards away. He was partially hidden by a row of trees that separated the parking lots.

Frank got out of the Camaro first and walked over to the van. Jimmy guessed he was doing a quick introduction of Tony, explaining how things were going to work. The conversation went on for several minutes. As the men talked, Tony got out of the Camaro but stood by it and lit a cigarette, waiting patiently.

As Jimmy watched the meet, he noticed several G-rides in the trolley station jockey for position, moving closer to the van. He got on the radio.

"Hey guys, I've got a good eye on our target. Don't get impatient and quit moving around. No one should get any closer," Jimmy said.

As he finished transmitting, Frank waved to Tony. Tony started to walk over to the van. As he walked, Jimmy noticed another G-ride, very obvious to him due to the tinted windows, moving closer to the meet. Suddenly, a handgun appeared out of the window of the van as Tony walked up to within a few steps of the window. He was oblivious as to what was happening until the last second when two quick shots were fired into Tony's chest. Jimmy could see the gun jump in Alfredo's hand, and as it did, things seemed to shift into slow motion for a moment.

Jimmy had grabbed his weapon as soon as he'd seen the gun appear, but he couldn't seem to move any further for a moment. As soon as Tony fell back, Jimmy seemed able to move again. He opened his door, wondering why the shots hadn't seemed very loud to him. Tony fell back to the ground while Frank ran to the rear of the van.

Several cars were backing recklessly out of parking spaces, tires screeching. Several vehicles accelerated towards the Dodge van. Alfredo threw open the driver's door and got out, gun still in his hand. He hesitated for half a second, apparently thinking about making a stand there, but thinking better of it he turned towards Frank. The two locked eyes for a fraction of a second. Jimmy could sense his confusion. Alfredo turned again and ran. He was running towards Jimmy.

Jimmy got out of his Expedition, hands shaking, and brought his AR-15 to a high-ready position. Alfredo was running towards him, his head turned the opposite direction, looking over his shoulder at the approach of numerous government cars. Alfredo fired a single round at the first car to stop next to his van. The driver, Ron Harris, had lowered himself and got out of his car on the passenger side. He reached out and grabbed Frank, pulling him to the ground behind his car. Alfredo fired another shot as he continued to run. Jimmy heard the thump in the metal as it struck the hood of Ron's car. One of the DEA agents drove up between the shooter and Ron's car. That agent also slid over to the passenger side of his vehicle and rolled out onto the asphalt using his vehicle for cover. As he came up over his hood, weapon in hand, Jimmy realized it was aimed at him. The DEA agent must have noticed it as well because he held his fire despite having a shot.

Alfredo realized he was rapidly becoming outnumbered. He turned east, continuing to run towards Jimmy, picking up his pace. Jimmy clicked off his safety, brought the sights of his rifle to eye level and fired two quick rounds into Alfredo's chest from about ten yards away just as he turned and his eyes met Jimmy's. Alfredo collapsed in a heap several steps away.

Jimmy lowered his weapon, keeping the muzzle on his threat, and moved up to him. The handgun, a Colt government model .45, lay next to Alfredo. Alfredo was trying to breathe, forcing air into his lungs with considerable effort.

Kicking the handgun away, Jimmy knelt down to Alfredo who was trying to say something to him. His badge hung from the chain around his neck. As he bent down, Miguel Martinez ran up to him.

"I, I thought I was going to get ripped off. I didn't know you were cops," he said weakly. He looked at Jimmy, then closed his eyes and stopped breathing.

"Fuck!" Jimmy shouted, taking a few steps then sitting down on the ground.

Miguel watched Jimmy for a few seconds, then took Jimmy's arm.

"Come on, man, let's get up. You don't need to be here right now," Miguel said.

Jimmy looked up at him, then took Miguel's hand. Once on his feet, Miguel led him over to his Expedition. There were numerous sirens whining, getting closer by the second as Miguel took Jimmy's rifle and laid it on the seat of his vehicle. Jimmy leaned against his car seat, looking questioningly at Miguel.

"Hey, Jimmy, you okay?" Miguel asked.

"What in the hell just happened? Jesus man. Did you hear him?"

"What did he say?"

"He thought he was going to get ripped off! Why the fuck would . . ." he cut himself off. "Where's Tony? Where's Tony?" he asked, steadying himself suddenly. He looked over towards Tony and then started running towards him. Several other agents were knelt around him.

Halfway to the van, Tony sat up. He was rubbing his chest. One of the agents helped him as he began to unbutton his shirt. Jimmy slowed but continued a fast walk towards his source.

"Holy mother of God," Tony said as Jimmy walked up to him. He looked up at Jimmy and half-grimaced and half-smiled. "Man, that hurt like a bastard," he said, taking the shirt off completely.

"Let's get the vest off too so we can have a look," Jimmy said.

Tony raised his arms and twisted his torso back and forth, testing his mobility. Then he reached around and pulled the Velcro straps apart that held the vest in place. He lifted the vest over his head, revealing two grapefruit-sized bruises that seemed to be getting darker by the minute.

"Dude, don't get up. Just sit there and relax. I want a paramedic to look you over before we do anything else," Jimmy told him.

Tony sat, looking past Jimmy to the body of Alfredo Saenz. Jimmy noticed the look, turned back for a moment towards the body, and then looked back at Tony who was now studying him.

"So, how are you?" Tony asked.

"Pissed." Jimmy lowered his voice a little and lowered himself into a catcher's stance beside Tony. "Man, I don't know what's going on with my life lately, but I really don't need this."

"Well, you'll have to tell me about it sometime." He and Jimmy locked eyes for a second, and Tony gave him a little smile, and then grimaced. "Oww. Jesus, it hurts. Better quit smiling," he said, giving a little chuckle. He grimaced again. "Laughing is worse. Hey, I'm going to charge extra for this one," he said.

Jimmy didn't respond, turning again to look at Alfredo's body. Then he scanned the controlled chaos around him. *Stupid assholes*, he thought to himself. *This didn't need to happen.*

"Hey, Jimmy," Tony said. Jimmy looked back at him. "Thanks."

"For what? Almost getting you killed?"

"The vest. I didn't want to wear it, but . . ."

"Don't mention it." He paused a moment then continued. "You're wife would have never forgiven me. Actually, she still might not."

A paramedic arrived seconds later and knelt down to Tony and started taking his pulse.

"How you feeling?" the paramedic asked Tony.

"Very abused. No, it's sore, but the only thing really bothering me a little is shortness of breath. Still, it's better than a minute ago."

Jimmy stood and was watching when Angelo came over.

"You all right, Jimmy?" he asked.

"Yeah, fine." Jimmy could feel himself getting angry and wasn't exactly sure why. There was the issue with the agents giving away their positions prior to the arrest, the fact that Alfredo had decided to shoot someone, the fact that he'd forced Jimmy into having to shoot him, and the fact that Alfredo had a connection, albeit small, to Carmen and Raul. Which issue bothered him the most was a tossup.

"You want me to call your wife and let her know what happened and that you're all right?" Angelo asked.

"No. No thanks." He hesitated. "We're separated. No sense in telling her anything."

"Jimmy, I know. But if she watches the news she's going to find out about this. It might not be a bad idea to give her a head's up that you're all right."

"I just don't want to deal with her right now."

"Okay, okay. How you doing?"

"I'm pissed, Angelo," Jimmy said. A tear ran down his cheek. "I'm pissed and I'm really tired."

"Come on then, let's get you out of here."

"Not until Tony gets transported. I want him checked out by a doctor."

"I'll make sure it happens, but why not get out of here before the press shows up?"

Jimmy wiped the single tear from his cheek. "In a minute. Seriously, I don't want to go until Tony leaves."

"Okay. But at least go sit in my car."

Ron Harris walked up to Jimmy and Angelo. "Hey, the heroin's in the van."

"Don't touch it, don't move it," Jimmy snapped.

Ron was a bit taken aback, but said nothing.

"It's a crime scene," Angelo said calmly. "Jimmy's right. Just leave it for now. We'll get it after the cops come and do their thing."

"Got it," Ron said. He turned and started walking away.

"Ron," Angelo said. Ron turned and walked back. "Get a roll of yellow police tape out of my trunk and let's get as much of this area taped off as possible. Make sure no one touches anything." He tossed Ron his car keys. Ron caught the keys, nodded and headed for his car.

As Jimmy stood watching everyone, his thoughts turned to Carmen. He wondered how she would react to what had happened. He wondered if she'd ever met Alfredo. He even briefly wondered how Angel would react to the news. *Damn, I shouldn't have let myself get involved in this case*, he thought, suddenly now angry with himself.

A few minutes later, Tony was stepping up into the back of the paramedic's ambulance. Jimmy walked over and nodded to his source. "Let them check you out good. I'll have someone bring you your car and escort you home."

"Thanks, Jimmy," he said as they prepared to close the door.

"If you need anything, call. In any event we'll talk tomorrow," Jimmy said.

"You take it easy, too, man," Tony replied as they closed the door.

"Okay, can we get you out of here now?" Angelo said.

"Yeah." Jimmy started walking towards his Expedition.

"Jimmy, you can't take your ride yet. The cops are going to want to see where you were parked, probably take a look at the rifle."

"Yeah, I know."

" I'll have Molly Hogan take you home."

"Just getting my keys and my wallet," Jimmy said as he kept walking.

He tried to avoid looking down at Alfredo's body as he passed by. Getting to the Expedition, Jimmy reached across the seat and took his keys and wallet from the center console. He saw his rifle lying on the seat. The safety wasn't engaged so he put it on. He turned to leave and this time did look down at the lifeless form of Alfredo. He could see a resemblance to Angel. As he looked, his knees got weak and he started to feel sick to his stomach. He fought the feeling and forced himself to look away and move.

As Jimmy got into Molly's car, a news van rounded the corner. It turned into the parking lot as they drove out. Jimmy could see one of the occupants of the van staring at him. He wondered what the reporter was thinking. His prior experiences with the press had all been negative and the thought crossed his mind that they'd probably butcher this story too.

Molly said almost nothing as they drove. She looked ahead, occasionally glancing at him. After Jimmy caught her looking over for about the fifth time, he turned to her.

"What?" he asked. She didn't immediately respond but then asked, "So are you sure you're all right?"

"I will be." He turned away and settled back into his seat, looking ahead. "How about stopping at that liquor store?" he said.

"You're not supposed to drink after a traumatic incident. Alcohol is a depressant and will only make things worse."

"Okay, mom. Stop at the liquor store," he said.

She looked at him a moment, then signaled and pulled into the parking lot. Jimmy exited the car and walked into the store. He selected about half a dozen of the airport-sized mini bottles of Jim Beam. He paid for them, then started stuffing them into his pants pocket as the clerk looked at him with some amusement. Jimmy opened the last little bottle and drank it down as he was walking out of the store.

"Hey, you can't drink on the premises," the clerk said loudly as he left. Jimmy ignored him, throwing the empty bottle as far as he could once it was drained.

"Jimmy. I don't know if anyone wants to interview you or if they need you to do anything else, but how about I take you home and they can call you if they need to see you," Molly suggested.

"Trying to get rid of me?" he suggested.

"No. Not if you need someone to talk to."

"Well I appreciate it, but I really don't think I need someone to talk to right now. And you don't have to worry. I didn't buy enough booze to do any real harm. Just need to relax a little and think things out. How about driving me up to the Cabrillo Monument."

"Where?" Molly asked.

"You know, the Cabrillo Monument. It's a state park. It's up where the lighthouse is on Point Loma, past the Fort Rosecrans National Cemetery."

"I've heard of the Fort Rosecrans National Cemetery, but I've never been there. Where is it?"

"Not from here, huh?"

"I've only lived here two years. Grew up in Texas."

"I'm sorry."

"I like Texas."

"Good. We have too many people in California already. Tell all of your relatives it sucks out here." Jimmy looked at Molly. She looked a little worried, glancing at him every ten or fifteen seconds.

"Molly, I'm just messing with you. I'm fine, all things considered. Let's just go up to the park. I guarantee you'll like the view." Jimmy gave her directions and thirty minutes later, they arrived at the park entrance. The ranger was just getting ready to close the gate and his guardhouse.

"Sorry, folks, we're closed. You'll have to come back tomorrow," the ranger said.

Jimmy took out his badge and credentials. "Official business. We're looking for a boat coming in from down south. We won't be too long."

The ranger looked over the credentials skeptically, and then waived the vehicle into the park.

"See how easy that was," Jimmy said. Molly smiled. A minute later they parked next to the monument and got out of the car.

"Oh my God. The view is fantastic up here," she said.

"On a clear day it is. You can see almost half of the county from here. It's a good place to come sit and look and think, except when you've got a zillion tourists under foot. This time of day it's not bad. In an hour, when it's dark, it's pretty amazing too."

"Yeah, but you can't get in after dark, can you?"

"I have a state parks master key. Don't remember how I came by it, but it has come in handy. Of course, if you come past nine p.m. the military police close up the access through the base."

Jimmy pulled another mini-bottle of Jim Beam from his pocket and drank it down. He tossed the empty into a trashcan. "Can't litter up here," he said, looking over at Molly.

"So now what?" she asked.

"Would you mind giving me about half an hour to go sit and relax? I promise I won't be much longer than that."

"I've got no plans. Take whatever time you need."

"Thanks."

Jimmy wandered out to the monument and sat down on the short wall built around it to protect the tourists from falling down the side of the hillside. He hung his feet and legs over the side and pulled out two more mini-bottles of bourbon. They were empty in minutes.

Well, you did what had to be done, Jimmy boy, he thought to himself. *Now what? Sure complicates things having it be Angel's brother*. Jimmy wondered what Angel would say to Raul on visitation days. He wondered how long his reach was from jail. Having to spend time in prison was one thing, but killing a family member was something else. He wondered if he should tell Carmen about his day. It seemed he'd have to talk to her, but he certainly dreaded the idea.

It was about forty-five minutes later when Molly walked out and sat down by him. It was starting to get dark and the breeze was chilly.

"Getting anywhere with those thoughts?" she asked.

"No, not really. I'm just sitting here trying to get up the nerve to go home."

Molly said nothing, but looked at him as he stared out at the city. An S-3 Viking, an anti-submarine warfare jet, was making an approach to the North Island Naval Air Station runway. It touched down gracefully.

"We live in a city whose core is military. One quarter or more of the Pacific Fleet is stationed here; we train Marines here, Navy Seals, send out submarines, build cruise missiles, you name it. It's a city that gets most of its support from those who train for war."

"Yeah, I suppose," Molly said, wondering where the conversation was going.

"So they train for war. You know, real war. We, on the other hand, wage a small kind of mini-war against a bunch of idiots who are trying to make money by flooding the streets of this country with drugs. Thousands of military guys training for war. We go out and shoot one bad guy about once every three or four years and it's a big deal, at least for a little while. Seems kind of stupid, doesn't it? Tomorrow or the next day I'll go into work and they'll make me go see a shrink a few times and everyone will ask how I'm doing and all that crap. Seems sort of silly when I look out and think about what the military does."

"Is that what you came up here to think about?" Molly asked.

"No. It just came to me while I sat here trying to get up the nerve to go home."

"Come on. Let me get you home. You've got to go some time and it's getting cold."

CHAPTER . . .

33

Jimmy walked into Carmen's living room and tried giving her a smile. She was sitting on the sofa. The television was on but she wasn't watching it.

"Hi, babe. How was your day?" Jimmy asked, trying not to give anything away about his day.

"Are you okay?" she asked with a worried look.

"Why wouldn't I be?"

Carmen got up from the sofa and walked over to him. She stopped in front of him and looked up into his eyes. "Some woman called. She said she was the head of your office. She was looking for you so she called here. She seemed concerned, so when I asked her what it was about she told me you were involved in a shooting."

Jimmy had been toying with the idea of not telling Carmen about the shooting but that was now out the window.

"I'm all right. She told you I was all right, didn't she?"

"Yes, but I tried calling you but you didn't answer your phone. You always answer your phone. Jimmy, I was really worried about you."

Jimmy pulled his phone from his belt clip and looked at it. He'd heard it ring a few times but had assumed the calls were from work.

"I'm sorry, hon, I was getting so many calls I couldn't take them all. I'm really sorry. I should have looked more closely," he said, trying to downplay the incident.

Carmen continued studying his face as he spoke. When he finally looked down at her, she threw her arms around him. As she held him, the tears started down his cheeks.

"Don't you ever let anything happen to you, Jimmy Maxwell," she said. "Don't you ever."

They stood holding each other for several minutes. When Carmen did pull away from him enough to look up, she saw his tears.

"You're not okay, are you?" she said, more as a statement than a question.

"I'm fine," he replied, wiping his face with his hands. He paused a moment then continued. "Really, I'm fine. It's just that I'm a little overwhelmed because I've never had anyone care about me like you."

"Really? Really, Jimmy?" It was her turn to cry. She pulled him over to the sofa and sat down, pulling him down next to her. He collapsed next to her, then threw his head back, resting it on the back on the cushion.

"I'm tired. Really tired," he said, looking up at the ceiling, fighting off more tears. The thought of having shot a man earlier bothered him, but he was feeling a numbness setting in. So many things troubled him about the incident that he couldn't seem to get an emotional grasp of the incident. What stuck in the forefront of his mind as he sat with Carmen was whom it was that he'd shot. How would he tell her?

Jimmy sat wondering how he would tell her, or if he could tell her what happened. For the moment, he took comfort in just holding her hand.

He found himself thinking back to the early days, when he'd first gone into law enforcement. He'd started his career with the philosophy that there was something good, or at least salvageable in everyone. He knew people did wrong things, sometimes even evil things, but he thought that if someone could just reach some of them they had a chance to be salvaged. Within a year, he knew his premise to be false. Oh sure, there were some that could be salvaged, but not all. His philosophy had changed. He now realized that there were people who had been involved in evil for so long that they were just a waste of air. They were on the earth to kill, steal, hurt or destroy their fellow man. He'd seen it. He'd been in home after home, alley after alley where people had been swallowed by evil.

Whether or not Alfredo Saenz was one of those people, Jimmy would probably never know. He certainly deserved to die based on his actions, but it shouldn't have come to that. Mistakes had been made. But what was that old saying—*shit happens*. Certainly everyone made mistakes, but he sure wished the mistakes of this afternoon hadn't been made. Well, he couldn't dwell on it. It was done.

"Hey, babe. I'm going to fix myself a drink," he said, letting go of her hand and standing after having sat with her for several minutes. He walked into the kitchen. He poured himself a double shot of Knob Creek, took a swallow, and then refilled his glass with what he'd drank before putting the bottle back in the cupboard. He turned to see Carmen looking at him.

"Jimmy, I'm not one to preach to you. You're a grown man." She walked over to him and took the glass from him. "But you don't need this." She sat the glass down on the counter and then stood on her tiptoes and kissed him.

"Oh, so that's what I need?" Jimmy said with a smile as she took his hand and led him to the bedroom. "Just let me call work first and check in with them."

The following morning, Jimmy went for a jog. He hadn't slept very well, but despite his lack of a full night's sleep, he seemed to have a lot of energy. It was Saturday and he'd let Carmen sleep in. As he ran, his mind raced through all the peripheral issues involved with what had happened the day before.

He hadn't talked with Carmen about any of the specifics of what had happened. He had that to look forward to. He'd have Raul to explain things to as well at some point. Then he had to decide about what to do, if anything, with Angel. His thoughts played out the options and he finally decided he'd go and see Angel and talk to him in person.

Once back at the house, he showered and then went to the kitchen and called Tony. He was home and doing well, even sounding a little upbeat as they talked.

Jimmy then called Tom and talked with him, letting him know he was doing all right. Tom reminded him that if he needed some time off he could take it and gave him the telephone numbers for the employee assistance program.

Jimmy finished getting ready and went into the bedroom. He sat on the edge of the bed and brushed back a lock of hair from Carmen's face. She stirred, then looked up at him, blinking a few times. He bent down and gave her a quick but tender kiss. She smiled, then took her arms out from under the covers and stretched.

"I'm going out, but just for a little bit. I don't expect to be gone for more than a couple of hours."

"How did you sleep?" Carmen asked.

"Not very well. But I'm all right. Maybe I can catch a nap this afternoon."

"I didn't sleep very well either. I kept having dreams that woke me. Dreams of losing you. I didn't like them one bit."

"Don't worry, babe, they were just dreams. I'm right here and I won't be gone very long," okay?"

Carmen didn't respond, but looked into Jimmy's eyes, studying him.

"You can talk to me about yesterday if you want to. I'll be here when you get back."

"I shot someone. There's not much more to tell."

"Jimmy, you need to open up to me. You can trust me." She paused a moment, looking into his eyes, searching for what he had hidden inside. "I do understand that you might need some time, that it might be painful, but when you're ready, I'll be here," she said.

"I know you will. You know, you said I can trust you. It's not about trust. I'm just not sure it's very productive to relive what happened. And I'm not sure I want to bring you into my world. It isn't always a good place to be. You should know that by now."

Carmen sat up, pulled her pillow from behind her and then leaned back against it as she scooted up, leaning back into the headboard.

"I do know that. You think I don't know about your world? Remember who I was married to? I didn't hear about everything firsthand, but I watched the news and picked up a few things about his activities from others, including you. I know there is ugliness in the world." She paused a moment then continued. "If I'm going to be part of your life, I want you to open up to me and let me share all of your life."

"I can't let you in to all of what I do. I wouldn't even if I could. I want to protect you," Jimmy said. "I want you living in your world. I want to be part of your world, but without dragging a bunch of crap into it from mine."

"Then I don't get to know you very well, do I? I don't get to see what makes Jimmy Maxwell tick. You see, I get cheated, Jimmy, and that's not fair to me. I know you want to protect me and I love you for it, but hiding part of your life from me isn't how you protect me. Please don't do that to me, to us."

A tear started to well up in his eye so he turned away. "I love you. I'll be back soon." He stood and walked to the door then turned around. Carmen was watching him. "You're right. We'll talk when I get home." Carmen gave him a worried smile, nodded but said nothing else.

Jimmy drove to the Metropolitan Correctional Center, and went into the lobby, waiting his turn behind two other people who were there to visit an inmate. When he got to the guard, he asked to speak with Angel Garcia.

"Sorry bud, you're not on the list of approved visitors."

Jimmy took his credentials from his pocket and showed them to the guard. The man examined them, nodded and remarked, "So why didn't you show me those to begin with?"

"You have a place for me to lock up my weapon?" he asked, not really answering the question posed to him.

"Yeah, right over here." The guard walked him over to a gun locker. "You'll need to lock up all your ammunition and any pocket knives. You'll also have to leave your cell phone and pager if you have one."

Jimmy filled the little locker, feeling quite a bit lighter when he was finished. He was then escorted to an elevator and was told to get off on the fifth floor. The elevator opened up to a waiting room where there was a table and several chairs. Jimmy entered the room and sat down. Ten minutes later, the only door into the room opened and Angel Garcia walked in wearing an orange jumpsuit. He stared at Jimmy for a moment, then approached him and sat down. Jimmy nodded, keeping his eyes locked on Angel's.

"I wanted to talk to you about a few things," Jimmy said.

"So talk."

Jimmy took a deep breath. "You have a brother named Alfredo Saenz?"

"I already heard. Who killed him?"

"Me. I didn't want to, but he gave me no choice. He shot a man, and was shooting at several other agents."

"He was always stupid. He always wanted to be in our business, but never had the head for it. He was just too wild, too reckless, and too trusting of strangers. Why were you there in the first place?"

"He was trying to sell us some heroin."

"And?"

"When our undercover officer came up to the car, I think Alfredo thought he was going to get ripped off. He panicked and shot the man."

"How do you know that's what happened?"

"That's what he told me."

Angel studied his face for a moment.

"So why are you here?" he asked. "You worried about me?"

"I'm worried a little about Carmen and Raul," he replied.

Angel again studied his face, not immediately answering. Then he turned away and looked down. "Raul likes you. He told me he likes you."

"He's a good kid."

"You got nothing to worry about from me. We may be on opposite sides of things but you've done me some favors." Jimmy looked at him questioningly. "You're taking care of Carmen and Raul and you've made sure that Raul comes to visit, that he doesn't know about Maria or my daughter."

Angel paused a moment, seemingly lost in thought, then continued. "I hadn't had a relationship with Carmen for a long time. Maria and Guadalupe are my family. I tried being there for Raul, but it really wasn't working very well."

"I don't really need to know . . ."

"Just listen. I'm glad you're there for them. I'm not going to be around and a boy needs a father."

"I appreciate that, Angel." Jimmy and Angel sat quietly for a minute, each lost in their own thoughts. Finally, Jimmy stood to leave.

"I need to tell you something else," Angel said. Jimmy sat back down and looked at him.

"Alfredo was married. They got divorced a few years ago, but I know they stayed in touch. She goes by Sylvia Castaneda now. She's loco. She's worked for me before. She can be quite vicious and vindictive."

"I know the name," Jimmy said.

"I thought so. She had one of your informers killed." Angel looked into Jimmy's eyes for reaction.

"You stay pretty well informed in here, don't you?"

"She wants to kill you for arresting me. Noble on her part maybe, but not necessary. I think she hopes I'll find her a job or give her some money if she kills you for me." He paused again, seemingly waiting for a reaction. When he didn't get one, he continued. "My people have never killed police in the U.S."

"So why would that bother you, her killing me?"

"Initially it didn't. But like I said, Raul likes you. And there're some other reasons that I'm not sure you really need to know. For now, just listen." Jimmy said nothing. "She heard that your informer was working for the police. She hooked up with him to see if he could lead her to you. Once she knew he couldn't, or wouldn't, and once she verified that he was working as an informer, she contacted Isidro Flores, the owner of the marijuana you seized. She let him know he was working for the feds."

"So how did she know Jesus was working for me?" Jimmy asked.

"I don't think she knew that your Jesus was working for you specifically but she'd heard rumors that he was giving information to the aduana. She hoped that he would be able to lead her to you. Your guy probably got drunk, or was just stupid and bragged about some work he'd done. I don't know the details about how she found out. Maybe he told her things she wanted to know in order to get her into bed."

"Maybe. He was never very smart when it came to women." Jimmy paused a moment, thinking. "Of course, that can be said about a lot of us, can't it?"

Angel looked at him without responding to the comment and then continued. "I wouldn't tell you any of this but for the fact that I know she wants to kill you," Angel said. "Once she finds out that Alfredo has been killed by federal agents, she'll quickly find out it was you. She will be even more motivated to kill you."

"So, do you know where I can find her?" Jimmy asked.

"I've already done you a favor by making you aware of the fact that she wants to kill you. Why should I tell you where to find her?"

"You're right. You've done a lot. But Raul needs me around, right?"

Angel looked at Jimmy, a smile slowly developing on his face.

"You've got a point," he said. "Do you think you can help me spend a little less time in here?"

"Probably. If the information is good I'll talk to the prosecutor. I'm reasonably sure it will help some." Angel looked at Jimmy for a moment without responding.

"If I tell you where she's at, what will you do?" he finally asked.

"Go arrest her."

"For what? She's not going to admit to having anything to do with your informer's death. She's not stupid."

"I'm a pretty good interviewer. I guess we'll just have to see how it plays out. If nothing else though I'd get a chance to talk to her."

"I don't think you're going to have any luck getting her to talk to you, but what harm can it do to try. I'm telling you again though, you need to be careful with her."

"Well if she points a gun at me she won't like what will happen. She'll be joining her ex-husband."

Angel thought about it a moment. "Alfredo and I were never close, but he was still a blood relative. Sylvia was his woman and that makes her family. Don't think you can make a habit of shooting us."

"Only in defense, Angel, only in defense."

Angel looked into Jimmy's eyes a moment then responded. "She lived at 293 Vista Point, San Diego, the last I knew."

"Thanks."

Jimmy got up and looked at Angel for a few seconds to see if he was going to say anything else. He didn't. Jimmy walked over to the elevator and pushed the call button. Turning back to Angel, he saw Angel looking at him.

"I'm not sure why you told me what you did, but I really do appreciate it."

"You didn't have to come here and tell me about Alfredo. I respect that you did, whatever the reason. And like I said already, Raul likes you. You take care of him, okay?"

"I'll do my best."

As Jimmy drove home, he thought about what Angel had told him. It seemed odd to him that someone of Angel's background and character would do anything to help a federal agent. It seemed even more odd that he'd want to help someone who was living with his ex-wife and son. Obviously the man had moved on to another woman and child, but Hispanic men didn't easily give up what was theirs, or what was once theirs. Was he being set up somehow? It didn't feel like it, but then who trusted feelings?

As his thoughts drifted from one thing to another, Jimmy found himself getting more and more anxious about having to talk to Carmen when he got home. He really wasn't ready to talk about the shooting, and he felt himself getting angry at the thought of having to relive the experience as he told her about it.

He pulled into the driveway and parked but continued to sit in his Expedition. He wanted to go see Carmen, to be with her, but he dreaded having to talk to her. He found himself again thinking about whether or not it was even right to be with this woman. He wouldn't be having these problems if he hadn't gotten involved with her. But he kept returning to the realization that he was in love. After about ten minutes, he finally talked himself into going inside.

"Is everything all right?" Carmen asked as he came in.

Jimmy nodded his head yes, then came over and sat down next to her. He said nothing for a minute. Just as he started to say something, Raul came into the room.

"Hey, buddy," Jimmy said. "How's it going?"

"Fine."

"Come over here and see me. I've got something for you," Jimmy said.

Raul walked over to the sofa and stood expectantly in front of Jimmy. "So have you been good today?" Jimmy asked.

Raul nodded his head yes, looking at Jimmy. Jimmy reached into his jacket pocket and took out a small customs' badge. It was affixed on a stickpin, made for use as a tie tack or jacket lapel pin. Jimmy took the back clasp off the pin and then affixed the badge to Raul's shirt pocket. "Now you're a federal agent. Of course, you have to be really good if you're going to be a federal agent."

Raul smiled and turned to go. He seemed proud of his promotion. "Hey, one more thing," Jimmy said. He reached back in his pocket and pulled out a candy bar. Raul took the candy and headed away. "Thanks, Jimmy," he said excitedly.

"Hey, he hasn't had lunch yet," Carmen said, starting to get up. "Raul, come here."

"Oh, let him have it."

"He can have half now, the other half later this afternoon," she said, catching up to Raul and taking the candy bar from him. He had already managed to get it unwrapped.

Jimmy smiled, got up and walked into the bedroom. He looked up to see Carmen's picture back on the wall. He smiled as he almost always did coming into the room, thinking of how lucky he was to be with a beautiful woman who loved him, but then realizing that there were many problems associated with it as well.

He lay down on the bed, kicking off his shoes. He closed his eyes for a minute, thinking he'd rest for awhile. A moment later he was asleep.

As he lay sleeping, he began to dream. He was at the Palomar Trolley Station parking lot. He had his AR-15 in his hand. Shots were being fired at him but he couldn't get his gun to work. No matter how hard he tried, the trigger wouldn't come back far enough for the weapon to fire. Someone was running at him. They were getting closer. He needed to take action but he couldn't move and his weapon still wouldn't fire. They'd be on him in a second. They turned, and the face he thought was Alfredo was a woman. It was Sylvia and she was pointing a gun at him. He forced himself awake just as she fired.

"Hey, no! No!" he said, sitting straight up in bed. He was soaked in sweat, his hair stuck to his forehead.

Carmen ran into the room, coming over to him.

"Jimmy, are you okay?"

"Uh, sorry. I'm sorry, I was dreaming I guess." He wiped some spittle from the corner of his mouth, then pulled off his shirt and wiped his face with it.

Carmen sat down on the bed, looking at Jimmy with concern. "You're a mess, honey. Come on, get up and get the rest of those wet clothes off. I'll go turn on the shower. You'll feel better after a nice hot shower."

Jimmy concentrated on slowing and regulating his breathing as Carmen rose to start the shower. He looked over at the nightstand clock. He'd been asleep nearly three hours. He felt almost too tired to move but he forced himself to stand. He undressed slowly, and then stumbled into the bathroom, stopping at the medicine cabinet to take several ibuprofens.

The hot shower helped and Jimmy felt almost normal by the time he'd dressed. He came out to the kitchen and sat down at the table, watching Carmen as she worked on the evening meal. She hadn't said anything when he entered the room, but after about a minute she walked over to the refrigerator, took out a beer, opened it, took a swallow, then brought it to Jimmy.

"Here, hon," she said.

"Thanks."

"You feel better?"

"Much."

Another few minutes passed. She finished what she was working on and then came and sat down next to him.

"What were you dreaming?" she asked.

"I guess I was reliving a little of yesterday. In the dream, I couldn't pull the trigger on my gun. I've had similar dreams before, but this one was a bit scary."

"It might do you good to talk about it. You know, talk it out so you can let it go."

"Maybe. Maybe not." He paused and took a long drink of beer. "I know I told you we'd talk, and I will, but not tonight. I'm just not up to it yet."

"Okay. Not tonight. But you need to talk soon, even if it's with the counseling services psychologist. You need to get it out. I wish you'd talk to me, but if you're not ready, you're not ready." Jimmy could tell that she was trying not to pressure him but he knew she was a little unhappy at his unwillingness to talk to her.

Jimmy looked over at her and smiled. "I'll talk to you about everything, and real soon. And I'm okay. Really. And you know what else?"

"What?"

"I love you more than I've ever loved anyone. I never thought I would ever love anyone like you. I still can't believe you exist in real life."

"Really, Jimmy?" She smiled and seemed to perk up a little.

"Really . . . Now what's for dinner?"

CHAPTER . . .

34

Jimmy thought about taking a few days off but couldn't stand the thought of sitting around the house all day thinking about the last few days and about all those things he needed to get done at the office. He assumed by now that Sylvia would know of her ex-husband's death by the hand of a Customs agent. She might even know that he was the man who pulled the trigger.

As much as it bothered him that she might try to have him killed, it bothered him more that she was responsible for Chuey's murder. He resolved over the weekend that he would have her taken off the streets one way or another.

Getting to the office Monday morning, Jimmy made the rounds, making it a point to say hello to as many agents as he could find. He wanted no question in anyone's mind that he was anything but okay. Everyone was friendly, but no one seemed to want to ask him about the shooting, and as a matter of fact, some seemed reluctant to talk to him at all. Several agents he ran into purposefully avoided him. He figured most of the agents didn't want to be responsible for saying or doing anything that might upset him.

As soon as Tom came in, Jimmy followed him to his office and closed the door behind them.

"Why you here? You can take some time off, you know," Tom said.

"I don't need it. There's too much going on that needs to be resolved."

"Maybe, but it'll still be here next week. You need to take a little time and make sure you're doing okay."

"Maybe. I'll be honest with you. I had a few nights that I didn't get much sleep, but I finally got some sleep last night. Anyway . . ."

"You go see the shrink yet?" Tom said, cutting him off.

"No. I'll call today and make an appointment. I think it's kind of a waste of time, but I know I'm expected to go."

"Well, you don't have to be a tough guy. It might be good to go talk about things that are bothering you."

"That's why I'm here. There are some things that are bothering me, and there's some things I need to update you about." Tom looked at him and listened. "I don't know if anyone told you about what happened last Friday, but I'm still bothered by some of things that went on out there. The fact is that if the agents in Angelo's group would have been better coordinated and less anxious to get Alfredo scooped up, it wouldn't have been necessary to shoot him."

"What do you mean? What don't I know about?"

"Just before the deal was going to go down, there were agents moving around in the parking lot. I put out over the air for everyone to sit still, but some of the agents were moving, trying to get closer, I'm assuming so they could be the first to rush in and make the arrest. I had a good eye on the whole deal, so there was no sense in moving around like some of them did. Alfredo saw a couple of cars sneaking in on him and it hinked him up. He told me he didn't know we were cops. He thought he was going to get ripped off." Jimmy paused a moment, waiting for a response. When he didn't get one, he continued. "All that jockeying around in the lot wasn't necessary. It almost got Tony killed. It almost got a couple of them killed, and it did get Alfredo killed."

"Okay, it sounds like there were some mistakes made. I'll talk to Angelo and maybe next week, once a little more time has gone by and we get a chance to review the shooting board's findings, we'll set up an office debrief so we can talk about the things that went right, and the things that went wrong. But now listen to me. I know you're upset about what happened, maybe more so because you were forced to take someone's life. That said, these things happen in law enforcement. That's why you carry a gun."

"I know, Tom, but this was a situation where it wasn't necessary because . . ."

"It was necessary," Tom said, raising his voice and cutting Jimmy off. "The guy shot someone. He was shooting at others. You did exactly what you were supposed to do."

"But, Tom, I . . ."

"No! Don't even go there . . . I know you're probably struggling with having had to take someone's life, but you've got to put this thing in perspective. This office is a place where new agents learn to be investigators. You know as well as I do that the office is full of new people, many right out of the academy. They spend four or five years down here learning how to interview, how to write a report, how to investigate and even how to do surveillance. Many of them have no prior law enforcement experience." He paused a moment then continued.

"Did you ever make mistakes learning how to be a cop?" Jimmy listened without saying anything. "Of course you did. Ever get scolded by a hard-ass training officer?" Tom paused another moment to let what he was saying sink in. "The important thing was to try to make sure the same mistakes didn't happen again. You know, last Friday was a tough day, but none of the good guys got hurt."

"But by the grace of God," Jimmy said. "I know there's a bunch of new guys, but we're supposed to be professionals."

"Jimmy, we're going to always have issues like this down here. Hopefully not issues with shootings, but issues with mistakes being made. So let's not beat anyone up too bad for wanting to go arrest the bad guy. It's up to guys like you to teach these new agents how to be good, competent, safe investigators."

"Okay, okay. I know you're right, but Jesus man, I sure wish they'd have listened."

"Well, I'll make sure Angelo or maybe even Arlene talks to them."

Suddenly, a smile broke out on Jimmy's face. "No, not Arlene. God, they screwed up, but not that bad."

Tom started laughing at Jimmy's remark. Jimmy didn't feel much better but he realized that Tom had a point, and being upset wasn't going to change what had happened. Maybe it was time to let it go.

"By the way, I don't know why you thought to have Tony put on that vest, but man, someone up there was really watching out for you two, especially him. Angelo told me that he was really surprised when he saw Tony get up. He thought the guy was dead for sure. You know he wasn't a big fan of Tony going into the deal but I think his opinion of the guy has been drastically changed."

Jimmy smiled. "Good. Tony's a good guy. You know, I don't know why I had Tony put on that old vest. Maybe the good Lord did have a hand in it. I'd also like to tip my hat to Bob Greene."

"He's one of the DEA guys in Webber's group, right?"

"Yeah. I don't know if you heard the story, but as soon as Tony was hit, Alfredo bailed from his van and then turned and fired a shot into Ron's car. Ron had driven up to go to the aid of Tony and Frank and once he got out of his ride he didn't have good cover. Bob Greene drove up between Alfredo and our guys, giving them pretty good cover. I think Alfredo was thinking about stopping and taking a few more shots at our guys. With Bob there as a distraction, he only got one other shot off, and that I think went into Bob's car. Anyway, that move by Bob was pretty ballsy."

"I'll let the DEA RAC know. Maybe you should write up a letter of commendation for him?"

"You or Arlene need to write the commendation."

"Oh, it'll be from Arlene, but you write it for her," Tom said with a smile.

"Figures," Jimmy said, shaking his head.

Jimmy settled back in his chair, pausing as he shifted gears in his thought process.

"So what else is on your mind?" Tom asked.

"I went and visited Angel on Saturday."

"Angel?"

"Angel Garcia. I went to MCC and had a chat with him on Saturday."

"What in the hell did you do that for?"

"I needed to find out what he intended to do, or try to do with me for shooting his brother."

"The guy you shot was his brother?"

"Yeah, well half-brother really. So, I needed to talk to him. Basically, I just wanted to clear the air and be up front with him. You know, let him know exactly what went down so there was no misunderstanding in what happened. He has his sources and you know how things get twisted around in the telling."

"And what makes you think he would believe you? God, Jimmy. I sure wish you'd have called and talked to me before you decided to go over there and talk to that guy. Did you let his attorney know you were going to see him?"

"No. But I wasn't there to ask questions about our case against him."

"I don't think that matters. You should have let his attorney know."

"Sorry, boss, but it was something I had to do. But you know it might have worked out for the best." Jimmy told Tom about the conversation and then about the issues with Sylvia. Saving the best for last, Jimmy then told Tom he knew where Sylvia lived.

"You're kidding? Why would he give you her address?"

"Well, maybe he was sincere in not wanting anything to happen to me for the sake of his kid. Maybe he really does feel like he owes me for not giving him up to his son about his other family, although I did tell Carmen. I didn't see any reason to bring that up. She'll never say anything."

"Maybe, but my guess is that this Sylvia either has some dirt on him that he wants buried with her," Tom said, "or maybe he just hopes that she'll kill you when you try to arrest her."

"Who says she's going to get buried? I'm not planning on going over there and whacking her. Of course, I'm not going to let her bury me either."

"I didn't really mean that you'd be the one burying her. Maybe he knows she won't talk, you know, if she's in custody, but out on the street she might say something to someone else in the business, like his old boss or someone like that. Then again, maybe he's hoping to get rid of some competition for his people that are still in business, you know, someone she's working for now."

"There's any number of reasons, but whatever the reason I believe his information to be good. I want to go hook her up. Not sure how I'm going to get into the house. The word of a convicted drug trafficker isn't going to be enough for a warrant."

"Go set up on the place, wait for her to leave, then have a marked unit pull her over. We'll interview her, see what she cops to and then maybe we can roll back into the place with paper."

"How about just going and knocking on the door?" Jimmy asked.

"Jimmy, you should know better. Now you're thinking just like those agents you initially came in here to bitch about. If she's violent, like Angel said she was, and she sees agents come to the door, what makes you think she's not going to go get a gun and then open the door and shoot you? If you want into that house, you'll have a warrant and you'll go in fast and hard. We're not giving anyone time to go arm themselves."

Jimmy looked at his supervisor, giving him a slight smile. "I knew the answer and what you were going to say the minute those words came out of my mouth. I'm glad you didn't disappoint me. I have to admit, it was a bonehead thing to suggest."

Tom thought for a moment before speaking again. "Are you sure you don't want to go home and take a few days off? Nothing's going to change over the next few days."

"I'm going stir crazy at home. I'd like to go out and do something."

"Well I think your crazy, but God bless you for wanting to work. Go grab whoever is here from the group that doesn't have anything more important going on. I'll join you guys in a few hours. If you don't find enough volunteers, let me know and I'll draft a few for you."

"Thanks, Jefe."

"Jimmy," Tom said as Jimmy was heading out his door. He turned and looked back at his supervisor. "You really sure you're ready for this? You're going to need to be firing on all eight for this."

"I'm fine. Besides, I'd like to get some closure on this."

"You just be sure you're getting the right kind of closure," Tom said. Jimmy gave him a little nod then turned and walked away.

Jimmy grabbed Deron, Bill, Jesus, Mitch and Shirley and headed out to 293 Vista Point. Forty minutes later, they were setting up around the residence. No one appeared to be home so they settled into quiet spots in the shade, watching and waiting. It was nearly a half hour before any activity was observed at their target residence.

"Hey, Jimmy, you see that car that just went in the garage?" Jesus asked.

"No, not from my position. Was it the gray Mercury? I saw a Mercury Cougar go by a minute ago?"

"Yeah. I got the plate. Let me give Sector a call and run it." Jimmy waited while the registration was checked.

"Jesus to Jimmy. It comes back to a 1995 Dodge stolen out of the bay area a couple of months ago."

"Looks like our P.C. on this place is starting to build already," Jimmy said. He got on the cell phone and passed the information on to Tom, advising that he intended to keep everyone out on the residence. Tom told him he'd send the rest of the group home to get some rest and then have them relieve everyone around ten p.m.

The wait continued with very little activity for the remainder of the day. Just before seven p.m., as it was getting dark, the garage opened and the Mercury Cougar that had parked there earlier came out and drove down to a shopping center about a mile away. Jesus, Shirley and Jimmy followed loosely while Deron and Bill stayed with the residence. The occupant of the vehicle, a Hispanic male, went to a phone booth located just outside a dry cleaning business. The man made several calls then got into the Mercury and drove back to the residence. Jimmy went to the phone booth, wrote down the number shown, and then called Sector Communications from the payphone, marking the phone booth in order to be able to later subpoena the numbers the man had called.

Just before ten p.m. Barbara showed up. She called Jimmy on his cell.

"Jimmy, where do you want me to set up?" she asked.

"Find one of the other guys and take their spot," he said.

"Why don't I take yours?" she offered.

"Thanks anyway, but I think I'm going to stay awhile."

Over the next twenty minutes, Sal, Gary and Greg also showed up, relieving the rest of the group. As everyone situated themselves, settling in for a long evening, Jimmy settled down into his car seat as best he could considering his legroom. He tried to put his seat back down but it didn't seem to make a difference in his comfort level so he returned it to its normal position. He was tired but anxious and he wanted to be present if something happened. He fidgeted for an hour in the cab of his SUV, trying to find a magazine he hadn't read or something to listen to on the radio.

"I don't know why a city this big has such crappy FM radio stations," he said aloud, turning the radio over to an AM talk show.

He was going to put off his call to Carmen until just before she went to bed, but he found himself so restless that he decided to call a little early.

"Hi, babe."

"Jimmy, it's getting late. You coming home soon?" Carmen asked. He detected a yawn with part of the question.

"Not for awhile. I'm on a surveillance that will probably go all night. Go to sleep and I'll check in with you in the morning."

"What are you doing?"

"I told you, I'm on surveillance. I'm working."

"You just went through a horrible experience a few days ago and they have you out working all night?" she asked.

"No one has me doing anything. I decided to be here be-cause I thought it was important."

Carmen sighed and paused a moment before continuing. "I'm not the kind of woman who's going to question what you're out doing, and I know you're an adult who can make his own deci-sions, but Jimmy, you've been through a lot. I'm worried about you. I really wish you weren't out there tonight. Whatever you're working on can't be that important . . . is it?" She paused a mo-ment, waiting for Jimmy to answer. He didn't respond.

"Why won't you talk to me?" she asked.

"Carmen, I do talk to you. This just isn't a good time for it. I am tired, so please forgive me for not telling you everything you want to know right now, but trust me when I say that I'm working on something that I think is very important. Look, I'm being safe, I have half my group out here with me, and I'll be home as soon as I can."

"Okay. Just be careful, okay?"

"Sleep tight," Jimmy said, hanging up.

The remainder of the night was uneventful. Jimmy might as well have gone home and got some sleep but he still had so much going on with his thoughts that he didn't think he'd have gotten much sleep anyway. He did manage a couple of fifteen or twenty-minute naps in his car. By morning, his legs were cramping and he had a stiff neck.

At a little past ten a.m., there was finally some activity at the residence. A Volkswagen Rabbit showed up parking in the driveway. A check of the registration on the vehicle showed it registered to a John Noble out of Laguna Nigel, California. Checks done on Noble showed prior drug trafficking convic-tions. The man driving the Rabbit appeared to fit the descrip-tion of Noble, a white male, 5'11", about thirty-two years old. He didn't stay long and when he left, Jimmy decided to just let him go. Probable cause for getting into the house was growing, although slowly.

By noon, Jimmy couldn't stay awake any longer and decided to go home and catch a nap. Carmen was at work so the house was quiet. Jimmy slept hard for about five hours, then woke, showered and headed back out to the surveillance. The only thing he'd missed during his absence was someone leaving several times in the Cougar to drive down to the shopping center to make calls from a payphone.

At six p.m., Jimmy's cell phone rang. "Maxwell."

"Jimmy, were you home today?" Carmen asked.

"Yeah babe. I got really tired so I came home and grabbed a nap and a shower."

"So are you coming home tonight?"

"I wouldn't count on it. I'm stuck out here on this surveillance."

"Jimmy, I don't understand. I really think you need a little break from all this for awhile. Can you tell me what is so important about what you're doing? Honestly, why do they need you?"

"Babe, please don't worry about this. I'm out here because I want to be, and because I have a vested interest in what we're doing. You might say that these agents are out here because of me. I wouldn't feel right about not being here with them if I'm the reason they're here."

"But you can't tell me what you're working on?"

"Not right now. I know you're probably tired of hearing this, but I really can't, and especially not over the phone. I'll try to give you the details when I get home. I'll call you tonight if I'm going to be late."

Carmen sighed and paused a moment. "Be safe," she said. The phone disconnected before Jimmy could reply.

Jimmy wasn't happy about leaving Carmen in the dark about what he was doing, but he couldn't think of a good way to explain to her the events of the last week without upsetting her or scaring her. He needed to have at least the safety-related problems solved before explaining to her that he'd killed her ex-brother-in-law.

As he sat thinking about whether it was right or wrong to keep Carmen in the dark about what he'd been going through the last week, the garage opened to the residence. The Cougar backed out onto the street and parked. The driver stood beside the car for several minutes looking down the street.

"Heads up, guys," Jimmy transmitted. "It looks like we may be getting ready to have an arrival. Our S-1 just moved the car out of the garage and is looking around." Jimmy heard his mike key several times as agents responded that they'd heard him without actually having said anything.

Two minutes later, a van came around the corner. There were two men and a woman inside. Jimmy wondered if it was Sylvia.

The driver of the van nodded to the driver of the Cougar who was now standing on the sidewalk near the driveway. The van turned into the driveway and then pulled into the garage. The man who'd been waiting on the street walked in behind them, greeting the driver as he exited the van. The garage door closed as Jimmy wrote down the license plate number.

"Sector, Alpha 353. Can you run TECS, registration and work up whatever else you can from the R/O information on California 9E42423?" Jimmy asked over the radio.

"Alpha 353, Sector, affirm. Standby."

"Like I'm going somewhere," Jimmy said to himself.

Several minutes went by as Jimmy waited for a response. He decided to give Tom a call to consult with him. Tom was parked a block east of the residence and Jimmy assumed he'd been able to see the arrival of the van.

"Hey, it's me. So what do you think?" Jimmy asked.

"Don't know for sure but this sure looks like a dope stash location and someone's making a drop. I guess it'll depend on what Sector comes back with. I'm guessing if the R/O is famous for something we should probably get a canine unit over here to run by the garage once it gets dark."

"Yeah, here we are waiting for a woman who likely set up a confidential source to get whacked and we're back working a stash house."

"I expected nothing less from you, Jimmy my boy. You've always been a magnet for this sort of stuff."

"Well, getting a dog over here sounds like a plan. It should be totally dark in another hour. But what if nothing comes back on the vehicle?"

"Maybe wait for it to leave, have a marked unit do a traffic stop and see who's inside. Maybe we'll get lucky and it'll be someone famous for something."

"Alpha 353, Sector."

"Go for 353," Jimmy responded.

"Your R/O is a Hector Paredes out of Los Angeles. Looks like he's under investigation for money laundering. There's a current investigation ongoing in L.A. and a little older one out of El Paso, Texas."

"Ten-four, Sector. How about faxing what you've got to my office," Jimmy said.

"It's on its way."

"So looks like we order up a canine. I'll put in a call," Jimmy said to Tom, who was still waiting on the line. "I think I'm going to head to the office and start working on the warrant. Can you meet with the canine unit and call me with the results so I can add it to the affidavit if it's positive? It's going to take me a few hours to get the damned thing written up anyway," Jimmy said.

"Yeah, I'll take care of it," Tom replied.

Two hours later, Jimmy was almost finished with the affidavit. Tom called just as he was wrapping it up.

"Hey, we got a dog alert. The canine officer almost got caught by one of the guys from the house when he came out to smoke a cigarette on the front porch. If he had come out thirty seconds earlier, he'd have seen the dog handler running his pooch along the bottom seam of the garage. We'd probably have had to go in and secure the place."

"Well let me add the dog alert to the affidavit and then get an A.U.S.A. to bless this thing for me. It's going to be tight getting this signed and served before ten p.m. I'll try to hurry, but I don't think I'll make it and I'm pretty sure we're not going to get night service."

"I think you're right," Tom said.

By the time Jimmy got an Assistant U.S. Attorney located, drove to meet her at her house, and then got the duty judge located, it was already 9:45. There was no way Jimmy was going to have his warrant signed, let alone executed, by ten p.m. It was going to be another long night.

Jimmy had the warrant signed and was back on surveillance at eleven p.m. Sitting in his Expedition, he realized he hadn't called Carmen. He wondered if he should call, ultimately deciding against it because he didn't want to wake her up. He'd apologize tomorrow after the warrant. Hopefully he'd have Sylvia in custody. Then he could tell her about everything and apologize for not talking about it earlier.

The night seemed to drag by, with most of the group taking turns getting naps in their cars. Finally the sun started to come up. Sal was left at the residence while the rest of the surveillance team from the night shift rallied behind a grocery store at the shopping center where their target had been making his cell phone calls. The half of the group that was able to go home and get some sleep started showing up as Jimmy pulled into the lot.

"Where're the donuts?" Greg asked. "Come on, it's the case agent's responsibility to bring donuts to these early morning ops."

"Sorry guys, I've been distracted. I blew it."

"Well, let's go home then," Greg said with a smile. Jimmy frowned and started to walk away, wondering how anyone could be in a good mood this early in the morning. As he walked to the back of his Expedition to start suiting up for the warrant, Deron drove up. He got out of his car with a large pink box of donuts.

"Sweet," Greg said, turning towards Deron. "Someone was thinking. Guess we'll be able to serve this warrant after all."

Fifteen minutes later, the group gathered around for a quick safety briefing, then got their stick assignments for the impending entry.

"Jimmy, I want you on perimeter in the backyard," Tom said as he made assignments.

"Bullshit! This is my warrant," he said. "Have one of the newer agents take perimeter."

"This topic isn't open for discussion. You were involved in a shooting less than a week ago and I'm not putting you in a position to get in another one this soon. You'll take the rear perimeter. End of discussion."

Jimmy was upset at this unexpected turn of events, and although he was unhappy about the decision, he understood it and was just too tired to argue about it. Wrapping up the briefing, the agents doubled up in cars, leaving the rest of the cars behind in the parking lot. Jimmy was ready to go and moved his vehicle towards the front of the train of cars that were staging to move. It always seemed to take longer than it should to get rolling on a warrant.

Finally moving, they drove back to the Vista Point address. "Sal, any change?" Tom asked over the air.

"A light came on towards the back of the residence, but nothing else," he advised.

"We're in route about a minute out. You've got the front perimeter."

"Ten four."

The train of agents stopped in the street about three houses from their target location, stacking up on the sidewalk, entry tools and weapons in hand. It was 6:30 a.m. A few people leaving for work watched with worried interest as they came out of their homes to find federal agents, guns drawn, moving towards a neighbor's house.

Jimmy quickly moved past his group, getting ahead of them and finding the gate in the side yard that opened to the backyard. He reached over the top and opened the latch. Once inside, he quietly closed the gate and then headed towards the rear of the house. As he moved, he heard the knock and notice.

Bang, bang, bang, bang, came the heavy pounding on the front door. "Federal agents with a search warrant demanding entry! Police with a search warrant demanding entry! Police with a search warrant demanding entry!" Once the third announcement was made, there was a loud crash and the splintering of wood as the door broke open.

The sounds became more muffled as agents rushed inside. "Police! Down! Get down!" Jimmy could hear doors being thrown open and the heavy footsteps of people moving inside.

In the backyard, Jimmy looked up to see a window screen pushed out. It fell in the yard within a few feet of him. He hugged the wall, his Sig .40 in his hand. Suddenly, a woman popped into view, hanging half in and half out of the window. Jimmy moved in front of her, trying to grab her with his non-gun hand. She noticed him move out of the corner of her eye and pushed herself back into the house before he could grab her.

The base of the window was even with Jimmy's armpits. He moved directly in front of the window, observing that the woman was standing in a bathtub. She stood frozen, looking at him as he pointed his gun at her.

"Just stand there, lady. Don't move," he ordered.

The woman stepped back and out of the tub. She continued to face Jimmy, staying focused on his weapon, but she started edging back away from him.

"Lady, I said don't move!" Jimmy yelled.

The woman turned briefly and looked at a cabinet behind her. The cabinet opened at a ninety-degree angle from Jimmy. It had no doors and it looked, from what he could see, like it contained towels and other linens. The woman continued looking back and forth, first at Jimmy and then into the cabinet.

Come on guys, get in here, he thought to himself. "Lady, don't you even think about it," Jimmy said loudly, realizing she was looking at something in the cabinet that she was thinking about grabbing. He hoped it wasn't a gun.

"Lady, I am telling you to stop!" Jimmy started to pull the trigger on his gun, the hammer creeping back as the trigger was pulled. "I will shoot you, you understand! Don't you move!" The trigger tightened further, the hammer creeping further back.

The woman suddenly focused all her attention on the gun in Jimmy's hand. She froze, her mouth falling open. Just then two agents rushed into the bathroom and grabbed the woman, forcing her to the floor. As they started handcuffing her, Jimmy finally eased up on the pressure on his trigger. He dropped his weapon to his side as they stood the woman up. From further inside the house he heard, "Code Four, we're Code Four in here." The house was secure.

"Hey, Greg, what's in that linen cabinet?" Jimmy asked. Greg looked around, then took a step over to the linen cabinet. He looked in, then smiled and shook his head. He pulled out a dinner plate that had a pile of what appeared to be cocaine on it. It was probably three or four ounces.

"That stupid piece of . . . I almost shot her! I thought it was a gun." Jimmy felt himself getting angry. He walked around to the front of the residence, stopped momentarily at the front door and said, "Maxwell, coming in!" He entered the house and walked back to a bedroom where the woman was sitting handcuffed.

"That stupid bitch almost got herself killed!" Jimmy said to Tom.

"Hey, calm down," Tom said.

"Who is she?" Jimmy asked.

No one answered immediately. Jimmy looked down at her. "What's your name?"

"Sylvia."

"Sylvia Castaneda?" Jimmy asked.

Sylvia looked hard at Jimmy, surprised at the fact that he knew her name.

Jimmy turned and walked from the room. As he walked back towards the living room, he saw three men seated in handcuffs on the sofa. He hadn't even noticed them when he came in.

"Jimmy, come here," Sal said quietly. Jimmy headed over to Sal who handed him two wallets. He opened them, finding badges inside. "Two of our friends are captains in the Baja State Judicial Police," Sal said with a smile. Jimmy smiled for the first time that day.

"Guys," Shirley said to them from a landing halfway up the stairs to the second floor. They looked up. "Come here," she said.

Jimmy turned again and noticed Barbara was in the living room. "Can you watch our new friends for a minute?" Jimmy asked her.

"Sure."

The two men bound up the stairs and joined Shirley on the landing. They followed her as she led them into the master bedroom and then to a walk-in closet. She stood at the door of the closet and pointed inside. They walked over and looked inside. There were three large cardboard boxes and a large suitcase, all filled with cash.

"Sweet!" Jimmy said, high-fiving both Sal and Shirley.

The search culminated in the discovery of no drugs other than the few ounces of cocaine found on the plate in the bathroom, but it was enough to guarantee the seizure of what Jimmy later found to be $589,000.00.

Jimmy went back to the room where Sylvia was being held. This time he took out his credentials and showed them to her, letting her study them. She looked at them, and then looked up at him questioningly.

"You speak English, correct?"

"Yes."

He pulled a chair over from a corner and sat on it facing her, removing a rights card from his wallet. "I need you to pay attention. You have the right to remain silent. Anything you say can be used against you in court. You have the right to speak with an attorney or to have an attorney present with you before any questions are asked. If you cannot afford an attorney, one will be appointed for you. Do you understand these rights?"

"Yes."

"I'd like to ask you a few questions. Are you willing to talk to me?"

"What about?"

"Simple things really. Like who lives here. Things like that?"

"Sure, I'll talk to you."

"Okay, good. So who lives here?" Jimmy asked.

"It's my house."

"What about these other guys? Who are they?"

"Friends. Two of them came by today to help me look into something."

"What's that?"

Sylvia looked at Jimmy but didn't answer.

"Okay, I'll move on," he said. "Who does all that money belong to that we found upstairs?"

"What money? I don't know anything about any money," she said, remaining expressionless.

"Come on, Sylvia. There're three large boxes and a suitcase full of cash in your closet. It's a simple question. Who does the money belong to?"

"Do I look like I have any money? I shop at Wal-Mart."

"You know, it's not illegal to have money in your house, so why not just tell me the truth? You were in the van that drove into the garage last night with the money."

Sylvia stared wide-eyed at Jimmy for a moment before speaking again. "I don't know about any money," she finally said.

"What about the cocaine? Who does it belong to?"

She sat silently. "You can't deny knowledge of the cocaine. I almost killed you over it. What were you going to do, try and flush it before someone got to you?"

Sylvia sat silently, saying nothing.

"Your husband got killed last week. You do remember that?" Jimmy said, trying to get her to say something.

"Yes, he was murdered by you people," she said venomously.

"Well, no, he was shot after he first shot one of our people, and was trying to shoot others," Jimmy said.

"That's not true. Why would he try to shoot anyone? He was a kind, gentle man."

"Well, I didn't know him, but I tell you the truth when I say that he shot someone else first and then shot at others."

"How do you know?" she spat.

"I was there. I watched him shoot a man, then I shot him."

Before Jimmy could even react, Maria jumped on him, knocking him backwards and onto the ground. She fell on him, trying to bite him, head butting him in a rage, but unable to get good solid blows with her hands handcuffed behind her back.

Shirley and Tom picked her up, still flailing wildly about as they practically dragged her from the bedroom. She was crying out loudly, "You filthy bastard! You murdering, filthy bastard! I'll kill you, you pig!"

Jimmy picked himself up from the floor and touched his neck. She'd managed to bite him in one spot good enough to draw blood.

Deron had been standing near the door. He walked over to help Jimmy up. "That went well," Jimmy said, shaking his head as Deron pulled him to his feet. Deron suppressed a laugh. Tom returned a minute later and approached Jimmy.

"Well, now that you have her in custody are you going to take a little break?"

"I'm going to go home soon and get some rest. I'm really tired. Good caper though, huh? Only bad thing is that our psycho woman there probably won't do much time for having a few ounces of coke."

"Don't worry about that right now," Tom said. "Maybe we can put together a money laundering case, and we still need to spend some time chatting with her about Chuey's murder. In any event I want you to take a week or so off. This will all be here for you when you get back."

Jimmy sat back and leaned against the wall. Tom and Deron watched him for a moment. Deron looked at Tom and then left the room.

"Sure you're okay?" Tom asked.

"Just not looking forward to going home and talking to Carmen about the particulars of the events of the last week."

"It isn't going away. You need to go home," Tom said. "When you get there, just tell her. Get it over with."

Deron came out of the kitchen with a couple of damp paper towels and handed them to Jimmy. He took them and wiped his neck.

Jimmy nodded and started to get up. "If I'm going to go home I better get busy processing some evidence and get the interviews of our other friends knocked out."

"I'll have it taken care of it," Tom said.

"You sure?" Jimmy said. "You guys are going to be here all day? Might get everyone home a little quicker if I help."

"Jimmy, go home, now," Tom said.

Jimmy smiled, nodded and walked out to his Expedition.

CHAPTER . . .

35

Jimmy woke up when Carmen sat down on the bed next to him. He looked up at her as she caressed his face with the back of her hand.

"Hi, babe," she said.

"Hi. What time is it?"

"It's almost eight. When are you going back to work?"

"Not tonight. In fact, Tom wants me to take a week or two off."

"I think you need it," she said, bending down to kiss him.

"Yeah." He sat up and stretched, then pivoted and threw his legs out of bed, remaining seated.

"What happened to your neck?" she asked.

"I was in a little scuffle at work this morning."

She started undressing. "You okay?"

"Yeah, where's Raul?" Jimmy asked. Jimmy knew she wanted more details about what had happened but he figured he'd wait until later, when he could tell her the whole story.

"With my mom. I thought I was going to be alone and I needed to think about a few things tonight. I think she knew so she offered to keep him. I'm glad I won't be alone, she said looking at him and giving him a little smile."

"Me too." He stretched again but remained seated, watching her as she finished undressing. When she finished, she looked over at him. He smiled as she stepped over to him. He pulled himself back under the covers, holding them open for her. Carmen lay down next to him, snuggling up against him. They lay together in each other's arms a few minutes without speaking and then Carmen rolled over farther and kissed Jimmy.

"So what did you need to think about?" he asked, coming up for air after a long kiss.

"Later," she said, continuing to run her hands over his chest and giving him kisses.

457

"Let me get up and brush my teeth."

"Stay put. Just hold me for a while more. Okay?" she asked. Jimmy pulled her closer to him. After a few minutes, he could hear her crying softly. He wanted to ask her what was wrong but decided to just hold her closer and let her get it out of her system. The soft sobbing stopped after a few minutes and Carmen reached down and started touching him intimately.

"I thought we were just cuddling?" Jimmy said with a little smile, looking into her wet eyes.

"Shut up and make love to me," she said.

An hour later, they sat at the kitchen table. They both had a beer open. As Jimmy started to say something, his cell phone rang. It was his daughter.

"Hi, sweetie. How's my girl?" Jimmy answered after seeing the number on his phone display.

"Hi, daddy. I'm calling to tell you I love you."

"I love you too. Are you being good for mommy?"

"Yes, but daddy, you haven't called me hardly at all the last week. What's wrong? When are you coming over to see me?"

Jimmy choked up a little, realizing it was true. He hadn't called, although he'd thought about her every day. He'd been so distracted that every time he thought about her something would come up just before he'd call. Tears welled up in his eyes as he spoke with her.

"I'll come see you soon. Maybe tomorrow I can pick you up from school and we'll go somewhere and have dinner together, just you and me," he offered.

"Okay," Nikki said, cheering up.

Jimmy ended the call and looked over at Carmen. She sat soberly watching him but gave him a little smile.

"You miss her a lot, don't you?" she asked.

"Yes. Yes I do." The two sat together silently for another minute.

"Carmen, about the last week. I'm sorry. I probably should have kept you more informed about what's been going on, but a lot has happened that I just didn't know how to break to you."

"You still haven't filed for divorce from your wife, have you?" she interrupted.

He looked at her wondering if that was all she was thinking about.

"You know I haven't had time. Besides, babe, you know I love you. Is that what's been bothering you?"

"I've been worried about what's been going on with you at work. But I guess I do think about the divorce issue whenever you get a call from home. I know you're still struggling with whether or not you should be with me."

"I'll get around to filing pretty soon."

"I know you love me, but this whole separation thing has been pretty hard on you, hasn't it?"

Jimmy looked at her for a moment before responding. "I never thought I'd ever get divorced. You know, I do believe in marriage and that it's supposed to last forever. I mean, I understand why people get divorced and I know there's good reasons for it sometimes, I just never thought it would happen to me. I guess I'm going through somewhat of an adjustment period." He paused again for a moment before continuing. "None of this changes the fact that I love you more than anyone else in the whole world."

"Except, you've got to be happy with yourself in order to truly love someone else. I know your faith has suffered quite a bit because of our relationship, too. Jimmy, I don't want to be responsible for taking you from your family or hurting your relationship with God. I talked to a priest a few days ago. I was worried about you, about us, about your lack of being able to open up to me about certain things. He told me that we shouldn't be together. You're still married to someone else and here we are living together. You think God is happy with that?" she asked.

"No. But I think he understands. I mean, he is a God of love, and we're together because we love each other, right? There certainly wasn't much love going on between Shirley and me and that was just as distracting from my relationship with God as anything else."

"Jimmy, there's other people to consider here. Despite the fact that your wife was a difficult person to live with, I'm sure she must have loved you. Certainly your little girl loves you and needs you."

"Carmen, you love me, you need me. Raul needs me. I need you as well. No one has ever loved me like you do. So what's going on? What are you trying to tell me?"

"I see struggle and conflict in you. I don't think you're sure that what we're doing together is right. Maybe you need to move out and get yourself together. Pray about what to do. Make sure you're doing the right thing. You know, I think the priest was right. God doesn't want us together right now."

"Are you suggesting that I shouldn't be here?"

"Yes I am. Maybe after some time, once you divorce, if you decide to do that, we can see each other again."

Jimmy was stunned. He'd been happy being with Carmen. The last six months had been the strangest rollercoaster of life he'd ever experienced, but he'd been happy in a bittersweet way. He'd never felt more comfortable and in touch with a woman in his life, or so he thought. He hadn't even considered the possibility that she would suggest a separation. He'd believed their newfound bond was strong and secure. He sat in silence, a dull pain of immeasurable proportion creeping into his heart.

"I don't know what to say," he finally said. He'd been thinking about the conflicts between his job and his personal life. They had spilled over into his relationship with Carmen and Raul, and Jimmy really didn't want them hurt because of him.

"I think you're wrong about why I should go, but maybe it would be better for other reasons."

Carmen looked at him, waiting for him to explain.

"The man I shot last week. It was Angel's brother." Carmen's eyes widened as she listened. "Alfredo?" she asked.

"He was trying to sell one of our sources some heroin. He shot the source thinking he was being robbed. Then he shot at one of our agents. I didn't have a choice."

"Oh, Jimmy, I'm so sorry. I can see why you didn't want to tell me about it."

"I knew that you and Raul would eventually find out about this. I figured Angel would say something to Raul during one of his visits. You know, I even went to MCC and talked to Angel about it last Saturday. I told him I shot his brother."

"My God, Jimmy! I'm sorry."

"It would probably be a problem for us as Raul gets older. I've been struggling with telling you about it for that reason. Then there's Alfredo's wife, or ex-wife. She's the person that got my source killed. As I looked into the murder, I learned that she'd made some threats against the agent that killed Alfredo. We've been out trying to locate her. She was arrested this morning. She's the one that did this," he said, pointing to his neck.

"Jimmy. What you've been through. I'm so sorry," Carmen said softly, shaking her head in disbelief.

"I've worried about the repercussions that all this mess was going to bring to you and Raul. What I didn't worry about was us, our relationship. That said, maybe I should go. Maybe I should have been strong enough when this mess started to just walk away to avoid putting you in danger. I disagree with your reasons for wanting me to leave, but still, there are reasons. Good reasons."

"Jimmy, I . . ."

"You don't have to say anything else. I'm a big boy. I have a job that I know is a service to most of the community I live in, but I also know that I do things that cause problems for some people. You don't need to be exposed to those problems. If I truly love you, want to protect you, I probably should leave."

Jimmy took a drink from his beer, got up and walked to Carmen's room. He packed his suitcase and walked to the front door. Turning to look into the kitchen, he saw Carmen still sitting in her chair. She was crying again. He turned and walked out the front door, got into his Expedition, and drove down to the corner. Once there, he pulled over and turned around, looking back at her house, a tiny little building among so many others. He wondered what other dramas were going on in the other houses he could see. He couldn't remember when he'd felt more depressed. He looked again at Carmen's house then put the vehicle in drive and drove away.

The next morning, Jimmy walked into his office and headed to his cubicle. Just as he was getting there, he bumped into Deron.

"Dude, I thought you were taking some time off? I didn't expect to see you for a week or so."

"Yeah, I thought about it, but what the hell. I figured you guys would miss me too much if I took that much time off."

"Yeah, like a toothache. The group was looking forward to having a little normalcy to their lives for a week or so." Deron smiled as he said it and punched Jimmy in the arm. "Actually, I'm glad you're back. We have duty tomorrow and Tom was going to have me take your spot."

Jimmy smiled and sat down at his desk. "Well, you're off the hook."

Printed in the United States
150749LV00007B/50/P